Raising a Gangster

Kerry Barnes

Once Upon A Book

A CIP catalogue record for this title is

available from the British Library.

ISBN 978-1-8380440-0-8

Ruthless

Ruby's Palace

Raw Justice

***

Cruel Secrets

Wicked Lies

Ugly Truth

***

The Hunted

The Rules

The Choice

***

Deceit

DEDICATION

To my dad

ACKNOWLEDGEMENTS

Robert Wood, my editor, for his time, his endless patience, and his determination to go the extra mile to ensure the book is the very best it can be and in the quickest time possible.
www.epworthediting.com

I want to thank the members of the NotRights Book Club and all the readers who have supported me.

Deryl Easton for her sound advice.

My beautiful cousin, Charlotte Capon, for the face of Peggy Reardon on the cover.

Raising a Gangster

CHAPTER ONE

South London, 1958

It was pitch-black outside by the time Peggy Reardon sat down with her cup of tea. A draught blew in through the small cracks in the window of the main room. She shuddered and stared into nothing.

There was no point in feeling any self-pity; besides, no doubt most of the neighbours in the street were all in the same predicament – piss-poor and living in a run-down row of two-up two-down terraced houses. Bleak was the best way to describe it.

She sighed to herself; at least she had her boys and her health. She peered down at her threadbare carpet slippers and wondered why on earth they were called carpet slippers; she didn't have any carpet, not even fancy lino – just clean floorboards and a bit of an old rug. She shook her head at the last of the coal glowing in the grate. Then her eyes scanned the empty mantelpiece. It once showed off a few bits of china passed down by her mother, Annie. But now the shelf was empty. Not that she had been very close to her mother, for no other reason than they had not been alike at all. Annie was quiet, sickly, and hard work at times, always taking to her bed. However, she had been very close to her father, Dillon, and having to sell his pocket watch had hurt her so much; even now the thought made her feel as though her insides were ripped in half.

She and her husband had sold everything of any value down at Camden Market before Reginald left and headed back to Ireland. She'd hung on to his promise that he would find work and come back for her and the kids. But then the weeks had grown into months, with not even a letter from him.

Many local men had found it hard when the docks closed. Until the1920s, Bermondsey had thrived. The docks secured enough work for the families to scrape by, but now, everything had gone, along with the odd little treat – a bottle of mother's ruin or a packet of tobacco.

Really, she knew in her heart that Reginald hadn't gone back to Ireland to find work. He'd buggered off to escape their life of poverty, so he could start afresh elsewhere.

She couldn't, though; now aged twenty-eight, she had been left with his debts and two kiddies to bring up.

She sighed heavily again. What was she going to do now? The old codger at Hartley's jam factory had fired her. The dirty ol' bastard had thought he could get his way. He assumed she needed her job enough to let him cop a feel. He was right, in so much as she needed that job, but she valued her pride more. He wouldn't have behaved in that way if her Reginald was about. Fiery he may have been, but a sniff that ol' Millard had pinched her arse, and there would have been murders.

She sipped her tea and blinked back the tears before getting up from the chair to stoke the remnants of the fire. The mirror on the wall was more for show, the last of her mother's possessions, but she rarely looked at herself: after all, what was the point? It didn't matter what she looked like; she had no husband or fella to smile her way.

The heat from the fire was minimal, and Peggy knew she had to hurry to bed before the house cooled to a bitter cold.

As she climbed the creaky steep stairs, she heard a gentle banging at the back door. Initially, she thought it was the wind blowing up. As she paused, she heard it again and instantly hurried back down and peered through the small window into the yard. Grinning like two Cheshire cats were her boys. Turning the key, she pulled the door open and ushered them in.

'What in the name of God are you two doing out? Jesus Christ, I thought yous were in bed. And look at the state of ya.'

Her eldest son of eight proudly pulled a hessian sack from behind his back and grinned.

She took it from him and peered inside. 'Bloody hell, Cyril. You can't be taking coal from our neighbours. Ol' Missus Peabody is sick, and Mr Bates next door is on his deathbed.'

'No, Mum, we didn't, did we, Howie?'

Peggy looked from her eldest with his lively grey eyes and confident grin to her youngest son, who always had a permanent smile and red flushed cheeks.

Howie shook his head but said nothing. He invariably

waited for Cyril to do the talking. Cyril was only a year older, but, already, he had the mind of a teenager.

‘So where’s it come from, then?’

‘The jam factory. We snuck around the back, and there was a bloody great mountain of the stuff.’

‘Oi, Cyril. Watch ya language.’

‘Sorry, but there’s so much coal all piled high and no one was there. Mum, empty the sack, and I’ll go back and get more. They don’t need all that, do they?’

Howie handed her his sack and flashed his big blue eyes.

‘No, no, it’s late, it’s dark and it’s dangerous out there. This is a treat, and it will do us just fine, although looking at the colour of you two, it will take all the coal to heat the water to scrub the black off your faces.’

‘Mum, I won’t get caught, and what’s the worst anyone can do, eh? Don’t worry about me, Mum.’ He looked at Howie and grinned. ‘We won’t be seen. The factory ain’t got any lights on. Honestly, Mum.’

Peggy chewed her lip. ‘Go on then, but if anyone comes, you drop the sack and run, all right?’

‘Me and Howie are gonna use the barrow and fill a big bag.’

She nodded. ‘Now, listen. If a bobby sees ya, you leave the barrow and scarper, right? You don’t want to get a name for yaself with the establishment.’

Cyril smiled. 'Yeah, o' course, Mum.'

Before Peggy could give any more words of advice, Cyril and Howie were out of the door. As an almighty gust of cold wind blew in, she shivered, and an unexpected tear trickled down her face. Quickly, she wiped it away. This was no life. Her two little boys feeling the need to scour the streets to steal coal to keep the house warm didn't sit at all comfortably with her, but it was a case of needs must. 'Reginald Reardon, what have you done to us?' she said aloud.

It was all wrong. She should have enough money to put more than bread and jam on the table and still have at least a few pennies left for the coalman. However, when Reginald had left that day to go in search of work, she hadn't a clue he'd not been paying the rent . . . or the coalman . . . or the butcher. In fact, wherever she went, there were hands palm up asking for money owed.

She closed the door, sat back down at the small table, and gazed around the room. Old crochet blankets covered the sofa to hide the ripped seats. The two steps that led down to the small kitchen were rotten and no doubt would soon collapse. And in her feeble attempt to cover the windows, she'd ended up having to dye hessian sacks and tie a pretty blue ribbon to soften the look. But they were still an eyesore and didn't add any relief to the sight of the walls blackened by soot. And now with no work, how was she even going to get through the next few weeks?

'Damn you, Reginald,' she hollered again. 'Why did you have to alienate everyone?' Everyone was in the same situation, and they would help anyone if they could, but he'd upset nearly every neighbour with his harsh tongue and lack of empathy, and now here she was left all alone.

But her pride, personality, and temperament meant that she didn't have the guts to ask anyone for help, all too afraid they would shut the door in her face.

Her eyes fell to a pair of shoes by the fireplace. Cyril had tied the laces in many knots and worn the soles so much, she could see the floorboards beneath. A tight feeling gripped her throat. He hadn't mentioned that his school shoes had bloody great holes in them. She cried another tear. It was all wrong. A thought came to her. Reginald had left an old pair of shoes under the bed. She could cut the leather and place it inside Cyril's shoes until she could afford a new pair. Eagerly, she got to work, using the old bread knife to cut the soles small enough to fit inside her son's shoes. Every few minutes, she peered through the window, hoping to see her lads walking up the path. Whatever was she thinking, letting them go off to steal coal? Still, what kind of life was this anyway? If her boys were to grow up on the wrong side of the law, whose fault was it but that bloody government. *They did sod all to help people like us*, she thought.

Peggy's real name was Margaret. She was born in Bermondsey but had moved to Ireland when her father went on the run for a reason she didn't know.

Luckily for the family, he was originally from Kilkenny and had relatives there, and so, right away, they offered him the cottage owned by his uncle. She was sixteen then and loved the countryside, but when she married Reginald, they moved back to Bermondsey.

She sighed again when she looked out of the window and

down the dark and empty path. If only she had the money to return to Ireland. However, that was such wishful thinking on her part. There was no family left to return to, and she was sure her husband had either died or had hooked up with a tart. He always did have a wandering eye. It was just a shame that she hadn't realised that fact until she was married and heavily pregnant with her first son. But, despite everything, she still loved the bastard.

Anxiously awaiting her sons, she was relieved when she heard the heavy wheels of the barrow. Jumping to her feet, she opened the door to find Cyril pushing the barrow, with Howie asleep on the front and the mound of coal on the back. She wondered how on earth her little son had pushed it all the way back from the factory.

She hurried towards him and took the handles, while Cyril leaned over and rested his hands on his knees, taking deep breaths.

'Howie was tired, Mum, or I would've loaded more coal.'

'Get yaself inside, and get warmed up. 'Ere.' She threw him a lump of coal. 'Stick that on the fire.'

As soon as she'd stationed the barrow by the coal shed, she scooped Howie in her arms and carried him inside. His cheeks were ice-cold against her neck.

'Cor, it's bleedin' taters out there, Mum,' said Cyril, still out of breath.

Laying Howie on the sofa, she then covered him in a blanket.

When she turned to face Cyril, she saw him rubbing his cold hands in front of the fire. 'I'm gonna make you a hot drink and get you thawed out.'

She hurried into the small kitchen area, put the kettle on the stove, and used her own cup to make her son a cup of tea. As soon as the kettle boiled and she'd made the tea, she returned to the main room.

Cyril was curled up beside his brother and purring like a kitten.

Another tear made its way down her cheeks. Feeding the fire with more coal, she sat in the chair, rested her head on the table, and fell into a nightmare-like sleep.

Peggy woke up before the boys, who were having a lie-in because the school was closed for the day. Gingerly, she stood up from the chair and stretched her aching back. The howling wind had died down, but the room was getting chilly. Creeping out through the back door, she shivered and hurried towards the coal shed. It had been so dark last night when the boys had returned that she didn't quite see how much coal they'd brought back with them. The generous mound on the barrow made her smile. But the clouds were heavy with rain; she could feel it in her bones. Out of necessity, she needed to shovel the coal from the barrow to inside the shed, before it got drenched and before any neighbours peered over the wall and saw it there. Using the handleless shovel, she scooped the coal and lobbed it inside the shed. Once she'd finished, she stretched her back again, scooped some more into the old scuttle, and dashed back inside.

The house was warm and cosy by the time the boys woke

up. Peggy had filled the tin trough with hot water and unwrapped a bar of carbolic soap, ready to give her black-faced boys a good soaking. Normally, she would have waited until Sunday night, but they needed one now.

As she made herself a cup of tea before waking the kids, she could hear the coughing coming from next door. Mr Bates coughed night and day, but this morning, the sound was so different – less violent and more like a wheeze. Feeling the heat from the fire envelope her, even in the damp kitchen, she wondered if the poor ol' sod had enough strength to keep his own house warm. She didn't like the sound of his cough or the apparent lack of movement. She could always hear the man go up and down the stairs, but, lately, the house was quiet except for the coughing. She had it from both sides – Mrs Peabody, the stroppy woman, and him, both coughing their guts up.

Cyril stirred and sat upright. 'Cor, did I fall asleep down 'ere, Mum? Aw, it's lovely and warm, eh?'

'Yeah. Now, Son, once ya bruvver gets up, I want both of you in that bath and scrubbed clean. Do you hear?'

'Yeah. Where are you going, Mum?'

'I'm gonna check on Mr Bates.'

Cyril rubbed his eyes and yawned. 'Ain't he dead yet?'

'Cyril!'

'Sorry, Mum. I just thought he would be dead by now. He's been dying for a year.'

'Hmm, yeah, well, he ain't dead yet, the poor ol' fella.'

* * *

Closing the door behind her, she trotted down the small path through the gate and into Mr Bates' yard. She sighed at the overgrown patch of garden that had once been quite a colourful sight before moody Mr Bates got sick. She tapped on the back door and waited; he didn't call out, though. And that was odd. He always called out. Gingerly, she turned the back door handle, opened the door, and called out again, but there was no response other than the sound of heavy wheezing. Hesitating before going in, Peggy felt as if she was doing something wrong. Mr Bates had never opened his door to invite anyone in, not that she knew of. She told herself she was going inside for a good reason, but as soon as she stepped over the threshold, she was taken aback. His kitchen, although untidy, was full of pots and pans, plates – which were piled high on the shelf – a beautiful china teapot, and even ornaments. As she ventured into what they called the main room, she was surprised again. A large rug almost covered the floorboards and a green three-piece suite dominated the room. A small table and two chairs made of mahogany were placed in the same position as her own – under the small window. Beside the fireplace was a brass scuttle, and on the shelf above the fireplace, there were more china ornaments and a large mirror. She wondered what it was like in what she called the 'Christmas room'. It was a small room at the front, a room that most of the street saved as their best, which they kept immaculate for use only at Christmas and on birthdays.

When she'd first moved into her home with Reggie, they'd had their ornaments, photos, and a polished table kept for best. However, since then, she'd had to sell off all of her knick-knacks as well as her most precious valuables.

She paused when Mr Bates coughed.

'Mr Bates, it's Peggy from next door, love.'

She couldn't make out the words through the heavy groaning, so she decided just to climb the stairs. If he told her off, then so be it.

A nasty smell made her cold nose tingle as soon as she reached the small landing. The smell and the wheezing were coming from the room to the left. 'Mr Bates, it's me,' she said, as she stopped dead in the doorway to his room.

Mr Bates was lying in his bed covered with blankets and propped up with three puffed-up pillows. His face was a gaunt and sickly grey colour.

'Holy Mary, Mother of God.'

Mr Bates' sunken eyes flicked her way. 'W-What . . . do you want?'

'Oh, Mr Bates, I want nuffin, love. I heard you through the wall. It's bleedin' freezing in here. Let me help you. You sound dreadful.'

Mr Bates coughed again and took three deep breaths before he looked back at Peggy.

'I'm fine. Leave me to die in peace, and d . . . don't you go snooping about . . . Th . . . this is my home, woman.'

'I'll not go snooping. Let me make you a cup of tea and get the fire going. You ain't well.'

'Didn't you hear me? I wanna be left to die in peace.'

The annoyance had somehow brought some life and spirit back into the man.

'Yeah and you *can* die in peace, Mr Bates, but not in the bloody cold. Now then, I will make the fire up and . . .' She gawped at the stinking chamber pot. 'I'm going to see if I can't get you cleaned up, warm, and more comfortable. I think I've got some medicine back indoors.'

Mr Bates sighed heavily. 'Bloody women.'

Peggy smiled. 'Yep, we're a right pain in the arse, ain't we?'

Picking up the chamber pot, Peggy took careful steps not to spill it, while tilting her face to the side, to avoid breathing in the stench. Once she'd disposed of the contents down the outside toilet, she opened the door to the coal shed. To her surprise, it was empty. But then, if the man couldn't get down the stairs, he couldn't pay the coalman to deliver more coal.

She tutted and returned to her house to fetch her scuttle.

* * *

Cyril and Howie were both in the bath.

'Ah, good lads. And make sure you scrub behind your ears. I don't want any black fingernails, neither.'

'Is he dead yet?'

'Cyril! No, he's not. He's very poorly, and I'm gonna heat up his house and make him a cuppa. Now then, where did I put that cough mixture?'

'In the cupboard above the mangle.'

'You don't miss a trick, do ya, Son?'

Cyril grinned, and his wet shiny cheeks glowed.

* * *

As soon as Peggy returned to Mr Bates, she got to work making up the fire.

The council and the welfare department had scheduled the terraced houses to be demolished, and the families were soon to be moved into the newer generation homes. For some, it was a blessing, but for others, it was heartbreaking. The new tower blocks were going up all around them, and the council were moving the families into the flats. The older residents loved the houses and their way of life, regardless of the fact that they were not fit for purpose and a health hazard, particularly to their lungs. The smoke and damp played havoc, and even in the depths of winter, you would see neighbours outside breathing in the fresher air.

Peggy would have loved to have been offered one of the brand spanking new flats. She felt ostracised from the community, all because of her husband's mean-spirited attitude. She realised that perhaps she was overthinking this because it played on her mind a lot, but after all the trouble he'd caused her, she felt so thoroughly ashamed as his wife. However, with all the rent she now owed, the council had placed her at the bottom of the list, and so she would need a good few quid before they would offer her a new home.

Some families had jumped the queue, of course, because their kids had either come down with measles, whooping cough, or, in some cases, diphtheria. But the authorities had deemed her lads fit and well, after being seen by the school nurse and the doctor, so her family were stuck where they were, and Peggy could only hope and pray that one day she would live in the sky, looking out over the shitholes of London.

The fire roared up the chimney and Peggy added more coal. She stood back and rubbed her hands together. It wouldn't be long before the heat emanating from the chimney warmed the two bedrooms upstairs. After putting the kettle on, she checked in the tea caddy. There, almost full to the brim, were tea leaves. A thought occurred to her. If Mr Bates couldn't make it downstairs to pay the coalman, he wouldn't be able to pay the milkman either. But as she looked around the kitchen, she noticed a fridge. 'Blimey,' she said, aloud. Gripping the big silver handle, she pulled the door open. She'd never seen a fridge – well, not in a house. Only in the factory had she seen one. There on the shelves were three bottles of milk, a slab of butter, and, wrapped in paper, were a good couple of pounds of sausages.

Using one of the china cups, she made Mr Bates a cup of tea. Carefully balancing the cup on its saucer in one hand and holding the bottle of medicine and a spoon in the other, she climbed the stairs.

''Ere ya go, Mr Bates. I've brought you a nice cup of tea to wash down this cough mixture. Now then, sit yaself up, if ya can.'

Mr Bates was in his late fifties but looked more like eighty. His thinning, straggly hair stuck up in all directions and his eyes glared suspiciously at her.

She placed the contents in her hands on the bedside table and helped him to sit up. He didn't stop her.

''Ere, take this,' she said, as she poured the thick dark liquid onto a spoon.

He did as he was told. Swallowing the mixture, he gratefully took the cup of tea.

'I've got the fire going, and I'll fetch ya your chamber pot. Did you fancy a bit o' bread and butter?'

'No,' he said, staring coldly at her. 'How did you start the fire?'

'I had some spare coal. Anyway, you drink your tea, and I'll come back in an hour or so. I'll make you another one and top up that fire. What d'ya say?'

Mr Bates nodded. 'Yeah, but don't you go snooping around or touching my stuff.'

'I have no intentions, Mr Bates, of doing any such thing. So, now, don't you go worrying. You just get warm and enjoy ya cuppa.'

'I'm dying, ya know.'

'Well, if you are, at least you'll be warm.'

* * *

Cyril was sitting next to his brother, huddled around the fire, when Peggy returned. She noticed the red mark across his shoulder. As she moved closer, she realised the red graze was from carrying the hessian sack. *This was no life*, she thought.

'Fancy a nice hot cuppa milk?'

Howie beamed and nodded, but Cyril just looked up sadly. 'I'll just have tea, Mum. Save the milk.'

She thought about the bottles of milk inside Mr Bates' fridge, but, instantly, she shook the bad thought from her mind. 'There's enough, love.'

Cyril appeared troubled. 'Mum, do you think Dad will ever come back, and if he don't, how are we gonna live?'

Peggy looked into her son's eyes and saw wisdom. 'Now then, don't you go worrying about all that kinda stuff. That's not for yous to concern yourself with. I'm gonna make some nice warm milk and no more talk of your farver, 'cos, Son, I have not an iota when or even if the man will come back. Anyway, we're doing all right, ain't we?'

Cyril nodded and looked back at the dancing flames.

As soon as the sun was higher in the sky, Cyril and Howie went out to play, leaving Peggy dusting and sweeping.

Once she'd finished with her own housework, she decided to return to Mr Bates. Politely, she called up the stairs, to let him know she was there before making him another cup of tea. She loved his kitchen; however, it was a stark reminder that she was penniless in comparison.

Mr Bates was looking a little better than earlier that morning.

'How ya doing? Did that linctus help?'

'Is that tea for me?'

She smiled and handed him the cup. 'I noticed that you've got some sausages in the fridge . . .'

'You want them, I s'pose?'

Peggy jerked her head in surprise. 'No, Mr Bates. I was going to cook them for you. Ya know, to get your strength up.'

Mr Bates sighed. 'Yeah, yeah, cook them all. They'll no doubt turn bad in a few days. Give your skinny little boys some to fatten them up.'

'Oh, really, Mr Bates? Are you sure? I mean, that's very, very kind of you.'

He sighed again. 'Call it payment for the cough medicine . . . and the coal.'

Peggy smiled. 'That's nuffin, Mr Bates.'

'More than anyone else would've done.'

'You look better. Now then, not that I was nosing around . . .' She paused when she noticed his raised eyebrow. 'But your lovely kitchen could do with a clean. Shall I . . . ?'

'If you must. But what do you want in return?' He tutted when he saw the disappointed look in her eyes. 'Sorry. Not used to people wanting to help me. I've pissed everyone off, over the years.'

'Never mind that. I'll give the kitchen a good clean, then cook you some lunch. The truth is, Mr Bates, I've done me own housework, and I'm not used to being idle.'

Unexpectedly, Peggy found herself telling him the story of how the manager at the jam factory had fired her and how her husband had left her and her children. Before she knew it, she was telling him her whole life story.

The expression on Mr Bates' face changed. His hard sallow features seemed to lift, to be replaced by rosy cheeks, and there was even a hint of a compassionate smile now.

Once she'd given his kitchen a good clean, she retrieved the sausages from the fridge and returned home. The amount of meat stuffed in the skins made Peggy's mouth water. Filling the pot with onions, carrots, and stock, she gently fried the sausages and lowered them into the stew. The aroma enveloped the kitchen and had Peggy wishing the stew was ready to eat. To make the meal go even further, she rolled some dumplings and popped them on the stove to steam. Pleased with her efforts, she filled a basin with warm water, washed her face, and tied her hair back into a bun. Looking at her reflection, she sighed. One day, she would have the money to have one of those modern cuts and to be able to buy hair lacquer to hold her hair in place. *If I ever get lucky*, she thought, *I'll buy myself a stick of lipstick.*

After stoking up the fire and laying the table, Peggy called out from the back door for her boys to come in and get cleaned up ready for dinner.

Cyril and Howie had hovered around the yard, tantalised by the cooking smells drifting from the house, and as soon as their mother called them, they were inside in a flash.

* * *

Peggy had poured a generous helping into Mr Bates' large bowl, and with a tea towel resting over the top, she left her boys to eat their food while she carried the weighty dish next door. Politely, she called up the stairs to say she was coming up, just in case he was in the middle of filling the chamber pot. To her surprise, he sounded more upbeat and replied, 'Come up.'

Carefully, she climbed the steep staircase and entered his bedroom.

'Cor, blimey, Mr Bates, you look a whole lot better.'

'Yeah, I guess I feel it,' he replied, pushing himself into an upright position.

'I hope it's all right. I've never been a good cook, but I've tried me best. Now then, you eat that, and I'll be back to wash up.'

Mr Bates took the bowl and stared at the steaming stew. 'Smells all right to me.'

Peggy smiled and was about to walk away.

'Don't worry about washing up, and, er . . . thank you.'

She smiled again and left.

* * *

Cyril and Howie had devoured their stew in the short time she'd been gone and were now wiping the sides of their bowls with a slice of bread.

Cyril looked up. 'Where's yours, Mum?'

'Now, don't you go worrying about me. I'll have mine later. Get yerselves ready for bed.'

As soon as they headed upstairs, Peggy cleaned one of their bowls and poured herself a small amount to satisfy her own hunger, careful to leave enough for tomorrow's dinner. She sat down and began to read a book, while listening to her boys giggling, and almost fell asleep as soon as their chattering stopped. By this time, she was ready for bed. A few embers remained, which glowed in the darkness, and she shivered as she entered her sparse bedroom. Most of the blankets were on the boys' double bed, so she put on a jumper and a long pair of socks and climbed under the threadbare sheets. It wasn't long before she was sound asleep.

* * *

Cyril lay awake worrying. His brother's soft purring told him that Howie was in a deep sleep. Quietly, he clambered from his bed, got dressed, and carried his shoes in his hands, as he crept downstairs, through the main room, and out of the back door. It was pitch-black, but Cyril wasn't afraid of the dark; he wasn't afraid of anything, except his mum running off like his father had.

He would have to find a way to put food on the table. The jam factory was his first port of call. After he'd nicked the coal the other night, he'd also clocked the back of the factory's loading bay, where lorry drivers pulled up and opened their back doors for the goods to be unloaded. He thought he might help himself at least to a bag of sugar from the Tate & Lyle lorry. However, as soon as he reached the factory, he noticed that the men had locked up the bay. He sat on the protruding low wall and waited in hope.

After a couple of hours of getting colder and colder, he got up and rubbed his frozen backside. He felt useless and tired, and so he headed back home. However, as soon as he turned the corner, he spotted a truck parked outside the pub. The double cellar doors that led down from the pavement were open and the driver was carrying barrels of beer on his shoulder down the steps. The light shone up against the dark backdrop, and Cyril decided to take a closer look.

Making sure he kept in the shadows, he crept his way towards the truck and spied a crate of whisky. His heart beat faster. No one was there. The driver and the landlord were busy down in the cellar. Without thinking, he snatched two bottles and scarpered along the main road. Just when he thought he'd got away with it, he heard a deep loud voice.

'Oi, you! Stop! I know who you are, you little shit!'

Cyril didn't look back; he ran as fast as he could in the cold air, which bit his face and burned his lungs. Turning sharp right, he could hear footsteps behind him, but nothing would stop him now. On he ran until he was in the alley that led to all the small gardens, or yards, as they were rightly called, including his own. But as the voice called out again, he decided not to go to his home but instead enter Mr Bates' place. Not wasting time by opening the gate, he hurdled it and ran to Mr Bates' back door, praying it wasn't locked.

He only hoped that the man shouting after him didn't see him go into Mr Bates' yard, or he would be well and truly done for.

Placing one bottle under his left arm and holding the other in his left hand, he turned the doorknob, and, luckily, it opened. In a panic, he closed the door behind him and sat down on the kitchen floor away from the window. Trying not to make a noise as he gasped for breath, he pulled his knees up to his chin and hugged himself. A million thoughts ran through his mind. If that man really knew who he was, he would bang at his house and get his mother out of bed. And if he got caught, his mother would be livid, ashamed, and, worse, sad.

But then his heart rate skyrocketed. Someone banged loudly at the back door.

'Oh, Christ. I'm—' He mumbled under his breath.

But he was cut short because from nowhere Mr Bates appeared in the kitchen.

Cyril looked up with wide eyes but was astonished when Mr Bates, dressed in a suit, totally ignored him and ripped the door open.

'What the bloody hell are you doing, banging at my back door this early in the morning!'

'Sorry, sir, but a young lad has just pinched two bottles of whisky and . . . Well, I thought, I, er . . . '

'I know you, and I know your farver. No one is in my house except me. Now, a word of warning: don't you ever knock at my bloody back door again.'

'Oh, er . . . Sorry, I didn't recognise you, Mr Bates. I, er . . . Sorry again.'

'Good. Now, fuck off.'

* * *

Cyril was totally shocked. He'd never heard Mr Bates speak like that before. It was pretty scary. The way he spoke so slowly, with such command, was alien to him.

Holding his breath, he waited for Mr Bates to shut the door and hoped that he genuinely hadn't seen him. He could then sneak back out and no one would be any the wiser. But he was in for another surprise when Mr Bates peered down.

'Get up, boy, and follow me!'

With the bottles hidden behind his back, Cyril stood up unsteadily. He watched Mr Bates take strong strides up the two steps and into the main room where he turned the light on and sat in the chair beside the fire. Cyril felt awkward but intrigued.

'So, lad, you've got a bottle of whisky, I see.'

Cyril clutched both bottles tightly behind his back.

'No use hiding them, lad.' He held out his hand to take one.

'I've got two,' said Cyril.

'Nah, lad, you've got one, 'cos one is now mine.'

Cyril had only ever thought of Mr Bates as an old man who liked gardening and who was now confined to his bed dying. He smirked. 'I tell ya what. You can have one for ten shillings. How about that?'

'Oh, is that right? And what do I get for not handing you

over?'

Cyril beamed more through relief at Mr Bates' softer tone. 'You get three shillings knocked off.'

'Take a seat, boy. You strike a hard bargain.'

'So do you wanna buy two, then?' asked Cyril, before he sat on the footstool brandishing the two large bottles with pride. 'Call it seventeen shillings for the pair.'

Mr Bates leaned back and steepled his hands, flicking his front tooth with his forefingers. 'Supply and demand, that's what the game's all about.'

Cyril frowned. 'What d'ya mean?'

'You pinched two bottles of Scotch just 'cos they were there, but tell me this? What were you doing out there when you should rightly be in bed?'

'I couldn't sleep.'

Mr Bates laughed. 'Right you are. So, you didn't plan anything, then? You just thought I'll have a nose around? See what I can nick?'

Cyril swallowed hard. He could see where this was heading. 'I'd best be going home.' He placed the two bottles on the side. 'You can pay me later.'

'Okay, lad, but listen to me. There's no point in nicking stuff that you can't sell. As I just said, it's called supply and demand.'

Cyril stopped in his tracks and glanced back at the old

man, who, somehow, didn't look so old now.

'Look, I'm not a thief as such. I just wanted to help me mum. Me dad's buggered off, and I have to be the man of the house. I only wanted to earn a few bob.'

Mr Bates laughed louder. 'Man of the house, eh?' He lowered his voice. 'Well, lad, your heart's in the right place, and you've got some bottle, I'll give you that, an' all. I tell you what. I'll give you thirty shillings. But I want you to do me a favour.'

Cyril chewed his bottom lip and looked Mr Bates up and down. 'What's the favour?'

'Go to McNalley the butcher and bring me back some meat.'

Cyril nodded. 'Yeah, sure. Give me a list and the money, and I'll go in a couple of hours. I'm . . . ' He yawned. 'I'm tired.'

Without waiting for the list, he waved goodbye and left through the back door.

CHAPTER TWO

Cyril woke up to find his brother already downstairs. He was about to turn over and catch some more shut-eye, but then he remembered the deal he had with Mr Bates.

As he climbed out of bed, he realised that he must have been dog-tired because he was still in his clothes from the night before. As his bare feet touched the wooden floor, he was pleasantly surprised. It was warm; in fact, the upstairs was toasty.

Peggy was buttering a wedge of bread when Cyril appeared. 'Not like you to lie in for so long.' She raised a questioning brow.

Cyril rubbed his face and scratched his head. 'It's lovely and warm, Mum,' he replied, ignoring her comment.

'Yeah, well, it's snowing, and I thought I'd best get this place warm if you two monkeys are gonna play outside today. No use in coming inside to a cold house. Now then, here's some bread and a cup of tea. I'm popping next door to make sure Mr Bates is okay. If you're going out, you wrap up warm. I can't have you two going down with pneumonia.'

Cyril thought about Mr Bates and his promise. 'I'll go next door, Mum. You stay in the warm.'

'Oh, I dunno, Son. He may not like it.'

'Honestly, Mum, he will be all right. Besides, he can only ask me to leave.'

Peggy looked at the blazing fire and sat down on the sofa. 'All right, love. You ask him if he wants a cup of tea and if there's anything he needs, anything at all. Tell him, I'll be around this afternoon. Oh, and can you take some coal and get his fire going?'

Cyril was nodding, while he pulled his shoes on.

In a flash, he was out of the door before his mother changed her mind.

He knocked first before he opened Mr Bates' back door and was surprised to hear him call out, 'Come in.'

The main room was already warm, and the fire was roaring up the chimney.

'Mum says I'm to make you a cup of tea and . . .' He looked at the fire. 'And make up the fire, but you've got that going yaself.'

Mr Bates smiled, and his eyes softened. 'You remembered our deal?'

Cyril nodded. 'Yeah, o' course. Have you got the list and the money?'

Mr Bates pulled a folded piece of paper from the inside

pocket of his suit. 'Just give him this and wait for the meat. It will be heavy, though. D'ya think you can carry it?'

Cyril smiled. 'I'm stronger than I look.'

'Go on, then. What are ya waiting for?'

Cyril looked at the untouched bottles of whisky.

Mr Bates laughed. 'I ain't forgotten your thirty shillings. Now, you listen to me. I'm trusting you, and you, lad, you need to trust me.'

Cyril paused in thought and decided that after the events of last night he *could* trust Mr Bates.

The snow was a good inch thick, and as he made his way towards the butcher's, he felt the wet soak into his shoes and sting his toes, but the thought of thirty shillings made him smile and walk even faster.

The butcher's at the end of the main road was a double-fronted property. He slowly gazed at the turkeys, geese, and lumps of meat hanging from hooks displayed in the window, wondering who in Bermondsey could afford joints of meat that size. Once inside, he looked down at the sawdust littering the tiled floor and inhaled the smell of fresh meat.

McNalley's two sons, Ernest and Gerald, were huge men but not as big as Malcolm McNalley himself.

Ernest was using a meat cleaver to chop through half a cow and Gerald was stuffing meat into skins to make sausages.

Cyril watched for a while, fascinated by the whole set-up.

He jumped when McNalley said, in a deep voice, 'What do *you* want?'

Cyril promptly pulled the note from his pocket, handed it to McNalley, and stepped back, intrigued by how the huge side of beef was being butchered.

'Oh, for fuck's sake.'

Ernest and Gerald stopped what they were doing and peered over their father's shoulder to read the note.

'I thought the man was dying?' said Gerald.

His father spat back, 'Well, Son, obviously he ain't gone yet. That's all I fucking need.'

'Dad, how much do we owe him?'

McNalley stared at the note and sighed. 'Half the bleedin' shop.'

'Are you kidding? We've been paying him for two years now, and he said the debt would die when he does. I sent sausages a week ago, and he looked like he was on his last legs then. He couldn't even breathe properly,' said Ernest.

'Well, he's still alive, and by the look of this list, he intends to stay that way . . . Fuck it, just prepare this lot.'

He turned to Cyril. 'What are you staring at?'

'I was wondering if you needed any help? I can work after school and at weekends.'

McNalley creased up his forehead as he peered closer.

'Ain't you Reggie Reardon's boy?'

Cyril nodded.

'Well, you can help by working off your ol' man's debt.'

Ernest and Gerald laughed, which annoyed Cyril.

'His debt ain't my debt.'

'You're a cheeky fucker, ain't ya,' growled McNalley.

'I could say the same about you,' retorted Cyril.

Before McNalley could ease himself from the counter to clip the Reardon lad around the ear for his cheek, he stopped and thought about Mr Bates. Mr Bates wouldn't like it if he smacked his errand boy.

'You should watch your mouth.'

Cyril stood silently and waited for the bags to be filled with meat. He wondered if in fact he could carry them, but then he thought about the thirty shillings. Come what may, he would get that meat back.

McNalley laughed when he handed Cyril the bags and saw how the weight instantly pulled the boy's shoulders down. Yet his amusement turned to intrigue when he saw how the scrawny-looking lad gripped the handles, straightened his shoulders, and marched with confident strides out through the door.

By the time Cyril had reached Mr Bates' back door, he'd stopped four times along the way. He couldn't feel his fingers, and his back ached as if it had been trampled on by a herd of elephants.

Mr Bates opened the back door and smiled, quickly relieving Cyril of his bags. When he took the first one, his eyes widened. It was so heavy that even he would have struggled to carry it, let alone two bags.

'Get inside, lad. Warm yaself up. I'll put this lot away in the fridge.'

While Mr Bates went into the kitchen, Cyril sat on the stool in front of the fire and rubbed his numb hands. 'Gerald thought you were dying. And Ernest mentioned something about the debt dying when you die, and his dad said they still owe you half the shop.' He didn't know why he told Mr Bates that information, but he felt a kind of affiliation to the old geezer. Besides, he didn't like Mr McNalley.

'They told you that, did they?'

Still facing the roaring fire, Cyril called out, 'Yeah, Mr McNalley and his fat sons were talking about you as if you should be dead by now.'

'The cheeky bastards. Yeah, they owe me a lot.'

He stopped when he realised that he was having a conversation about his business with just a kid. Then he smiled to himself when he thought back to his younger days. He was probably just as direct and confident as Cyril.

Yet there was one boy who was more upfront than him and that was his old and best pal, Dillon Docherty, Cyril's grandfather and Peggy's father.

It was so obvious that Cyril didn't take after his father Reginald because he was a proper idiot, but Dillon wasn't. In fact, Cyril was a lot like Dillon; not so much, perhaps, in his looks, but in his ways.

Mr Bates sighed, feeling guilty about the past.

'Listen, Cyril. You keep this business between me and you a secret, right?'

Looking away from the fire, Cyril frowned. 'Business, Mr Bates?'

'Yeah, son. You can run a few errands for me, but you keep them to yaself. I'll pay you a few shillings, but you keep your mouth shut.'

Cyril beamed. 'Yeah, o' course I will. I only told you about what the McNalleys said 'cos I thought you should know.'

Mr Bates nodded and walked over to a large pot on the shelf to the left of the fireplace. He pulled the lid off and scooped out a handful of shillings.

Cyril watched in amazement. 'Cor.'

Mr Bates counted out thirty shillings. 'There, that's yours, and before you go, look in the fridge. All the meat on the top shelf is for your mum. Best I keep it here, though. It will go off, otherwise.'

Cyril's heart was beating fast with excitement. His mum would be over the moon. Quickly, he jumped up and headed to the kitchen and opened the fridge. 'Blimey. Can I take some now?'

Mr Bates sat in his armchair, smiling. 'Yeah, of course you can. And tell your mum, not to worry about popping in anymore. I'm up on me feet now. You, though, pop in after school tomorrow, right?'

Cyril pulled four pork chops from the fridge and smiled. 'Mum will do you a dinner an' all, for this lot.'

Mr Bates shook his head. 'There's no need. I can cook me own. I enjoy cooking.'

Cyril frowned. He'd never heard of a man cooking before, but he nodded politely and left. The feeling as he walked up the garden path was of relief and pride.

As soon as he was inside, he placed the meat on the table and emptied his pockets of the shiny silver shillings.

Peggy was sewing up a hole in her cardigan when she suddenly gasped. 'What in God's name!'

She jumped up from her seat and rushed over to the table. 'Oh, my word, Cyril. Where did you get this lot from?'

'Mum, it's thirty shillings, for the rent and . . . whatever else.'

Worry now dulled her excitement. 'Cyril, where did it come from?'

He flicked his eyes to the left. 'Mr Bates gave it to me.'

Suddenly, her face flushed red as she gripped his arms. 'Oh my God! What did he do? Did he touch you? Did he hurt you?'

'No, Mum. What's the matter?'

'Well, why would he give you thirty shillings and . . . ?' She looked at the open bag of meat. 'And all of this?'

'It's all right, Mum. I just went to the butcher's for him and fetched him his meat, and he said we could have all of the meat on the top shelf in his fridge.'

'And what about the money?'

'Oh, bloody hell! Do you have to ask, Mum?'

'Enough of the language, and, yes, Cyril, I have to ask.'

Cyril sat awkwardly on the edge of the table and told her what had happened last night. He'd decided that there was no point in leaving out any details.

Peggy listened intently, but a rush of sadness and guilt came over her. Her eldest son was running around the streets in the dark, looking for an opportunity to make a few shillings because he felt he needed to be the man of the house. He was mentally older than an eight-year-old – she knew that – but even so, he was only a lad still in primary school.

Cyril peered up at his mother's face. 'Sorry, Mum. I was only trying to help.'

'Aw, you, ya daft beggar. There's no need to say "sorry". It's my fault. I should be the one taking better care of us.' Her eyes were suddenly drawn to the shillings. 'Cyril, if I go out tonight, would you promise me you will stay inside and look after Howie?'

Looking at the money, Cyril swallowed back the lump that was forming in his throat. He nodded as he looked down before sauntering away. History was repeating itself. His father had done exactly that. It was that same eager, excited expression, whenever there were a few shillings in the pot. He would go out using some excuse and come back drunk. The cupboard would be empty and the rent man would be banging at the door. Now his mother was about to do the same.

* * *

At 8.00 p.m., after they'd sat down to a hearty and tasty meal, Cyril joined Howie in front of the fire to play a game of marbles. He couldn't even look at his mother when she said she was going off out. Instead, he sighed and said 'goodbye', staring at the glass balls that Howie was winning from him. He would have easily beaten Howie, but not this evening. He was heartbroken. As much as he loved his mother, he felt so disappointed that she would use the money to go out, instead of paying off the rent, or the coalman, or even filling the cupboards with food.

By 10.00 p.m., he and Howie had climbed into bed, and within minutes, Howie was dead to the world. However, he couldn't sleep. He lay there with his arms folded in front of him, while his eyes stared up to the ceiling. Trying to excuse his mother's want for a night out, he racked his brains to make sense of it all. He'd seen her crying after the rent man had belittled her, and he felt sad when she sighed into the empty cupboards. Turning on his side, he closed his watery eyes and hugged himself to sleep.

It was 2.00 a.m., when Cyril heard the back door open. He would have gone back to sleep, if he hadn't heard a heavy thud and then silence. Quickly, he sprang from his bed and hurried down the stairs to find his mother lying on the floor. His first thought was that she was drunk, just like his father used to get. Legless. However, when he turned on the gaslight, he momentarily froze. His mother was bleeding from a gash at the side of her head. The blood covered her face, her neck, and her hands. Her jacket was ripped and so was the top half of her dress. It was her Sunday best dress as well.

With a dry mouth and his heart beating fast, Cyril rushed over to help his mother to the sofa, but as he lifted her arm, she didn't move.

'Mum!' he cried, as he leaned closer to her face. 'Mum!'

His voice wavered in panic. 'Mum! Wake up! Please, Mum!'

Her stillness frightened the life out of him, and as much as he felt he was the man of the house, this situation was beyond his capability. 'It's all right, Mum. I'll get help.'

He stepped over her lifeless body and leapfrogged over the fence. Without knocking, he opened Mr Bates' back door to find him sliding his feet into a pair of slippers. Again, Mr Bates was smartly dressed, even though it was so early.

'I heard you, Cyril. What's going on?'

Cyril was breathless with fear. 'It's my M . . . Mum. She's hurt bad. Please come.'

He didn't wait for a reply but rushed out of the house and

jumped over the side fence again. To Cyril's great surprise, Mr Bates was hot on his heels, having done the same.

When they arrived inside the house to where Peggy was lying unconscious, Mr Bates pulled Cyril aside, so he could take over and tend to the situation.

Relieved to have Mr Bates with him, Cyril stepped back and watched him carefully scoop his mother up in his arms and gently lay her on the sofa.

The gaslight showed every cut and bruise on Peggy's face, and the nasty deep claw mark just above her left breast. For her own dignity, Mr Bates placed the torn part of her dress over her exposed breast and then checked a gash on the side of her head. 'Boil a kettle, lad. Do you have any towels or sheets, so I can clean her up?'

'Shall I run for the doctor?'

'No!' He then lowered his voice. 'Not just yet, boy. Get me some sheets first to clean her up.'

Cyril rushed to the foot of the stairs but paused and turned back to see what Mr Bates was doing. Then he heard him whisper into his mother's ear. The tone was harsh. 'Who the fuck did this to you, Peggy? Tell me.'

With those words ringing in his ears, Cyril ran up the stairs. He'd not even contemplated that someone had hurt her.

As he ripped open the cabinet doors at the end of his bed, he found a new clean bed sheet and quickly tucked it under his arm. He glanced at his brother gently snoring. *It would take a bomb exploding outside to wake up Howie*, he thought.

Tearing back down the stairs, he placed the bed sheet on the floor by Mr Bates and then hurried to the kitchen to put the kettle on.

'Cyril, go to my house. In the kitchen cabinet, by the window, you'll find a bottle of brandy. And bring some sugar, if you don't have any.'

Cyril was just pleased that Mr Bates was taking over and seemed to know what to do. Within what seemed like seconds, Cyril was back, with a bag of sugar in one hand and a bottle of brandy in the other.

'Good lad. Now, make a sweet tea and add a measure of the brandy. Bring over a bowl of warm water.'

'She ain't gonna die, is she?'

Mr Bates shook his head. 'No, son, but she's hurt bad. So, you just do as I tell you.'

Cyril nodded, rooted to the spot. His eyes were like saucers.

'Well, go on, lad. Get the tea and the water.'

With his hands trembling, Cyril poured the hot water into a teapot, put sugar and a generous helping of brandy into the cup, and then added the tea. He hurried over to Mr Bates with the drink and then returned to the kitchen to pour the rest of the hot water into a plastic bucket; he didn't have a bowl. Once he'd topped up the bucket with cool water, he hurried back to Mr Bates and watched him at work.

Holding and supporting the back of Peggy's head, Mr

Bates put the sweet tea, laced with brandy, to her lips and allowed some warm liquid to go into her mouth. Slowly but surely, she sipped the tea and then her eyes flicked open.

'Take it easy, girl. Don't rush to get up or else you'll faint again.'

Peggy rested her head back and took a few deep breaths.

'That's it, girl. You just rest while I get this cut cleaned up.' He turned to face Cyril. 'Lad, go upstairs and see if you can find a dressing gown or something for your mum.'

Cyril frowned, but as young as he was, he assumed that Mr Bates wanted a quiet word with his mum, and so he did as he was told, but, again, he paused at the first step and listened.

'Peggy, who did this? Give me a name, will ya?'

'No, Mr Bates, I don't know.'

'What were you doing?'

'I went to the Black Horse to play poker.'

'Alone, Peggy?'

'Well, yeah. I had Cyril's money, and I wanted to make a few more shillings . . .'

'Easy, girl, take another sip of this.'

Cyril was still fixed to the spot. He had to hear the rest of the conversation.

'Did you win?'

'Yeah, I did. I won three pounds. I was on me way back when . . . well, when I was bashed up.'

Cyril felt his blood run cold with guilt. He'd assumed she'd gone off to get drunk, when all she'd tried to do was to go out to earn money for her family. However, he was surprised that she'd gone to play poker. He knew she owned a pack of cards, but he'd been oblivious to the fact that she could play. Intrigued, he stayed where he was on the step.

'So did this attacker take your money, then?'

'Yes, Mr Bates. He ripped me best frock, as you can see. I should never have hidden the money down me top.'

'And you didn't see who it was?' asked Mr Bates, suspiciously.

'I . . . er, I don't want no trouble. I'm on me own, with two little 'uns, as ya know.'

'Yeah, and I should have looked out for ya more than I did, instead of wallowing in me own self-pity. Well, Peggy, you ain't on your own, girl, now.'

'Mr Bates, I ain't no charity case . . .' Her voice trailed off into a whisper.

'Peggy, I was supposed to look out for ya. Your farver asked me to keep an eye out when you moved back with that good-for-nuffin husband of yours.'

'What? Why would my dad . . . ?'

Cyril sensed his mother was getting tired; however, he

really wanted to know himself.

'Never mind, all that. All you need to know is that your farver and me were mates. Let's leave it at that for now. Now then, Peggy. Who robbed ya?'

'Mr Bates, please, it doesn't matter. I was stupid to even think I could walk into a poker game and walk out with the winnings.'

'Are you telling me there was more than one fella who beat you up?'

'No. I thanked them all, put my money in a pouch, and left the pub. I then stuffed the notes down me bra. When I got near the corner of our street, the next thing was I was thrown against the brick wall and tossed about like a rag doll. But listen. Please leave it. I don't want attention drawn to me. I just want the incident left alone.'

'Who was *it*, Peggy?'

Cyril strained to hear, but his mother was whispering, and so he never got to know who it was. However, what he did get to understand was that Mr Bates was probably kind to him because he was friends with his grandfather.

* * *

Once Peggy was cleaned up and in her dressing gown, she sat upright sipping her tea with less sugar and no brandy. Mr Bates left her to it; he told her he needed to sort something out.

Later that morning, Mr Bates returned with a bag of meat, to cook some breakfast, and he'd also brought with him some old comics he'd collected over the years. He sent the boys upstairs out of the way.

Cyril could sense that the man had more to talk about with his mother.

After an hour or so of flicking through the old comics, Cyril jumped up when he heard Mr Bates call them down. Cyril and Howie found Mr Bates in their kitchen cooking up a feast, which amused them both. They'd never seen a grown man cooking before. He'd made bacon sandwiches all round. The fire was stoked, and the room seemed less gloomy. Cyril felt in some ways relieved as if his responsibility of being the man of the house was being relinquished, even if it was just for one day.

Cyril sat next to his mother and leaned into her. 'Are you all right, Mum? Do you need the quack?'

She patted his hand. 'No, I'm okay. I'm just a bit shaken up, is all.'

He looked at the bandage around her head. 'That looks more than a bit shaken up, Mum.'

'The head always bleeds a lot, but don't you go worrying about me. Mr Bates has made sure that I am okay. And, Son, you did good with your quick thinking.'

'You gave me a right fright, Mum. I thought you were dead.' He glanced down and noticed her bruised knuckles. He knew then that she must have put up a damn good fight.

'It will take more than a bash on me noggin to finish me off.'

‘Oi, son, don’t go pestering your muvver now. You skip along outside and get some fresh air in ya lungs, and take Howie with you.’

Cyril was about to have a go back, until he realised that Mr Bates was merely helping out, and he was grateful.

* * *

Outside there was that kind of stillness in the air that only arises when it has been snowing. The snow was deep enough to make snowballs. Howie was rolling the snow, determined to build a snowman.

But Cyril was uneasy. He couldn’t help but worry about his mother and the fact that they were skint. He would have to find a way to earn a few bob. And his concern turned to anger at the idea of a grown man beating up his mother. He wandered around the garden with his hands in his trouser pockets kicking the snow. He wished he was older and strong enough to bash the man up who had hurt his mother. He imagined using a metal pole and smashing it around the man’s head until he was unconscious and on the floor bleeding, like he’d seen his mother.

A snowball hit him on the side of the head and pulled him instantly from his raging thoughts. He shot a cold, harsh look in the direction from where the snowball came to find two lads, one a good foot taller than him and another one the same size. They were laughing and ready to launch another snowball. If it had been any other day, Cyril would have laughed and engaged in a good snowball fight back, but not today.

'Throw another one and I'll black your eyes.'

The lad who was the same size as Cyril dropped his, there and then, but the taller boy, with the dark eyes, dark hair, and hands like shovels, ignored Cyril's comment and launched a tightly compressed snowball that hit Cyril clean on the jaw and knocked him backwards. 'Black me eyes, would ya? I'd love to see you try, you scrawny little runt.'

Almost foaming at the mouth, Cyril's eyes were red with anger. '*Scrawny*! Bloody *scrawny*! Why, I'll flaming well knock you on your arse, you lanky piece of dog shit!'

Howie stopped what he was doing and quickly stood by Cyril's side. He remained quiet, but that rosy countenance, along with its permanent grin, prevailed.

The tall lad then glared menacingly at Cyril, but his friend seemed more worried about the crazed look on Howie's face.

'Reckon you'll knock me on me arse, yeah? I'd like to see you try.' The bigger lad was already flexing his fingers before holding them up ready to take a boxing stance.

Cyril was taking deep breaths through his nostrils. As if the world had changed colour before his very eyes, he ran towards the gate, and without opening it, he jumped over and hurtled head first into the tall lad. Before anyone could say 'fight', Cyril began punching and swinging his arms, landing hard and fast jabs into the lad's ribs. So fast and furious was Cyril that the bigger lad was now pushed against a wall, fervently trying to stop the barrage of blows.

It wasn't until Mr Bates called out that Cyril, now breathless, stopped and stepped back.

The true colours of the world he lived in came back. There before him was a lad doubled over, with bruised cheeks and blood dripping from the corners of his mouth.

Howie was still grinning as if all this was normal.

In contrast, Mr Bates wasn't grinning. He pulled Cyril away. 'What on earth's going on?' he bellowed. But as soon as the tall lad straightened up, Mr Bates recognised him. 'Cor, you must be Marsden's boy. If so, what are you doing in Bermondsey? Your farver lives in Poplar.'

'We . . .' He tried to catch his breath, but he was not prepared to risk taking his eyes off the lad, who stood like a rabid dog, ready to have another go at him. He wiped the blood away from his mouth and then gave a look of spite. 'We moved into the road two days ago. They've condemned our house.'

'What were you two fighting over, Cyril?' Mr Bates asked, while still clutching him by the collar.

Cyril shook himself free. 'That great long streak of pi . . . pilchards called me "scrawny" and hit me on the sly with a snowball.'

'Oh, is that all? Well, since you two are gonna be neighbours, you'd best make up, or you'll be warring every frigging day. Now, be real men about it and shake hands.'

Cyril narrowed his eyes and looked the Marsden lad up and down, but he wasn't going to be the first to put out his hand.

'Well, go on, then, Cyril. Shake on it,' demanded Mr

Bates.

Just as Howie was about to do likewise, he slipped in the snow. It was a sight to behold as he slid around like a cartoon character from a *Tom and Jerry* show. And it was so hilarious that the Marsden boy burst out laughing.

Even Cyril saw the funny side and decided there and then that this day shouldn't end in anger. 'I'm Cyril Reardon and that's me brother, Howie.'

A huge hand slid from out of a long sleeve, and Cyril then realised that if this lad had got a punch in, he himself as sure as hell would have been on his back. Gratefully, he shook hands and felt the strength behind that grip.

'Me name's Frank, Frank Marsden. This, here, is me mate Freddy. He's staying with me while his mum is nursing a baby.'

The soft-faced lad smiled. 'Yeah, number nine, I think.'

'Nine kids!' shrieked Cyril. 'Blimey.' He looked at the bruises on Frank's face. 'I'm, er, well, sorry.'

Frank held his head up and laughed. It was a very deep laugh for a young lad. 'I'll remember next time not to call you "scrawny", eh?'

'Right, I'll leave you all to it,' said Mr Bates, before he marched back along the garden path to see to Peggy.

Cyril looked Frank up and down again. 'So, how old are you?'

As Frank grinned, his cheeks flushed and his dark eyes narrowed even more. 'I'm nine. What about you?'

'I'm nearly nine, so we may be in the same class at school.'

Frank nodded and looked over at the sad attempt at a snowman.

* * *

By the time it was dark, all four boys had thoroughly got to know each other and were hoping it would be snowing tomorrow, so they could have another fun-filled time after school building snowmen and having a few snowball fights.

Cyril and Howie were by now frozen to the bone, but they were, nevertheless, full of laughs and smiles as they warmed their hands by the fire.

Peggy was still very pale but able to walk about. The cut to the head wasn't as bad as it had looked previously, just as she'd thought.

However, Mr Bates had spent the day ensuring her needs were taken care of, and he only left to go home after he'd cooked a stew and loaded the fire with coal.

With a crochet shawl around her shoulders, Peggy began to rise from the sofa to pour the boys a bowl of stew each, but the second Cyril saw her get up, he waved his hands.

'Mum, it's all right. Sit down. I can do whatever needs doing.'

Peggy, grateful for the offer, nodded. 'Go and dish yourselves a bowl each. The stew's still warm, and, I have to admit, it tastes lovely. He's a good cook, is that Mr Bates.'

From nowhere, Howie piped up, 'Is he gonna be our new dad?'

Cyril pushed his brother gently. 'Don't be bloody stupid. Mr Bates is old enough to be our grandfarver, and, anyway, we don't need a dad, do we? We're fine on our own.'

Peggy listened to her son, trying to remember if he'd ever been a child. He had such an old head on his shoulders. 'Mr Bates is our neighbour, and we will treat him with respect. No, he is not your new farver, but he is still to be spoken to politely.'

'I am polite,' replied Cyril.

'Sometimes, Son, you're too brazen, and it can come across as rude. You'll get away with it once you're a grown-up, but, for now, try to ask less frank questions.'

Cyril laughed. 'Me new friend is called Frank. Cor, Mum. He's like a giant, but he's all right.'

Peggy lowered her voice. 'Yes, Cyril, I heard how Mr Bates had to break up a fight.'

'Well, Mum, we're mates now. This lad, Frank Marsden, he's my age, and he's sort of a lot like me, Mum, only much bigger.'

* * *

Once Howie looked as though he was about to fall asleep, Cyril decided to take him upstairs. He knew his mother was in no fit state to carry him up the stairs herself.

Howie, who had his head resting on the arm of the sofa, stirred, wiped his dribble from his cheek, and flicked his eyes open.

'Come on, Howie. Let's go to bed.'

Howie loved his sleep. Slowly, he dragged his weary body up the stairs and climbed into bed. He was out like a light before his head had even hit the pillow.

Cyril covered him over and returned downstairs to make his mother a cup of tea.

Peggy sensed he wanted to talk and waited before the cup was in her hands before she patted the footstool. 'Sit down, Son. Tell me, what's on your mind?'

Cyril eagerly sat down.

Peggy was watching him carefully; she could sense his brain ticking away, trying to articulate the right words.

'Mum, I didn't know you could play poker. D'ya think you could teach me?'

Peggy screwed up her dainty nose. 'Why on earth would you want to play poker? Crikey, look what happened to me! You don't want to learn the game. Just be a boy and do your sums and your spellings.'

'I do all my schoolwork. I got best marks in sums, and the

teacher gave me a sweet for my English, but I really want to learn poker.'

'But why, Cyril?' She sounded tired.

'Probably for the same reason you did, Mum.'

Even though Peggy felt drained, she had to smile because her little lad had a bloody answer for everything, and he was often right. 'Fetch me the pack of cards. The cards are—'

She didn't get to finish before Cyril was up off the stool and diving into the kitchen drawer that held all their paperwork from the rent book to her marriage certificate.

She sighed but decided not to ask how the hell he knew where everything was in the house.

Instead, she took the pack from him. 'How many playing cards are there in a pack?'

'Fifty-two.'

Intrigued, Peggy asked him to shuffle the cards. She wondered if he'd been shown already. But once he tried, the cards flew all over the place. She then knew where to start, and Cyril being a quick learner, she guessed it wouldn't take too long. 'First, Cyril, you need to play an easy game, like pairs or Fish—'

'Mum, I want to learn *poker*.'

Peggy sighed. 'One lesson you must get right first is to listen before jumping in. In fact, Cyril, saying less and letting someone else speak will gain you knowledge about them rather than the other way round. There, that's your first lesson in poker. Keep your mouth shut.'

'Now I want you to learn the deck of cards before you even think about playing a game of poker. You need to know every card in the pack, and once you've done that, then you can tell me what you know. We can play Fish just to get you used to holding cards and . . . and . . .'

'Mum? What is it?'

Peggy shook her head. 'Nuffin, Son. It's just late and I'm exhausted. Why don't you pick all those cards up and count them to make sure there are fifty-two. Then you can get yaself off to bed.'

Cyril decided not to protest but to do as he was told. His mother was particularly white, and so he thought it best to get out of her way. 'Goodnight, Mum. Er, can I play with these?'

'Yes, Cyril. You can have them. I don't think I ever want to play the game again. Well, not outside the home.'

As he skipped up the stairs, he gripped the well-used pack of cards and held them to his nose. They had a strange smell. It wasn't nasty. The cards just looked old and had a fusty odour. Once his mother was better, he would ask her more about this game of poker.

CHAPTER THREE

By Monday morning, the snow had begun to melt. Both Cyril and Howie were not excited about the prospect of walking in all the grey slush, certainly when there was no option of at least a few snowballs to throw along the way.

Just as Cyril tied his shoes up, there was a loud bang at the door.

Peggy was still a little light-headed. 'Go and see who it is, Cyril, but check through the window first. Don't answer, if it's the rent man.'

Cyril hurried into the front room and gently pulled back the corner of the curtain; there like a soldier stood his new mate Frank Marsden. Excitedly, Cyril opened the door and dragged the strapping lad inside. 'Mum, it's me new mate, Frank.'

Peggy pulled her dressing gown tighter around herself and stood up from the table. 'Well, invite him in. Don't leave him . . .' She paused, as Frank stepped into the house. 'Ah, you already have.' She looked Frank up and down. 'What did ya muvver do? Stand you in horse manure, did she? Gawd, blimey, you're a tall 'un.'

Frank laughed. 'Pleased to meet ya, Mrs Reardon.'

'And you too, Frank.'

'Now then, you three. Don't get all wet and filthy before you get to school or you'll be miserable all day. Oh, and make sure you eat the school dinner, Cyril.' She looked at Howie. 'I've no need to tell you.' She laughed as she poked his pot belly.

As soon as they were outside, Cyril tapped Frank on the shoulder. 'Listen, I'm sorry. Ya know, I felt bad, bashing you up like that.'

Frank shrugged his shoulders. 'It's all right, but don't tell me dad. He'll only go and thump me, if he finds out I've lost a fight.'

'I don't suppose you have lost many, though, have ya?'

'Nah, but I've not had many, either.'

Just as they reached the end of the street, Frank stopped dead and looked ahead. 'Cor, what d'ya suppose has gone on over there? Look, Cyril, there's bobbies everywhere.'

'Come on, let's go and ask,' replied Cyril, as he ran towards the pub.

Frank and Howie followed but then held back and watched when Cyril confidently approached the tall policeman.

'What's going on? Is someone dead? Anyone been murdered?'

The officer bent down and tapped the side of his nose. 'Get off to school and mind ya own business.'

But Cyril wasn't going to accept any brush-off. 'Well, it *is* me business. I *live* 'ere, and if there's a murderer on the loose, I wanna know.'

'Get off to school with ya.'

Cyril looked at the hive of activity surrounding the pub. The cellar door was open, and a light shone up and onto the pavement. The orange glow from the leaded windows made the pub look so inviting against the gloomy backdrop of the Bermondsey streets.

Cyril stepped off the pavement and joined Howie and Frank on the other side of the road. They were just as intrigued. 'He won't tell me nuffin, but I bet ya, someone's been murdered, all right.'

'It's the landlord. It's gotta be,' said Frank, in his deep monotonal voice.

'What? How d'ya know that?'

''Cos, look over there.' He nodded in the direction of the pub. 'See that lady? She's crying, and she's in her nightclothes, so she's got to be the missus of the landlord. So I think he's been murdered. Look, Cyril! See that copper? He's giving her a cup of tea.'

'I can see you're gonna be a detective when you grow up. Blimey, the landlord murdered. I wonder why?'

'Someone don't like him, I fink,' replied Howie.

Both Frank and Cyril burst out laughing.

'Well, that'll be loads of people, 'cos my ol' man reckons

he's one nasty bastard.'

Cyril smiled. He liked the way Frank spoke and the fact that he swore as well. 'How does your dad know him? I mean, I thought you came from Poplar?'

Frank shrugged his shoulders. 'I dunno. He just knows everyone, and everyone knows him.'

'Oh, that's right. Mr Bates, me neighbour, knows your dad an' all.'

'Yeah, ya see everyone knows him. What's your dad do?'

'My ol' man? Huh, he buggered off to Ireland, so I don't rightly know, but if he ever comes back, I'll tell him to sod off.'

The rest of the walk to school had Cyril and Frank chatting for England. It was as if they had the same ideas about life. It was a first for Cyril because he trusted no one and didn't care much for the lads in the street; he found them a little too young for him. He had enough to contend with, just by looking out for Howie, but that was a different matter altogether because they were related by blood.

The day dragged and Cyril spent most of his staring out of the window. He couldn't stop thinking about the murdered landlord. As his mind ran away with him, he remembered that his mother had been to that pub to play poker, and what with Frank telling him that the landlord was a right bastard, he wondered if it was in fact the landlord who had attacked his mother. He just wished he'd heard the conversation fully between Mr Bates and his mother. He'd planned to tell his new mate about the incident, but something bothered him, and his imagination began to put forward all kinds of weird scenarios to find the cold truth. So Cyril decided today that he would keep his thoughts to himself.

As soon as lunchtime arrived, he joined Frank in the queue. 'It's a shame you're not in my class.'

'Yeah, but even so, I can meet you at break and lunch. What's the grub like?'

Cyril screwed his nose up. 'It's all right if you like lumpy mash and boiled cabbage.'

As soon as Frank held his plate out to the dinner lady, he got double helpings.

Cyril marvelled. 'Hey, why does he get that much?'

Zena, the greasy-faced, red-headed dinner lady, flared her nostrils at the cheek of Cyril, but she decided to answer anyway. ''Cos one ice cream scoop of mash won't even fill his boots, whereas you, little lad, will be bloated on half a scoop.'

Cyril looked across at her and grinned. 'So, I bet you eat ten scoops to fill your boots.'

'Enough of your lip. Move along.'

Frank was still laughing by the time they sat at the table. 'Cor, Cyril, don't your mouth get you into trouble?'

Cyril positively beamed with delight. 'That's what me mum says. But she also says it gets me back out of it an' all.'

* * *

The white clouds of snow had gone and all that hung in the sky were the heavy clouds of rain.

The sweet smell drifting from the jam factory had Cyril's stomach rumbling. He hoped that his mother was well enough to have cooked them all a filling dinner from the meat that Mr Bates had put aside for them. He dawdled because Howie was dragging his heels. If he was being honest, he was a little annoyed with his brother because it meant that he couldn't keep up with Frank. Frank had to be home early. He never mentioned to Cyril why, though. They told each other just enough, until they could fully trust one another.

As soon as Cyril and Howie had skipped through the back door, the aroma of steamed bacon pudding made Cyril's mouth water. His mother looked surprisingly well. Her face was glowing more from the cooking than anything else.

'Dinner will be in about an hour . . . Oh, I think Mr Bates wants you to run an errand for him.'

Cyril had those mad ideas crashing through his mind again: Mr Bates, and the dead landlord. 'Okay, I'll pop around now.'

'Darling, listen to me. You be careful. You can always say "no".'

Cyril looked up and tilted his head. 'What do you mean?'

Peggy stirred the gravy and tasted the contents using an old wooden spoon. She winced as the boiling hot liquid touched her lips. 'I know Mr Bates has been very kind to us, but I don't want you being his gofer. You do have homework, and . . . well, anyway, all I'm saying is you can always say "no".'

Cyril didn't know what the word 'gofer' meant, but he had a pretty good idea, and it was okay, as long as he got paid.

He knocked, out of politeness first, before letting himself in. Surprised that Mr Bates wasn't by the fire, he called out, 'It's me, Cyril.'

In a second, Mr Bates appeared from the front room, looking a little sheepish. It was a far cry from the confident – almost arrogant – expression that he usually wore.

Looking over Cyril's shoulder, he asked, 'Have you locked the back door behind you?'

Cyril shook his head but acted right away, by locking the door. He sensed there was serious business afoot.

'Everything okay, Mr Bates?'

Mr Bates stared for a moment. 'Sit down, Cyril. I want to have a discussion with you, man to man.'

Cyril sat instantly on the footstool, now mightily intrigued. He had never heard anyone use that expression 'man to man'.

'Okay, son, it's like this. You see, me and you, well, we're pretty much alike, wouldn't you say?'

Eyeing Mr Bates cagily, Cyril nodded. 'I reckon so.'

'Good. Right, I am gonna trust you with something that I wouldn't even trust me own brother with. Now, I know you're only nearly nine, but you have a good head on ya shoulders and a cute mind that knows when to keep ya mouth shut. Am I right?'

Cyril nodded.

'Hmm, where were you late Saturday night around midnight, but possibly later?'

For a minute, Cyril thought Mr Bates sounded like a policeman, and then a torrent of dark thoughts ran through his mind. 'Er, I could have been anywhere. I don't sleep.'

A frown flickered its way across Mr Bates' forehead. 'So were you in my living room, playing Scrabble with me, then? Only I can't remember if it was you who beat me or someone else. 'Cos, I'm sure I owe them five quid.'

Cyril was really warming to this man. He grinned from ear-to-ear and straightened up. 'Oh, that was definitely me, Mr Bates. We played Scrabble, drank Coke, I spelled out the word "dinosaur", and I beat you fair and square. If ya remember, you had a Scrabble board, didn't you, Mr Bates?'

Totally bemused, Mr Bates wondered if there was anything Cyril couldn't work out for himself.

'So,' continued Cyril, 'if anyone asks if I've seen you, I can tell 'em I was around yours all Saturday evening until the early hours playing Scrabble and drinking Coca-Cola until I got tired. Then I went home.' He paused and looked confused for a moment. 'Hang on, Mr Bates, don't you mean *Sunday* night?'

Mr Bates inclined his head. 'Why would I mean Sunday night?'

'Well, on the way to school, I saw the police outside the pub, and a woman in tears, so I reckon the landlord was killed either last night or early this morning.'

Mr Bates frowned heavily. 'What's that got to do with me?'

'Well, did you kill the landlord of the Black Horse?'

As if someone had stabbed him with a sharp instrument, Mr Bates nearly jumped out of his skin. 'What the fucking 'ell are you on about?'

Cyril flinched so much, he almost fell off the footstool; he didn't like the look on Mr Bates' face. 'Oh, sorry, I thought you . . . Oh, never mind.' He felt sick and wished he'd kept his thoughts to himself.

Grabbing Cyril by the shoulders, Mr Bates pulled him close. 'Who the fuck said I killed him, eh?'

'No one,' replied Cyril firmly. 'It's just that with me mum playing cards at that pub, and her getting attacked, and then you being all cagey, like, I just thought . . .'

'Yeah, well, lad, you think too much. Of course I didn't kill the landlord of the pub.'

'Okay, er, but do I still get the fiver?'

'You'll get your money but only once the week is over. Got it?'

Cyril nodded hard. 'Yeah, I've got it.'

With that, Mr Bates held out his hand for Cyril to shake on it.

As Cyril hopped over the fence, all he could think about was the five quid to hand over to his mum. He knew, though, he couldn't divulge how he'd come by this large sum of money. As far as he was concerned that was men's business.

After they'd all sat down to eat the mouth-watering bacon pudding, they heard a commotion coming from Mr Bates' house next door.

Peggy rose from her seat and hurried to the front room window to find the police outside and Mr Bates being helped into a police car.

Cyril kept his face down on his food; he knew he needed to keep his mouth shut.

It was Howie who wanted to know what was going on, but Peggy shrugged her shoulders and didn't answer.

A cold feeling ripped through Cyril. Had his mother been in on the murder? Was that what it was all about?

As Peggy cleared away the empty bowls, she peered back at Cyril and smiled. It was an odd look, as if she knew his thoughts and was in some way approving them.

Two hours passed quietly following the commotion next door when a hard knock at their own front door had Peggy up in a flash and rushing to the window.

'Who is it, Mum?' called out Cyril.

'The police, love.'

As his mother opened the door, Cyril could see two

officers towering over her. One of them looked past his mother and glared his way.

'May we come in, Mrs Reardon?'

Peggy stepped aside and allowed the two officers inside. They respectfully wiped their feet and joined her in the front room.

Cyril glared at the two of them, and, without being prompted, he grabbed his brother's arm and said, 'Come on, Howie. It's time for bed.'

Howie didn't argue. Once they reached the top step, Cyril pushed Howie into the bedroom and told him to get his pyjamas on, while he stealthily listened to what was being said downstairs.

'Mrs Reardon, there has been an incident. Joseph Shields, the landlord of the Black Horse, has been murdered, and we understand that you were at the pub on Saturday night.'

Cyril wondered whether he should wander back down the stairs casually and pour himself a drink or stay put and strain to listen.

'I was there. Yes, that's right.'

'And what time did you leave?'

Peggy shrugged her shoulders. 'I can't remember. Why?'

Cyril sensed the police officer who was asking the questions was getting annoyed.

'Oh, come on, Mrs Reardon. It was only two nights ago.

Think! What time did you leave?'

There was a long pause before the officer asked the same question again.

'I don't know what you want me to say. If I cannot remember, then I cannot remember, so there's no point in you raising your voice.'

'Look, Mrs Reardon, we know that you were there to play poker. The other players have already confirmed it, and that does not bother us. We are trying to find the person responsible for Joseph Shield's murder. So what time did you leave the pub on Saturday night, or was it during the early hours of Sunday morning?'

'Sorry, I still can't remember.'

Cyril could hear the exasperation in the officer's voice.

'So Jack Gibbs tells me you won the pot. Three pounds in total.'

'Yes, I did.'

'Jack also told me that Joseph Shields was not happy and made accusations that you cheated.'

There was a long pause again, but Cyril held his breath and listened.

'Well, Mrs Reardon?'

'Sorry, officer, was there a question in there?'

'Don't get smart, Mrs Reardon. Did Joseph Shields accuse

you of cheating?'

'No, not that I remember. He wasn't happy that he lost the pot, but he never accused me of cheating. Perhaps he did, once I'd left the pub. But I wouldn't know about that, would I?'

'Mrs Reardon, three pounds is a lot of money, so where is it? I am assuming you wouldn't have spent it already. Am I right?'

Cyril suddenly felt his insides tighten. His mother never had the three pounds on her when she returned home. He assumed the landlord – if it was him – stole it from her, and now the police would know that he attacked his mum and . . . His mind was running away with him again.

'Why do you need to see the three pounds?'

'Because, Mrs Reardon, we have every reason to believe that he attacked you and stole the money from you, and that makes you a key witness with a reason to seek retribution.'

Cyril's heart was beating so fast, he thought they could hear it downstairs.

'That is silly, and do I honestly look like a murderer? Me?' She laughed. 'Now hold on a second while I fetch the three pounds.'

Cyril hoped that by some miracle she had a few quid stashed away. Suddenly, his eyes were wide when she appeared at the foot of the stairs. She winked as she walked upstairs past him, and then, as pretty and proud as Grace Kelly, she glided back down the stairs.

'There you go. There's my winnings. I suppose you are gonna take them off me now, ain't ya?'

Cyril heard a different voice, a deeper and older voice, and he assumed it was the other officer.

'No, Mrs Reardon. You are not under arrest. We don't have a search warrant. Thank you for showing us, and I'm grateful for your co-operation.'

Cyril heard his mother showing the two officers to the door, and then, just before he was about to make his way back down the stairs, he froze when he heard the older officer say, 'And Saturday night, early into Sunday morning, Mrs Reardon. Where was your eldest son? Cyril, isn't it?'

'Oh, blimey! Cyril? Well, as young as that lad is, he's a law unto himself, that one. So to be honest, I couldn't rightly say. But come on. Surely my little 'un isn't a suspect, is he?' She laughed again.

'No, he isn't a suspect at all. Tell me, Mrs Reardon, could your son have been next door at Mr Bates'?'

'Well, to be honest, I wouldn't be surprised at all. My Cyril pesters the life out of the man. I suppose it's not having a farver or grandfarver in his life, so Cyril likes the company of an older man. They play board games and stuff. Why?'

'Oh, we just want to tie up a few loose ends. Good evening, Mrs Reardon.'

Cyril heard the door close and before he joined his mother, he went over the conversation in his mind. She'd lied. He'd never ever been to Mr Bates' home to play board games. Mr

Bates specifically mentioned Scrabble. He obviously knew it was a board game although he'd not played it. It felt as if Mr Bates and his mother were concocting something between them. And where did his mum get three pounds from? She'd told Mr Bates it was nicked off her. He decided he would ask his mother outright.

However, the minute he stood in front of her, he could see she was shaking. What he'd heard upstairs was not the person he faced right now. His mother was white-faced, and her eyes were huge. She was a different person from the one he'd heard dealing so confidently with those policemen.

'Mum, what's really going on?'

Holding a tea towel in her hands, she twisted and turned the thin rag. 'Oh my Gawd, what a bloody nightmare.'

Cyril placed his hands on his hips and spat, 'Did Mr Bates kill that geezer, then?'

'What? N-No, o' course he never. What gave you that idea?'

Cyril was at first puzzled and then he became annoyed. ''Cos I heard you tell that bobby I was probably with Mr Bates playing board games.' He paused, perplexed. 'Although I guess that don't make much sense, 'cos I saw the police outside the pub on me way to school. That landlord must have been murdered last night or this morning.' He stared off again in deep thought. 'I reckon that Mr Bates must be a robber or a cat burglar or something like that, and that's why he wanted me to be his alibi and to say I was with him playing Scrabble on Saturday night.'

Peggy tilted her head to the side. 'Well, you must stop all this surmising. It will only get you into trouble, and Cyril Reardon, you shouldn't be earwigging, should you? This ain't no little 'un's business.' She suddenly chewed her bottom lip, as if in deep thought. 'Listen, darling . . .' She paused and sighed. 'The truth is, babe, I really don't know what happened to that bastard, the landlord, except we had a fight, and I think I came off worst. I ain't sorry about him being murdered neither. If it was anything to do with Mr Bates, then I don't want to know. He's been good to me, and there is more good to come our way. So let's just leave it at that. If any copper comes snooping around you, you say nuffin unless I say you can. Understood?'

Cyril smiled. 'Yeah, all right, Mum. Don't worry about me. I ain't silly, ya know.'

'I know, Son. I bleedin' well do know that.'

* * *

It was almost 8.45 a.m. the following day, when Frank came knocking on the front door to walk to school with Cyril.

As Howie stopped at the kerb to tie his laces, Cyril saw Mr Bates looking a little worse for wear, marching along the street. He was dressed in a suit and wearing a long dark-grey overcoat. Grey stubble covered both his cheeks and chin, and his hair wasn't so sleek as before. Their eyes met, and Mr Bates held the stare for a second before he nodded and winked. It was an unspoken gesture that assured Cyril that as far as he himself was concerned, he'd kept to his side of the bargain.

It was only when Cyril was in his sums lesson that he cast his mind back to the policemen's visit to their house last night after Mr Bates had been carted away. And then his thoughts returned to the murdered landlord. It should be shocking – even worrying – but if the landlord had been responsible for hurting his pretty, kind mother like that, then who cared. If he was old enough, he wouldn't have just killed him: he'd have smashed the life out of him first. His mind now turned to all the shenanigans going on between his mum and Mr Bates following the injuries to her. Three pounds was a lot of money. He smiled ruefully.

The teacher called his name, and instantly he snapped out of his gaze.

'Cyril Reardon, are you paying attention?'

Cyril looked at the sum on the blackboard and grinned. 'Yes, Miss, the answer is three hundred and sixty-five.'

'That response just shows that you are not paying attention because I didn't ask you the answer to a sums question. I said that the school will be shut tomorrow, and you are all to let your parents know that we will be having builders in to repair the snow damage to the roof.'

'Sorry, Miss.'

He wished for a moment that he could stop thinking about the dead landlord and Mr Bates, so he turned his thoughts to something else, but his mind was like a revolving door.

CHAPTER FOUR

The last school bell of the summer term sent a wave of excitement as the holidays began. Some of Cyril's school friends were going to the seaside to stay with relatives, and some were off hop picking or 'hopping' as they called it.

Cyril wasn't doing either. He'd never been to the beach or the countryside, so he could only imagine what it was like. He could go mudlarking on the banks of the Thames. He'd watched the older kids picking through the thick claylike mixture, finding odd pieces of silver or gold coins.

Cyril found himself wondering what it would be like to go on holiday. Even just to see the countryside, and enjoy anything other than the gloomy streets of Bermondsey, would be a godsend.

As soon as the school gates opened, the children flooded out.

Cyril waited for his brother Howie, who, as per usual, was dragging his heels. Frank had already begun marching on ahead. He'd wanted to walk with Cyril, but he had chores to do.

‘Hey, wait up, Frank. What are you up to tomorrow? Would you like to go over to the river banks and see if we can find any Roman coins?’

Frank stopped dead. ‘Er, no, I can’t. We’re all getting ready to go hopping. I think there’s a lot of us going. Ain’t you an’ all?’

Cyril looked at the pavement and shook his head. ‘No, we never go. Me mum can’t afford it.’

Frank felt awkward; even when they’d lived in Poplar, they would always go hopping. It was a yearly trip to the countryside where they all picked the hops, soaked up the sun, drank Pepsi-Cola, and earned a few shillings. The men got drunk on milk stout, and the women often joined them, laughing and singing.

‘We’ll only be gone for a week or so, and when I get back, we can go mudlarking, if you like?’

‘Yeah, yeah, sure. You have a great time and fetch us some Pepsi back.’

Frank gave Cyril a sorrowful expression and continued on. He felt sad for his new mate, not being able to join them. He knew just how much fun Cyril would have if he could come along.

* * *

Peggy was staring at a letter when Cyril and Howie wandered up the garden path. Quickly, she tucked it in her apron pocket and put on her best smile, but she was soon frowning when she saw Cyril’s flat expression.

‘What’s up with you? You look like you’ve found a penny and lost a pound.’

Cyril tried to smile, but he was annoyed with the world right now. ‘Nuffin.’

Peggy grabbed his shoulders and stopped him from walking past her. ‘Don’t give me “nuffin”. Tell me, babe. I’m all ears.’

He looked up and noticed the wisps of hair stuck to her face. She’d been sweating from the hot weather and housework, no doubt. ‘Everyone’s going hopping.’

‘I’m sure not *everyone’s* going. There will still be some lads your age hanging about, wanting to kick a ball, surely?’

‘Yeah, I s’pose so,’ he replied, as he began to walk away.

‘Go and take your school clothes off . . . Oh, and see if they fit ya brother. He can use them when you go back to school. I’m sure you’ll grow another few inches before you go back.’

Howie followed Cyril up to the bedroom. He was quiet, even more so than normal. Unbeknown to Cyril, Howie was feeling left out. It had always been him and Cyril, but, now, it was different, since Frank was on the scene. ‘Cyril.’

Cyril sat on the bed and started to pull his shoes off. ‘Yeah, what’s up?’

‘Now Frank’s going hopping, can me and you play again?’

Cyril pulled the other shoe off and sighed. He knew he’d

neglected Howie. 'Yeah, sure. How about we go down to the river tomorrow and see what boats are coming along?'

Howie's face lit up; he loved to watch the boats.

After they'd all eaten their evening meal of shepherd's pie, there was a knock at the door. Peggy told the boys to stay where they were. She wasn't expecting a call, not after eight o'clock. She fingered the letter in her apron pocket and felt her heart beating relentlessly. As soon as she opened the door, she stepped back. There as tall as the door frame and just as wide stood a dark-haired man with a heavy brow and a sour face.

'Hello, can I help you?'

The tall man removed his hat and suddenly appeared awkward. 'Hello. Mrs Reardon?'

Peggy nodded.

'I'm Frank's farver. Your boy is friends with my boy.'

'Aw, Gawd. Yeah, I should have guessed right away. He is your spitting image. Come in.'

Peggy stepped aside as Mr Marsden walked in.

'Hope you don't mind me calling?'

'No, not at all, Mr Marsden. Is everything all right? My Cyril hasn't got into any trouble, has he?'

'No, no, he's fine, and please call me Henry. Everyone does. The thing is that my Frank has taken a real liking to your boy, and he said that you didn't have any plans to take your boys hopping this year. I came to ask if it's all right if I take

Cyril with me?'

Peggy felt uncomfortable. She'd paid off some of her husband's debts, but she still owed the butcher and the loan shark, so money was scarce. 'I, er, well, the thing is . . .' She fingered the letter in her apron again.

Henry knew the circumstances and quickly said, 'It won't cost a penny. Frank has room in his tent. We get the milk train early in the morning, and the ticket inspector doesn't really count the kids.'

'Oh, right, well, I would say "yes", but, to be honest, I have two boys, and my Howie would be . . .'

'Sorry, I meant *both* lads. Frank mentioned Cyril's brother. It won't make any difference. The kiddies have too much fun to be pestering me.'

Peggy was taken aback. The sour expression had faded to a soft look. She knew Henry Marsden had a reputation that meant no one in their right mind would want to get on the wrong side of him. But his tone was so gentle and his intentions extremely kind.

'That's very generous of you, Mr, I mean, Henry. Are you sure you don't mind?'

He winked. 'I don't mind at all. If they give me any trouble, they'll get a clip round the ear. It's only the same as my own boy. They have to work a bit to earn a shilling or two, to pay for their Cola and crisps.'

Peggy nodded. 'When are you going?'

‘We leave at five in the morning from London Bridge station. Can you have them ready by then? They only need some old clothes and a toothbrush. They can meet at mine and follow us. We’ll only be gone for a week or so.’

Peggy was thrilled that her boys could have a holiday in the countryside, and it wouldn’t cost her a penny. She knew she had to get some money together before they were evicted. The rent man was a bloody evil bastard, and the last time he called, he wanted either what he was owed or another way of paying. She’d felt her anger rising then and had been about to kick him between the legs, but he saw the look on her face and laughed at her. Then he’d handed her the letter: she had a few days to pay up or get out.

* * *

It was 4 a.m., and both Cyril and his yawning brother were up and full of excitement.

Peggy had used two of her father’s military style faded green rucksacks to pack their clothes, toothbrushes, and a paper bag full of her own home-made toffee for the trip.

‘Now, listen up, boys. Mr Marsden has been very kind in taking you two along, so I don’t want to hear that you’ve been rude, cheeky, or naughty. You do just as he asks ya, and . . . ’ She looked at Cyril. ‘No thinking you know best.’

Cyril nodded. ‘I’ll be good. I promise.’

Peggy looked into her son’s wide eyes and scrutinised them for any signs of skulduggery lurking behind them. Kissing him on the top of his head and then pinching Howie’s chubby cheeks, she sent them on their way.

* * *

Cyril, with Howie in tow, hurried along the road to Frank's house where there was a crowd gathered. As they approached, the sound was like a buzzing beehive. Cyril noticed the children were all carrying bags and blankets. Quite a few of the women had their hair up on a scarf, while some had their aprons on and others wore a lightweight coat over the top. Sticks and canvases protruded from Army rucksacks, and even a large copper pot was being carried by two older women.

Frank's face lit up when he saw Cyril and Howie, but he couldn't drop what he was holding to greet them. It appeared as if everyone was trying to find ways to lug along as much as they could carry.

Then, suddenly, the crowd became like a train of people, banging and rattling, in single file towards London Bridge station.

Cyril gripped his brother's arm in excitement. 'Stay close, Howie. Don't go wandering off.'

Frank was weighed down with all sorts and was out of breath trying to talk to Cyril. Still, he didn't like to complain and get a thick ear from his father.

The sun hadn't even broken through before they all reached the early morning milk train.

The women quickly pushed the children through and Mr Marsden nodded for Cyril, Frank, and Howie to head on through as well. The ticket collector at the gate was in a panic. No matter how many times he tried to get everyone in an orderly queue, he felt like he was herding cats. One woman produced two tickets but pushed her four children through, saying, 'I am with her or him', and more little children squeezed through the ticket collector's legs and sprinted towards the train. By the time the crowd was all aboard, the ticket collector was sweating and shaking and had given up. Every year was the same. They would leave him holding only ten tickets, but more than thirty people were on that train. He knew the ticket inspector would have the same issues. Children would hide under their mothers' skirts or start moving about the train, and it would be nigh on impossible to keep count.

Frank, Cyril, and Howie managed to get a seat all together. Opposite them was Frank's father, who sat alongside two women, both holding babies. One of them was Agnes Stokes. She was a buxom woman, dressed in a plain grey dress down past her knees and wearing pit shoes on her feet. Her hair was hidden inside a scarf. Many of the women on the train had the same style – the land girl look. Next to Agnes was Shirley Mills, a prettier woman, in her late twenties, with bleached blonde hair just visible through her scarf. She had a mouth like a sewer that made Cyril grin at her choice of words. She wasn't as pretty as his mother and certainly wasn't as serene or graceful, but her bossy and forceful demeanour made Cyril warm to her. He wasn't so sure about Agnes, though; she seemed to peer at him and his brother with beady, watchful eyes.

Cyril and Howie had never been to the countryside. All they'd ever known was the River Thames, the streets of Bermondsey, or the hustle and bustle of Camden Market or Billingsgate Fish Market. The nearest they'd got to the countryside was the trip to Covent Garden to see the masses of flowers and enjoy their sweet aroma – a far cry from the markets at Billingsgate or Smithfield.

As soon as the whistle was blown, the train set off and the chitter-chatter began.

It was a relief for Frank that he could unload his baggage and get comfortable.

Howie stood up and had his nose pressed to the glass to stare out, but Agnes swiftly grabbed him, and in the process, she nearly dropped the baby she had in her arms. 'Get ya arse on the seat. We all wanna look outta the window, ya know.' The harsh way she ripped him away from the door was too much for Howie. He sat down on his seat and stared at the floor.

Cyril glared at Agnes in disgust and placed his arm around Howie's shoulder, whispering in his ear, 'Take no notice of the fat ol' cow.'

'What did you say?' snapped Agnes.

'Aw, Aggy, leave the lads alone, will ya? They're doing no wrong. It's their holidays as much as yours,' said Shirley, as she winked at Cyril.

'Yeah, well, best they know who's paying for them, 'cos it ain't their muvver, is it?'

'Oi,' came a deep growl from Henry Marsden. 'You mind ya business, Agnes. The lads are in my care, so you shut it about who's paying and who ain't. Sister or no sister, you remember who's paying for *your* flaming holiday while your ol' man pisses it up down the White Swan.'

Agnes suddenly turned cherry red; she hadn't expected a man to interject in women's gossip – especially her own brother.

'All I was saying—'

Henry Marsden held up his hand for her to stop. 'Don't bother. Shut it. It's nuffin to do with you.'

Agnes pulled the wriggling plump baby closer to her and stared out of the window, now feeling very chastised.

Cyril guessed there was tension here, but he didn't really understand what all that was about. Still, he didn't have to worry, as it seemed that Mr Marsden was looking out for them.

As the train continued on its journey, the scenery changed drastically from miles of buildings, where you could see the small back gardens of the Victorian dwellings to larger expanses of greenery, until they were finally chugging along through stunning fields of all colours.

Cyril felt his chest fill with excitement and his blood pump fast. It was so bright and open that he wondered if this was what Heaven was like. The rocking motion had already sent Howie off to sleep and had left Frank and Cyril to talk about what they could do once they were off the train and after they'd erected their tent.

'I've got a torch. It was me grandfarver's, so we can have light in our tent. I've got Coke and crisps for a midnight snack, too,' said Frank, grinning.

Cyril looked around and whispered. 'Why don't we go out

and see what's about when everyone's asleep?'

Frank glanced at his father. 'I dunno. I don't wanna get in trouble.'

'Okay, well, I've got some of me mum's special toffee, although the last time I ate some, I chipped me back tooth. We can add that to the midnight snack.'

CHAPTER FIVE

By 9.00 a.m., they'd arrived at Sevenoaks station. Cyril was eager to get off the train and breathe in the warm clean air. The skies seemed bluer and everywhere appeared vibrant and fresh. However, anywhere was better than where he came from. Even the birds had coughs back there. Howie was wary of Agnes; he hurried on behind Cyril, before he got manhandled again.

In single file, they all walked along the country road until they came to a double gate. Beyond that they could see oast houses. Cyril had never seen anything like it. There were horses and carts carrying men and large canvas bins. A man dressed in a cream shirt and loose beige trousers was giving the adults directions. Cyril looked at Mr Marsden and waited to be told what to do. It then became apparent that the adults would sleep in the wooden huts, and the children could pitch a tent and sleep outside, if there wasn't any room in the huts. Everyone seemed to know the drill. At the end of the row of huts was a makeshift shop where the owners of the fields sold cider and a few bits and pieces – mainly basic things like soap, bread, and tent pegs. In front of the huts were improvised kitchens called cookhouses. They too were basic, but they enabled the families to cook and make tea.

The fields stretched for miles, and to Cyril, who had never been in a field before, let alone a hop field, the sight sent goosebumps along his skin. The heavy green bines grew up the poles and across strings in rows along the fields, which made them look like a row of tunnels.

Each family was allocated their own row that stretched across a field. They were each supplied with a bin.

The bins were very large canvas sacks held up by poles at the ends. The hops were cut from the bines before they were picked and thrown into the bin. Once a bin was full, someone would call the tally man over to weigh the hops, and he would then keep a record before he put a new bin up.

The money collected at the end of the day would pay for the drinks and food. The men drank the beer, and the women joined them for a milk stout, and, if they were lucky, a bottle of gin.

Cyril could sense the sudden joy as everyone settled into their huts or tents, and it was as if the stress and depression from their days of living and working in London had somehow lifted from their faces. The women sang, the men whistled, and the kids ran around laughing.

With heat on his face and the sun tickling his nose, Cyril felt as if he'd stepped into another world. The feeling was of a community of fun and of good times. In that very moment, when he looked about him, he wanted to freeze time, to stay on that farm, to breathe in the spicy, almost evergreen pine needle smell of the hops, and to feel the warm breeze touch his face.

'Cyril, come on. Me dad's got our row ready,' called out Frank.

A loose chicken bemused Howie, and he was happy to squeeze the life out of the poor bird.

So Cyril ran after Frank to see how it all worked.

A man on a machine called the bird's nest was high above the bines, cutting them free so they would fall to the ground ready for picking.

Henry Marsden got to work right away by picking the pale green hops and showing Cyril how it was done.

Frank already knew, so he didn't need showing.

'If we fill this bin by two o'clock, then,' said Henry Marsden, 'I'll have a few coppers for your Pepsi and a packet of Spangles.'

Cyril beamed and got to work. He stood next to Mr Marsden and admired how nimble his huge hands were when picking the hops. As everyone worked away, the songs became louder and merrier and even a little cheeky. It was a while after that when they called the tally man, and Cyril watched as he weighed the canvas bin. The load was worth a few shillings, and both he and Frank were handed a couple of pennies to get their drinks and sweets.

As they headed back to the huts, a crowd of lads their own age were playing footie, and so Cyril and Frank joined in. The dry ground caused the air to fill with dust as they ran and kicked the old leather football.

Howie wasn't interested in the football. He was happy tucking into a spam sandwich that Shirley had made for the boys. It was then that Cyril learned that Shirley, with the potty mouth, was Frank's aunt – his mother's sister. Frank's mother had been taken strange and was ill in an asylum, but Frank didn't really want to talk about it, so Cyril never broached the subject after that.

'Cyril, get your collar up, son. Your neck's red raw from the sun. You'll be sore, come morning, babe.'

Cyril lifted his collar and smiled when she handed him a spam sandwich and a bottle of pop.

'Don't go running around until that pop and food have had time to settle or you'll be sick.'

Cyril smiled and then blushed when she winked at him. 'When I grow up, I'm gonna marry a girl just like you, Shirley.'

'Aw, give over, you little charmer.'

As the sun went down and the gnats buzzed overhead, Cyril sat back and noticed the stars in the sky. He'd never seen stars, not in Bermondsey, only in the books at school. He lay back and stared, now left wonderstruck.

Frank sat around a fire in front of the cookhouse, browning off some sausages.

Shirley had already put Howie to bed on the spare straw-filled mattress in her own hut. The fresh air had well and truly knocked him out. The men were playing cricket, each holding a bottle of beer, and the women were washing their pots and pans or cooking food for the next day.

The whole experience for Cyril was perfect, from the smells of the open fire, to the aroma of the nearby lavender fields, along with the laughing and singing. He never wanted it to end.

That night, both he and Frank fell asleep in seconds. There was no midnight feast, just a gentle purring from two happily tired young lads.

* * *

Bright and early the next morning, Cyril and Frank climbed out of their tents and stretched. The smell of cooking had tantalised their taste buds and after having a quick wee, in the somewhat rudimentary toilets, they both hurried over to Shirley, who was using what looked like a home-made frying pan that could cook up to twenty sausages at once. With her baby resting on her hip and a Woodbine dangling from her lips, she prodded and poked the contents of the pan.

'Grab yourself a slice of that bread and a sausage and sit over at that table.' She pointed to the trestle table with plastic cups and tomato sauce already laid out. 'And have yourselves a bit of breakfast, while it's still hot.'

Cyril was starving. All the fresh air had his tummy rumbling. As he sat at the trestle table and squirted a decent helping of sauce over his black sausage, he noticed Mr Marsden gently put his arm around Shirley's waist. She blushed. Cyril watched as Mr Marsden kissed the top of the baby's head. He looked different dressed in loose trousers with his braces dangling down. His hair was wet and swept back.

‘Frank, is your dad soft on your Aunt Shirley?’

Frank looked down and nodded. ‘Yeah, I like me Aunt Shirley. She ain’t like me mum. As ya know, me mum’s ill, and so Shirley helps out.’

‘I bet she does,’ replied Cyril, as he watched the affection between the two adults.

Cyril swallowed the last of his bread and butter and hopped down from his seat. ‘Frank, d’ya think your dad will let us go exploring today? Only, I really wanna see what the countryside has to offer. How about you?’

Frank looked over at his father and sighed. ‘I best stay here today and fill that bin. Tomorrow, if I work hard now, he may let me go off.’ He smiled at Cyril. ‘But he can’t stop you from exploring. You go, Cyril, and let me know what’s out there, and then I’ll come with ya tomorrow. ’Cos if I ask right now, me dad will say “no”. But I can work on him today.’

‘If I find anything worth having, Frank, I’ll bring it back for me and you to share.’

Frank laughed. ‘What like, Cyril, a rabbit or a bunch of flowers? ’Cos there ain’t much out there but fields, woods, and rivers.’

‘I might catch me something good. Me mum always says “If you walk around with your eyes shut, you’ll never see nuffin.”’

Howie was too busy with the animals on the farm to be bothered with Cyril. Not having a dog or even a mouse of his own, Howie was fascinated and excited to play with the ducks, geese, and the two sheep.

Cyril was told not to go too far and to be back well before it got dark.

As Cyril looked across the fields to a wooded area, he decided that it would be as good a place as any to go exploring. With his shirt collar up and his shorts rolled down a couple of inches, he set off. Passing bees and butterflies and the sweet smells of the meadow flowers, he came to a river. The water was so clear as it bubbled over the rocks. He stopped and bent down to scoop a generous helping to cool his dry mouth.

A quarter of a mile or so further on, the river became wider and quite deep in some parts, and that's when he came upon a fisherman. Cyril stopped in his tracks, half hidden behind a tree, and watched the man, possibly in his thirties, thread a worm onto a hook and cast the line out. The trees were sparse just around that part of the river, resulting in the sun reflecting off the water. The man sat still, patiently waiting, but Cyril didn't know about the etiquette of being quiet while someone was fishing.

'Hello, Mister. Wot ya doing?'

The dark-haired man with heavy eyelids, who was sitting on a plaid blanket, turned to face Cyril and looked him up and down. He suddenly beamed. 'Well, hello, there. I'm fishing. Come and join me. I suppose you are one of the hop pickers. Lovely day for it.'

Cyril smiled at the man's posh voice and the way his face seemed to lift a few inches. That wasn't the typical reaction he got from most grown-ups. He was usually told to go off and play, or the less polite would tell him to sod off.

He quickly walked over and sat next to the man. 'So, have ya caught anything?'

The man put out his hand for Cyril to shake. 'I'm John Dulcie, and you, my young fellow, are?'

'Oh, me? Yeah, my name's Cyril Reardon, named after me grandfarver on me farver's side. Pleased to meet ya.'

'Well, young Cyril, in answer to your question, I have caught a few rainbows.'

'Rainbows?' Cyril frowned.

'Yes, rainbow trout. Look, you can see them in that bucket.'

Cyril stood up and peered into the big white bucket where there were three good-sized trout struggling to swim.

'Cor, are you gonna take 'em home for dinner?'

Dulcie laughed. 'No, I will put them back. I don't eat fish.'

Cyril's eyes were wide. 'Can I have 'em for my supper, in that case?'

Dulcie laughed again. 'If you must. I am actually a vegetarian, so I don't eat meat or fish.'

'You can't have any muscle on ya, then.'

He looked at the fishing rod and noticed another one on the

grass.

'D'ya reckon you can teach me to fish? I see you've got a spare rod.'

The man stared at Cyril for a few moments. 'I will teach you to fish, and you can have that spare rod. It's an old one, but it works, and maybe you can return the favour.'

Cyril's eyes lit up. 'Blimey! What? Are you gonna let me keep the rod?'

'Yes, I might do.'

Cyril watched as his new friend, Mr Dulcie, showed him how to wind the reel and thread it through the loops on the rod and then how to attach the hook before finally securing the worm. He stood behind Cyril and guided his hands and arms to cast out. 'Now, you see that float? When that starts bobbing up and down, that means you have a bite. At that point, you give the line a sharp tug and then reel the fish in.'

Cyril was a fast learner, and within a few minutes, he had a bite and yanked hard on the line before he excitedly began winding the reel and pulling in whatever he'd caught. He laughed with excitement. 'Blimey, that was quick. There must be loads of fish in that part of the river.'

Dulcie laughed along with him. 'Yes, there would be because the fish swim to this point from a small stream that flows directly from a trout farm.'

Cyril was still pulling and tugging at the rod to reel in the fish that he could only assume was massive. 'So why don't you fish from the trout farm, then?'

‘Oh, no, no, that’s private land. The fish belong to Lord Chambers, a friend of mine, at the estate up there. It’s too easy to fish from the lake, anyway.’

The fish finally came to the surface, and that’s when Cyril noticed that it didn’t look like the ones that Mr Dulcie had caught.

‘Oh dear, we might as well cut the line, young Cyril. That one is a pike. It’s no good to man or beast.’

‘Oh, I was hoping to have that for me tea tonight.’

‘Never mind, you can catch good trout by standing in the water, you know. Why don’t you strip off and get in. The further out you go, the greater the chance of throwing that line into the deeper part, where there are lots of fish.’ With that, John Dulcie used his razor-sharp fisherman’s knife to cut the fish free from the line.

Cyril looked at his empty line and quickly whipped off his shoes. ‘Can I have another hook and a worm, Mr Dulcie?’

Passing Cyril a barbed hook, the man winked. ‘There you are, and here is a good juicy worm. Now, try to go in deeper, but take your shorts off. You don’t want them getting wet and ruined, do you?’

‘I’m all right, Mr Dulcie. They could do with a wash, anyway.’

Cyril was threading the hook and not taking much notice of Mr Dulcie until, that was, he felt a hand on his shoulder. ‘You like your fishing rod, don’t you, Cyril, and you want to keep it?’

'Yeah, I think it's great, and I can catch me supper now.'

As soon as Cyril had the worm wriggling on the hook, Mr Darcie slowly slid his hand down Cyril's back and then inside his shorts.

Cyril stopped dead and felt not only uncomfortable but uneasy. This wasn't normal; this wasn't right. His mother's words rang in his ears. 'Cyril, those are your private parts, and no one must ever touch them. If anyone tries to do so, you must run as fast as you can, and you *must* tell someone.' He had never understood why anyone would want to touch his private parts, but if his mum said it was wrong, then it was wrong.

She had also told him that if any man tried to hurt him, then he either ran, or, failing that, fight with every ounce of strength with any weapon to hand.

'Get off me!' demanded Cyril, as he spun around and tried to remove the man's hand.

But John Dulcie was strong. He gripped Cyril's shoulder so tightly with his other hand that Cyril winced to the point where he felt almost paralysed. Dulcie's other hand then moved to the front of Cyril's shorts.

'Get off me, I said!'

Terrified and yet angry because the man wouldn't let go, Cyril pulled his leg back and booted Mr Dulcie in the shin, but his bare foot did little harm to the man, only more so to himself. Now really afraid, he struggled and tried desperately to pull away.

It was no use, and the expression on Dulcie's face was one of evil satisfaction. Unexpectedly, he changed tack, throwing Cyril to the ground before climbing on top of him.

So scared that he would die, Cyril looked to the side of him for a tool, a weapon – anything – to hurt the man. He couldn't run or escape. The man's weight was too heavy for Cyril to push him off. But there, right beside him, was the knife that the man had used to cut his line. He reached and stretched his arm, desperate to get hold of that knife. And while Mr Dulcie was fiddling with his own trousers, Cyril had enough freedom to stretch a little further and grasp that knife with the tips of his fingers and pull it closer until he had a grip. So petrified, Cyril didn't think what would happen if he stuck that fisherman's knife into the man's flesh. All he could think of was escaping with his life. He was absolutely convinced that Mr Dulcie would kill him and cut him up as fish bait.

As soon as Dulcie had pulled his trousers down to his knees, he lunged forward.

Cyril held the knife blade upwards, and when the man forced himself on top of Cyril, Cyril thrust the knife into John Dulcie's side like a hot knife through butter.

Dulcie froze for a moment and stared at Cyril before he pulled himself to his knees and looked down at the bloody knife still firmly gripped in the kid's hand.

Unsure how much damage he'd sustained or even if the wound was fatal, Dulcie tried to get to his feet, pull his trousers up, and get away from the boy, who now looked like a child possessed by demons. The wide eyes and flared nostrils were sure signs that he was no pushover, and if he didn't get away soon, then the crazed boy could stab him again. The strength was draining from him, and as he placed his hands on his side, he felt the blood pumping out. This was no superficial graze. This was bad, and if he didn't get to his car soon, he would bleed to death in the woods. No one would know where he was. Nothing was spoken between them, as Dulcie, or, as he was otherwise known, Lord Parker-Green, tried to put pressure on the wound and walk away. He had to get away from the place before the kid screamed blue murder and accused him of all sorts. But to Parker-Green's horror, the boy jumped to his feet, brandishing the knife and almost daring him on. Parker-Green didn't look back but hurried away as fast as his shaking legs would take him.

As soon as Mr Dulcie was out of sight, Cyril gasped for breath and blinked a few times. Then he looked down at the blood and the knife. Spinning around to see if there was anyone about, he realised that there was no one, just him and the knife dripping with blood. And if he hadn't been holding the evidence, then not even he would have believed what had just taken place.

Cyril heard a car engine start up and guessed that Mr Dulcie had scarpered. He let out a deep breath and shook all over. It was all a shock. His eyes looked at the blood on the ground and then at his shirt. He was covered in claret. How could he ever explain that? And if the man were to die, would he go to prison forever? How would his mother cope? And Howie, how would he get on without him? With fear surging through his veins, he waded out into the river and furiously scrubbed the blood from his shirt using his fingers. The stain was beginning to fade, but it was still there. 'Christ alive!' He bent down, grabbed a handful of mud, and began rubbing it all over the pink stain, until, finally, it turned to a muddy colour and the water eventually washed it clean.

As he returned to the bank, he noticed the man's belongings. Two fishing rods, a box with fishing hooks and floats, a leather bag, and the plaid blanket lay on the bank. Cyril listened again for anyone approaching, any noise at all, in fact, but apart from the sound of the running water of the river, there was no one. He crouched down to inspect the leather bag. It was made from good quality leather and would probably bring him a few shillings down the market at home. He unzipped the side pocket and slid his fingers inside; he could feel a few coins, some paper, and what felt like a pocket watch. Quickly, pulling the contents out, he was wide-eyed with wonder. Not only were there a few shillings, but there were also some pound notes, and, yes, what looked like a *gold* pocket watch. On inspecting it carefully, he saw it was hallmarked, and a huge smile crept across his face: so the watch was solid gold.

If he took all the stuff back to the tent, there would be questions, he thought. How could he even explain what had happened? And did he have any right to keep Mr Dulcie's stuff? But he did feel he had the right. The man was certainly not kosher. Why else would he throw him to the ground and dive onto him with his trousers around his ankles, unless he was going to kill him?

Away from the clearing there was thick undergrowth, which was more densely populated with trees. Cyril gathered up Mr Dulcie's belongings and hid them in the overgrown foliage and stepped back. No one would spot them there. But when he looked back, he decided to take with him the rod he had used earlier; after all, that one was given to him by the potential murderer. He grabbed the bucket of fish, poured the water away, and with the rod under his arm and the fish in the bucket, he headed back. He would tell Frank, but he would never breathe a word to another living soul.

As soon as he reached the field and saw some of the pickers merrily singing and picking, while others were larking about, he felt at odds. He peered back over his shoulder and then down at the fish. His hands shook, and a sick feeling rose from his stomach and made his ears tingle. Suddenly, he felt the ground reach up towards him and everything went dark. It was a few minutes before he came to, and he then had to take a few deep breaths before he felt better. Sitting himself upright, he looked again at the fish in the bucket and the rod by his side. But that vision of Mr Dulcie and his weird expression as he lunged towards him made Cyril feel sick again. Why did he have his trousers down? What was the man going to do to him? He wondered if Mr Dulcie had made it to the hospital or had died on the way. He held his hands in front of him and turned them over. A tear trickled down his face, and his mother's words shot through his mind once again. 'If you can't get away, you use a weapon or anything to hand.' Well, he had, and he would do it again. It was all about that look in the man's eyes that had told him he'd been in danger – real danger.

Once Cyril reached the cookhouse and Shirley saw what he had in the bucket, she called to Henry and Frank to come over and see what they would have for supper.

Frank was excited to see Cyril and to hear how the heck he'd brought back three trout and a rod. But with one wink and a nod from Cyril, Frank knew there was more to hear. While Henry got cleaned up and then helped Shirley with the cooking, Frank grabbed Cyril's arm and pulled him away. 'So what's going on, Cyril? How did you get that rod?'

Cyril looked behind him. 'Listen, Frank. I've got a secret, right? I promised to share everything with you, right?'

Frank nodded quickly, desperate to hear the tale.

'I got us four pound notes and there's another fishing rod and the floats and hooks, but I left everything back there, further up the river in the bushes. I couldn't bring them back 'cos your farver would ask questions, and, well, the thing is this, Frank. This geezer, right. Well, he tried to murder me.'

Frank put his hand to his mouth to stop himself from laughing.

'Nah, Frank, seriously, yeah, listen to this. At first, he put his hands down my shorts, and then he pushed me right on me arse and then got on top of me. I swear, Frank, he was gonna kill me.'

Hearing that, Frank stopped laughing and tilted his head in disbelief. 'Why would the man wanna kill you?'

'Frank, I can't prove all of this, but I stabbed him.'

Frank pushed Cyril. 'Give over, Cyril. Stop it. I really thought you were honest.'

'Frank, come with me, then, and I'll show ya. I ain't no liar, and I only told you 'cos I thought I could trust ya. I mean, you've hardly said two words to me. You ain't gonna go telling anyone, are ya?'

Frank stopped dead and looked Cyril up and down. 'You *are* telling the truth, ain't ya?'

Cyril sighed and then nodded. 'It was 'orrible, bleedin' scary. I thought I was a gonna.'

'Go on then, Cyril. Show us where it happened.'

They hurried through the woods and followed the river until the trees became few and far between and the river widened. And there, just by the bank, was the knife. Cyril had forgotten to hide it.

'See, look, Frank, there's his knife, and look at the mud.' He pointed to the blood just visible on the damp clay.

Frank picked up the knife and turned it around in his hand. 'Cor, this is a nice blade. I bet this cuts through anything.'

'Yeah, yeah, Frank. Look, what are we gonna do about the other stuff? How are we gonna explain that we've got the other rod and the box of fishing gear?'

Frank was still admiring the knife. 'Did you stab him hard. I mean, did it go right in, or what?'

Cyril stood with his hands on his hips. '*What*? Frank, are you really *listening* to me?'

Frank looked up and smiled. 'Yeah, I'm listening, but you said you would share whatever you found fifty-fifty. How about you have everything else, and me, I want this knife. What d'you say?'

Cyril laughed. 'Whatever, Frank. Now, come on. I wanna

show you this box and his fishing gear. I bet it's worth a few bob.'

Cyril, with Frank on his heels, clambered through the undergrowth until he found all of Mr Dulcie's belongings. He felt more relaxed with Frank there. After retrieving the box, he carried it to the river bank and began lifting each compartment out until he got to the bottom and found some bags of sweets. ''Ere, look at this lot, Frank. Blimey, the ol' codger must have had a sweet tooth.' He pulled out a packet of Army and Navy sweets and threw it to Frank. 'There ya go.'

Frank caught the packet with one hand and peered inside. 'Cheers, Cyril.'

As they sat side by side on the bank, sucking on the sweets, Cyril turned to Frank. 'You won't tell anyone, will ya? I mean about me stabbing that man?'

Frank turned the knife around in his hand. 'If he was to come back right now, Cyril, I'd stab him meself.'

Cyril nearly choked on his aniseed twist. 'Would ya? Really?'

'Yeah, I would. I'd stab him a hundred times and then float him down the river.'

'Hmm, so you won't tell anyone, will ya, just in case the ol' git did die? 'Cos then they would lock me up for murder.'

Frank placed his arm around Cyril's shoulder. 'You are me best friend. I'll never say a word. But can I keep the knife?'

Cyril nudged him. 'Sure, as long as you don't go digging

me with it.'

* * *

By nightfall, the camp was quietening down and the trout was cooked to perfection, shared between Henry, Shirley, and Frank. Howie didn't like fish. And Cyril still felt sick; he only ate the baked potato.

'That was the best meal I've had in a long time. Thank you, Cyril. So how did you manage to talk the fishing rod off someone?' Frank's dad laughed.

Cyril quickly responded. 'I caught six fish and let this geezer have three for his missus, so he gave me his spare rod, saying it was no good to him.'

'Well, I bet the trout were worth more than the rod. Cor, they cost a pretty penny, they do. So this was a right treat, son.'

Cyril was taking it all in; he had no idea that the fish were worth so much money. And he knew where there were plenty more. As soon as they returned to their tents, Cyril pulled out his rucksack and began emptying the clothes.

'What are you doing, Cyril?' asked Frank, as he fiddled with his torch. 'I think the batteries are flat.'

'I'm going fishing up at the lake where there are hundreds, even millions, of trout. I'm gonna catch as many as I can carry and sell them to the hop pickers for a shilling a piece. What d'ya reckon?'

Frank laughed and shook his head. 'Are you really going

fishing? In the dark?'

''Course! Are you coming? 'Cos, then, we can carry more between us.'

Frank nodded. In his mind, it seemed that Cyril had more fun out of life than he did. 'Yeah, all right. And if any bloke tries to murder us, I'll stab 'em with me new knife.'

Cyril giggled. 'What, like fish food?'

Quietly, they crept out of the tent and made their way through the woods until they found the river and followed to where it widened. Cyril searched the undergrowth again for the leather bag and the box, and as soon as he found them, he emptied the contents and placed them into his rucksack. The bait box still contained a few worms, so they were set to go.

Frank eventually got his torch to work, and soon they were able to follow a small stream that flowed into the river behind them from the trout farm further upstream.

As the boys trudged along for a few hundred yards they came across a clearing. It was dominated by a huge house. A new barbed wire fence had been erected with signs saying PRIVATE PROPERTY – KEEP OUT. Cyril managed to pull the two lines of barbed wire apart and allowed Frank, with his long legs, to squeeze through first, before he himself climbed through.

The moonlight was bright enough for Cyril to spot the large lake just below the house. He stopped and stared. 'Cor, Frank, look at that, mate. Fancy living in a big house in the middle of a field with your own woods and a lake all to yaself.'

‘I dunno. It’s a bit too big, but I suppose it’s better than my house.’

An owl hooted and a fox shot out from a bush, making both of the boys jump.

Slowly, they caught their breath, and, walking gingerly, they followed the stream towards the lake. ‘I wonder what they would do if they caught us nicking their fish?’ asked Frank.

‘Nuffin. We’d just have to take ’em back, I suppose. I mean, what can they really do? I’ll just say we didn’t know, and that I can’t read or write.’

Frank laughed. ‘And I reckon they’d believe you an’ all.’

As Frank shone the torch on the stream, he could see a trout stuck on the rock in the shallows. ‘There, Cyril. Look, you can grab that one with your hands.’

Cyril dropped his rod and rucksack and jumped into the stream. With both hands, he grabbed the fish and threw it onto the grass.

Frank instantly snatched the fish and plunged his knife into its head. ‘You can’t let it gasp for breath; you’ve got to put it out of its misery.’

Cyril nodded. ‘Yeah, I guess so.’

‘I love this knife. It’s really sharp. Hey, look, there’s another fish. Bloody hell, Cyril. They are just hovering there.’

Cyril wasted no time in grabbing the fish and then going

for another one.

'I reckon these little ones have escaped from that lake, but I bet the bigger ones are trapped,' said Cyril, now pointing to the silver appearance of the lake.

'Cyril, we can just catch these. We don't need to go up there. Besides, what if we get caught?'

Cyril peered up at Frank. 'I never took you for no chicken, Frank.'

With his eyes narrowing, Frank glared back. 'I ain't no chicken, Cyril.'

'Well, come on, then, Frank. What are you waiting for?'

Frank moaned under his breath but followed Cyril anyway.

A few hundred yards further on, they came to the enormous property set in its own grounds above the lake. Cyril was struck by wonder at the size of the beautiful house. Every window was bathed in a soft orange glow, and on the roof, there were at least a dozen chimneys, which looked as though they had been designed especially for this house. The driveway was grand. It was lined with bushes and hedges, which appeared to have been cut with scissors. He truly had seen nothing like it.

Both Cyril and Frank remained vigilant in case they could be spotted. But the house was far enough away; if anyone should suddenly appear, Cyril reckoned he and Frank would have a good head start to get away.

Once they reached the lake, Cyril sat down and just gazed.

It was stunningly still and so peaceful, until, every so often, a fish would flick its tail and cause ripples.

'What are you doing now, Cyril?'

'I'm putting a worm on a hook. I wanna see how big these fish really are.'

Remembering what he'd been taught, Cyril cast out and was pleased that the float was bright enough for him to see. Bingo! Almost in a flash, the float was dragged down. Cyril yanked at the rod and then began reeling the fish in. It was a fighter and tough to pull, but the fish didn't stand a chance, and it was on the surface before he could say 'Birds Eye fish fingers'. He was proved right about what he'd said back by the stream: this trout was three times the size. 'Quick, Frank. Sort this one out. I'm gonna catch another.'

Within thirty minutes, they had ten fish in the bucket. Frank looked at their catch and the weight of it.

'I think we'd best go, Cyril. I'm not sure how far I can carry this lot.'

Cyril knew he had a point and began taking his rod apart and packing up the fishing gear. Just as they were off, they heard a deep loud voice.

'Oi, stop, right there!'

Frank and Cyril turned to see who was shouting; to their horror, a man stood aiming a rifle, with a young lad standing by his side.

'Stop, or I'll shoot!'

Cyril couldn't believe for a moment that a grown man would actually shoot at them.

'Leg it, Frank.'

Frank didn't have a chance to consider any alternative. He ran, and without thinking to ditch the bucket, he gripped the handle tightly and tore along the stream towards the barbed wire fence. The fish were sliding up the sides, but Frank continued on.

Cyril was right behind him, though, dragging his rucksack along.

Bang! The gun fired and both Frank and Cyril automatically ducked.

'Jesus! He's really shooting at us.'

Then they heard the young lad shout, 'Shoot them, Father! Shoot them!'

Suddenly, Frank lost his footing and tumbled over. Cyril rushed to his side and grabbed his hand to pull him up. 'Come on, Frank. We've got to get out of 'ere. Get up!'

But Frank had twisted his ankle, and he was now yelping in pain.

Cyril, however, would not leave him there like an injured dog. He yanked at Frank's arm. 'Come on. Get up.'

Frank yelped again as he put his weight on the ankle, but the fear of being shot gave him the strength he needed to get away.

As Cyril clutched Frank's arm, Frank manged to grab the handle of the bucket, and, again, they were on their way. Once they reached the barbed wire fence, Cyril knew they were nearly safe. The other side appeared to be common land with no sign telling them that it was private property. Carefully holding the barbed wire apart for Frank to climb through, Cyril then launched his rucksack and climbed through himself.

Cyril and Frank ducked again when they heard another bang. Cyril was angry. He knew that man and his son couldn't shoot him, not when they weren't on his property. What bloody right did they have?

Frank was still hobbling when Cyril threw his rucksack over his shoulder and held Frank up to support him.

Out of breath and with their ears banging as their adrenaline pumped around their bodies, they never expected the man's son to follow them through the fence, until the boy suddenly pushed Cyril hard in the back, knocking him flying. Cyril spun around to see the lad was older than them – probably around thirteen. The man, who Cyril could only assume was his father, was not in sight. There was just Frank, the toffee-nosed boy, and himself.

'You thieving poachers. Hand back the fish and your rod and everything you have on you as compensation, or I will get my father to shoot you dead as trespassers.'

Frank's usually deadpan face changed. He was in pain with his ankle, and he wasn't going to be bullied by an older boy or anyone ever again.

'If you want it, you snotty prick, then you can come and

get it.'

Cyril was gobsmacked by Frank's deep angry voice.

'Come on, toff. Come and get it.'

Cyril's eyes widened as he watched Frank straighten up. Suddenly, Frank looked like a giant, almost the same size as the toff.

Then Cyril saw something gleaming in Frank's hand – the knife. 'Oh Gawd,' he mumbled, under his breath.

Cyril looked over the lad's shoulder to see if his father was there with the gun, but he was nowhere to be seen in the darkness.

'Come near me or me mate, and I'll slice your face off.'

Cyril swallowed hard; even he was scared. Frank's tone was sinister, and it was at that point he knew his best buddy really meant it.

The toff laughed like a girl and then shook his head. 'Oh, dear, dear me, you silly little boy. I am the lord of this land. You are mere farm workers. I can have you shot. Now, hand over the rod and everything else you have before I call my father over to put a bullet through your heads.'

The cocky look on the toff's face had Frank flaring his nostrils. 'Like I said, come and take it.'

The young man smirked. 'Do you know who I am?'

'I don't give a rat's arse who you are. You ain't taking my stuff without taking a clumping from me first.'

'I am Lord Chambers' son, and my father owns most of the land around here, so I will take what I want, if it's on our land.'

Cyril glared at the sign behind him. 'This bit ain't your land, though, is it?'

The toff looked Cyril up and down and curled his lip.

'You guttersnipe,' he yelled, as he lunged forward. And with his fist clenched, he punched Cyril in the chest making Cyril stagger back and gasp for breath.

Frank was about to rip into Lord Chambers' son when Cyril growled like a wounded bear. He ran with his head down straight into the lad's chest, and then, in a frenzy, he grabbed him by his buttoned-up shirt collar, holding him within easy reach, while he threw a hard punch connecting with the toff's chin.

Frank was amazed by the speed at which Cyril could fight. Small he may be, but he was fast. However, the toff was a great deal bigger, and although he was hurt, he managed to push Cyril off and punch him in the face twice before Frank intervened and pulled him away. The older lad then turned on Frank by giving him a nasty right hook to the side of Frank's face.

Cyril was still clutching his split lip when he saw Frank glare as though he was deranged at the toff. In a deliberate, almost slow-motion reaction, he snatched him by the back of his head, and with the knife in his other hand, he used it to make a deep cut down the lad's chin.

Suddenly, like a banshee, Lord Chambers' son screamed

and put his hands to his face and then pulled them away to look at the blood. He was so panicked by the sight of his own blood in his hands, he turned and ran towards the fence. But, without thinking, when he tried to dive between the lines of barbed wire, he got his tweed trousers caught by the seat of his pants, and as he tugged and tugged, he lost his balance and toppled over. Stupidly, though, when he grabbed the barbed wire to restore his balance, he injured himself even more.

Cyril didn't hang around to help or see how much damage the toff was doing to himself. He snatched his rucksack and clasped Frank's arm to hurry him away.

Frank grabbed the bucket of fish and hobbled along with Cyril's help.

With the black clouds obscuring the moonlight, and the tall leafy leaves making it hard to see where they were going, the boys followed the river until they came to a familiar field. In the distance, they could see the fires by the cookhouses.

They paused for a moment to catch their breath.

'What shall we tell your ol' man?' asked Cyril.

'Nuffin, unless he knows we've not been in the tent.' Frank pointed at Cyril's bucket. 'You can say that you went back and fished for those from the river. He won't say much to you, will he?'

'What if that lord's son grasses and the police come asking questions?'

'I dunno, Cyril. I guess I'll be in a lot of trouble, eh?'

Cyril sat down for a moment. 'Nah, ya won't. Listen, if they come and accuse us of stabbing him, I'll just say he chased us but he got caught up in that barbed wire.'

Frank sat down beside him and laughed. 'Silly beggar. Fancy getting caught up like that. I bet he's cut to bleedin' ribbons now, eh?'

Cyril laughed. 'Served him right.'

'Thanks for not running off and leaving me to get shot.'

Cyril nudged his arm. 'You're me mate. Mates don't leave you in the shit. Ever.'

CHAPTER SIX

Luckily for Cyril and Frank, Lord Chambers didn't take the matter to the authorities. So, no police came looking for the boys.

The Londoners were coming to the end of their week away. Cyril didn't relish going back to the gloomy streets of Bermondsey although he had missed his mother. The sun had browned their faces, bleached their hair, and given them a twinkle in their eyes.

Howie had caught the sun the most because he was forever spending time with the pig farmer and the piglets, which meant he was constantly being dunked in the steel bath to remove the stench, after which, he was told to run about to dry off. With his dark hair and now chocolate-coloured skin, anyone would have mistaken him for an Italian.

Henry helped Shirley to pack away their belongings. The load was lighter as they had made sure they'd used up everything they had.

Cyril's rucksack, however, was heavier, but no one took much notice.

Frank hung on to his knife and hid it well in his bag.

They had a few hours before they would catch the train home. Cyril hovered around the tuck shop area with Frank, debating whether to buy chocolate or hard-boiled sweets, when the boys heard a car approach.

Cyril turned to see who was coming. He assumed it was more hop pickers ready for the next week and the last of the hop picking season. Seeing the familiar tall bony-looking gentleman step out of his car, dressed in a suit and wearing a trilby hat – in this weather as well – his eyes widened. *What was Mr Bates doing here*? he wondered.

He didn't approach Mr Bates, but he watched as Mr Marsden hurried over. Cyril stared as Mr Bates removed his hat and nodded to Mr Marsden to indicate he wanted a private word. Cyril could see the men whispering to each other, and at that point, they turned and looked his way. Cyril guessed they were talking about him, but he had no idea why.

He turned to Frank. 'What d'ya reckon that's all about?'

'I dunno. But that's Mr Bates, your neighbour, ain't it?'

'Yeah, well, I'm gonna see what he's doing 'ere.'

He slapped some pennies into Frank's hand. 'Hard-boiled, I think.'

Cyril marched down towards the men and passed Howie on the kerb strangling the life out of the cat with his overzealous hugs.

Before Cyril even reached the two men, Mr Bates looked up and beckoned him over.

Cyril hurried to the men and stopped dead, trying to read the anxious expression on Mr Bates' face. 'Wot you doing 'ere, Mr Bates?'

'I've come to pick you and your brother up.'

'Why?'

''Ere, Cyril,' said Henry Marsden. 'That's enough questions. You just do as Mr Bates says. All right, son?'

Cyril looked at Mr Marsden. 'Of course I will do as I'm told, but what's going on? Is me mum all right?' He then clocked Mr Bates giving Mr Marsden a look of unease. Almost immediately, Cyril felt his insides turn out and a nasty, sick feeling made its way up to his mouth.

'Is me mum all right? What's going on?'

Mr Bates put his hand on Cyril's shoulder. 'Your mum's all right, Cyril, but you need to come with me. It's only for a couple of days or so.'

'But if Mum's all right, why can't I see her?'

Mr Bates was not a patient man at the best of times, but he didn't have either the time or the energy to answer a hundred and onc qucstions from Cyril. 'Listen, Cyril, we have to go now, all right? You and ya brother. Your mum is in the police station.' He held up his hand before Cyril said any more. 'I will explain in the car, but, right now, we have to go. The police will be on their way to question you about stuff, so I am going to take you to my other house, away from here. Now, Cyril, do you understand what I'm saying?'

Cyril gave a firm nod, looked at Mr Marsden, and offered his hand.

Mr Marsden was surprised that the little lad was so mature. He shook hands and smiled. 'Good lad. We will see you in a few days, eh?'

As Cyril walked away to fetch his belongings, he heard Mr Marsden say, 'Well, I never knew the lad was Dillon's grandson. Cor, I wonder if he takes after the ol' man?'

Then Cyril paused and waited to hear the answer.

'He's a lot like him, well, in his ways, that is.'

'Well, God 'elp Bermondsey when that boy reaches a young man, if he's half the man his grandfarver was,' replied Mr Marsden.

Cyril wondered if that was a good thing or a bad thing. However, right now, he was more concerned about his mother. He trusted Mr Bates, and so he quickly scooped up his belongings and hurried over to Frank. He whispered, 'I've gotta go, Frank. I can't say why, but I'll be back home soon.'

Frank's shoulders drooped in disappointment. He was thoroughly enjoying Cyril's company; it was as if they were brothers. He didn't have a brother, only cousins over in Poplar. He watched Cyril hurry back and grab Howie and their rucksacks, and he continued gazing as his friends made their way to the car that was idling in the entrance to the farm. Then he saw Mr Bates open the back door of the car for Howie to climb into. He was expecting Cyril to do likewise. A grin crept across Frank's face when he saw Cyril skip around to the front, while Mr Bates could only shake his head in disbelief.

Frank smiled to himself at the cheek of Cyril. He thought about what Cyril had once said. 'Yeah, my mouth gets me in trouble and back out again.'

* * *

Cyril was silent and he sat still until Mr Bates was a mile along the country lane.

'I didn't know you had a motor, Mr Bates?'

'Hmm, there's a lot you don't know about me, and to be frank, lad, that's how I like my life to be. It's one long mystery.'

'Is our mum okay? And why is she at the police station?'

Mr Bates looked in the rear-view mirror at Howie who was just gawping out of the window.

'Is he always like that – in a dreamworld with a grin on his face?'

'Mum says our Howie is what you call a kind-hearted lad.'

'Oh, is that what they call it?'

'Mr Bates, why is Mum in the police station? Is it about the landlord's murder?'

Mr Bates couldn't put off the inevitable. Knowing what Cyril was like, there would be endless questions. He understood Cyril, though. The boy, as young as he was, wasn't stupid. In fact, he had intelligence that few his age had. And then there was the smartness behind those inquisitive eyes. 'Yes, they have pulled her in for questioning because she was the last person who had any grievance with the landlord.'

Cyril's palms began to sweat, and his knees shook. The thought of his mum going to prison was unbearable. 'But what are ya saying, Mr Bates? She may have been the last person who had a grievance with the landlord, but she wasn't out that night he was murdered. She was at home, with me. I can tell the police that.'

Mr Bates put his foot down and took off his hat, tossing it over his shoulder onto the back seat. 'Cyril, the police know that your mum was probably one of the last people to see the landlord alive, because Saturday night she was playing poker with him.'

'But that was Saturday night, Mr Bates, not Sunday night, when he was killed.'

'The landlord wasn't murdered on Sunday night. He was murdered in the early hours of Sunday morning, after the poker game. He was knifed through the chest. But his wife didn't discover his body until Monday morning when she went to change the barrels. He'd apparently been murdered on the street and his body was thrown down the cellar from the pavement doors. So they believe whoever murdered him had a reason, and that, son, is your mum.'

Cyril said no more but mulled over everything that Mr Bates had just said.

Sensing that Cyril was chewing over his thoughts, Mr Bates tapped the lad's knee to console him. 'Listen, Cyril, you have to trust me. Not that you have any reason to, but when we get to my cottage and we are out of earshot, then I will explain everything to you. But you have to be bloody grown up about all of this.'

'I understand, Mr Bates, as long as you have a bloody good idea of how to get my mum out of the police station.'

Mr Bates grinned. Cyril reminded him of himself as a young lad. 'Don't you worry about your mum. I won't let anything happen to her.'

Cyril sank back into his seat and tried to calm down. He could feel tears welling up in his eyes, but he quickly blinked them back. He was a man now, not a kid, and men didn't cry.

After a good half an hour, Mr Bates slowed the car down enough to turn into a drive. Cyril gripped the seat for a moment because the drive itself was so overgrown with hanging vines and foliage that he thought the car would end up in a hedgerow. However, a few seconds later, a small cottage came into view.

Cyril hopped out before Mr Bates had even opened the door. He stretched and looked around. The cottage looked a bit dingy, but his mother always said that you should never judge a book by its cover. He noticed to the right of the cottage a pile of logs and an axe. *This was different*, he thought. A proper log fire inside, no doubt.

While Mr Bates unloaded the boot, Cyril walked up to a window and peered in.

Pleasantly surprised at the inside of the building, Cyril, still with his nose pressed to the glass, called out, 'It's a bit of all right, Mr Bates, eh!'

‘Cyril, take a bag or two, would you, please?’

Cyril hurried back to the car and relieved Mr Bates of all the luggage he seemed to be laden down with. He tapped on the window to wake Howie, who had fallen asleep after three minutes into the journey.

Mr Bates was taken aback by how much Cyril could carry and nodded out of respect.

Once they were inside, the relief from the sun was instant because the stone walls kept the heat out. Mr Bates walked on ahead through the small hallway directly into the kitchen where he offloaded his and Cyril’s bags. He then turned to Cyril and pointed to the door on the right, which led into the main room, the living room. Cyril had seen it from the outside, but inside, it was even better. The walls were gleaming white, unlike his main room at home, where everything was blackened with soot.

The floors were covered with thick rugs so only the bare floorboards were visible around the perimeter of the room. The open fireplace was huge compared to his at home, and there on cabinets and on the mantelpiece were photos and ornaments.

‘Cor, it’s lovely, Mr Bates.’ He turned to face him. ‘So why do you live next door to us in shitty Bermondsey, when you have got all this lot?’

Mr Bates nearly choked. ‘Bloody hell, Cyril. You don’t hold back, do you?’ He gestured for the two boys to take a seat. ‘Me and you, Cyril, are gonna have a chat.’ He looked at Howie who was just gazing around the room.

Cyril waved his hand. 'It's all right, Mr Bates. Howie won't say nuffin.'

'No, I don't suppose he will. Right, then, down to business. Your mum has been arrested for the murder of the landlord. But!' He paused and took a deep breath. 'They have nothing on her other than the fact she was the last person to have any gripe with the man. So, for the moment, they have her down at the station.'

Cyril was still perplexed and screwed his nose up. 'But why did I have to say I was with you that night?'

'Look, Cyril, the odds were that the filth would have dragged me in over it and tried to pin it on me.'

Still confused, Cyril asked, 'Why would they even think it was you, Mr Bates?'

Mr Bates didn't answer right away; instead, he walked over to a small drinks cabinet and poured himself a brandy. 'Okay, I went to prison many moons ago, for a very long time, and so, see, the likes of me, well, we get pulled in if there is a serious crime like a murder in the vicinity of where I live.'

Cyril was now getting the picture. 'So did you go to prison for murder, then?'

'Yes, if ya must bloody know.'

'Was my grandfarver involved? Only, I know you and him were mates.'

Staring into nothing, Mr Bates swigged his brandy. 'No, Cyril.'

‘Are you sure they won’t put my mum in prison?’

Mr Bates snapped out of his gaze. ‘Yes, I’m positive, Cyril. They have nothing on her, and just because she was the last person to have an argument with the man doesn’t make her a killer. So . . .’ He looked at his watch. ‘This time tomorrow they will have to let her go. The reason I came to collect you is that the boys in blue can do some nasty shit to get her to make a false confession – like have you and your brother put in temporary care – and then it’s a bastard getting you back. They play all kinds of dirty tricks. So that’s why I got you here, so they can’t get their hands on you – for one, to make you talk, and for two, to take you away to the social services.’

‘Jesus, Mr Bates, does me mum know all of this? I mean, won’t she be worrying?’

Mr Bates smiled. ‘Listen to me. Your mum is a very tough lady. She knows what to do. And not only that, but I have a bloody good lawyer who will have her out of there in no time – in fact, as I just said, this time tomorrow, to be precise. He told me what the police are up to, so he knows what to do, and that’s why you two are here . . . Are you with me, now?’

‘Why are you helping us, Mr Bates?’

Mr Bates sighed heavily and took another swig of his brandy. ‘Because, lad, at one time, your grandfarver was my best mate. He was like a brother, he was, but I let him down a long time ago. He wrote to me and asked me to look out for your mum, and I didn’t, until recently, when she came to my bedroom to help me get better. So, let’s just say, I am repaying a big debt.’

‘Mum never talks about her dad much. Will you tell me about him?’

‘Your lovely mum keeps a lot to herself. I’ve just found out how much bleedin’ debt your farver left her with. But, yes, Cyril, one day I will, when you’re old enough to understand his ways, and mine, funnily enough. I will tell you, and maybe, you will learn a thing or two.’

PART TWO

CHAPTER SEVEN

Cyril stared at himself in the hallway mirror. Mr Bates' suit was a little snug around the middle, but at least the trouser bottoms weren't swinging around his ankles. The navy blue was a respectable colour, and he had to admit to himself that he looked smart. The white shirt was pressed, and the final touch was achieved by adding a slim blue tie and a slap of aftershave.

Just as he stood to the side to admire his side profile, Peggy called out. 'Cyril, love, you won't be long, will you? You may wear a smart three-piece, but that don't make you a man ready to be out all hours.'

'Mum, me and Frank are off job hunting, up the West End.'

He straightened his tie and smiled again.

'You ain't even finished school, so what are you on about?'

'We will in a few weeks, and we wanna be ready when we

do, Mum. Don't you go worrying, now. I'll be back before midnight.'

Peggy laughed. 'All right, Cinderella. Mind you don't get into any trouble. D'you hear me, Son?'

'Mum, when have I ever brought trouble to your door?'

'That's a really good question, Son. Where do I bloody start? How about the time you just managed to swerve borstal because you nearly brought London Rail to a halt? I mean, Cyril, fancy taking all the nuts and bolts off the tracks to sell for scrap. And I wouldn't have minded, but you'd bleedin' nicked the replacements before the company even had a chance to fit them. I thought a near brush with the law would have kept you on the straight and narrow, but not you, eh?'

Cyril was still admiring himself in the mirror. He smiled when he heard the humorous tone in her voice.

'And you had the council take on an extra six months of laying the new road because you and the boys kept nicking the tar blocks. The coalman nearly went out of business 'cos the neighbours weren't buying the coal and —'

'Mum, I'm not going to get in any trouble, not tonight.'

Suddenly, Peggy appeared and looked Cyril up and down. 'Well, look at *you*.'

'What d'ya reckon, Mum? Mr Bates' suit looks smashing on me, don't ya think?'

Peggy raised her brow. 'You sure look fine, Son, but maybe a little too old in those clothes.'

'There's nuffin wrong in that, is there?'

Peggy sighed. 'Well, only in the fact that people will treat you as a lot older, and let's face it, you're still only fifteen, and you should look and act like it.'

Cyril noticed the sad expression in her eyes. 'What's wrong, Mum?'

'I dunno, Cyril. Sometimes, I look at you and see a man. In fact, I don't know if you were ever a little lad. With your farver running off the way he did, somehow it made you believe you were the man of the house, and you had it firmly fixed in your brain that it was your job to see us all okay. But it wasn't, Son. It was my responsibility to look after us all, and I feel at times that I failed you and . . .'

Cyril stepped away from the mirror and placed an arm around his mother's shoulders. 'You never failed me. Ever. Me ol' man buggering off probably did me a favour in some ways. We've had Mr Bates, and he's taught me a lot, you know. Not like me dad, who only showed me that getting drunk on the last few shillings only leads to bloody misery and being skint. Well, I ain't ever gonna be skint. Not all the time I have a hole in me arse.'

'Cyril!'

A cheeky giggle left Cyril's mouth. 'I'll be a very rich man, even a lord one day, and I will wipe those tears of yours away and replace them with diamonds. You'll see, Mum.'

'Aw, give over, Cyril. You just get yourself a good job and live a decent life. We did all right in the end, didn't we? We've got this new flat, with all its heating, a Formica kitchen, and no more dirty, stinking walls, or rats, or coal to worry about. Look at the huge windows and the little balcony. I can see right across London now. What more could we want, eh?'

Cyril felt a lump in his throat. It hadn't been easy, not one little bit. The whole street, barring Mr Bates' house and theirs, had once been vacant. It had been a dismal place then. Even Frank and Mrs Peabody had been rehomed in the new flats before Cyril and his family were allocated one. A whole year went by living in a run-down derelict street before the news came that they were going to be moving. Cyril knew it was Mr Bates who had been influential in securing a move.

He had been off to school one day when he'd spotted Mr Bates and the dreaded rent man talking. It was the very next day when some official turned up with the offer. He recalled his mother's face; she seemed to light up like the gas lamp, all beaming and shiny. She was so excited, she could hardly get the words out, she was so out of breath. 'A two-bedroom flat, in one of the new blocks, with heating and a new kitchen!'

Cyril had danced around the living room, enjoying her elation and soaking in her happiness.

However, Cyril had never forgotten the trip to Kent and the adventurous week of hop picking. He'd also never forgotten the huge house – that mansion – and the lord's son whose father owned it. He'd learned so much that week and the days that followed. As Mr Bates had promised, his mother had been released on the hour. The police had had no evidence, and so the case was closed. He remembered the glance that passed then between Mr Bates and his mother; it was a knowing look, an expression of accomplishment. And he remembered searching the house high and low for the potato peeling knife; it never did turn up. He realised that day that his mother wasn't as strait-laced as he thought she was. When he asked her why some people lived in a mansion, and others didn't, she explained about the world of the gentry. The list was endless, what with the aristocrats, the toffs, the snobs, the dukes, the lords, and the barons.

Cyril had never forgotten those words that left his mother's lips: 'Cyril, you can never be a lord. You have to be born a lord and to be born into money.'

He just couldn't understand how someone could be automatically entitled to so much wealth without having worked a day's hard graft for the privilege. It angered him when he recalled the young lord telling his father to shoot them for taking a few fish to eat. He was glad Frank had cut the toff's face, and he hoped he had a scar by now. And he still held that anger for the rich who really didn't deserve to be so, and that sympathy for the poor, who really didn't deserve to be in that state either.

'And, Cyril, make sure you take your key. I can't leave it on the string anymore. Apparently, there are some nasty gangs going around breaking into flats and scaring the bejesus out of the pensioners. Two old dears were startled only last week in the lift. The bloody sods nicked a butterfly brooch off one lady's hat, and, then, they even tried to snatch the other old lady's bag, but when she bashed them around the head and the lift door opened, two men were waiting there, and so the sods scarpered. Anyway, Cyril, they have been known to break into the flats, so, I'm just saying, watch yaself and take your key.'

Cyril felt in his trouser pockets, and there, sure enough,

was the key. As soon as he opened the front door, he saw Frank with his hand poised to knock.

Peggy laughed. 'Bloody hell, Frank, you've grown again over the holidays. I think you must be the same size as your farver now.'

Frank blushed. 'Yes, Mrs Reardon. In fact, I'm a little taller. He's getting a right belly on him now, though.'

Peggy laughed. 'It happens to all you men, if you let the beer get the better of you. Now then, off you go, and keep out of trouble.'

'Always, Mrs Reardon,' replied Frank.

As soon as they were in the lift, Frank grinned. 'Mr Bates' suit fits you like a glove, and what d'ya think about this whistle? It was me ol' man's, but he's too fat now to fit in it.'

'It looks great on ya, mate. D'ya reckon we'll pass off as twenty-one, or what?'

Frank shrugged his huge lintel-sized shoulders. 'There's only one way to find out.'

* * *

By the time they reached the Dorchester Hotel, their plan was in place. The size and the grandness of the building made both Cyril and Frank step back and take it all in.

Cyril's idea was more or less just a theory, but it was a plan that would be the start of a new way to earn a few bob, if it worked.

As they pushed their shoulders back and held their heads high, they marched confidently through the large doors and right past the concierge. Once inside, they surveyed the grand foyer. The place reeked of money. The tall pillars looked as if they'd been made from gold, something out of a Greek mythology book. The chairs were covered in red and purple velvet, and the floor was made of highly polished marble. Everywhere they looked, it shone like glass. The bellboys marched from the reception and on to the lifts carrying suitcases, and one young employee even held a chihuahua dressed as a baby. The manager walked around with a permanent grin smacked across his face, and in among the hustle and bustle of the staff were the wealthy clientele.

Cyril guided Frank over to a less conspicuous place where two chairs were partially hidden by what looked to be a big palm tree. They realised that there was less chance of them being noticed, although it was hard not to be aware of Frank with his dark hair and tall build.

Cyril, on the other hand, could really weave in and out among the crowd, and no one would even recall him being there; it was just how he liked it too.

They sat for a moment and watched until Cyril spotted exactly who he was looking for. 'There, Frank. See that group?' He pointed to some people standing by a table near the bar area.

'Yeah, Cyril, I can see them.'

'Good. Keep watching.'

As Cyril studied the slim woman surrounded by three men,

he clocked her dress, her shoes, and her bag. She was roughly his mother's size, and the dress was obviously some very expensive design. The fur around her shoulders was probably worth more than the contents of his family's entire flat. She was attractive, with dark hair piled high on her head. Her thick black lashes, like butterfly wings, fluttered as she laughed aloud. She was holding a cocktail glass. Cyril guessed she was drinking a Martini cocktail, and, in her other hand, she held a long black cigarette holder. As soon as she popped it in her mouth, one of the men was there at the ready with a lighter.

Cyril imagined his mother there standing next to the rich woman. What a stark contrast that would be. He could easily picture his mum in her plain short skirt and an ordinary jumper, with a string of cheap pearls he'd nicked from the market, and wearing shoes with the heels worn down and her hair tied back with a plain band.

'Right, Frank. Get yourself off up to the bar and order a pint of bitter and a glass of white wine.'

Frank frowned. 'Wine?'

Cyril shook his head, slightly frustrated that his friend wasn't on his wavelength. 'Yeah, 'cos white wine won't stain, will it? Anyway, buy the drinks and hang around over there. Look, she's gone off to powder her nose. As soon as she's in sight, walk past and tip the wine down her frock, but make sure it looks like an accident.'

Frank didn't see any point in questioning it. He only hoped that Cyril knew exactly what he was doing. He got up and did as Cyril instructed. He didn't have any qualms over not being served, but he did almost choke on the bill. Once he had the drinks firmly in his grasp, he watched the ladies' room for any signs that the posh woman was on her way back. He knew he had to get to her before she reached the table, or the three men would cause a problem.

Suddenly, she appeared and was heading his way. He swallowed hard and focused on his plan of action. He had her in his eyeline. Fortunately for him, she was searching for something in her bag. She didn't look up until he bumped into her, and at that point, he spilled the entire contents of the glass of wine down the front of her dress.

Instantly, she gasped as the cold drink splashed onto her neck and through her thin outfit. Almost as a reflex action, she then tried desperately to pull the front of the dress away from her skin.

'For God's sake! You bloody great oaf. Now look what you've done. This dress cost a fortune and now it's ruined.'

'I-I'm so sorry, Miss. I-I didn't mean to.'

'Christ, now I'll have to change. Why don't you look where you are going, in future?'

With that, Frank turned to Cyril and smiled.

Cyril wasted no time. Quickly and quietly, he followed the woman up the grand staircase and along the corridor, noticing which room she disappeared into. Immediately she was inside, he spotted a cleaner pushing a trolley that was laden with towels, toiletries, and laundry bags. 'Bingo,' he mumbled, under his breath.

Once the cleaner let herself into the room at the far end of the corridor, Cyril quickly grabbed a laundry bag from the trolley, placed a white towel over his arm, and then knocked at the room the posh woman had just entered.

'Who is it!' bellowed a female voice, in a tone that was clearly angry.

'Compliments of the manager,' came a voice from outside the room.

The door was flung open, and there wearing a well-fitted petticoat stood the woman, with a face like thunder. 'What compliments?'

'My manager saw what happened downstairs, and he has offered you a dry cleaning service. There is absolutely no charge, and you will have your dress brought back first thing tomorrow.'

The woman stared for a moment before snatching the laundry bag and shoving the dress inside. 'Well, if he's offering a free laundry service, I should throw in my other dresses. After all, the management should be more careful who they let into the hotel. The man who did this to my dress was some bloody great oaf who was obviously three sheets to the bloody wind,' she spat, as she opened the wardrobe door. Pulling four dresses from their hangers, she threw them into the laundry bag.

Cyril could hardly believe his luck with the way the plan was working.

'Miss, might I also suggest that we have your shoes cleaned? I know our manager wouldn't want to have an unhappy customer.'

'Quite right, too,' she replied.

She spun around and went into the room to look for her shoes that she'd thrown across the room in anger. Gathering them up, she threw them into the proffered laundry bag.

'And you can tell the manager—'

The sound of the phone ringing put her off her stride.

Cyril felt his heart was in his mouth. He prayed it wasn't the manager or he was well and truly in the shit.

Moving across the room to the phone, she picked up the receiver and said, 'Darling, I will be along in a jiffy. Now then, why don't you book a table for the four of us, and I will see you soon. Toodle-pip, my sweet.'

Replacing the receiver, she strode over to the door and handed Cyril the bag, before she waved him off and slammed the door.

With the laundry bag in his hands, he hurried along the corridor. He then realised that it would hardly look good for him to walk out of the Dorchester with a laundry bag bearing the hotel's logo; in fact, it would look highly suspicious. He stopped and leaned against a wall, in a recess, to give himself time to think.

The lift bell rang, and the door opened ahead of him. From out of the lift stepped a very smart-looking man, possibly Spanish or Italian, followed by one of the hotel's bellboys, loaded up with luggage. The boy put the suitcases on the floor before he unlocked and opened the room for the guest to enter. He then began to take the cases inside.

Cyril heard the smartly dressed man ask the bellboy if he had all the luggage. Cyril's intuition that the man was foreign was confirmed.

When the bellboy left the room, Cyril saw him shut the door behind him, and then walk towards the lift. But because the bellboy had stepped backwards and then turned immediately in the direction of the lift, Cyril could see why he had not spotted the one remaining case left outside the room.

Cyril's eyes scanned the corridor, and, to his relief, he was alone. With the bellboy now in the lift, and the corridor still clear, he rushed up to the suitcase, grabbed it, and ran to the staircase. On opening the suitcase, and without unzipping the interior, he placed all the dresses and the pair of shoes inside. He struggled a little to get everything to fit and to shut the case, but by sitting on it, he finally succeeded. With his adrenaline at a peak, he hurried down the staircase and out through the foyer where he spotted Frank standing well back behind the palm tree. Catching his attention with a wink, he strode confidently out through the hotel entrance. As soon as he'd turned the corner, Cyril managed to bring his heart rate down.

Seeing Frank approach him, he yelled, 'Fuck, Frank, we'd better leg it, mate. I dunno what I've half-inched, but I may have just nicked stuff off a Mafia man.'

As they ran, they both began to laugh until they were in hysterics, and they had to lean against a wall to catch their breath.

'Crikey, for all we know, we might be running with a dead body in the suitcase.'

‘Well, if it is, I bet it’s a midget.’

By the time they were on the bus home, Frank was ready to take on the world. England had won the World Cup, his father was teaching him to drive, and now the plan had gone so well that Cyril’s infectious optimism was rubbing off, and he too felt he could conquer Mount Everest.

‘Me and you, Frank, we’re gonna be rich, just like them toffs, just like that lord. Me, well, I’ve just gotta come up with the right plan.’

CHAPTER EIGHT

With large grins on their faces, Cyril and Frank appraised the suitcase. Both surmised that there was something very special inside it. Neither of them even considered that it may contain only a few pairs of underpants or a couple of shirts.

The lift to their block opened, and they both nudged each other before going inside with the ominous suitcase. They had agreed that apart from the woman's clothes and shoes, the rest of the contents in the suitcase were for sharing equally. In fact, that pact had stood intact since they were nine years old. Six years later, they were still honouring their promise to each other. Once the lift jolted to a stop at the second floor, Cyril could have kicked himself. He'd obviously pressed the wrong button for his floor. He was even more pissed off, though, when the doors opened and he and Frank were faced with three young men, all around twenty years old.

The tallest one, Nigel Deacon, otherwise known as Nut Nut, stood in the middle with his chest out and with a cocky sneer across his face. His hair was a light ginger colour and his cheeks were pitted with acne scars. His brother, Neville, the lad to his left, was more heavily built, with auburn hair and a pale skin. His strikingly brown and intense eyes gave him a vicious look. Gavin Pearson, the young man to his right, was the shortest. Unlike the other two, he had light-brown hair cut very short, and he looked completely gormless.

'Well, lads, look what we have here!' said Nut Nut, as he

held the lift door open while his two sidekicks stepped inside.

Cyril gripped the suitcase tighter. He guessed the strangers were out to cause trouble and would more than likely try to take the suitcase. However, Cyril had worked hard and taken a great risk to secure his mother a dress for the local tea party that everyone was going to. But because she couldn't afford a nice rig-out, he'd had to think of a creative way of ensuring she had one.

The lift door closed, leaving Cyril and Frank pushed against the back while the three bullies glared at them and then laughed in their direction. Nut Nut pressed the button for the next floor up. He knew where Reardon and Marsden lived.

'Nice leather suitcase you have there, and I am guessing that it ain't yours. So where did you nick it from? You see, I'm one of those Good Samaritans that likes to do the right thing and return stolen goods to their rightful owner. But you ain't the owner, are you?'

Cyril looked at each one in turn, quickly working out a plan to get out of this intimidation.

'It ain't nicked. It belongs to me farver, who's a copper.'

Nut Nut laughed. 'Oh, 'ark at this little toerag. A copper, yeah? You lying bastard. And I hate liars, don't I, Neville? Don't I, Gavin?'

Neville and Gavin, who now acted like Tweedledum and Tweedledee, replied in unison, 'Yep, Nut Nut, you do.'

Moments later, the lift doors opened onto the third-floor walkway. As Cyril and Frank attempted to squeeze past, Nut

Nut pushed Cyril back, stopping him from exiting the lift.

'Get off me!' yelled Cyril, as he tried again to leave the lift.

'Mouthy little fucker, ain't you!' replied Nut Nut, as he pushed Cyril even harder in the chest.

'I said, get the fuck off me!' yelled Cyril, now livid that he was being stopped from moving. Unexpectedly, he felt as if the world he knew was once more changing. The dreaded red mist descended, and, without thinking, he grabbed the suitcase with both hands and used it to barge his way out of the lift.

Nut Nut was taken aback and lost his balance, grabbing one of his mates to stop himself from tumbling. But Neville had nothing to grab hold of to stop himself from falling, and both men fell backwards, out onto the walkway.

The whole incident took place almost in slow motion, which gave Frank the chance to make sure that Nut Nut and Neville remained on the deck. In one fluid movement, he lifted his leg and pounded Nut Nut in the chest. He followed that up with a hard kick to Neville's face.

With only Gavin left on his feet, Cyril, who was never slow on the uptake, took his opportunity to ram him in the face with the suitcase, which he did, repeatedly, until Gavin tumbled backwards out of the lift and half onto the walkway. But Cyril wasn't finished. Standing over him, he stamped on his face over and over again. He didn't stop until he was breathless.

Nut Nut managed to get to his feet to take Frank on, but Frank punched him hard before he could get a blow in. Frank then grabbed Nut Nut's collar, and with a powerful right hook, Nut Nut fell backwards from the blow.

It was at that point, Cyril really saw the dark side of Frank. He watched his friend pull his fisherman's knife from inside his jacket pocket, and in one easy slice, he cut Nut Nut's ear clean off.

The lift door was opening and shutting because Gavin was slumped across the entrance.

Cyril grabbed Frank's arm, picked up the suitcase, and said, 'Let's get moving, Frank, before we get fucking nicked.'

Frank looked at the shrivelled piece of ear and tossed it over the balcony. 'No one will ever try to rob us again. Fuck 'em.'

Cyril was hurrying along the walkway shaking his head. 'Frank, who's in yours?'

'No one. Me dad's at Shirley's.'

'Good. Let's get inside. I can't go home like this. Me mum will worry.'

They stopped at Frank's front door and peered down the walkway to see if the three guys had recovered. There was no movement, so, quickly, they hurried inside and slammed the door shut behind them.

'Bloody hell's bells, Frank. You do realise you cut that bastard's ear clean off, don't ya?'

Laughing, Frank said, in his deep tone, 'Of course! And

what about you, Cyril. Christ, I thought you were gonna kill that guy. I don't think he has much of a face left. You ripped his mouth wide open.'

'Did I?'

Frank stared for a moment and wondered if Cyril had lost the plot. 'Didn't you see what you did, mate?'

Cyril placed the suitcase on the floor and shrugged his shoulders. 'I wasn't gonna let those no-good scumbags take what's rightfully ours. Anyway, me mum deserves a pretty dress for that do of hers. Let's forget about them. They probably deserved worse than what we gave 'em. Me mum said there's a gang of thugs going around the estate, and I bet they're part of it.' Cyril threw his head back and laughed. 'And they ain't a full army now, are they? They're an ear short of a cornfield.'

Frank didn't get the connection but laughed anyway.

The atmosphere turned serious. 'I think we've done some crucial damage, Cyril. D'ya reckon we'll get our collars felt for it?'

Cyril looked at the blood on the seam of the suitcase. 'No one actually saw us, and those cocky bastards won't admit to any defeat. If they call the coppers, then they're as good as grasses and wimps, so, nah, I doubt it. Anyway, we were only defending ourselves.'

'What, with a knife, Cyril?'

'It was *their* knife, Frank, that *you* managed to take from them. Right?'

Frank frowned. 'What? No, it was . . .' He stopped when he saw Cyril shaking his head.

'Oh, I see. Yeah, that's right, Cyril. They had the knife first.'

'Now then, let's see what we've got 'ere. And if there's nuffin much, I reckon a real leather suitcase will fetch us a tidy few quid down the market.'

Frank carried the suitcase into his bedroom and closed the door behind Cyril. 'Go on then, open it.'

Cyril unzipped the case and allowed it to fall open from the weight equally distributed on both sides. He removed the laundry bag and then unzipped the segregated compartment on the left-hand side.

They stood silently, just staring at the contents. They then both looked at each other in wide-eyed amazement.

'Well, I'll be buggered with an ironing board. What d'ya make of that, Frank?'

Frank was still staring at the grey metal gun, which had been carefully held in a padded compartment.

'How much do you suppose we'd get down the market for that thing?'

Cyril blinked. 'What? We can't flaming well sell *that*! Jesus, I'll end up in borstal.'

'So, what d'ya reckon we should do with it, then?'

Cyril shrugged his shoulders. 'Nuffin, for now. But I tell

ya what. It's a lovely tool,' he replied, as he took the gun from its compartment and turned it around in his hand. 'It's heavier than I thought it would be.' He then held it up, aiming at the window. 'Cor, it's a really tasty piece of weaponry. I wanna keep it. Ya never know, I might need it one day.'

'Open the other side of the case, Cyril. See if there's anything we can divide up.'

When Cyril unzipped the right-hand side, his heart sank. He really hoped it would be loaded with money. But, instead, all he saw was a bag of washing powder. 'Oh damn it, I thought we'd be in for a few quid. Instead, the Mafia man's brought washing powder to wash his smalls, no doubt. Ah, well, I guess I can use it to wash the wine out of that dress.' He sighed and looked at his mate, who looked equally deflated.

'I tell you what, Frank. That suitcase there . . . I bet it's worth a lot of money. Let's get it checked out. Sorry, I thought it might have diamonds or something valuable in it. D'ya mind if I use your sink just to wash out that mark on the dress, before I hang it up in me mum's wardrobe? I tell ya, Frank, she'll be over the flippin' moon. My mum swanning around in a posh frock, what a sight that would be! And look at the shoes. They're proper soft leather. They ain't any ol' tosh.'

'Yeah, I agree. Right. Go on, then. Use the bathroom.'

Cyril grabbed the dress and the bag of washing powder and made his way to the bathroom. The layout of the flat was exactly the same as his own, except he had to share a room with his brother, so there were two beds in the second bedroom. Just along the hallway on the left was the bathroom.

Cyril filled the basin with warm water and poured in a small amount of powder. He scrubbed at the stain, which came out right away. But then he noticed that the washing powder didn't produce any lather or bubbles. A feeling of excitement came over him.

'*Frank*!'

Frank heard the tone in Cyril's voice and ran to the bathroom to find Cyril holding the bag of powder as if he were holding a baby. 'Frank, this ain't *washing powder*. I reckon it's *drugs*.'

'Get out! Really?'

Cyril nodded. 'Well, it ain't washing powder . . . Oh, damn. I just wasted some on the dress.'

'What do you think we should do with it? 'Cos I don't know much about drugs, Cyril.'

Cyril walked back into the bedroom and placed the powder back inside the suitcase. 'Me neither, Frank, but, for all we know, this could be our lucky break, mate. I don't know how much this is worth on the street, but that's our next mission. We need to find out.' He paused in deep thought. 'But we need to be careful, 'cos if we're asking the wrong people, it could come back to bite us on the arse . . . I know a man who I can trust with me life. I'll have a word with him tomorrow.'

Frank rolled his eyes. 'You'd better know what you're doing, Cyril, 'cos the Mafia ain't a joke, and neither is getting caught with drugs. I mean, I haven't ever taken drugs in me whole life.'

'Me neither, and that's the way it's gonna stay. I don't want to put anything in me body that shouldn't be there. Except for a few beers, now and then.'

Slowly, Frank opened the front door to check the coast was clear. Then he stuck his neck right out to see if the three hoodlums had crawled away to the rock they'd come from. They had, so he stepped aside and watched Cyril hurry a few doors along and enter his own flat.

* * *

'Is that you, Cyril?' his mother called out.

'Yep. I'll be with you in a minute.'

'All right, love. I'm just gonna finish me cuppa, then I'm off to bed.'

Cyril hurriedly removed the dresses from the suitcase, slid them onto some hangers, and hung them on the outside of his mother's old oak wardrobe. His eyes wandered around her little bedroom and his heart sank. The rickety bed was covered in a faded bedspread; the light on a nightstand, which was balanced by being shoved against the wall, was also faded, and the pink tassels on the fringes were sparse. There was nothing inviting about his mother's room at all. Not compared to the pictures in the magazines. He had to find a way to earn some real money and give her a better life. He placed the leather shoes in front of the wardrobe under the red dress, and then, before he headed to his own bedroom, he stepped back to admire his work.

Saying not a word, he slipped out of Mr Bates' suit, checked it over for any scuff marks or rips, and then, once he was satisfied, he hung it also on a hanger and slipped into his striped pyjama bottoms.

Howie didn't move, sleeping like a log.

That was until he heard his mother screech, 'What on earth is *this*!'

Cyril grinned at the excitement in her voice.

Howie, though, just sat up straight and rubbed his eyes. 'What's going on, Cyril?'

'Mum's just seen her new party dress.'

Howie huffed. 'And where did you nick that from?'

Cyril smiled at his brother and then tapped the side of his nose.

'Cyril! Cyril! Where on earth did you get these from? They're worth a bleedin' fortune. They don't look like market dresses to me.'

Cyril glided into his mum's bedroom again, laughing. 'That's 'cos they didn't *come* from the market. They came from the Dorchester Hotel, no less. Some silly posh bird was throwing them out, so I took them out of the bin.'

Peggy raised her eyebrow. 'Oh come on, Cyril. That's not true. And knowing you the way I do, I bet there was mischief involved.'

Cyril winked. 'Well, they did come from the Dorchester Hotel, and the lady was posh, and she did give them to me. In fact, she almost threw them at me.'

Peggy held the red dress up against herself, feeling the richness of the material.

Noticing the happiness on his mother's face, Cyril knew he'd done the right thing. She really looked so much prettier and classier than the woman from the hotel.

'Aw, Cyril, the shoes fit like a glove. Oh my Gawd, they feel like socks on me feet. I shall only ever wear these for best. So what else did you manage to get?'

'Nuffin, really. I only got you a few bits of clobber, so now you can go to the ball.'

'My, my, Cyril. I *will* be the belle of the ball, an' all. Dressed in red, heads will turn, lad, heads will turn.'

'Good. An' so they should. Right, I'm off to bed. I need me beauty sleep.'

Pleased with himself for being the one to put a smile on his mother's face, Cyril slept like a baby. He gave no further thought to the fight, the gun, and the drugs.

CHAPTER NINE

By 6.00 a.m., Cyril was up, Peggy was beginning to stir but still in her bed, and Howie was sound asleep. Cyril wanted to get out while the darkness afforded some decent cover. He'd already decided to leave the suitcase, with the gun and the drugs inside, under his bed, and, instead, go and pay Mr Bates a visit, if he was in, which couldn't be guaranteed, even at this early hour.

Since Mr Bates had recovered from the lung condition that he'd thought would kill him, he had become a very busy man. Nevertheless, he always had time for Peggy. Every so often, he would bring along a big bag of meat, and last Christmas, like Scrooge himself, he'd brought the biggest turkey, and along with it came a fridge he'd bought, much to the delight of his mother, who had made sure that no matter how many times a sticky hand touched the large long silver handle, she would make it her mission in life to polish it clean, to the point that she would then stand back and admire her addition to the kitchen.

Daybreak cast light on the entrance to the lift. For a second, Cyril stopped and just gazed at the bloodstains. For what he'd classed as a tussle had turned out to be more than that. He tried to recall what he had done to the guy on the floor, but he couldn't remember. The disturbing memory was of Frank cutting Nut Nut's ear off. He shuddered but turned and peered over the balcony, although he couldn't see anything on the floor below. Once the lift door opened, he sidled in and looked carefully at the floor. Like the outside, the inside was also covered in claret. 'Oh shit,' he mumbled, under his breath. Perhaps they had gone overboard with the belting. But then he remembered that he and Frank had been confronted with three thugs intent on stealing his suitcase. He smiled proudly and huffed, 'They deserved every clump they got.'

Three long taps followed by two slow taps was the code for Mr Bates. He waited, wondering if Mr Bates was even up at this hour. When the door opened, Mr Bates ushered Cyril inside before quickly closing the door.

'Right, go into the living room. You're lucky I even answered the door again.'

'*Again*? Mr Bates, what's going on?'

'What's going *on*?' He raised his voice. 'I can only bloody guess what's being going on, but I was the one who got questioned over it. So, Cyril, do you wanna tell me what you were up to yesterday?'

Cyril sat down in the armchair that was positioned against the long window while Mr Bates sat opposite.

Cyril wondered why on earth the police would question Mr Bates over some stolen property from the Dorchester Hotel, which was two bus rides away. He screwed his face up, determined not to give anything away. 'What did they say, Mr Bates?'

'They asked me if I had anything to do with three lads

who'd been beaten half to death, one having had his ear sliced off.'

Cyril deflated his chest. 'Oh, *that*,' he stupidly replied, along with a relieved sigh.

'Oh, *that*! Oh, *that*! So tell me, lad, what were you up to, if beating three young men up comes down to just saying "Oh, that", as if "oh" was nuffin?'

Cyril felt his cheeks redden. He hadn't thought it through before he'd opened his mouth, and he could have kicked himself. He didn't want to lie to Mr Bates, as he he'd come to see him to discuss business, which, in fact, was to do with what he'd been up to yesterday.

'Well, actually, Mr Bates, that's why I'm here, really.'

Mr Bates sensed that there was something more serious to discuss. 'Go on, lad.'

'Do you know anyone who buys drugs?' He couldn't think of any other way to ask, other than coming straight out with it.

Mr Bates' sleek features for a moment looked almost vampire-like. He could just have easily played the part of Dracula.

Cyril swallowed hard as Mr Bates, with his lips now pursed, stared at him, his eyes almost boring into his soul. Cyril hadn't seen this expression before and he didn't like it either.

'Why?'

'I, er, oh, never mind. Sorry, I shouldn't have asked. Anyway, I managed to get Mum a nice dress, and I'll have your suit dry-cleaned and back to you before next week.' The words almost tripped over themselves as Cyril shot up out of the armchair, ready to leave.

'Sit, boy!' demanded Mr Bates, as he got up and placed a hand on Cyril's shoulder, pushing him back into the armchair. 'Don't rush off. I asked you a question, and I want an answer. Now then, let's start again. Why do you want to know if I know anyone who buys drugs? Because, Cyril, that isn't like asking me what football team I support, now, is it?'

'Okay, okay, I know you and me Grandpop were villains, and I know that you still do what you do, and it ain't none of me business. I trust you, Mr Bates, so here's the thing. Me and Frank came across a bag of powder, and, well, it definitely ain't washing powder, so we think it's a bag of drugs, perhaps cocaine or heroin.'

'What colour is it?' asked Mr Bates, in an even tone.

'It's white.'

'It's more than likely cocaine. And how much does it weigh?'

Cyril leaned forward. Mr Bates had him interested now. 'Dunno, might be half a pound.'

'Are you fucking serious?'

Cyril nodded. 'Yeah, 'course. The truth is, I nicked it by mistake. I just needed a suitcase to carry the dress I acquired for me mum. Anyway, when we got back from the hotel, we unzipped the case to find a bag of white powder.' He deliberately left out the fact that he'd also found a gun in there as well.

'Did anyone, and I *mean* anyone at all, clock you leaving the hotel with the suitcase?'

Cyril shook his head. 'No, and I reckon by the time the Italian noticed it was missing, we were probably on the bus home.'

'Italian?'

'I dunno. He was dark-skinned, that was for sure. He could have been Spanish, Italian, or an Arab, although he didn't have a tea towel on his head.'

'Bloody hell, boy, you could have the Mafia on your arse. Right, what do you want to do, Cyril? 'Cos, son, getting involved in selling drugs is a very, very dangerous and risky game. You're just fifteen years old. I know you get up to no good, but we probably all did at your age. But jumping from the odd little tickle to peddling drugs is a serious prison sentence and . . .'

He paused and got up. 'Do you want to be a crook, Cyril, or get a decent job and earn an honest living, not looking over your shoulder all the time?'

'Come on, Mr Bates, even if I got a good education, I couldn't even afford the suit for an interview. I don't speak the Queen's English, and I don't know what I wanna do to earn a living. But I do know I wanna live in a big house, drive a flash motor, and have money in me back pocket for a few beers.'

'It's all or nothing, Cyril. It's like rolling the dice, because if you go down that road of villainy, you either make it big, or you end up in the clink wondering why the fuck you didn't just get a nine-to-five job and stay out of trouble.'

Cyril looked around the room and noticed the paintings on the wall, the new sofa, two high-quality armchairs, and the new coffee table. Mr Bates even had a fancy unit that housed his bottles of spirits. The most luxurious additions were the floor covering – there was no lino or rug here but wall-to-wall carpet – and the floor-to-ceiling curtains. It was a pivotal moment for him: if he wanted what Mr Bates had – all the luxury items, the nice trappings of success – then there was no point in working in a factory and bringing home the same pitiful monthly salary.

'You do all right though, Mr Bates, don't ya? I mean look at this place. You've got it rigged out all fancy.'

Mr Bates sighed. 'But, Cyril, look at me.' He raised his hand to demonstrate the finery in the room. 'All this and me sitting in a chair alone, with no wife, no kids, and fuck all of any importance. So why is this not enough?'

Cyril frowned.

''Cos, lad, I was in and out of the nick. Me lovely lady, Annie, such a sweet woman, stayed with me until I got an eight-stretch, and then she buggered off with me pal. I didn't blame her at the time, although I wanted to kill him, but the truth is, it was me own fault. I got greedy. I didn't know when to call it a day, and now I collect monies owed to me and can afford luxuries, but – here's the point – I have no one to share it with.'

Cyril tilted his head. 'Monies owing to you?'

'Yes, Cyril. In the early days, I had a lot of money and used to lend it. But don't get me wrong: I let them pay it back when they could. Some took the piss. They had a word of warning – Mr Bates style – but some genuinely didn't have the money at the time. So, years on, when they're back on their feet and are able to pay me what they owe, I treat meself to something nice. It don't make up for the loneliness, though.'

Cyril drank in everything that Mr Bates was saying. For a moment, he felt sorry for the man. He then said something that he didn't even realise what he'd said until the words came out of his mouth.

'You may not have kids, but you've been like a dad to me.'

Mr Bates' eyes suddenly widened. 'I never wanted kids.'

'Sorry, I only meant that you've been there for me. Perhaps saying you've been like a dad was going too far.'

Mr Bates laughed. 'I dunno, Cyril. You really can talk your way out of trouble, can't ya. Right, anyway, back to this drugs stash you have. First, tell absolutely no one.'

'Frank knows.'

Mr Bates nodded. 'Well, he's a lad of just a few words, that one.'

'You're right. He won't say a dicky bird.'

'Second, that is a lot of cocaine, if that's what it is. And it's worth a lot of money.'

Cyril's eyes shot open. 'How much?'

Mr Bates waved his hands. 'Look, forget that for now. The thing is, you don't know who you've nicked it from, so you need to stash it away somewhere safe and wait. Someone out there is gonna be pretty pissed off, and word will get about soon enough. So we need to know who owned the drugs in the first place. If you suddenly start peddling cocaine in large amounts, the Italians, or whoever, will come for you, and with that amount of cocaine in a suitcase, it's sure to mean they'll have a right hefty mob behind them, and you, son, will end up in a suitcase yaself at the bottom of the friggin' Thames.'

Cyril felt a chill run through him at the thought and wondered if it was excitement or nerves.

'Okay, Mr Bates, but do you know roughly how much it's all worth?'

Mr Bates rolled his eyes. 'Now, lad, don't you go getting carried away, right? I don't want you to go making yourself busy, trying to sell that shit because, mark my words, the Italians, or the Arabs, or whoever, will know. They only have to get a clue that someone is selling this shit, and then they'll find ya and kill ya. These drug peddlers don't mess about. They are serious gangsters – ruthless, in fact.'

'I ain't silly, Mr Bates. I won't go flogging it. But I don't know enough about it. I have some serious homework to do. So how much, d'ya reckon?'

Rubbing his bristly chin, Mr Bates then peered into space. 'A hundred quid, perhaps? It could even be more. It depends how hard it is to get hold of at the moment and who's willing to buy it if it's top quality.'

Cyril was breathless. 'A hundred *quid*? Bloody hell!'

'Cyril! Listen, say nothing and fucking do nothing, right?'

Cyril sat up straight.

Mr Bates' tone was not to be taken lightly, and besides, he never usually swore.

'Okay, Mr Bates, I promise. Shall I just hide it and wait a few days?'

'A few *days*? No, you daft sod, we need to wait a few *months*. Christ, if you're serious about this, Cyril, you'd better learn bleedin' well fast, and do as you're told, right?'

Cyril stared him straight in the face and nodded.

'And don't get anything on loan because that also draws attention. You just go about ya business as if nothing's changed, and don't even think about the money. I need to do a bit of digging.' He sighed. 'First, I'd better try to find out who the blazes you've gone and nicked it from.'

Cyril watched as Mr Bates relaxed into his armchair, and then he saw a generous smile creep its way across the man's face.

'So,' he sniggered, 'you gave that little gang what-for, did ya?'

'Who were they?'

'Nigel Deacon, for one. A right little bastard, he is. I knew his farver an' all. Funny, 'cos I had a toe-to-toe with him many years ago. Such a horrible tribe that lot. Well, anyway, watch out. Because I don't think that hiding will necessarily make 'em think twice about giving you any more grief, or Frank, for that matter. The police questioned me about it because, like I said, any trouble, they always knock at my door. What a joke, eh? Do I look like a teenager? Mind you, the police were probably just doing a routine check. I don't think they'll be feeling your collar. Word has it that those lads have been robbing a few of the flats, and they've even stooped to robbing the old people on the estate.'

That pricked Cyril's ears. 'No way. So, d'you think it was them?'

Mr Bates nodded. 'Yeah, they're cocky bastards, they are. But, Cyril, be careful, 'cos I do believe they have a firm, and Nigel has a cousin called Red or Rhett from Hackney, who, by all accounts, is a nutcase.'

'Hmm, well, I ain't worrying over anything that ain't happened yet. I best get off home and hide that powder somewhere safe.'

Mr Bates got up and placed a hand on Cyril's shoulder. 'Crime is always only a short win, Cyril. You're a bright lad, and you can make something of yaself by doing it the right way.'

'I would love to go to university and become a lawyer or an accountant or something like that, but let's face it, I ain't the type that would fit in, and I don't have the money to pay for it. But you watch me, Mr Bates. I will be rich one day.'

Mr Bates squeezed Cyril's shoulder. 'You are your grandfarver all right.'

'Let's hope I'm a bit smarter than he was, 'cos he ended up skint, didn't he?'

Mr Bates' face suddenly fell in a sea of sadness. 'Yeah, I'm afraid he did.'

CHAPTER TEN

Cyril waited until his mother left the flat to go to her new job at the chocolate factory. He'd just watched her spray lacquer over her hair, which was piled high, and then run a quick slither of lipstick over her lips. He smiled to himself.

She was happy. Not that they had much, but life was better living in the flat rather than the house, although that was now razed to the ground. She'd returned to the odd game of poker and was grateful to be escorted by Mr Bates once a month up town. She won more games than she lost, and the cash was enough to cover the rent and buy a few treats, including the pretty flowered dresses – which brightened up her face – her pink patent handbag, and matching shoes. She made sure that all the wardrobes contained decent clothes. The family had nothing expensive, but gone were the days of wearing holey jumpers and cardboard in their boots.

She would roll her eyes and then smile when he'd place a few shillings on the table, and she was past caring where he'd got them from. He didn't like to lie, and yet he didn't want her worrying. He'd learned a few things about his grandfather, and so when his mother ruffled his hair and said, 'Aw, Cyril, you are so much like me dad, he would have been proud of you,' he knew that she was wise to the world of crooks. Perhaps she had seen so much in her hard life that she wasn't so averse to falling off that straight path trodden by the law-abiding citizen.

As soon as she was out of the door, Cyril retrieved the suitcase from under his bed, wrapped the gun and the drugs inside an old shirt, and got to work removing the wooden panel that lined the bottom of the wardrobe. He almost bent the kitchen knife trying to prise it out, but as soon as the nail loosened, he removed the panel and then placed the gun and drugs inside before carefully putting the panel back.

He got up and sat on the end of his bed and thought about his future. Mr Bates had a point: he either became a villain or he found a half-decent job – thereby never having to risk spending time inside a prison cell. His mind went over and over the pros and cons. He had to ask himself if he would ever be satisfied with clocking into work for the eight hours a day and then returning to sit in a flat, with the only excitement being a few beers on a Friday or Saturday night. The thought of a hundred pounds for that bag of white powder weaved its way through his brain like a whisper beckoning him to take the risk. A hundred pounds would be the equivalent to a year's wages from the local factories, meaning he wouldn't even have to punch a card into the clocking station and spend eight hours a day doing something he hated.

He wanted to own a business, own a house, and drive a flash motor. He wanted the handmade suits, the Italian leather shoes, and to smell of expensive aftershave. Mr Bates always smelled good, always wore classy clothes. It gave him a bit of an edge. And he wanted to be like that too.

A commotion from the bottom of the flats snapped Cyril from his thoughts. He jumped up and peered out of the window to see a car being unloaded and a woman bellowing at the driver. 'You'll regret the day you ever crossed me. Go on, then. Fuck off back to your wife. You were never any good to me, anyway.'

Cyril chuckled to himself as he watched the suited and booted man drag suitcases and boxes from the back seat of the car while a well-dressed woman kept screaming in his earhole.

'Mind me fucking hatbox, you clumsy bastard.'

'Oh, for God's sake, Sonia, will you stop screeching? You'll burst my eardrum. I am not going back to my wife, I want to be on my own. I never bloody asked you to move in anyway, so stop screaming at me.'

Cyril continued to watch the commotion and then he noticed a very young woman, with striking red hair that shone like chestnuts in the sun. She was dainty and dressed in a black-and-white polka dot dress and black patent shoes. Her long hair was tied up in a black bow, and she stood with her arms folded just staring as if this fracas was a usual event.

Suddenly the woman stopped screaming and grabbed the young girl by her arm. 'Come on, Flossie. Fuck him. Help me carry the bags back to the flat.'

'Mum, get off me. I know the bloody way.'

'Well, don't just stand there like a peacock! Grab a bag and help, will ya!'

Cyril noticed the girl's face as she turned towards the flats. His stomach felt odd, and his heart beat faster. She was probably the same age as him, and her face, although stern, was almost catlike, with almond eyes and rosebud lips. Her cheek bones were high and chiselled, and the way she walked was so controlled and serene, to him she looked like one of those models in the magazines.

'Flossie, get a bloody move on, before someone pinches all our belongings.'

Cyril spotted that when they were out of sight there were quite a number of bags left behind. He hurried from the bedroom, quickly straightened his hair in the mirror, ran along the walkway to the stairwell, and jumped the stairs two at a time to stand guard over the boxes and bags until he saw Flossie – as he now knew she was called – and her mother return for them.

Before they could say a word, he said, 'Would you two ladies like a hand carrying your bags up?'

Flossie's mother looked questioningly at Cyril and screwed up her face. 'Why would you wanna help us? Got your eye on me daughter, have you now?'

Gobsmacked, Cyril bit back. 'No, I was just being a gentleman, that's all, but if you don't need me help, then, carry on, missus.'

Flossie's face lit up, and she giggled. 'That told you, Muvver.'

'Shut ya mouth and get your arms full, girl.'

Flossie looked at Cyril and rolled her eyes. It was at that precise moment that Cyril felt he had been stabbed in the heart by Cupid's arrow. 'I'm Cyril Reardon. Pleased to meet you.'

'Flossie Hever, likewise.'

Cyril picked up a heavy-looking box and walked towards the lifts with Flossie holding a hatbox. 'So are you moving in then, Flossie?'

She shook her head. 'We never really moved out. We only stayed at me mum's fella's for a few weeks until he got pissed off with her.'

'What was that, Floss?' yelled her mother, who was now impatiently smacking the lift button.

'Nothing, Mum.' She sighed.

After three more trips, every bag and box was inside their flat on the fourth floor. Flossie's mum thanked him and ushered him out of the flat at breakneck speed.

In fact, she was so quick that when he turned around to say goodbye, he found the door was slammed in his face. Still that didn't bother him because he and Flossie had shared a few looks: one was a laugh behind her mother's back and then there were a couple of shy glances.

With his mind on the new girl Flossie, he didn't see Frank until he almost bumped into him. 'Hey, mate, where've you been?'

Frank had his hands in his trouser pockets and wore a face like a smacked arse. 'To the asylum. Me mum's sick.'

Cyril had never seen Frank look so sad. 'Oh, sorry, mate. Is she bad?'

Frank nodded. 'Yeah, she won't last the week, they reckon.'

'Aw, no. D'ya fancy having a wander around the market to take your mind off it?'

Frank gave a lipless smile. 'I'm not really in the mood, Cyril.'

'D'you wanna be on your own?'

Frank shook his head. 'Not really. D'you fancy coming to mine, though? 'Cos I don't really wanna face anyone, and me ol' man's at Shirley's.'

They headed along the walkway to Frank's flat and went inside straight into the kitchen where they both sat at the table.

'You never speak about your mum, Frank.'

'Nah, it's, er . . . I guess it's a sore subject. Me mum has problems. Her brain ain't right, ya know. She gets these violent tempers that the doctors reckon ain't normal. It's something in her blood. I dunno. Me dad had to put her in the asylum. At first, he hoped she could get treated, but, as the time went by, the doctors told him she'll probably never get better.'

'Cor that must be hard, eh, Frank? I would miss my mum badly. I suppose you do, eh?'

Frank slowly shook his head. 'No, not at all because all my memories of me mum ain't good ones. She tried to kill me a few times. Luckily, me dad caught her. I remember this one time I was in the tin bath, and then she had her hands around me throat and my head was under water. I couldn't breathe. I fought and fought, but she was so much stronger than me. It was bleedin' frightening.' He paused and looked up to find

Cyril with his mouth open.

'Blimey!' said Cyril.

'I was under the water with me eyes open, and then I saw me dad, and, instantly, I was out of the water gasping for breath. All my dad would scream was "Why? Why? Why?" I dunno, none of us knew why she wanted to kill me.'

Cyril watched as Frank stood up from the chair. He turned to the side and rolled down the top of his trousers to reveal his right buttock.

Cyril gasped at the swirls of scarred skin. 'Jesus.'

'She sat me in the fire, and it was me Aunt Shirley that saved me that time. That's when she and me Dad called the authorities. It broke me dad, ya know. He got a bit nasty with everyone. He's all right now, mind you, and me Aunt Shirley's always been good to me.' He pulled his trousers back up and sat down.

'So, if your mum did all that to you, why did you want to visit her?'

'She's dying.'

'I guess you wanted to say goodbye, you know, just in case, like . . .'

Frank looked across to Cyril and screwed his nose up. 'No, I wanted to hear her say she was sorry before she pegged it, but she just looked me up and down and said, "What the hell do you want?" I shrugged me shoulders and stared at her thin, gaunt face and wondered if behind those dark eyes lurked the

Devil. I just couldn't stop staring at her. Then she grinned, and she had hardly any teeth, but it was that sick look, as if she was laughing at me. It was as if she hated me. So I just turned around and left, and I won't be going back.'

Cyril felt the lump in his throat when he saw his mate's shoulders droop in utter sadness.

'Well, Frank, you tried, mate. You can take a horse to water, but you can't make it drink.'

Frank shook his head. 'I don't know what you mean, but you're probably right.'

* * *

That evening, Peggy dished up a large tray of shepherd's pie and invited Frank to dinner. It was not that he needed an invitation – he usually got fed if Peggy was laying the table. 'Open that drawer there, Howie,' she said, pointing to the free-standing cabinet that was always empty.

'Cor, what's all this, Mum?'

'Those are what the factory manager calls "seconds". He said I could help meself.'

Howie placed the large box of chocolates on the table, removed the lid, and eyed each and every one of them.

'It's like Christmas.'

Peggy smacked his hand away. 'Now then, no touching until you've washed your hands and eaten your dinner.'

She looked at Frank. 'How are you, babe? Your dad told

me what's going on. If you wanna talk, I'm all ears, love.'

Frank gazed at Peggy for a while. 'I didn't even know her, really. I know you more than her.'

For a moment, Peggy felt so sorry for Frank. Shirley Mills and Henry Marsden had filled her in on the truth behind his mother being in an asylum. How she had repeatedly abused Frank and tried to kill him. And she knew that was the reason why Henry kept a watchful eye on Frank – because he didn't want him to get out of hand and go off the rails. She also understood Frank's father was just grateful that it hadn't affected Frank mentally, and, on the outside, he did seem a well-adjusted lad.

Peggy used her wide knife to score the crispy top of the shepherd's pie and then used an egg slice to lift a generous helping onto each plate. She drained the spring greens and placed some on the side, adding a knob of butter, before pouring gravy over the top.

As soon as she placed it under Frank's nose, his face lit up. 'Cor, my favourite.'

'I know, lad. I'm sure you can smell it right down the walkway, 'cos you always turn up just when I'm about to serve.' She ruffled his hair.

The small table in the kitchen could just about seat the four of them, now the lads were getting bigger. Howie was taller than Cyril and plumper, but he still had a very young face and dimples. Cyril was still slim, but he wore a man's expression. His grey eyes sparkled, especially when he was being cheeky.

Peggy wondered if that's how he always seemed to get out

of trouble. Because she knew damn well he was often in it. However, her Cyril was never not going to be up to something or other; it was in his bones, in his blood, and it had been passed straight down from her father, no doubt.

As soon as they had finished and used the last of the bread to wipe the plates clean, Howie opened the box of chocolates, but Peggy tapped his fingers again. 'You can take the rubbish down for me first, and then we can all have a chocolate.' She turned to Cyril. '*Opportunity Knocks* is on soon. There're four beers in the fridge and some Battenberg cake.'

Frank beamed again because he loved watching the TV. He didn't have one at home, and Peggy had only recently acquired one, so it was a novelty.

Just as they were seated with a beer in their hands, and the TV was warming up, they heard a high-pitched scream, like that of an injured fox.

Peggy's heart was in her mouth. She jumped up from her chair and flew to the lounge floor-to-ceiling window. Throwing it open, she leaned over the balcony looking for Howie. She knew that sound; it was odd and piercing, and it was from her son. She'd only ever heard it twice before; once when a rat had bitten him when he was two years old, and the other time was when he trod on a nail that went straight through his shoe and up through the sole of his foot. She panicked trying to see where he was, but she could only see the shadows of three, possibly four, men. The bins tucked under the balcony of the first floor restricted the view to the lift and stairs.

In a panic, she grabbed her shoes and pelted along the

hallway. 'It's Howie, that noise. It's him!' she cried. 'And I can see the outlines of men down there. Quick, Cyril!'

'What!' screeched Cyril, as he and Frank leaped from their chairs and hurried behind Peggy. Cyril was still holding his unopened bottle. The thought of anyone hurting his brother sent him into that place where the world changes. Feeling every inch of his body alight, he suddenly pushed past his mother and ran to the stairwell, jumping down the stairs four at a time. So much was rushing through his head at the thought of his little brother hurt or being beaten. 'Christ!' he mumbled, under his breath. *Had those men who he and Frank had bashed the life out of come back out for revenge? Maybe*, he thought, *Mr Bates was right and they'd come here firm-handed.* Mr Bates had warned him. But he couldn't think about that now: he needed to get to his brother.

As soon as he leaped from the last few steps, he saw them. The fact that there were six men didn't bother him one bit. He looked down at the tarmac to see Howie curled in a ball, his cheek swelling like a balloon and his whole body shaking. Cyril had seen enough to tell him that his little brother was traumatised, and it sent him into a rage like never before. Every nerve was alight, every muscle throbbed, and his pulse beat like a war drum. His brother was sweet and kind, and he wouldn't hurt a fly. He did no wrong, and he couldn't fight his way out of a paper bag. He wouldn't even have known what was going on. Cyril ground his teeth and flared his nostrils.

He gripped the bottle and glared, looking to see who was in charge.

The biggest, ugliest man, with black teeth and white eyelashes to match his light ginger hair smirked. He stared at

Cyril and bared his teeth while he kicked Howie in the stomach. A daring glare with a curled lip would have worried anyone because this was Red Deacon, a cousin to Nigel Deacon, a woman-beating, obnoxious, nasty piece of work who terrorised the streets of South East London. He'd got away with it for years, and at twenty-three, he was a first-class bully who took what he wanted and from those he wanted too. He wore a smart suit, but no amount of smartness would change the fact that he had a face that only his mother could love and teeth that would give a great white shark a run for its money.

'So, you must be Cyril Reardon, then, who fucking hurt me cousin. You shouldn't have done that!'

There was no time for talk. Cyril felt the anger surge through him like the red-hot lava from an erupting volcano. In one fluid movement, he launched himself at the ginger-haired man; he guessed he was Red Deacon. He lowered his head like a bull and rammed him in the chest. Then, as the man staggered back, trying not to lose his balance, Cyril pulled his arm back, and with all his strength, he hit the guy around the head with his unopened bottle. Even though the thump was loud, Cyril didn't notice Deacon's eyes roll back. All Cyril could do was lash out. Again and again, he smashed the bottle around the man's head as though he was tenderising a cheap piece of meat.

'I'll fucking kill ya,' he yelled.

He couldn't hear the commotion behind him. All he wanted to do was to kill the ginger-haired bastard, and he wouldn't stop until he had. On the point of hitting Deacon again, he missed because the bloke had sunk to his knees just after the bottle had finally smashed into millions of pieces. It was time to take stock of what had happened. Reality had at last smacked him in the face. When his eyes began to focus, he saw the blood dripping from his hands and the broken bottle. But something warm and sticky trickled down his face.

He heard his mother yell. As he turned around, he gasped when he witnessed his sweet, inoffensive mum pounding another man in the head with the heel of her shoe. It was like hammering a nail into a piece of wood.

'Take that, you fucking scumbag, and that!' she yelled, as she smashed him again.

Then he saw Frank fighting two men. He was more controlled, with his arms in a real boxer's stance, and each jab or right hook was precise. The two men were being punched left, right, and centre. They didn't stand a chance. One copped a nasty blow and toppled over. The second man ran like a chicken. Then Cyril saw the knife in Frank's hand and watched the remaining lad finally leg it away.

In all the fracas, it was Mr Bates who shocked him the most. He was wielding a bat and using it to beat the other men about the head as if he was whacking a rounders ball. He seemed to fight with little effort as if it was child's play.

All around him was carnage. He had to grab his mother before she got hurt, and as he tried to pull her away, he saw something in her eyes he'd never seen before; it was a rage that would terrify anyone who crossed her. The guy was trying to get away from her. Blood poured from his head, his nose, and his ear. She had well and truly battered him, but she was still gripping him with one hand while trying to smash him with her shoe to injure him some more. 'No one hurts my boys! No one!' she screamed.

Out of the six members of Deacon's gang who had started the fight, only Red was left on the tarmac, now groaning but trying to get to his feet.

Mr Bates grabbed Cyril and Peggy. 'Get Howie upstairs quickly and wash the blood off that shoe, and you, Cyril, get cleaned up.'

Frank was out of breath, but he managed to scoop Howie up like a forklift truck and take him in the lift to their third floor.

Peggy was running alongside him looking at Howie's beaten face. 'It's gonna be all right, Son, I promise.'

Cyril stared at the state of Deacon. 'Fuck.'

About to head back to his flat, now things were under control, Mr Bates pulled Cyril aside. 'I said a while ago that Deacon's cousin will wanna throw his weight around. Well, let's hope that's the end of it. Now, go and get cleaned up before the police show themselves.'

Cyril took one last look at Deacon's bloody head. Then he ran up the stairs and hurried along the walkway and into the flat, slamming the front door behind him.

Peggy and Frank laid Howie on his bed. 'Cyril, get a bowl of water, will you, love? I wanna see what those bastards did to him. Christ, if he's badly hurt, I will swing that fucking fishwife, Sheila Deacon, off her tower block. Fancy raising bloody evil bullies like that. I swear, she will come a cropper.

I've never liked her, anyway.'

Frank helped undress Howie; he looked so frightened. His eyes were wide and his permanent grin was gone. As Frank tried to pull the shirt over Howie's head, the younger lad winced. It was too painful for him to straighten up.

But Peggy helped, and between them, they had Howie's top off. Peggy stepped back with her hands to her mouth. Howie's chest was purple, and there was even a bootprint on his ribs.

Tears tumbled down her face. 'Oh, my little lad. It's gonna be all right. You're safe now, and I promise you, no one will hurt you ever again.'

Cyril returned with a bowl of warm water and a flannel. He swallowed hard as he wiped his brother's swollen face; his left eye was completely closed. 'I'm sorry, Howie. I never knew those men would come looking for me. You didn't deserve this.'

Peggy pulled him away. 'Get up to Mr Bates, and see if he's got any painkillers, strong ones.'

Cyril nodded and did as he was told, while Frank stayed and helped Peggy get Howie into his pyjamas. She knew how to check for internal injuries, but, even so, the bruises were horrific, and she wished she'd seen them before she'd beaten one of the men with her shoe. She would have made sure she killed him.

Looking at Frank's hands and then his shirt and trousers, she said, 'You get in the bathroom and wash your hands. Check there's no blood on your shirt, or I'll have to shred it and flush it down the loo.'

'We didn't murder anyone, Mrs Reardon.'

'Listen, son, do you know the definition of murder?'

Frank shrugged his shoulders. 'You are responsible for someone's death.'

Peggy shook her head. 'Well, that's partly correct, but if you hurt someone badly enough, and they die from the injuries within a year and a day, it's still classed as murder. And the way Cyril has bashed that Deacon bastard, he could die next week from internal head injuries. Just 'cos he was alive when we left him don't mean he won't die, and the filth will have us up as accomplices.'

Frank said no more and hurried to the bathroom and scrubbed his hands. On the wall opposite the toilet next to the bath was a long mirror. He carefully studied every inch of his clothes, and, lucky for him, there was no blood.

He returned to the bedroom to find Peggy kneeling beside Howie's bed and stroking his head. Frank felt sick. Poor Howie's face was a mess. It was so swollen, he looked like a purple pumpkin. And if he hadn't cut Nut Nut's ear off, then those men wouldn't have sought revenge and poor Howie wouldn't have been caught in the middle. Guilt was a horrible feeling; it was one that he had never felt before and never wanted to again.

Frank could hear Cyril running back along the walkway and then the sound of the front door being slammed shut.

Holding a bottle of liquid, Cyril said, 'Mr Bates gave me

this. He said only to give Howie a teaspoonful or he'll be asleep for a whole week.'

Peggy took the bottle and removed the lid. Carefully, she placed it to Howie's lips. 'Try to sip a little. You will feel so much better, my angel.'

Howie sipped the liquid before he curled into a tighter ball.

Peggy placed the blue candlewick bedspread over him and gently kissed his forehead before ushering Frank and Cyril into the living room.

'Cyril, get those clothes off, and, Frank, fetch me the scissors. They're in the drawer by me bed. Cyril get cleaned up and put a clean shirt and a fresh pair of trousers on. If the police come calling, you have been in here all night. Where is your pack of cards? Get them on the table. We'll say we've been playing cards.'

Cyril and Frank didn't argue. Cyril went to his bedroom, quickly got changed, and returned to the living room, while Frank fetched the scissors from Peggy's bedroom.

'Good. Cut up Cyril's clothes as small as you can. I don't wanna clog up the lav. But we need to get rid of that shirt, and . . . for Christ's sake, Cyril, wash your hair, will ya? There's blood all over you.'

Cyril ran his hands through his hair and felt the sickly liquid. 'Well, it ain't mine.'

'No, it's probably full of that ginger-haired bastard's blood and brains. Now, get a move on. And while you're at it, wash me shoes. I can't flush them away.'

‘If the police call, what do we do about Howie?’

‘You leave all the talking to me, d’ya hear? This is just a precaution because, hopefully, that nightmare of a family will keep their mouths shut. Nothing worse than getting a name as a grass, is there? And I will pay their mother a visit soon, to remind her of the fact, and also to give her a bloody piece of my mind. Who the hell do they think they are, bashing a kid? And a defenceless kid when all’s said and done.’

Cyril could hear the anger in her voice as her pitch got higher.

‘I have a good mind to go there right now and punch the life out of her. See how she likes it. Gawd help me, I should have caved her spiteful face in years ago.’

Cyril looked at Frank, who, in turn, shrugged his shoulders.

After flushing the strips of his shirt down the toilet, Cyril scrubbed his mother’s shoes and headed for the kitchen to find her wearing her nightdress and a bright-pink quilted dressing gown.

‘How do you know that family anyway, Mum?’

Peggy’s face was tight, and her movements were quick with temper. She put the kettle on and lit up a cigarette, taking a deep drag. ‘The ol’ tart went after your farver when I was expecting you. I warned her to stay away, but she laughed in me face and said, “I can give your ol’ man what you can’t.”’ She took another deep drag. ‘If I hadn’t been heavily pregnant with you, I would have swung for her and your farver, the bleedin’ good-for-nuffin sod.’

'How did you know I'd had a run-in with this Deacon family?'

Peggy sighed. 'I ain't blind nor deaf. Besides, Mr Bates told me.' She held up her hands. 'Not that he was grassing on you two. No. He warned me in case there were any repercussions. Well, it looks like there bleedin' were.' She shook her head, exhausted. 'He's only fourteen. How dare they!'

'I don't think they'll ever touch Howie again, not after the fight they've just had. And I bet they didn't expect you to join in, Mrs Reardon,' said Frank, through a held-in snigger.

Cyril sensed the tension leaving and laughed out loud. 'Cor, yeah, you don't need a hammer, do ya, Mum?'

Peggy blushed and then laughed herself. 'And what about you, Cyril? You were Taurus, the Bull, out there. I didn't even see your arms move as you smashed the great oaf with the bottle.'

'Er . . . Mrs Reardon, you won't say nuffin to me dad, will ya?'

Peggy stubbed her cigarette out and gave Frank a look of confusion. 'What d'ya mean? That you helped defend Cyril, my Howie, and yourself against six *grown* men. I'd like to think he'd be proud. A chip off the old block, wouldn't ya say?'

Frank sighed. 'I dunno about that. He don't like me getting into bother.'

'Well your farver could fight when he was younger, and he

often did. By all accounts, he was a proper good bare-knuckle fighter as well. You must take after him. Anyway, I won't mention any of this, babe. Let's just pray the police won't call.'

* * *

Cyril lay in bed in deep thought. The evening had opened his eyes. He had seen his mother in a new light. Maybe she had been like it all along, but he had only ever seen her as his sweet, kind-hearted mum. That expression in her eyes when he tried to pull her off the guy she was beating with her shoe would stay with him. He saw it when he closed his eyes. How quick she was to ensure that any evidence was stripped and flushed, as if this wasn't new to her at all. He cast his mind back to when the landlord was murdered and she had the three pounds on her person, but he'd heard her tell Mr Bates that her attacker had stolen it, and she'd been so controlled when the police had called that day. Maybe Mr Bates had given her three pounds or maybe he hadn't. Either way, it was possible that perhaps his mother had a side to her that she had never wanted him to see. A smile slid across his face, when, as clear as day, all the little snippets of the past suddenly made sense. His mother could play the innocent housewife, the single mother of two, who was always trying her best to bring up her two lads on the pennies she had. Yet, behind that inoffensive bright smile, there was a woman who had seen more than most. Perhaps she had witnessed far more of her father's villainy than she had ever let on. Cyril could only assume that his mother was clever to his own naughty little ways, but instead of coming down hard on him, she either turned a blind eye or just watched from afar.

CHAPTER ELEVEN

It was a month after the fight, and no one had come near or by. Word had spread since everyone on the estate loved to gossip, and it also changed the way they treated Cyril and Frank. The teenagers and even the young men in their early twenties went out of their way to say 'Hello' or 'How's it going?' It was as if, for the first time, they had suddenly become visible.

Eager to get the cocaine sold and have that money in his back pocket, Cyril was up with the lark, dressed and ready to pay Mr Bates a visit. As he walked along the walkway, he could hear a car revving up and then stalling. He looked across to see Mr Marsden's car parked awkwardly, and then, as he looked more closely, he saw Frank in the driver's seat. He smiled to himself. Frank was having a driving lesson, if he ever managed to get the old banger into first gear. He thought about the money he could earn from the powder. Frank wouldn't have to drive his dad's old car; he could have a new one.

As Cyril sauntered up the steps, he stopped dead. Flossie appeared. Cyril immediately beamed. 'Hello, you look pretty, Flossie. Off anywhere nice?'

Flossie's face looked glum. 'Not really. Just to Martin Fords to buy a new dress. My dad sent me a postal order for two pounds. It's my birthday tomorrow. It'll be my sixteenth.'

‘Oh, I didn’t know . . . Er, are you doing anything nice?’

Flossie looked behind her. ‘No, my mum’s having my aunts around to a tea party. She’s baking the cake now. But I don’t even like cake.’

‘Do you fancy coming out with me?’ He gulped once he realised that he had actually asked her out. He felt his cheeks go hot and his mouth felt as dry as a bone.

‘Yeah, why not,’ she replied, her face now instantly lighting up with interest. ‘It’s got to be better than staying around here. Where do you want to take me?’

Cyril hadn’t thought that far. ‘How about I keep it a surprise, and I’ll call for you at seven o’clock?’

Flossie was now really excited; she loved surprises, as long as it didn’t involve sitting around drinking tea and eating cake with gossipy old women putting the world to rights and giving her a lecture on men. ‘Oh, can you make it eight o’clock? You see, my aunts and my mum’s mates will all turn up at three, and by six, they’ll be on the gin, and by eight, they won’t even notice me gone.’

‘Eight it is, then. Er, Flossie, have you got any mates?’

She tilted her head to the side. ‘Yes, I’ve got a best friend, Trudy. Why?’

‘Well, what about bringing her along? I could bring my mate Frank, and you might feel less kinda awkward, if you know what I mean?’

‘Yes, I’ve seen Frank. He’s the big fella that lives along

the way from you.'

Cyril nodded. 'Yeah, him.'

'My mate Trudy likes the look of him, you know.'

'Even better, then. Right, eight o'clock, by the bins would be best, tomorrow night. It's a date.'

'See you then.' She winked as she skipped down the stairs past him.

Normally, nothing ever fazed Cyril. He never felt nervous or uneasy, except when it came to women, and Flossie in particular. He now had even more reason to get that cocaine sold. He had a girl to wine and dine.

* * *

Mr Bates opened the door and flicked his head for Cyril to come inside.

'All right, Mr Bates?'

'Yeah, son, and how's your brother? I haven't seen him out and about.'

Cyril's upbeat mood plummeted. 'No, that kicking he got has knocked him for six. He's a nervous wreck. He won't even go to school. Me mum says he doesn't have to go, and she even gave the bloke from the school board an earbashing.'

Taking a seat opposite Mr Bates, Cyril leaned back and crossed his legs. His confident posture didn't go unnoticed.

'You need to be careful, Cyril. That fight you had seems to

have given you a name. The cocky little walk and the flash hairdo, they only draw attention.'

Cyril sat up straight. 'I dunno what you mean.'

Mr Bates lit up a cigarette and blew the smoke up in the air as he stared at Cyril. 'Yeah, you do, Cyril. A pat on the back and all those compliments. Men telling you they respect you for seeing off the Deacon mob. It can go to your head. I know, mate, because it's human nature. If you get treated like a top dog, you act like one. But there's a difference. Act like you can take on anyone, and that's what will happen. The wannabes will always crawl out of the woodwork and want to fight you. But you need to keep your nose clean, lad. Don't draw attention to yourself, right?'

Every word that Mr Bates said made sense. He nodded. 'Yeah, all right. I'll keep low for a bit. Oh, I've got a date, though, with Flossie Hever upstairs.'

Mr Bates smiled. 'As long as she ain't like her muvver. Now, that one's a real piece of work. She's had more men than I've had Capstans.'

Cyril laughed, but, really, he wasn't one for disrespecting a woman.

'So what brings you here, Cyril?'

Leaning forward, Cyril kept his voice low. 'It's been a few weeks now, and I was hoping I could start selling that cocaine.'

'Hmm, so I take it you've decided on the path you want to take, then?'

Cyril nodded slowly. 'I can't work in one of the factories, it's just not me. I saw the toffs in the hotel and the lord that owned the mansion, and I want to live like that. I want money, I want to buy me muvver nice clothes, not nick them from a rich woman at the Dorchester or the Ritz. I want a lovely motor. If it means I risk going to prison, then so be it, but I ain't living a boring life stuck on this estate with bugger all to live for.'

Mr Bates laughed. 'Well, it doesn't surprise me. Really, it's in your blood after all. Right then, this cocaine. Like I told you a long time ago, it's all about supply and demand.'

Cyril was now comfortably seated to listen to the facts and absorb the information like a sponge.

'To flog drugs, you need buyers. The rich and stupid are your customers for cocaine, but you don't want to be running around with packets selling bits here and there. You need a buyer who will buy a big amount. There's less risk of getting caught that way. Now, the one issue you will have is if the sale of your cocaine ever gets back to the person you stole it from. Then, Cyril, you will have a bigger threat than the Ol' Bill knocking at your door.'

'So where do I start? I mean, I know I've got the drugs, but I don't have the contacts. I was hoping that we could go fifty-fifty, if you put me in touch with a buyer.'

Mr Bates sucked in his bottom lip. 'There's your first mistake.'

Cyril frowned.

'Fifty-fifty, for just a name? That's well over the odds, lad.

You're too quick to give your money away. Now, I do have contacts, and I'll get rid of the cocaine for you, but fifty-fifty? No, lad. Let's just say you will owe me a favour.'

Cyril rubbed his hands together. 'Fine by me. Do you want to see the goods?'

'*Me*?' Mr Bates almost gasped. 'No! Don't bring it all here, for Christ's sake. Just show me a small sample. Leave it with me and give me a week. Oh, and weigh it, will you? So we know how much you've got there.'

Cyril didn't hang about. He pushed himself out of the chair and headed off. 'See you in five, Mr Bates.'

By the time he was back home, his mother had left for work and Howie was sitting in front of the TV set watching cartoons. He would have tried to coax his brother out for the day, but he needed to get the ball rolling to sell his powder. Once he had the money, he would treat Howie to something special, although he didn't know quite what just yet.

Using a kitchen knife once more, he removed the panel of the wardrobe to reveal the suitcase. After opening the side zipper, he stared at the clear bag. Perhaps it weighed more than a bag of sugar. He hurried back to the kitchen and grabbed the scales and weights to weigh the cocaine. Sure enough, it was well over the weight of a bag of sugar. In fact, there were two and a half pounds of gold dust. Using an old envelope, he poured a small helping inside, folded it up, and placed it into his top pocket. Once he'd put everything back inside the wardrobe and replaced the panel, he hurried up to Mr Bates' flat.

Three long taps followed by two slow taps and Mr Bates opened the door. He looked up and down the walkway and stepped aside for Cyril to come in.

'There you go,' said Cyril, handing Mr Bates the folded envelope. 'Oh, and there's two and a half pounds of the stuff at my place.'

The open-mouthed expression on Mr Bates' face told Cyril that he was in possession of a lot of drugs.

'Leave it with me.'

'Thanks, Mr Bates. I know it probably don't sit well with you, but it's what I want to do. You do understand, don't ya?'

With a nod and a chuckle, Mr Bates shut the door.

* * *

Cyril was mentally counting the money in his head when he literally bumped into Shirley, who had her head down, not looking where she was going.

'Sorry, Shirley . . . What's up, love? Why are ya crying?' asked Cyril, as he grabbed her arms.

'Oh, it's nuffin, Cyril. It's only that flaming perv at the jam factory.'

Cyril felt the hairs on the back of his neck stand up. He remembered. So the manager at the factory was at it again, just like he had when he'd tried it on with his mother. Years ago, he had overheard her telling a neighbour that the manager had tried to touch her up, but when she'd told him where to get off, he'd fired her on the spot.

'What's he done this time?'

Shirley looked up and sniffed back the tears. Until that point, she hadn't realised that Cyril had grown up. His serious expression and the concern in his eyes made her feel like a child.

'He said I would get promoted to shop-floor manager if I went on a date with him. I told him I was not that kind of girl, and so he fired me. He really thinks he's something special all because he's in charge of the wages an' all. And I needed that money for me holidays. I wanted to take my Terry hopping again. Everyone's going, and it looks like I won't be.'

Cyril sighed. 'Mr Marsden wouldn't leave you behind, Shirley.'

'The truth is, Cyril, Henry is good to me. He always has been, since, well, since I was left with little Terry and on the bones of me arse. Well, we have an understanding, if you know what I mean. And he's a diamond. But I don't like to take advantage of his good nature.'

'I think his good nature will fly out of the bleedin' window when he hears about that perv down the factory.'

'Oh, no. No, I can't tell him. Henry would end up back inside, and I can't have that.'

Cyril suddenly thought about the days they had spent hopping and how much he and Howie had enjoyed it. 'Shirley, if I get the money together for you, Terry, and me brother, would you take him? The poor little sod hasn't left the house since the fight, and I know he was like a pig in shit on that farm.'

Shirley pulled a handkerchief from the pocket of her full flared skirt and blew her nose. 'Oh, I dunno, Cyril. It ain't cheap, love, and I can't ask you to pay. You ain't even got a job.'

'But if I could pay, would you take me brother?'

She nodded but gave him that look, as if to say 'What are you up to?'

Cyril winked. 'Leave it to me, and I'll let you know if I can come up with the money by next week. And why don't you talk to me mum? She's down at the chocolate factory. I bet she'll get you in there. And me mum likes it there an' all.'

'All right, I'll come calling tonight. Let her know, will ya?'

Cyril nodded and was about to walk on when he had a sudden thought about something Shirley had just said. 'Oh, what do you mean by "He's in charge of the wages"?'

'You know. He's the one who goes to the bank on a Friday afternoon carrying his flash briefcase and collecting the wages to hand out as if it's his own bloody money. I bet Mr Hartley would hate him an' all if he ever met him.'

Cyril listened intently. 'So he goes to the bank, collects all the wages, and walks back to the factory, does he? What, *alone*?'

'Yeah, the cocky little shit thinks he's so high and mighty

now. Well, I hope someone runs him over one day. Playing with people's lives like that.'

'Is Frank in?'

Shirley nodded. 'Yeah. I don't think Henry has the patience to teach him to drive anymore. Frank was moping over his corned beef sandwich, the last I saw of him. Anyway, I've got to dash. Terry's got football practice. He's with Henry's sister. She's a moody bitch, she is.'

Cyril laughed at the way Shirley spoke. She always amused him.

Frank took his time answering the door, and when he did, he had a face like a deflated balloon.

'What's up with you?'

'The car's engine's flooded, me dad can't get it started, and he blames me.'

Cyril barged past and quickly sat himself at the kitchen table. 'Listen, Frank, you and me are gonna be rich, mate. You won't need to drive your dad's old banger 'cos you'll soon have a new car of your own.'

Frank clutched his hands together and leaned forward. 'So what's the plan, Cyril? 'Cos I'm guessing, mate, you have one.'

Cyril chuckled. 'Well not quite yet, but I will have, come next week. First, me and you need to get up to the jam factory and follow that ol' pervy bastard Millard, the manager, to the bank and back. I wanna see his exact route 'cos, next Friday,

I'm gonna rob the nonce.'

Frank laughed and shook his head. 'Are you serious?'

Cyril nodded, with a huge grin plastered across his fresh face.

'That's robbery and carries a long stretch.'

Cyril nodded again. 'But only if we get caught, which, Frank, we won't. Trust me, I'll have a watertight plan.'

'I dunno.'

'You what? How can you not know, Frank? Look around. Do you wanna be living in a flat like this all ya life?'

Frank looked at the small kitchen. It was new and clean, but it was small, and the replica of every flat in the block, including Cyril's. They all had the same wallpaper, the same cabinets, and even the same lino. 'No, but I don't wanna go to prison either.'

Cyril stood up. 'All right, Frank, never mind. I'll go it alone, but although we share everything fifty-fifty, I won't this time. Not if I'm on me own.'

Frank jumped up. 'Wait . . .' He sighed. 'All right, I'm in. So what's the plan?'

Cyril spun around with his famous half-smile that merged into a smirk. 'Right, so we follow him today to the bank and back again. We clock the route he takes and the times. He may decide to go a different way next week, but all we need to do is to follow him and see what or who else is about. We'll check the ideal spot to relieve him of his briefcase and then get away.'

'In case, Cyril, you've forgotten, we don't have a getaway car, and besides all that, he'll see our boat races, and that will be us in Wormwood Scrubs.'

'I've got a week to sort out the finer details, but for now, Frank, we need to check the route out, so stop moaning like an old woman, and let's get going. Oh, and by the way, tomorrow night, me and you have a date.'

'You *what*?'

Cyril laughed. 'Not with me. With Flossie and her mate, Trudy, I think.'

Frank raised his eyebrow. 'Trudy sounds like a doll.'

'Yep, and if she's anything like Flossie, she'll look like a doll, an' all, so get yourself cleaned up and be ready by eight o'clock tomorrow. We're off up town.'

Frank rolled his eyes, but, secretly, he was excited. Being mates with Cyril was always exciting, if not somewhat risky.

* * *

Standing with their backs to the factory, Cyril and Frank waited for Mr Millard to leave the premises and head for the bank to collect the money for the wages. Frank was as nervous as if he was robbing the man today.

Millard didn't even look around. He walked so confidently, marching along the road in his lightweight suit and his trilby and allowing the large shiny leather briefcase to swing by his side.

Cyril walked behind him, itching to get a closer look at the case. He had to know if it was possibly secured to his wrist. But there was no chain visible. He backed away before Millard clocked him, and as the manager turned the corner, the boys waited. As soon as they were in sight of the bank, they stood together and watched. Within five minutes, Millard was out of the building, and this time, he appeared more vigilant for his own safety before he set off on his way back to the factory. Cyril and Frank held off until he was out of sight, and then they followed. Cyril had to be sure of the return route.

‘’Ere, the daft git is going back the same way he came. I reckon he does that every Friday,’ whispered Cyril.

‘So what will we do then, Cyril?’

Cyril pointed down the street. ‘Look, Frank. Those houses are ready for demolition. No one walks down there, ’cos no one lives there. If we nab his briefcase in this road, no one will see us.’

‘He will, though, Cyril.’

‘No shit, Sherlock. Just leave that little problem to me.’

Frank was relieved that Millard was out of sight, and he hadn’t spotted them loitering. ‘And you’re sure about this, Cyril?’

‘Yes, I hate the bastard. He sacked me mum years ago, which left us skint. So I don’t care that I’m gonna rob him. The factory will pay out the wages, anyway. But I bet that ol’ codger gets fired for the cock-up.'

Cyril stopped in front of the flats. 'Frank, we've only got until tomorrow to get ourselves spruced up for our date. I was thinking of getting one of those collarless suits.'

Frank frowned. 'A bit girly, don't you think? Next, you'll wanna wear one of those frilly paisley shirts or a striped suit like Andy bloody Pandy.'

Cyril grinned. 'Mick Jagger and the Beatles are wearing them. Soon, everyone will be.'

'Not me, mate,' growled Frank.

* * *

Saturday morning arrived, and Cyril checked all of his pockets for some money. All he could find were a few shillings. He sat down on his bed and sighed. He only had a few hours to get his hands on enough cash to take Flossie out for a slap-up meal and a dance. He had to make a good impression because he knew that, secretly, he had really fallen for her.

Laden with clean bed sheets, Peggy swanned into his room, and, right away, she noticed the sad yet thoughtful look on Cyril's face. She recognised that expression. 'So what are you up to, Cyril Reardon?'

He looked up and sighed. 'Nuffin.'

'Don't give me *nuffin*. You're up to something.'

Placing the sheets on the bed, she sat beside him. 'Come on, Son. Tell me, what's going on?'

'I've offered to take Flossie Hever out on a date, a foursome with Frank and Flossie's mate Trudy, but . . .'

Peggy sighed with relief. 'Oh, is that all? And you haven't got the money, is that it?'

Cyril nodded. 'I suppose I could take her on a picnic.'

Peggy jumped up. 'You will do no such thing. You, my lad, will take her out somewhere special. Wait there.' She hurried to her bedroom and fished around at the back of the wardrobe until she felt the silk dress. She unhooked it from the hanger and returned to Cyril, who was looking pleasantly puzzled.

'See this dress?' She grinned. 'The one you said the woman threw at you? Well, I hardly think she would have. This dress is probably worth more than the whole of the inside of this flat.'

Cyril frowned. 'No way. It's just a dress, Mum.'

'No, it ain't, babe. This is a *Chanel* dress. Only the very rich wear stuff like this, and it's worth a fortune.'

Cyril stared at the very plain black garment. 'It don't look much, though, does it?'

She shook her head. 'It looked a million pounds on Audrey Hepburn, and it's all the rage, if you mix in those posh circles. I know you got it for me, but those other dresses are beautiful, and it means I'll never be stuck for an outfit for a posh do ever again. But you see this one? It really needs to be dressed up with real pearls, the long gloves, and the Chanel handbag. I'm not that type of woman, Cyril. That dress says a lot about who you are. One day, you'll understand. So take it and sell it. It's worth about twenty pounds, if not more. And it's immaculate.'

Cyril's eyes were wide with excitement. 'Blimey, Mum, twenty quid? That will buy us a moped an' all.'

She smiled and nodded. 'Go on, lad. Get up town and flog it.'

'Mum, would you mind if I gave some of the money to Shirley to go hop picking?'

Peggy knew her son would have a good reason to hand over money to Frank's aunt. 'No, babe, I don't mind at all, but can I ask why?'

'That Millard bastard fired her for the same reason he fired you all those years ago, and she was so upset that she couldn't afford to go and . . . ' He got up and closed the bedroom door. 'Our Howie needs a holiday, Mum. He won't leave the house, and I remember how he was when we went hopping. He loved it. He might feel safe there, and so if Shirley took him, well, I just thought . . .'

Peggy's eyes welled up with tears, ready to tumble. 'Aw, Cyril, you are such a good boy.' She threw her arms around him and hugged him tightly. 'I love you, my little lad.' She finally let him go and sniffed back her tears. 'Go on with ya. Get the best price you can, and remember, it's real Chanel, so take no less than twenty pounds.'

After carefully wrapping the dress in paper, as if it were a baby, and then sliding it into a bag, he was on the point of leaving when he heard his mum call out.

'Cyril! If anyone who wants to buy it starts to ask questions, then walk away. Don't draw attention to yourself, and don't let anyone take it around the back of the shop. You keep it in your sight until the money is in your hand.'

'Got it, Mum,' replied Cyril. He knew how to work a sale, but he always heeded any advice his mother offered. If anything, it would put her mind at rest.

'You ought to try Mr Izzy Ezra, the jeweller, down the Old Kent Road. He buys all sorts and will give you a fair price, but only if he really wants the dress. But don't bother with the markets, if not. Oh, and there's another little shop off Carnaby Street, Mrs Mockford's. Now, she might be interested. I know she buys expensive bags.'

Cyril had got as far as the front door when he stopped. He wanted to ask his mother how she knew these people, but then, when he glanced up at the clock in the hallway, he realised he didn't have time. If he was going to flog the dress, and get his hair cut, and buy a new suit, and . . . the list was endless.

'Cheers, Mum. See you soon. Oh, I nearly forgot. Shirley's coming around tonight, to ask ya about a job at the chocolate factory,' he called back.

* * *

Cyril knew where the jeweller's was down the Old Kent Road. He decided to go there first since it was the nearest of the places on his list; it was only a short bus ride away. But as soon as he had the road in his sights, a beaten-up old Humber Sceptre stopped in front of him and a head with a mop of dark waves popped out of the passenger window. 'Cyril!' came the upbeat voice.

Cyril knew that voice. It belonged to Ronnie Blake, Freddy's elder brother.

'All right, Ronnie?'

'Yeah, Cyril. Where you off to?'

'The Old Kent Road.'

'Jump in, mate. Marcus, me pal, 'ere, will give you a lift, won't ya?'

Cyril peered in to find a tall and well-built lad, almost the same size as Frank. 'If you're sure?'

Marcus River smiled. 'Yeah, of course, Cyril. Ronnie tells me you had a run-in with the Deacon family. He said you bashed up Red.' He laughed and looked Cyril up and down. 'You must have some fist on you then.'

Cyril remembered Mr Bates telling him not to go larging it up and acting all cocky, so he lowered his face. 'Just got a few lucky ones in, that's all.'

'Hop in, Cyril. I'm going that way.'

'Cheers,' said Cyril, as he climbed into the back of the car. 'Nice motor.'

Marcus laughed again. 'Polite an' all, eh? This is a right ol' rust bucket, but it still goes, so it will do until I win me next fight.'

Cyril's ears pricked up. 'Are you a boxer, then?'

Marcus focused on the road ahead as he pulled away. 'Yeah. You should come down the club, because it sounds like you could win a few fights in the ring.'

Cyril shook his head. 'Not me, Marcus. I wanna keep me charming good looks for the birds.'

Ronnie chuckled. 'You're a flash fucker, Cyril, and no mistake. Anyway, me and the lads are going down the Pagoda tonight. They've got a band on. Do you and Frank wanna come? Freddy's coming.'

Cyril felt grateful that he was invited. And since the fights with the Deacon lads, he seemed to have grown immensely in popularity, but he had his heart set on taking Flossie out. 'Next time, Ronnie, only tonight, me and Frank are on a date.'

'I never took you for a queer boy, Cyril.'

'And so you shouldn't, Ronnie. Me and Frank are meeting two little gems. We're going out for a meal and a few drinks.'

'Next, you'll be up the aisle with a bun in the oven.'

Cyril laughed. 'Not me. Babies can wait. I'm gonna make a fistful of money first, just you see. Any babies I have will be eating their dinner off a solid silver spoon. Talking of which, can you drop me just there, by the jeweller's?'

Marcus slowed the car down and stopped outside the shop. He turned to face Cyril. 'Nice to meet you.'

Cyril grinned. 'And you, Marcus. Good luck with the next fight.'

Ronnie ruffled Cyril's hair. 'Give us a shout about next weekend, you and Frank, because we may be going up west. The more the merrier.'

Cyril smiled. 'Yeah, I'll be up for that.'

* * *

As soon as he was out of the car, he waved them off and straightened his shirt before entering the jeweller's. A bell rang as he walked in, and the smell of the wood polish hit him. The parquet floor and the rows of cabinets gleamed. Behind the counter stood a very tall and slim lady with auburn hair and a sweet face. She gave him a friendly smile. 'Hello.'

Cyril checked the woman over. She was roughly the same size as his own mum and that of the posh lady from the Dorchester. 'Good morning. I have come to see Mr Ezra, but, looking at you, I really think it's you who would be more interested in what I have.'

The lady's cheeks lifted and blushed slightly. 'And what would that be?' She tried not to chuckle at the young man's confidence.

He removed the dress from the bag and laid it across the counter carefully, appreciating its value.

'Beautiful,' said the lady, as she softly touched the material. 'Chanel?'

'Yes, from Coco herself.'

The lady couldn't help but chuckle. 'Coco no less, right? Hmm, it's certainly very exquisite.'

'Yep, and brand new.'

The lady checked inside the collar and then held the dress up.

'Go on, put it up against you. I bet it will fit like a glove. Audrey Hepburn wore the same one, and . . . well, let's just say, you would knock spots off her.'

Caught up with the idea of owning a Chanel dress, the lady did just that, turning to face a glass cabinet and hoping to see a reflection of herself. No sooner had she spun around than a smart man appeared, dressed in a suit with a gold watch dangling from his watch pocket.

Cyril smiled. 'I was just saying, this lady would give Audrey Hepburn a run for her money in that dress. Wouldn't you agree, Mr . . . ? Is it Mr Ezra?'

The man nodded and peered at Cyril with a suspicious frown.

The lady quickly folded the dress and laid it back down on the counter, but not before Mr Ezra noticed how much she had already fallen in love with it.

'Go on, *Mrs Ezra.* You take your break. I'll see to this young man.'

The woman nodded, kissed her husband on the cheek, and disappeared through the back door.

'Clever move, young man. So it's a Chanel dress known as the "little black dress". How much?'

‘Thirty pounds. It’s brand new, and now Mrs Ezra’s got her heart set on one, it’ll save you a few quid come Christmas, or . . .’ He paused, realising that he didn’t know if the Jewish community celebrated Christmas. ‘Or perhaps your wedding anniversary, or whatever.’

Mr Ezra nodded. ‘You have a good point, but I may not want my wife to wear a dress like that.’

Cyril guessed right away that Mr Ezra wouldn’t be buying his flannel, and he knew he didn’t have time to mess about. ‘Mr Ezra, I will sell this dress today, either to you or to someone else, but I don’t have time to play games. Either you’re interested or you’re not.’

The self-assured manner in which the young man spoke had Izzy Ezra pricking up his ears. ‘Okay, I know how much these dresses cost. I have an eye for good quality clothes, so—’

Before he could finish, Cyril jumped in. ‘So what’s your best price? No messing about.’

‘Fifteen pounds.’

‘My mum said you would drive a hard bargain. So, I will take me business elsewhere.’

‘Oh, yeah? And who’s your mother?’

‘Peggy Reardon.’

Izzy Ezra beamed. ‘Dillon Docherty’s daughter? Well, in that case, twenty pounds, for you.’

'Twenty-two, Mr Ezra, and we have a deal.'

For the first time in history, Ezra nodded without bartering down the price to squeeze that last pound. He was taken with the young lad's attitude. He reminded him of Dillon and Arthur Bates. He had been very young himself when he'd done business with them. Peggy's son was so much like them in the way he spoke, walked, and even winked. He wondered if the young lad would end up being a two-bit scallywag, or, like himself, run a lucrative, if not illegal, racket.

As soon as the money exchanged hands, Cyril winked and left, thanking the man, as he closed the door behind him.

It was Cyril's lucky day; a bus pulled up, and now he was on his way home to share his earnings with Frank. And he also had enough cash to put a little aside for Shirley to take his brother hopping and some for a set of wheels for him and Frank.

* * *

At 8.00 p.m. on the dot, with Frank dressed in his new suit and with his hair cut neatly behind his ears and Cyril dressed in his new collarless shirt and with his hair trimmed at the back but with the front left long – the new fashion – the boys stood at the bottom of the steps, by the bins, waiting for the girls.

'So, Cyril, this whistle ain't too much, is it?' asked Frank, tugging at the sleeves to bring them down to cover his long arms.

Cyril laughed. 'It's light grey. Christ, I nearly bought a purple one. If the Beatles wear 'em, then so can we. You look fine, Frank. Stop getting nervous.'

'I ain't been on a proper date yet.'

'Me neither, so just act like this is old hat to us, yeah?'

Frank wiped the sweat from his brow. 'Yeah.'

They could hear the giggling before the girls appeared. Trudy was shorter than Flossie and had her dark hair cut into a short bob, with a poppy hair clip placed at the side. She was a bigger girl, with larger breasts and thicker thighs, but that didn't stop her from wearing a mini skirt like Flossie's.

Frank was taken with her right away; he wasn't one for fancying the 'Twiggy look'. He liked meat on the bone and Trudy's big round brown eyes and long black eyelashes attracted him instantly. Placing her bag over her right arm, she linked Frank's arm as if she'd been dating him for weeks. Frank raised his brow, followed by a satisfied smile.

Flossie appeared incredibly shy as she walked by Cyril's side, holding her bag in front of her with both hands.

'So, girls, we've booked a table at The Talk of the Town.'

Flossie stopped dead. '*What*? Seriously, Cyril? We're going to the Hippodrome?'

Cyril nodded. 'Yep, birthday girl. This is your treat.'

Trudy squealed. 'Well, I never. Blimey! The Talk of the Town, no less.' She clapped her hands together. 'I am so excited, us going there.'

Frank felt confident enough to put his arm around her shoulders and join in with the excitement.

With the girls giggling, both Frank and Cyril glanced at each other with a nod and a wink that said, 'We did it.'

* * *

The waiter showed them to their table and offered a wine menu. Cyril glanced at the other tables and noticed that the men were drinking either spirits or wine. He didn't like either much, so he settled for a Coke. Frank joined him, and the girls each had a Cherry Coke.

The three-course set menu was reasonable considering they were in a high-class establishment with stage shows for entertainment thrown in.

'I've never been wined and dined before,' said Trudy looking around, taking it all in.

'Well, we ain't ya type of fellas that go for a bag o' chips and the pictures on a shilling.'

Flossie was looking at the older women, dressed in their classy evening gowns and pearls. Some wore real gold necklaces with gems or even diamonds that shone from the dazzling lights. She wanted to be like them; she knew she had the figure – she just didn't have the clothes.

Cyril wasn't too bothered about the place; he was there to get to know Flossie.

'So, Cyril, you seem to know what a girl likes.'

'I try me best, Flossie.' He stared for a little longer than he should and watched her blush as she shied away from his penetrating gaze. 'So you like this place, then?'

She nodded. 'It's classy, Cyril. This is upmarket and Ritzy. I was born to live this life, and I would have if my mum hadn't left my dad to go screwing every fella this side of the river.'

Cyril chuckled. 'Rich was he, then, your ol' man?'

'I don't know, to be honest. My mum said he was, but, sometimes, I wonder if she even knows what the truth means.'

Cyril gently placed his hands on hers. 'Don't you worry, Flossie. I'm gonna be rich. I mean proper rich, like a lord.'

Flossie gazed into Cyril's grey eyes. There was so much life in them; it was as if his soul was having a party all of its own. 'Is that so, Mr Reardon?' She smiled back.

'Yeah, me and Frank have our own business.'

Flossie smiled, wondering if he was teasing her.

'Ain't we, Frank?'

Frank was so busy getting to know Trudy, he didn't even hear Cyril.

Cyril just shook his head and looked back at Flossie. 'Well, they've hit it off, eh?'

As if a light had come on, Flossie sat up straight. 'I think, Cyril, we may have, as well.'

Cyril squeezed her hand with excitement. This would be the best night of his life.

CHAPTER TWELVE

The following Tuesday afternoon, Frank and Cyril both stared at the yellow and black Lambretta Model D 125 and then at each other.

'So, take it or leave it, boys,' said Petrol Pete.

'Frank, you've got to take it for a spin,' said Cyril, looking at Pete for the nod.

'Sold as seen, lads.'

'No way, mate. If I'm parting with my well-earned dough, then I wanna ride that thing to make sure I ain't buying a pile of shit.'

Pete wiped his greasy hands down his boiler suit. 'Go on, then, but you smash it up, and you're paying, right?' He spat the cocktail stick out of his mouth and fumbled inside his overalls for the keys. 'There, and I *mean*, don't you crash that beast.'

Frank laughed. '*Beast*? You're joking, ain't ya? You mean bumble bee! The bloody colour of it!' He took the keys and started it up. With confidence, he revved the engine, dropped it into gear, and began to set off. He wobbled a little to start with, though, as he rode along the cobbled street under the arches.

As soon as he returned, he handed the keys to Cyril, who'd never ridden a bike let alone something with an engine, but Cyril, being Cyril, was pretty sure he could. He gunned the engine like Frank had, but as soon as he put it into gear, he shot forward and nearly fell off. Regaining his composure, he tore off, along the street, veering from left to right.

Petrol Pete had his hands on top of his head. All he could say was, 'Fuck me, he's gonna kill himself.'

Frank laughed as he watched his mate stutter and restart the bike, shaking his body back and forth, as if he was having a seizure. Then, as Cyril tried to make a U-turn at the end of the road, he didn't quite make it; instead, he ended up riding straight into a metal bin.

Petrol Pete threw his monkey wrench onto the pavement, in a temper. 'I fucking knew I shouldn't have trusted him. That's it! You two are paying for that bike. He's just rode into a sodding bin! A bloody *great* bin. How could he not see *that*?'

Frank was now doubled over, crying with laughter. In fact, even more so, now that Pete was livid. Try as he might, Frank just couldn't keep a straight face.

Finally, Cyril stopped the bike and looked behind him. 'Rides like a dream.'

Frank had tears streaming down his face. He just couldn't contain the laughter. Cyril's matter-of-fact face, as if riding a bike like a kangaroo was okay, had sent Frank into hysterics.

'You can bloody well hand over the money, now you've smashed it into the sodding dustbin,' hollered Pete.

Cyril rolled his eyes. 'Oh, leave off. I didn't do any damage.'

'Damage! *Damage*! The fucking headlight's hanging off.'

Cyril turned to find the headlight dangling by a single wire. 'It must have been loose. You wanna knock a few bob off for that. See, I knew we had to take it for a spin, or we would never have spotted that.'

Frank still couldn't stop laughing even when Cyril handed over the last of their cash.

Regardless of the money in his hand, Petrol Pete was still livid. 'Cyril, just so you know, you ain't never gonna be the next James Dean.'

Cyril winked and grinned. 'Nah, see, me, I'm gonna be the next Paul Newman.'

'Look, mate, give the keys to Frank, will ya, or you won't have a bike left by the time you reach home.'

'Jesus, Pete, that's nuffin a few spins around the block won't cure. I'll be whizzing around London in no time.'

'God help anyone on the streets when you're out and about, then, is all I can say.'

* * *

No sooner had they reached the estate than Frank got to work trying to teach Cyril how to ride the Lambretta. It was clear from the onlookers that Frank was born to ride, but Cyril was like a fish out of water. Still, he persevered and managed at least to stay on and not stall the thing anymore. Once the lessons were over, they pushed the bike to the garages below the flats. Mr Marsden had rented one for his car, but there was plenty of room to keep the scooter in there as well.

'Right, Frank, I've bought the black paint. We need to cover up that yellow paint, or else we'll look like a poxy wasp whizzing around, and you know me, I don't like to draw attention.'

Frank chuckled and was swiftly nudged by Cyril. 'What's so funny?'

'Nuffin, Cyril. I just think with you in charge of the scooter, looking like a bumble bee will be the least of your worries.'

'Well, anyway, we need the wasp looking like a blue-arsed fly.'

Frank nodded, still contemplating the paint job to be undertaken.

'Good lad, Frank. I'm off to check Millard's route again. I wanna be sure we can make a smooth getaway.'

Frank felt his breathing speed up. 'And you're a hundred per cent sure about this, are you?'

'Yeah, 'course I am. The ol' bastard deserves it, Frank. Just 'cos he's a manger, it don't give the prick the right to pinch the ladies' arses. It just ain't proper. The bloke's a weasel. Trust me, Frank, this will be a doddle, and we'll be a few quid in, and, hopefully, he will get his comeuppance.'

Frank shuffled nervously.

'Listen, Frank, if we get caught, I will hold my hands up, and I'll say I bullied you into it, and you had no idea what I was up to, all right?'

Frank nodded. 'I s'pose so.'

'Think of the money, the new suits, the new scooter, even a car.'

Frank smiled, but, underneath, he felt very uneasy.

* * *

The sun was at its peak and Cyril removed his jacket and carried it over his shoulder as he whistled a Beatles tune all the way back to his flat.

Entering it, he saw Shirley having a cup of tea with his mum.

'Here he is, my lad. Look at him. Like butter wouldn't melt.'

Shirley laughed. 'Yeah, Peggy, he does have the face of an angel but the mind of the Devil, no doubt.'

She looked at Cyril and winked. 'Your mum's just got me a job at the chocolate factory.'

'Oh, that's good, but are you still taking our Howie hop picking?'

Shirley grinned from ear-to-ear. 'Yeah, and your mum is coming along as well. I've been telling her all about it. We'll have a right laugh. We can join the men down the pub, since the kids ain't babies anymore. I reckon I could drink Henry under the table, on gin an' all.'

'I do like a drop of gin meself,' said Peggy. 'I haven't had a holiday in . . . Er, I've never *had* a holiday. I'm excited. It'll do my Howie the world of good. I'll have our bags packed by next Thursday night.'

Suddenly, Cyril had a thought. 'Mum, if I give you the money, will ya buy me and Frank a ticket as well?'

Peggy gave Cyril a sideways glance but thought better of asking why, not in front of Shirley. 'Yeah, of course I will. You'll have to get your case packed, if you're coming.'

'Will do.'

'Cyril . . .' said Shirley, hesitantly. 'Thanks for . . . well, you know.' She looked at Peggy, hoping that Peggy knew why she was grateful to Cyril.

Peggy placed her hand over Shirley's. 'You looked after my boys all those years ago when I didn't have two farthings to rub together, and he's returning the favour, ain't ya, lad?'

Cyril gave them his cheeky half-smile. 'Yeah, 'course.'

* * *

It was Friday morning and Cyril was up and pacing the floor. He wasn't so worried about the robbery himself; he was more concerned about Frank bottling out. If he did, he would have to rethink how he was going to do it alone. He stopped pacing and stared at the two makeshift balaclavas. He would have laughed, if he wasn't so anxious. There on the table were two sleeves from an old baggy jumper. He'd cut them off, tied each top with rubber bands, and cut two holes for the eyes. He looked down at his trousers and black shoes. All was in order. The old clothes were ready for the bin, so he didn't mind chucking them out afterwards. The hessian sack was on the table, along with a heavy monkey wrench, which he really hoped he wouldn't have to use, but, if push came to shove, he would batter the bastard.

As soon as Frank knocked at the door, Cyril jumped out of his skin. He made a mental note to himself that he needed to calm his nerves. 'All ready, Frank?'

Surprisingly, Frank seemed very relaxed. 'Yeah, Cyril, the scooter's downstairs. I've covered the number plate in soot. The wasp is now a black panther, and me tool is sharpened and ready to use.'

'Tool?' asked Cyril, nonplussed.

Frank's eyes narrowed. 'Yeah, me tool.'

Cyril looked down to find Frank gripping his fisherman's knife in his huge hand.

'Gawd, give me strength, Frank. What the fuck are you doing with that thing?'

Frank looked sheepish. 'I just thought if Millard gets saucy, I'll stab him, or cut a finger off, or, I dunno.'

Cyril stood with his hands on his hips, shaking his head.

'Listen, Frank, the plan is to just push him over, grab the suitcase, jump on the scooter, and scarper. Jesus, Frank, you do love to cut someone, don't ya?'

Frank changed the subject when he saw the makeshift balaclavas. 'You don't think me barnet will fit in that, do ya?'

'I dunno. Try it on.'

Frank was chuckling as he tugged the jumper sleeve over his head.

'See, it fits like a glove,' said Cyril, laughing.

'It fits like a glove, but how the hell do I know where I'm going?'

Cyril looked at the home-made balaclava and realised he'd cut the holes too low down. All he could see were Frank's rosy cheeks. He chuckled and replied, 'It needs a few minor adjustments, that's all.'

Frank pulled the balaclava off and laughed. 'I bet Dick Turpin didn't have to put up with all this bollocks.'

* * *

By 2.00 p.m., the sun was blisteringly hot and Frank was sweating buckets. 'Cyril, I'm baking in this jacket, and don't you think it looks silly? I mean, look at us, both in black trousers and long black jackets. I know you said to look inconspicuous, but we stand out like two sore thumbs. Everyone's in short-sleeved shirts, and there's us looking like we work in a funeral parlour.'

‘Shush and stop moaning. Right, get your balaclava on and start her up. Millard should be turning that corner any minute.’

‘Oh, shit!’

Frank was starting the engine when he looked down the road, only to see Millard side by side with another man.

‘What now, Cyril?’

Cyril stared for a few seconds. ‘Frank, ride along the road. It’s all derelict around ’ere. There’s no one about. Ride past them and turn around and leave the bike running. We’ll both tackle ’em. I’ll grab the case, and you ride. I’ll jump on the back.’

‘Are you sure?’

‘Yes, Frank. That other geezer looks a wimp.’

Before Frank had the chance to think, they rode down the street past Millard and the accompanying man.

Cyril was surprised that Millard hadn’t even looked at them. He was too busy chatting to the young man. Frank pulled over, thirty yards ahead of them. Anyone else would have thought it was strange to see two young men wearing makeshift balaclavas and walking together down a derelict street.

Frank jumped into action and pulled the unassuming young man away from Millard.

The young man lost his balance and went flying onto his backside. The balaclava covering Frank’s face looked so intimidating that the young man curled himself into a ball in fear of his life.

Cyril had intended just to snatch the briefcase but when he saw the spiteful look on Millard's face and thought about this bastard touching up his mother, he simply couldn't help himself. He punched Millard hard on the side of his face, but when Millard stood his ground and tried to whack Cyril with the case, Cyril went into a frenzy and punched and punched until Millard dropped the case. Then Cyril fly-kicked him into the kerb.

Cyril was panting through anger; he'd just used all his strength to give Millard a good hiding.

It was Frank who grabbed the briefcase out of Cyril's arms. 'Come on. Let's get out of 'ere.'

Frank dragged Cyril to the Lambretta and pushed the briefcase into his chest. 'Fucking hold this and get on.'

Cyril snapped out of his frenzy; for the first time, he took orders from his best friend. Once he'd hopped on, they were away. Two left turns followed by two right turns found them under the arches. Cyril was off the scooter before Frank even had time to come to a standstill. He opened the briefcase and there ready to blow in the breeze were the used banknotes.

'Fucking handsome!' he said, as Frank climbed off and stared at all the money.

Wasting no time, Cyril lifted up the seat of the motorcycle, retrieved the hessian sack, emptied all the cash into it, and threw the briefcase, the two black jackets, and the balaclavas into an empty yard. They then rode away in their bright shirts, looking completely different from any description that Millard or the young man could have given when questioned by the police.

As soon as they reached the garages, they jumped off the bike, lifted the garage door, and wheeled the scooter in, careful to look around first, to see if anyone had spotted them.

'Frank, wash the dirt off the number plate, just in case the Ol' Bill get nosy. I'm gonna take this cash to the flat before anyone sees us.'

Frank was now shaking; the deed was done, and he was nervous. He had to wipe the number plate clean and calm himself. All he could do to stop the shakes was to think of all that money.

Cyril opened his front door and left it ajar for Frank. He hurried to his bedroom and tipped the money onto the bed. Like Frank, his hands were shaking but more through excitement. He had never in his life seen that amount of cash.

As soon as the door slammed, he spun around. 'In 'ere, Frank.'

But it wasn't Frank who appeared.

'Oh, shit! What are *you* doing here?'

'I could have been the police, Cyril.'

Cyril knew he couldn't hide the money. 'Mr Bates, look, I was, er . . .'

Mr Bates shook his head. 'Out on the thieve, by the look of

things.'

Cyril's eyes were round and large. He didn't know what to say or what to make of Mr Bates being there in his flat. 'Sorry, Mr Bates, but did you want something?'

Mr Bates nodded slowly. 'A word.'

Cyril stood rigid.

'You and Frank went out in suits, and you came back in bright shirts and no jacket in sight, so me, I can guess what you've been up to, and many won't, but some will. You need to think things through, lad, if you don't wanna end up inside.'

Cyril sighed. 'I suppose you want a cut, then?'

Mr Bates shook his head. 'No, I don't. I wanted to tell you, so that next time you get up to no good, you come back in the same clothes you went out in. Have what you need for a job in a bag and bloody change elsewhere. Jesus, you have a lot to learn.'

Cyril nodded. 'Okay.' He was still waiting for a ticking off from his mentor.

However, all Mr Bates said before he left was, 'Come and see me later. I have a buyer for your cocaine. And come alone. I deal with you only, Cyril. Don't send anyone to my door, will you?'

Cyril was still shocked at being caught with all the money. All he could do was nod.

'Good lad. Oh, and by the way, don't ever leave your front

door open again. Not now, son, not ever.'

Cyril nodded again. He felt like a naughty schoolboy, but, in reality, and after today's little earner, he knew he was far from it.

The door slammed shut, and Cyril sat back on the bed and let out a deep breath. Mr Bates was right; he should never have left the door open or gone out in black and returned in the colours of the rainbow. He just hoped that no one had spotted him.

Frank knocked at the door, but even though Cyril knew it was Frank, he still called out, 'Who is it?'

'It's me, you crank.'

Cyril opened the door. 'Quick, in me bedroom.'

'So how much is there?'

Cyril laughed. 'So much, mate, that I ain't had enough time to count it.'

He grabbed a pile of notes and threw them Frank's way. 'You count that lot.'

'We pulled it right off, eh, Cyril?'

Cyril didn't answer until he had counted a hundred pound notes.

'And, my son, this is just for starters. The main course will follow. Mr Bates has a buyer for the drugs, so me and you, Frank, we'll soon be rolling in it.'

Frank stared at the money. 'I tell ya what, Cyril. This is easy money. I ain't working down the factory or as a grease monkey under the arches. Fuck that. Look at all this.'

Cyril chewed his lip. 'I got an idea, right? We need to case a few of these factories, follow the wage collectors, and make a plan, 'cos we could clean up within a month. I mean, really clean up, and we'll have ourselves a right tidy stash of money.'

Frank wasn't so nervous now; he knew this was the way forward, and just having that money in his hands, he saw his life as going only one way, and that was up.

* * *

Three weeks passed, and all seemed okay. There was no talk from the factory that Mr Millard had been robbed, and Mr Bates had taken the cocaine and returned with two hundred pounds. For Cyril and Frank, everything in the garden was looking rosy.

That was until one evening when Peggy, Cyril, and Frank sat around the table playing cards in the kitchen. A heavy bang at the door had them all looking nervously at each other.

Peggy got up. 'Stay 'ere, boys. That sounds like the police to me.'

Frank turned from red to white as a sheet.

'Frank, don't look so guilty. I'm sure you've done nuffin wrong,' Peggy said, with a confident smile across her face.

As soon as she opened the door, Cyril and Frank strained

to listen.

'Are you Mrs Reardon?'

'Yes, why?' she replied, in a flat tone.

'I am Inspector Jones, and this is Inspector Limes. We would like a word with your son Cyril.'

'What about?'

'Well, Mrs Reardon, we would like to talk to him. Is he in?'

'I said, what about?'

Cyril and Frank could almost hear the frustration from the policemen at the door.

'A robbery.'

'What!' screeched Peggy. 'And why on earth would you turn up at my doorstep at nine o'clock at night? I really hope you're not enquiring if my little lad was involved, are you?'

Cyril wanted to laugh. His mum could give as good as she got, that was for sure.

'He owns a black scooter, doesn't he?'

'Owns? No, there was an old black scooter dumped around here a few days back, mind. I guess boys will be boys. You know what they're like. I don't suppose you were much different when you were a lad.'

'So he doesn't own a black scooter?'

‘No, he don’t own one. Why?’

‘There was a robbery three weeks ago on the Friday afternoon. Two lads were on a black scooter wearing balaclavas. A man was injured, and the robbers stole a substantial amount of money.’

‘And you think because my young lad rode around on a dumped black scooter that he committed a robbery! Oh, officer, you must be scraping the barrel with that one.’

Cyril listened, but it was as if he was listening to a stranger, not his mother. Then he heard a deeper voice, and it sounded as if it was coming from an older officer.

‘No, Mrs Reardon, we wouldn’t be asking your son to help with our inquiries just on the fact that he may own a black scooter. We’re not that daft.’

‘So why my son, then?’

‘Because your son is friends with Frank Marsden, and Frank’s mother was sacked by the man who was robbed, so it would give both Frank Marsden and your son a motive, as well as the black scooter, and the description of the size of the two lads.’

‘Well, Inspector, someone has been telling you porky pies, ’cos I do know for a fact that Frank’s *muvver* is dying in her bed at Cane Hill Asylum.’ She grinned with satisfaction because she knew that they meant Frank’s Aunt Shirley. ‘And, sorry, but when did you say this happened?’

‘It was a Friday, three weeks ago, in St Saviours Road.’

Cyril felt uneasy, and Frank, who had not moved an inch, now had a sickly green pallor.

'Couldn't have been my lad, nor young Frank either. On that Friday, they were down in Kent with me.'

'Can you prove it, or, more to the point, can they prove it?'

'Oh, hang on. I do believe I can. Wait there.'

Cyril and Frank remained silent, as Peggy entered the kitchen. She put her finger to her lips and then snatched her purse from the side.

Frank had no idea what was going on, but the calm expression on Cyril's face gave him hope that they weren't to be carted off anytime soon.

'There you go, officer. Look, those are four train tickets for me, Cyril, Frank, and my youngest Howie.' Her voice suddenly turned from being accommodating to the officers to now being thoroughly annoyed. 'Now then, you have no real reason to ever knock at my door and have the flaming neighbours gossiping. My lads have a good name, and I don't want your presence suggesting otherwise. I might not be a fucking lady or a duchess, but I am a hard-working woman with two law-abiding lads who do no wrong. So, a word of warning. If you ever knock at my door again, you make sure you have a bloody good reason, or I'll be making a formal complaint.'

'Does your son own a black jacket?'

'Nope, never has done! Black is for funerals. Is that all, officer? Because I have company, and, like I said, unless you have proof that my lad has broken the law, then bye-bye.'

Peggy slammed the door shut in their faces and returned to the table, where she sat down and calmly picked up her hand. 'None of you peeked at me cards, did ya?'

With his eyes like saucers, Frank's mouth was too dry to speak.

'No, Mum. It's your turn, anyway.'

* * *

It took a few minutes for Frank to settle down, and by 10.00 p.m., he was tired and decided to call it a night. Peggy had offered him Howie's bed because Howie was staying on at the farm to help out with the pigs. But Frank wanted his own space and time to think.

As soon as he was gone, Peggy got up and put the kettle on. She was silent, and Cyril knew that she wanted to have a serious talk. After the kettle whistled and screamed, she poured the hot water into a teapot and placed it on the table. Retrieving two cups and the milk jug, she sat down. Not looking at her son, she poured them both a cup of tea and stirred hers slowly. 'So, Cyril, you've decided what career you wanna take, then, 'cos I'm very sure that that little earner wasn't for a college fund, was it?'

'If I've let you down, Mum, I'm sorry. I never want to cause you any trouble, you know that. And thanks for . . . you know, remembering to save the train tickets.'

Peggy looked up, her eyes glassy. She sighed. 'I suppose it's one of those things. You're clever, Cyril. You always have been. Your brain is too smart for mundane work, and you want the finer things in life. When you were a little lad, you simply couldn't understand how those lords could just be born into money, and you thought it was unfair. And you see, Cyril, life is unfair. It's a cruel world, an unjust world, and the biggest crooks are the bloody government and those lords.' She sipped her tea. 'Son, if you're kind to those who deserve it, then I don't mind what you do. I've seen enough heartache come to the kindest people.'

'I will have you dressed in the best, Mum, and dining at the finest restaurants, you'll see. And one day, Mum, me and you, we'll live in a mansion, like those lords.'

Peggy smiled. 'I quite like me little flat. I don't need a mansion. I have all I want. Our Howie is happy, Cyril. That saying, "happier than a pig in shit", describes Howie perfectly. He is. Mrs Muggeridge can't run that pig farm on her own, and she told me, if after a month Howie wants to stay, there is a live-in job for him. That fight nearly sent him over the edge, but when he's around animals, he has that sweet smile back on his face. See, he wasn't born to live in London. He was born with a yearning for a simple life. He should have been born to a farmer.'

Cyril poured himself another cup of tea. 'I knew going back there would make him better, and I'm glad he's got a job because he couldn't go back to school. The thought of it even made him sick.'

Peggy nodded. 'Well, the school board will have to get on with it, and that's that.'

'I'll get him some clobber and send it down to him.'

‘Clobber? The lad only needs wellies, bloody long johns, and a bar of soap.’

‘Next week, I’ll visit him, just so he knows I ain’t forgot him.’

CHAPTER THIRTEEN

As Mr Bates took his pint over to the bay window of the Cedar Arms pub, he eased himself in behind the oak table and relished the warmth coming through the window. A few of the locals nodded politely his way, but most knew he liked his own company. The lifeless beer annoyed Mr Bates, and he called over to the landlady, and none too discreetly either. 'Joanie, a gnat has more gas in it than my pint.'

Joanie rolled her eyes but followed it with a smile. Mr Bates was a regular and had been for thirty years, on and off, in between jail time. She knew he was one of the old school villains since her own father knew that crew many moons ago, and he was full of stories of what the gang had got up to. She was glad that now Mr Bates was old, he probably didn't have the strength or the energy for any more skulduggery.

While Mr Bates waited for Joanie to bring a fresh pint over to him, he pulled out his tobacco and rolled a cigarette. As he let it hang from his lower lip, he searched his pocket for his lighter.

The light from the side door suddenly disappeared when a very large man stepped inside. Mr Bates looked his way. The man was dark-haired and dark-skinned, too dark to be Spanish, though, and he wore a devilish expression. His eyes were black like a shark's, with no soul. And his beige suit suggested he was foreign, maybe Mediterranean. Mr Bates wondered what a man like that would be doing in Bermondsey.

As the man scoured the room, his eyes rested on Mr Bates.

Mr Bates felt his stomach churn over because the foreigner was staring at him and heading his way. An avalanche of thoughts ran through his head until he stopped at the obvious reason for why the man had joined him at his table – the drugs.

'Would you join me for a drink?' he said, in a slow but firm voice.

The foreigner nodded. 'I will have what you are having.'

Mr Bates called over to Joanie to bring over two pints.

'So, did you want to speak here, or shall we go somewhere more private?' asked Mr Bates, feeling beads of sweat coating his brow.

'I want to try your English beer first. Then I will take you to meet the boss.'

Mr Bates accepted that the foreigner was being polite; however, his undertone was laced with intimidation.

Joanie was waltzing over, wiggling her arse as usual, but balancing the two pints carefully so as not to spill a drop. 'There you go, Mr Bates. See, more gnat farts than you can count.'

Mr Bates would have smiled, but he needed that drink to moisten his dry throat. This was probably the last pint he would ever enjoy. He just hoped that they wouldn't torture him and instead give him a clean death.

'So, can I ask, are you from Greece or Mexico?'

The huge evil-looking man laughed and waved his enormous hands to suggest he was not. He swallowed half the pint in one swig.

Mr Bates wondered if he actually savoured his drinks. 'Where are you from?'

'Colombia, Mr Bates. Colombia.'

The tight feeling around Mr Bates' throat immediately increased; he felt as though an invisible wire was about to garrotte him.

The man finished his pint. 'Come! The boss is waiting. We have a car outside – do not try to run.'

Taking his jacket from the back of the chair, Mr Bates followed the Colombian to the black Jaguar XJ6. Two other men, almost as big, stood by the car. As soon as Mr Bates climbed in, they took up their seats on either side, almost squashing their guest.

The journey was undertaken in silence, and it was then that Mr Bates assumed he wasn't coming back. He hadn't been shoved in a boot, or had his head covered, for that matter. So, this would be his last journey, and he prayed he wasn't entering the gates of hell. The saying you live by the sword, you die by the sword came to mind. However, in his heyday of working in the underworld, he wasn't a brutal man who tortured people. He would fight hard for what was rightfully his, and he would use weapons, but he never resorted to agonising torment. He didn't really need to; he had a name and could handle himself. He was more of a planner, the man who read architectural drawings, who masterminded a heist. He lent money to those who needed it, and those who wouldn't pay back what they owed were dealt with. He didn't get his hands dirty – not now he was so much older, and besides, most of the loans were paid up. So, as much as he could fight, he rarely needed to. He sensed the power emanating from these two muscular henchmen on either side of him. He knew damn well that there was no way he could fight these guys.

The car pulled into an underground car park. They were in the centre of London somewhere, but Mr Bates had not really taken much notice since he assumed he was off to meet his Maker. The building was new and the concrete unpainted. The Colombian to the left of him got out of the car, allowing him to climb out himself. He wasn't dragged or shoved.

He followed them to a lift's entrance, and shortly, the lift came to a halt. After the Colombian had pulled open the black cage doors and then the main door, Mr Bates found himself in a huge sparsely furnished room, which included a large desk, a couple of office chairs, and two sofas. He was, however, taken by the far-reaching views across London.

That was, until his eyes were drawn to the man behind an impressive desk who seemed to dominate the room. He was very young and smartly dressed in black trousers and a white shirt. His olive-skinned face was freshly shaven and his hazel-coloured eyes were lively and appeared to hold intelligence behind them. Yet Mr Bates couldn't help but wonder why these huge Colombian men would bring him here to meet a kid.

It wasn't until the young man spoke that Mr Bates realised he was no idiot.

'Sit, Mr Bates,' said the young man. 'My name is Carlo Sandos, and I guess you are wondering what it is you are doing here? Or perhaps, Mr Bates, you already have a good idea, and, if that is the case, then, please . . .' He poured two glasses of dark liquid and handed one to Mr Bates. 'Please sit down and tell me about the cocaine that you sold to the Hells Angels for a mere two hundred English pounds.'

Mr Bates sat on the blue velvet chair edged in gold, and, in one mouthful, he gulped back the drink. In any other circumstances, he would have savoured the single malt whisky, but considering the predicament he was now in, if he could have got his hands on the bottle, he would have drunk the lot.

'So, Mr Bates,' said Sandos, as he perched on the edge of the desk, a few feet above the Englishman.

'Mr Sandos, I am afraid there is not a great deal to say. A few weeks ago, a kid asked me if I knew where to sell cocaine. He said he had pinched a suitcase from the Dorchester Hotel, and when he got home, he found that inside it had a bag of cocaine. That's it, really.'

Sandos grabbed the bottle of whisky and poured Mr Bates another glass.

'Thank you,' said Mr Bates, as he knocked the drink back in one gulp. 'This is good stuff.'

'So was my cocaine. It had not been cut, it was pure, and you sold it for half its value. So . . .' He paused and refilled Mr

Bates' glass a third time. 'I want the truth. How did you know about the drugs, and who else is on your firm?'

Mr Bates tilted his head and frowned. 'My firm, Mr Sandos? I don't have a firm. Look at me. I'm a man who just flogged a load of gear for a kid who happened to get lucky.'

Sandos jumped up from the desk. 'Lucky! There were four men, two with guns, who robbed my man. They robbed his suitcase from his car. They stopped him at the traffic lights with a gun to his head. So, now, let's start again. Who were the other men who robbed my man?'

It was at that moment, Mr Bates realised either he kept his mouth shut or he got Cyril to confirm his own story. But first, he needed to know if Sandos would hurt a kid.

'Tell me, Mr Sandos, what would you do if you found my story to be true, and your man had lied? That he was in fact forgetful, and, stupidly, he left his suitcase outside his bedroom door in the Dorchester Hotel, where a young lad found it?'

Sandos' eyes narrowed, and he stared for a moment. 'Why would my man lie? He has no reason to.'

'Really? Well, let's look at this from your man's point of view. He'll know that it's going to look very foolish if he comes to you and says "Sorry, I left my case outside my room, and it got pinched." Of course, he will make up a dramatic story. I think, in his circumstances, I would have done exactly the same.'

Sandos was still staring as he listened. 'This boy of yours interests me. Who is he? I will ask him myself about what happened, and if he's telling me the truth, then, perhaps, I will let you go.'

Mr Bates shook his head. 'There's no way I'm telling you where he is. He's a fucking *kid*, for Christ's sake. He's only just turned sixteen years old. He went to the Dorchester to pinch a dress for his muvver to go to a dance, and then he saw your man's suitcase, so he nicked that too. The lad's just a little chancer, that's all. I'll get you your money back, but, please, Mr Sandos, leave him out of it.'

Very slowly, Sandos' hard-faced expression began to soften, and a glimpse of a smile appeared. 'Sixteen, you say?'

Mr Bates nodded. 'Well, yes. He's sixteen now, but he was fifteen at the time, and I dunno about what you do in your country, but 'ere, we don't hurt our kids, and he is, as I've said, just a kid.'

Sandos' smile vanished as quickly as it appeared. Slowly, he shook his head. 'In my country at fourteen, you are a man.'

'Yes, I guess it's different in Colombia. You have to be a man there, but here, well, he doesn't know the world.'

'Mr Bates, you have my word that I will not hurt this boy as you call him, if he says exactly as you have said. But it was his choice to sell my drugs. He may have only been fifteen at the time, but he has to learn that actions have consequences. He owes me. End of. But, rest assured, if the boy does what I want, he will live.'

Mr Bates was usually good at working out a lie from the truth, but the Colombian's eyes were now dark and still. In short, he didn't believe him.

'It's up to you, Mr Bates, but think about this. If you do not tell me where this boy lives, then I will find him anyway, just as I have found you, but I will not give him a chance to tell me his version of what happened. I will just shoot him.'

Sandos walked around his desk sat down on his chair, pulled the side drawer open, and retrieved a photo. He then flipped it across to Mr Bates. 'That is my little brother. He's fifteen, and as much as our father thinks we are men, I know he's a little boy with big ideas. I promise you, if your boy is telling the truth, I will not harm him.'

Mr Bates glanced at the photograph of two young lads; the older one had his arm around the younger lad.

'Okay. He lives at number 33 in my tower block. And I'm guessing you know where I live?'

Sandos nodded. 'And his name?'

'Cyril. Cyril Reardon,' replied Mr Bates, as he lowered his head, hoping to God that Carlo Sandos would be true to his word.

* * *

With the sounds of the Beatles singing 'Can't Buy Me Love' on the radio, Cyril was engrossed in his task. He was placing all his money behind the false panel at the bottom of the wardrobe when there was a knock at the door. He assumed it was Frank, ready to worry over what they would wear tonight on their double date with Trudy and Flossie. He pulled the door open with a beaming smile only to find two of the biggest men he'd ever seen in his life standing there like Frankenstein and his brother.

'Cyril Reardon?' asked the uglier of the two.

Cyril nervously shook his head. 'Nah, mate. No one by that name lives 'ere. Try the fifth floor.'

The man laughed. 'I was being polite. You need to come with me now, or I will shoot your friend Mr Bates.'

Cyril's eyes nearly popped out of his head. 'What d'ya mean, "shoot Mr Bates"?'

The other Colombian used his hands as a gun sign. 'Pop.'

'Look, I . . . er, I can't just leave.'

'Yes, you can, and now, or he dies. It's very, how you say, "easy"?'

Although Cyril was usually an incredibly quick thinker, right this moment, he was stunned.

A meaty hand grabbed his arm. 'Come quietly or come screaming, but, either way, you will come with us now.'

Cyril felt the strength of the man and decided he had nowhere to run or to hide; basically, he was fucked. He heard the door slam shut behind him and wondered if he would ever see that flat again, or his mum for that matter. It was at that moment, he realised that if he wanted to become a small-time villain or a major player, this would be what life was like. It was a dog-eat-dog world. He had no idea who the men were, but it didn't take an Einstein to work out that they weren't English.

Like Mr Bates, Cyril was shown into the back seat of a

Jag. He was accompanied by two more heavyset men.

Cyril could feel his stomach churning and it wasn't quiet either, but, right now, he didn't care how he sounded; he was shitting himself. *So would anyone else be, in his shoes*, he thought.

He decided not to say a word. He would only speak if he had to because he knew that his mouth often got him into trouble, and today, he wasn't going to take any chances.

In around forty minutes, Cyril watched as the driver pulled into an underground car park. Once he was hurried into a lift, then rushed along a number of corridors and through various doors, he arrived at the top of the building. Finally, he entered a somewhat minimalist room, although the view from the windows overlooking the City was impressive. Ahead of him was a dark-haired swarthy man, of medium build, who was sitting behind an impressive oak desk. In front of him was Mr Bates, who was sitting with his head lowered in shame.

As Cyril was marched forward to face the occupant behind the desk, he was struck not just by the man's looks – which to Cyril's eyes looked distinctly South American – but his age. The guy wasn't much older than him. And he clearly had plenty of hired muscle. But far from being terrified of being here, Cyril was drawn to the possibilities of what crime could offer him.

Then Cyril turned to Mr Bates, whose expression of guilt made Cyril feel so sorry for him. After all, Mr Bates had helped his family to get out of the gutter.

'So, you must be Cyril Reardon. I am Carlo Sandos,' said

the young man.

Cyril stared for a second. He'd expected some fire-smoking dragon of a man, not someone so young to be in charge. However, it was obvious that he was, since all the huge minders in the room surrounded him, and he was the one behind the desk wearing the flash suit.

'What do you want? Only I was very busy.'

Sandos' eyes narrowed in anger, but there was surprise too. He'd expected a pathetic, uneasy sixteen-year-old thief, who would be quaking in his boots, not a spritely confident Londoner.

'Busy? *Busy*? Busy, Cyril Reardon, selling my drugs that you stole, you mean.'

Cyril suddenly realised what the hell was going on, and his cockiness hit the floor. 'Oh, shit. Hey, Mr Sandos, let's talk about that. Look, I'm sorry. I only nicked the suitcase. I didn't know there were drugs inside. I nicked it because I couldn't walk out of the Dorchester carrying a laundry bag with their name printed on it, now could I? Look, mate, I know from your point of view it was wrong, but I didn't know the suitcase had anything of value in it. I thought it would hold just a few smart bits of clothing.'

Suddenly Sandos grinned and his whole face looked like a teenager's – not the face of a man in charge of a very lucrative and dangerous business. 'You stole the suitcase because you wanted to hide a *laundry bag*? But why?'

Cyril looked at the bodyguards, who stood with their legs apart and their hands together. *Impressive*, he thought. These were real gangsters here, with guns. The top guy had status, and money, and a quick glance at Sandos' gold wrist watch confirmed the guy was loaded. 'I stole a few dresses for me mum to go out. She didn't have any real nice dresses, ya see. Well, anyway, I thought I got lucky when I realised I had pinched a load of drugs, but . . .' He sighed. 'But it looks like I didn't, don't it? Can you let Mr Bates go, Mr Sandos? He didn't have anything to do with it? It was all my idea. Ya see, I live in a poxy two-bit tower block with sod all chances of getting a decent job and earning real money. I know, I took a chance, but wouldn't you have done the same?'

Sandos nodded to his men to escort Mr Bates from the room.

But as Sandos' bodyguards moved to help him from the chair, he leaned across the table. 'You fucking promised me you wouldn't hurt him, and I really thought you were a man of your word, but I was right: you're not a man, you're a child.'

Sandos banged his fist down on the desk, making everyone jump. 'You are wrong, Mr Bates. You assume too much. I *am* a man of my word. I won't hurt Cyril Reardon or you. I want to talk to him alone.' He held up his hands.

Dejectedly, Mr Bates turned towards Cyril. 'I'm sorry.' It was all he could say.

But Cyril wasn't worried. He could see something in Carlo Sandos' eyes that told him he was safe.

He patted Mr Bates' shoulder. 'It's okay. Just wait for me downstairs 'cos I have no fucking idea where I am. And what's more,' he said – looking towards Sandos and his men –

'I'm going to need a lift home, ain't I?'

'My men will drive you back,' said Sandos.

As soon as the men left, Sandos returned to his chair, and Cyril sat in Mr Bates' vacated chair.

'I know what you're thinking – that I am young, maybe too young to be a boss.'

Cyril gave a half-smile and shrugged. 'Maybe, Mr Sandos, maybe not, but what's it to do with me? I mean, I can see that you are a very dangerous man, rich an' all, and I fucked up when I stole the flash suitcase. I can pay you back, but I'll need a little time to find that kinda money.'

Sandos swung gently on his chair, with his hands steepled, obviously in deep thought. 'Yes, you can pay me back. First, though, I have business to attend to. Come with me.'

Cyril did as he was told and followed the Colombian to a side door. As it opened, the strong wind hit Cyril, almost bending him double. As they walked up two steps, onto the roof of the building, Cyril took a moment to gasp for air. He had never been so high up in all his life. Then, as he gazed around, he noticed three men; one of them was being held down on a chair. He too looked South American. Then it dawned on him who the guy was. It was the man he had stolen the suitcase from. *This is serious shit*, he thought.

Cyril continued to follow Sandos over towards the three men.

The man in a very smart pinstriped suit, who was being held down, looked as if he might throw up at any minute.

'Please, please, I beg you,' he cried.

Cyril could see the smart man's legs were limp with fear, but it was also obvious the guy had no idea what was about to happen to him.

'Take off your watch!' growled Sandos.

The man's fingers were all over the place as he fumbled with the strap, until, finally, the watch was in Sandos' palm. The two stared for a few moments, until Sandos finally nodded at his goons, who still had him pinned to the chair.

Cyril was still baffled but only until he saw the man being dragged to the edge of the building. With just one swing, he was hurled into space. The scream was loud, but the thump as he hit the ground was sickening; no one would have survived that.

'Jesus!' bellowed Cyril, as he clutched his head in shock. 'Oh my God, you've *killed* him. Shit!'

He knew then that this was no game. Sandos had ordered the death of a man just by the flick of his head and a nod. Cyril's stomach churned over, and he felt the vomit rise to burn the back of his throat.

Still gripping his head, he glared at Sandos. 'You killed him, just 'cos he left the suitcase outside the room!'

Sandos' unconcerned expression spoke volumes. 'No, of course not. He is dead because he *betrayed* my trust. He told me he was hijacked at the traffic lights by four men with guns, and they took two suitcases, but, as we both know now, you stole just one. So I believe you. I knew in my heart he was lying, but this is what happens when someone, as you say in your country, "screws me over".'

He suddenly glared with an anger in his eyes that had Cyril quaking in his boots.

'And don't you ever talk to me like that again, or you will be next. You need to show me respect.'

Cyril listened to his words, but they were drowned out by the sounds of the crowd gathering down below. He heard a woman screaming and guessed the man was a real bloody mess. He looked at Sandos' stony-faced expression. 'Don't you ever wonder that that could be you one day?'

Sandos shot the boy a glance. 'Is that a threat?'

Cyril shook his head. 'No, not at all. But don't you worry about anything? I mean, you've just had that geezer thrown off the building, and anyone, me even . . .' He held his hands up. 'Anyone could grass you up. But I won't.'

Sandos nodded. 'Yes, but by the end of the day, I will know who you are related to, who you care about, their address, date of birth, and their exact movements.'

Cyril knew now was the time to shut his mouth, before Sandos lost his temper, or he would also be blancmange on one of London's streets.

'Come with me, Cyril. We need to discuss business and how you can pay off this debt.'

'What about the police? I mean, come on, they'll be crawling all over this gaff. You've just had a bloke thrown off the roof? There must be a right mess down there.'

Ignoring Cyril, Sandos marched on ahead.

'Mr Sandos, do you think you'd better, like, get out of this place?'

Sandos stopped and spun around. 'You are a child, and you propose to tell me what *I* should do? I didn't ask for your opinion, and yet you give it to me anyway. *My* men wouldn't dare speak to me unless *I* asked them to.'

Cyril looked Sandos up and down. The man had his hands on his hips and a discerning look on his face. 'Okay, okay, I understand that you are some top boss, but me, I just come from Bermondsey, with fuck all, and I didn't even leave school with certificates, so, sorry, mate, but I don't know how all this works. What I do know is, I ain't used to dealing with people like you, so forgive me, if I don't kiss your arse. I was just saying, maybe we'd better scarper, like.'

Once again, Sandos' serious demeanour mellowed into a soft smile. 'Come with me, Cyril. Let's talk.'

Cyril glanced behind him, unsurprised by bodyguards on his heels. Sandos led Cyril down a private staircase, through a door marked PRIVATE, and finally into what appeared to be his apartment.

'Take a seat, Cyril. Do you drink?'

Cyril sat down and shook his head. 'Nah, not really, but I'll have a Coke if you have one.'

Sandos nodded to one of his men to fetch a bottle.

'So, Cyril, it is obvious to me and you that my man that I had in London seriously let me down. As you would say "He fucked up." So, I need a man to work for me. I think you have the balls to be his replacement.'

Cyril waved his hand. 'Oh, mate, listen. I ain't up to all this kind of bollocks. I mean, I wouldn't be throwing people off tower blocks, and, come on, Mr Sandos, I'm just sixteen years *old*. What do I know, really?'

Sandos leaned forward, with what appeared to be his boss face on now. 'To start with, let's talk about how you are going to pay me back.'

Cyril's hands became clammy. *Nice one, Cyril*, he thought. *You've really taken on something now.*

'You are smart, I can tell that. I need someone to find me serious buyers. I need safe people, men who I can trust, because, Cyril, this game is all about trust.'

Leaning back on his chair, Cyril scrutinised Sandos' face. He wondered if the man was deadly serious. 'Why me, though?'

Sandos shrugged his shoulders. 'It was something my father told me when I was sixteen, and at that time, I had to make some very harsh decisions. He said, "Always trust your gut instinct, because it knows the truth before your brain does."'

The man who scared him at his own front door returned with a bottle of Coke and placed it gently in Cyril's hands.

In that moment, Cyril felt like he was in a dream. The

situation was so surreal. 'Look, I tell you what, I will make some enquiries . . .' He sighed. 'But I'll be upfront with you. I don't really know any of the big buyers, but I'll do me best, and if I fail, then, at the very least, you can have your money back for the drugs.'

Sandos gestured with his hand again. 'I don't want the money back. What I want are the names of the people who I can do business with.'

Cyril took a few mouthfuls of his drink and then nodded. 'Okay. But it won't happen overnight.'

'I know, and I have time.' He paused. 'Do you know much about cocaine?'

Cyril grinned. 'Well, it don't wash clothes, that's for sure.'

Despite not understanding the joke, Sandos couldn't help but laugh at what Cyril had just said. It was the way he spoke and his facial expression as he said it. He was a charmer, that was for sure. *And that, he thought, could be an attribute that would work well for both of them.* Sandos smiled inside. The boy may only be sixteen, but there was a maturity and a confidence that even his brother of a similar age back in Colombia didn't possess.

As Sandos stood up, Cyril followed suit.

'It was good to meet the thief who stole my goods from my top man.'

Feeling unsettled, Cyril shook Sandos' proffered hand and spun around to leave. 'Oh, Mr Sandos, how do I keep in contact?'

Sandos grinned. 'You don't. But I will.'

* * *

As soon as Cyril stepped out of the lift, he clocked Mr Bates leaning against a wall, smoking a roll-up. Hurrying over to see him, he just hoped Mr Bates wouldn't suffer from the stress of everything he'd put him through.

'Are you okay, Mr Bates? You kinda look a bit white, like.'

Mr Bates stubbed out his cigarette, looked about, and grabbed Cyril's shoulder. 'Let's get the fuck out of here.'

'It's all right, Mr Bates. We're safe, now, but we need to talk.'

The police were still outside the building, and the crowd were all competing with each other, trying to get a look at the gory mess left on the pavement.

'Let's just get away from here, first. I'll call a black taxi.'

'Hang on. Sandos' men can take us back.'

Mr Bates shot Cyril a death stare. 'You *what*? No, thank you.'

* * *

Once they are away from the building and heading for the main road, Mr Bates lit up another cigarette, and that was when Cyril noticed just how much his hands were shaking. Whatever Sandos' men or the boss himself had said to Mr Bates, it had well and truly put the wind up him.

A black taxi was approaching with its 'For Hire' sign lit up, and Mr Bates ran towards the kerb to wave it down. As it glided to a smooth stop, Mr Bates said, 'Get in, lad, and we'll talk at home.'

Getting back proved quicker than expected. As soon as the taxi pulled up outside their tower block and they were safely inside Mr Bates' flat, the colour in his cheeks seemed to return.

Cyril was still silent as he watched Mr Bates pour a generous measure of whisky into a tall glass. He knew he must wait until Mr Bates was ready to talk.

'So, Cyril, what did he want?'

'He wants me to pay off the debt by fixing him up with drug dealers, and I told him I don't know of any, but he seemed to think I could find that information out.' He sniggered. 'Silly bastard, I know *nothing* about it.' He looked up and raised his brow. 'So, I guess, Mr Bates, you'll have to tell me.'

'*Me*?'

Cyril nodded. 'Well, you know people, obviously, 'cos you sold the shit and to the wrong person who grassed. So, Mr Bates, we do know one firm that can't be trusted.'

For a second, Mr Bates stared at a man, not a boy. 'Christ, Cyril, do you know what you are getting into? If you start being the middleman to the fucking Colombians, you could seriously jeopardise your life expectancy.'

'I don't have a choice,' replied Cyril, in a matter-of-fact

voice, almost spelling each word out.

'Christ, this is a ball-ache and a half.'

'It may be a ball-ache, but, Mr Bates, I have no fucking choice, unless I wanna go skydiving. In case you didn't hear, Sandos' men flipped a guy off the top of that bleedin' building back there.'

Mr Bates swigged more of his whisky and rolled his eyes. 'Fuck it. Right, you and Frank will have to come with me, and I'll start by introducing you to a few faces. But – and I mean but – don't ever go alone. Frank's a big lump, and you'll need men, big men at that, to accompany you. And I see you knock about with the Blakes. That Freddy's a lump as well. It may be an idea to have them with you, if, of course, you can trust them.'

Cyril sat forward, listening carefully to everything Mr Bates told him.

'So, Cyril Reardon, you may be sourcing buyers, but you do know now that you have the backing of the most fucking feared men in London.'

Cyril tilted his head to the side. 'Who's that, then?'

Mr Bates shook his head in disbelief. 'The *Colombians,* you twat. First things first. You, lad, need to look the part, right? I will introduce you to Larry McKendrick. He's a hard bastard, with a mob that are ruthless. You need to walk smart, act smart, and bloody think smart. He don't like wimps or weasels.' He looked Cyril up and down. 'So I think he'll probably like you.'

'And I will have something he wants. See, I remember what you said, Mr Bates – it's all about supply and demand.'

A loud laugh filled the room, more through relief, though, than anything else.

It was well into the night by the time Cyril and Mr Bates had hatched a plan, and as Cyril left to go home, Mr Bates sat pondering. He recalled the little eight-year-old with the look of an angel, his blond wavy hair always pushed behind his ears and the round grey eyes so full of that thirst for knowledge. Now Cyril was on the verge of manhood, with a boyish twinkle and a light-hearted way of talking, but he had a cunning about him all the same. He knew then that by the time Cyril reached twenty-one, he would run a tidy firm of his own. He just didn't know how reckless Cyril would become, but he hoped that he would be sensible enough to know when to call it a day. He closed his eyes and prayed that Cyril was tough enough to handle the job he was tasked to do. He knew what the Colombians were all about, and seeing a young man in charge made him nervous. Did Carlo Sandos have a lot to prove, and would he see Cyril as easily dispensable? One thing he was sure of and that was he was as much to blame as Cyril for getting into this mess, so he would try his utmost to be the one to help him get out of it.

CHAPTER FOURTEEN

Cyril and Frank had treated themselves to new suits and Italian leather shoes to add to their expanding wardrobes. Their outfits defined who they were – confident young men who weren't afraid to take a chance on what life held in store for them.

The money from the robbery provided more than enough for Frank to buy a car. Cyril warned him about purchasing anything too flashy to draw attention towards them, but, instead, to buy something with plenty of power.

They also invested in a newer motorbike – one that would definitely get them away from any robbery. Cyril had tried to ride it, but he nearly wrote the bike off, so it was down to Frank to do the driving.

Frank had got used to Cyril calling the shots: it was how he liked it.

Since Cyril's plan to rob Mr Millard had worked, Frank was more than happy to go along with his friend's scams. Cyril rented a lock-up close to where Freddy Blake lived, so that anything they got up to would not be seen by nosy neighbours in his tower block.

* * *

Flossie raised her eyebrow and gave a pretend wolf whistle when Cyril appeared at the door. 'You look nice, Cyril,' she said.

Cyril grinned. He knew he looked good in the suit and the shoes, but he was still a gentleman.

'And you, my duchess, look a million dollars. So you've had your hair done, I see?'

Flossie turned her head. 'I didn't think you'd notice.'

'Of course, I would, babe. Here, this is for you.' He smiled and handed her a small box.

'Blimey! What's this for?'

'Oh, let's just say, me business is doing good. Go on, open it, and if you don't like it, they said I can change it.'

Flossie opened the lid and her face instantly lit up. 'Cyril! It's beautiful. Oh, do it up for me, will ya?' she said, as she handed Cyril the silver necklace with the silver dove charm.

'You like it, then?'

'I love it. I ain't got any jewellery, not proper stuff. I will treasure it.'

Cyril fastened the clasp while Flossie pulled her hair to one side. Then, spontaneously, he kissed her neck.

Slowly she turned around and gazed into his grey eyes and then lowered her eyelids, waiting for him to kiss her on the lips.

Cyril wanted to wait to ask for permission, as his mother had always told him never to take for granted that a girl would want to be kissed. But she didn't push him away when he kissed her neck. He decided to go for it, and if he got a slap, then so be it. Gently, he leaned forward and carefully brushed his lips past hers. He noticed she had her eyes shut, and so, again, he brushed her lips, and then, as if all the fireworks on New Year's Eve had gone off inside his stomach, he had a surge of excitement and couldn't hold back any longer. Placing his arms around her waist, he pulled her close and kissed her properly, hoping that she would respond. Then he felt her arms slide over his shoulders and around the back of his neck as she too pulled him close. Pins and needles invaded his entire body, and for the first time in his life, he felt his legs go to jelly.

As she drew away, she giggled and blushed.

'Come on, Cyril, let's not leave Trudy and Frank waiting, eh?'

Cyril held her hand as they skipped down the stairs.

'Blimey, Frank, is that yours?' squealed Flossie.

'Yep.' He looked at Cyril. 'And Cyril's, but I'm the only one driving until he gets his licence.'

Cyril felt his heart melt. His mate Frank was the best pal anyone could have. The car wasn't his as well; it was just Frank's.

Trudy sat in the front as if it was her rightful place and Cyril kept quiet. He knew Frank had taken a liking to Trudy, although she wasn't his type. She was a little too loud and brash for his taste.

His Flossie was serene, graceful, and although she didn't speak the Queen's English, she had a sweet way of talking. As Cyril climbed in the back, Flossie sidled up to him, clutching his arm. 'So your business is really doing well, then?'

Frank shot a glance at Flossie through the rear-view mirror but said nothing.

The Pagoda was packed and most of the clientele were in their late teens or early twenties. No sooner had Frank stuck his head in the pub than he saw Ronnie and his mates, who were over near the bar.

'What's ya poison, Frank?' shouted Ronnie, over all the chatter.

'It's all right, Ronnie, we're on our own tonight.'

Ronnie then spotted Flossie and Trudy and nodded to Frank in acknowledgement.

Flossie looked around and noticed that all the girls wore fashionable clothes, and for a moment, she felt a little dowdy, until one of Ronnie Blake's sisters, Tilly, paid her a compliment about her hair. That was enough for Flossie to feel a million dollars. She never dreamed that she would be standing in a pub with grown men and women, and, to top it all, be greeted and treated as if she were 'a somebody'. It was obvious to the girls that Frank and Cyril had gained respect; they had no idea why, though.

But plenty in the pub did. Word had it that Cyril and Frank were on the make. They were the new boys in town and were given a level of admiration that neither could have foreseen just a few months ago.

As Cyril went to the bar to order another round, Marcus River appeared by his side. 'Hiya, Cyril.'

Cyril glanced at the man's black eye and flattened nose. 'Cor, shit, I take it you lost the last fight, then?'

'Nope. You wanna see the other fella. It will take a good taxidermist to pack his face out.'

Cyril laughed. 'Have you got any more fights lined up?'

'Nah, not at the moment. I did get hurt, to be honest. I won, but I'm still getting headaches. I need a break.'

Holding the four tall glasses between his two hands, Cyril paused for a moment. He looked Marcus up and down. 'So, Marcus, who do you work for? Is it just the Blakes?'

Marcus frowned. 'Yeah, mate. I've known the Blakes all me life. In fact, I'm dating Tilly.'

'Look, mate, if I need a bit of muscle, are you up for it? I'll pay ya.'

Marcus looked down at the tan brogues and then back at Cyril. 'Looks like you and Frank are doing well. Yeah, Cyril, call me, mate.'

Cyril returned to the table and handed out the drinks. Trudy and Frank were like a married couple, both with their arms linked. Flossie, meanwhile, was soaking up the atmosphere.

As soon as 'A Hard Day's Night' by the Beatles came on the jukebox, the pub erupted. The men were singing at the top of their voices, and the girls were dancing. Even Trudy shuffled past Frank and began wiggling her chubby arse.

The night proved to be a success. The girls had seen the lads in a different light, and they wanted more. Trudy wasn't slow in coming forward. 'Ya know what, Frank? If you were to ever propose to me, I'd kind of like one of those simple-looking rings – you know, nuffin too flashy. What about you, Floss?'

Frank looked at Cyril and rolled his eyes.

'Oh, me, well I wouldn't mind any ring, really. For me, it's more about being with the right man,' she said, as she squeezed Cyril's knee.

'Yeah, of course, and Frank's definitely the right man for me, ain't ya, Frank?' giggled Trudy, her eyes now glassy from the four bottles of Babycham followed by two cherry brandies.

Frank stiffened. He had other ideas, and as much as he liked Trudy, he had no intentions of getting married just yet.

Just as they were about to get into Frank's car, a voice called after them. 'Oi, are you Cyril Reardon?'

Cyril removed his foot from the rear footwell of the car and stood back to see who was calling him. The road was dark, but the streetlamp shone enough to see a slim man, roughly the same age as him.

Frank shut his door and joined Cyril in the road. Standing next to the stranger was another man, a well-built lad, and to his left was a very tall guy, with a scar that ran the length of his face from his eye to his jawline.

'Who wants to know?'

The man stepped closer. 'I'm Johnnie Carter. A word of warning, Cyril. This is my fucking manor. I don't wanna see the likes of you muscling in on business that's nothing to do with you. You may have scared off the Deacons, but don't think you can lord it over me on *my* turf.'

Flossie attempted to get out of the car, but Cyril swiftly closed the door on her.

The last of the punters from the pub, the Blakes – Ronnie, Freddy, and Keith – along with Marcus River, were walking towards Frank's car and could see some men surrounding Frank and Cyril.

They hurried along to see what was going on. It soon became clear what the problem was. Ready for a fight stood Johnnie Carter and his firm.

Ronnie wanted to drag Cyril and Frank away. Carter was a nasty piece of work, but, in fairness, he did run the manor. However, something inside Ronnie made him hold back. It was like watching a Mexican standoff.

Marcus, however, hated Johnnie Carter with a passion because he'd not only been battered by two of his mates in his time, but when he was twelve years old, it was Johnnie who had kicked dirt in Marcus' face. However, things were different now. Marcus wasn't twelve or skinny or afraid. That humiliation had made him want to learn to box.

Taking his jacket off, he handed it to Ronnie and marched over to Cyril.

'You can pay me back later, mate,' he whispered.

Cyril knew then that this would not be a verbal conversation, although he wasn't ready for a ruck, either. He had been taken a bit by surprise, but as he looked around him, he realised that if he didn't stand up for himself now, then all the praise and pats on the back for beating up the Deacons would be a thing of the past.

'Your turf? What the fuck! Are you a gardener, mate, 'cos, all I see is a dirty, dusty road, and a gobby twat making threats. Now fuck off.' No sooner had the words come out of his mouth than he realised he had just declared war on a well-known gang. And judging by the expression on each of the Blake brothers' faces, he had just fucked off the wrong person. Now he had thrown down the gauntlet, he knew he had a fight on his hands. The first thing that came to mind was his suit and the shoes. 'Bollocks,' he mumbled under his breath.

Unexpectedly, Freddy, who Cyril knew from way back, when they were only eight years old, marched over to Cyril and also stood by his side.

'Four on three, is it?' bellowed Johnnie Carter.

But Freddy, a lad of few words, spoke up. 'You're just a bully, Johnnie Carter, and your firm are bullies, so if you're gonna have a fight, I'm here to see it's done fucking fair and square. No tools.'

'And who the fuck d'you think you are?'

‘He’s with me,’ said Cyril.

Carter stopped and inclined his head, giving Cyril a nasty sneer. ‘You really think you’re hard, don’t ya? A fight with the Deacons, and now you think you can run the manor.’

Cyril stepped forward. ‘I don’t wanna run any fucking manor, but I don’t take too kindly to being called out in the street in front of me bird. I ain’t done you any harm, and yet you seem to think you can throw your weight around to intimidate me. Well, I have news for you, Johnnie Carter. I ain’t scared of you or your firm, so, unless you want this to get messy, I suggest you turn around and fuck off.’

Carter looked at his two sidekicks and laughed. ‘Did you hear that, lads? That fucking little boy has just told us to fuck off.’

Carter was laughing along with his two minions while Cyril was raging. He hated the words ‘little boy’ or anything that insulted his appearance or inferred he was immature.

Frank chuckled because he knew that that was one of Cyril’s pet hates, but no one expected what came next.

Cyril ran forward and before Carter could take his hands out of his pockets to defend himself, Cyril leaped into the air, and with one almighty crack, he headbutted him straight across the bridge of his nose. As Carter fell back and tried to regain his composure, Cyril tore into him, throwing punches so fast and so hard that the now battered young man didn’t stand a chance. He staggered backwards and landed with his head on the kerb. That’s when Cyril reached down, grabbed Carter by the hair, lifted him up, and then rammed his head face down into the kerb again and again, until he felt someone pulling him off. His hearing sounded fuzzy, as if he were underwater, but he could still hear the words. 'No, Cyril, you'll kill him.'

As he turned to see who was talking, he realised it was Freddy.

Then, like before with the Red Deacon incident a while ago back at the flat, he looked around to see the carnage. Frank was kicking the tall lad, who, by now, was already battered and lying on the floor, and Marcus was punching the hell out of the other one of Carter's sidekicks.

Cyril gasped for breath and then straightened his jacket; when he peered down at his shoes and saw they were ruined, he wasn't at all surprised.

Carter lay with his face covered in blood, but the moans and groans were enough to know that Cyril hadn't murdered him.

Frank stopped when Ronnie pulled him off.

That just left Marcus, whose opponent already had his hands up in surrender.

Carter knew he needed the hospital, but he still slowly sat upright and peered up at Cyril. 'This ain't over.'

Cyril shook his head. 'Nah, you're right there, mate. This *ain't* over, because you fucking threatened me, and you were ready to hurt me, weren't ya? All because you think you own this area. Well, you don't own it, you idiot, we all grew up here. And you! I've never even met you before. So, let's get one thing clear. See us lot.' He pointed to the men standing by Frank's car. 'Us lot, *we* run this manor. Any tickle, and it's ours, any knocked-off gear, they come our way, so if you want a so-called manor, fuck off back to where you came from.'

All the while Carter maintained his glare, he kept wiping the blood away with the back of his hand. 'You shouldn't have done that.'

Cyril turned and walked away. 'All right, Frank, Freddy, Marcus?'

All three men nodded in return. 'Let's get out of here,' said Cyril. 'We've got a business to run.'

The drive back to the tower block was spent with Flossie fussing over Cyril. Really, she was proud that her fella was a real 'rucker', and he'd fought like a man. Trudy, however, didn't fuss over Frank at all. But she excitedly went on about how hard and brave he was.

Cyril and Frank would have lapped up the attention, but they had more pressing issues to deal with, so as soon as the girls were dropped off, Frank drove back up the Old Kent Road to their lock-up. They'd rented it with the contents inside, which included a table and four chairs. There was electric already wired up and ready to go, so Frank had popped in a light bulb.

It was only a few minutes later when Marcus, who had Freddy in the car, pulled up outside. They were vigilant and looked around them before disappearing inside the lock-up.

Cyril was already seated, and Frank was leaning against the wall. 'Come in, sit down,' said Cyril, as he popped open a bottle of Coke. 'D'ya fancy a bottle?'

Marcus and Freddy shook their heads. They were still a little stunned from the fight they'd just been involved in, and there was Cyril, as cool as a cucumber, sipping a Coke.

'So, this Johnnie Carter has a firm and from what he said, he's worried that we're gonna take over his manor. Now that tells me he has a good earner going on there, but, to my mind, lads, he shouldn't have threatened us. Where does the prick come from?'

Marcus chuckled. He was enjoying the idea that they could take over Carter's mob. 'He comes from North London. He moved down here about six years ago. I was twelve when his lot moved into the Elephant and Castle.'

'Good, so he can fuck off, then, can't he, back to North London. What's his business? Do any of you know?'

Marcus took a seat. 'They sell tobacco, fags, you know, that sort of shit, but it's Carter's uncle who runs the show. Really, he has protection rackets. Johnnie's only young, and so are his brothers, but their Uncle Harry has them on his firm. You need to be careful, Cyril.'

Cyril grinned like the cat that got the cream. 'Sounds like a challenge to me, lads, but, first, we need to talk. I've got some business lined up, but I need me own firm.'

Freddy laughed. 'A firm? I've only just left school, Cyril.'

'Yeah, but who said we've got to be thirty years old? Fuck it. You wanna earn good money, then we ain't gonna earn it by doing a nine-to-five job, are we?'

'I'm in,' said Marcus, eagerly. 'Fuck it. I need the money. I'm gonna marry my Tilly, and she deserves a decent wedding.'

Frank looked at Freddy. 'What you gonna do with your life, Freddy, 'cos there ain't no one in your family that went to Oxford or Cambridge, is there?'

Freddy sighed. 'No, I guess not. I think me dad's assuming I'll turn out like me bruvvers. I reckon I shouldn't let him down.' He laughed, and as if the tension in the room had disappeared in a nanosecond, they all joined in and creased up.

Cyril looked into each pair of eyes, one after the other, and he knew from that minute they were the three men who he could trust with his life.

'So who's up for taking over from the Carters?' said Cyril.

Marcus nodded. 'Me, I'd fucking love to.'

Frank held his hand up. 'I'm in.'

Freddy looked from one to the other. 'It's the uncle, though. He has a nasty mob.'

Cyril shrugged his shoulders. 'And your point is?'

'All right, I'm in.'

'Good, because I've got a few things up my sleeve, starting with – as I'm told – the hardest men in London. My new Colombian friends.'

Marcus and Freddy both frowned in shock. Freddy even gasped. 'Are you serious?'

Cyril nodded slowly but deliberately. 'Yeah, I am. A rich Colombian drug dealer has, shall we say, a little issue with me, and . . .' He paused when he saw the terror on his three friends' faces. 'Don't panic, lads. I think I have everything under control. If I can find a buyer for a load of cocaine, then I'm off the hook. But I've got an idea.'

Frank sighed. ''Ere we go.'

'The Colombian needs my help. Why he chose me, God only knows, but, if I get a buyer and get in his good books, then who better to have on the firm than the biggest ugliest Colombians that can put the shit right up ya, with a grin and a mouth full of garlic.'

'You have big ideas, Cyril,' Marcus stated.

'I know, but I like to call them plans.'

* * *

It was 1 a.m., by the time Cyril put the key in the door. He crept along the hallway and into the kitchen to pour himself a glass of cold water. As he ran the tap, he noticed his knuckles were bruised, and a little swollen, so he held them under the tap to cool them down. *Was this really the life that he wanted*? he asked himself. Fighting, stealing, and the constant fear of being murdered, or, worse, his family murdered. It was all well and fine keeping up the bravado in front of the lads, but he wondered if, after the last few weeks' events, this was really the road he wanted to take. He was sixteen, a kid really, and, already, he was taking serious risks. He realised that he had stepped onto a rollercoaster that would be forever on the rails. There was no coming off. The Colombian wanted a buyer. And he himself also wanted the same lifestyle, and now he had just created a firm to make a shedload of money.

A key being inserted into the lock of the front door pulled Cyril from his thoughts. He dried his hands and poked his head out of the kitchen. He let out a sigh of relief when he saw it was his mum. And it was at that point, he knew he was on edge.

'Cyril, 'ave you just got in?' asked Peggy, as she kicked off her shoes and removed the chiffon scarf from her head.

'Yeah, I was just having a glass of water. Did you have a good night, Mum? It's not like you to stay out so late.'

Peggy carried her bag into the kitchen and placed it on the table. 'I couldn't leave. The pot was big. Still, I won in the end.' She chuckled as she emptied all the money from her bag out onto the table.

Cyril's eyes were alive with excitement. 'Fucking 'ell.'

'Oi, Cyril, mind ya language.'

The notes spilled onto the floor, like autumn leaves in the wind.

'Mum, you've just won yourself a flaming fortune. You don't need to work in the factory. Look at it all.' Cyril laughed as he picked the notes up from the floor.

'Cyril, listen to me. I don't *have* to work. I've got more than this pugged away, but I *want* to work. I like to work and meet people. I love the chatting and the laughs, and I do have a few laughs. This is for retirement or if you boys ever need some. Put that kettle on, babe.'

Cyril filled the kettle, placed it on the stove, and pulled two cups from the cupboards.

'Mum, I'm gonna be rich an' all.'

Peggy took a seat and studied her son. 'You already look the part, what with your smart suit, and classy shoes, but look at your brass bands.'

Cyril turned around. 'What?'

'I can see you've been fighting again, Son.' She pointed to his bruised and grazed knuckles. 'Don't make too many enemies because they may come back for revenge when you least expect them to.'

Cyril could see that his mother's statement was said in such a way that she had lived this kind of life herself. He decided not to pry but changed the subject to talk about Flossie.

'Yeah, I like her, Mum. She ain't like her mate Trudy, who is rough, but, mind you, Frank likes her.'

'Cyril, you wanna hope that Flossie ain't like her muvver, 'cos she's not a nice woman, I can tell you that for nuffin. No, she is dog rough, that one.'

'No, no, Mum, my Flossie is a good girl.'

'Your Flossie now, is she?' she teased.

'Yeah, Mum. I guess she is.'

CHAPTER FIFTEEN

Within days, Mr Bates had arranged a meeting between Larry McKendrick and Cyril.

Cyril paced the floor of Mr Bates' living room. 'And this McKendrick geezer supplies South London with every drug there is. So how the hell can I convince him to buy cocaine from the Colombian?'

Mr Bates seemed to have aged a lot in the last few weeks. His face appeared gaunt once more and he had that familiar yellow tint to his skin he'd had a few years ago. He had stopped accompanying Peggy to the poker games – not that she needed a chaperone anymore.

'Listen to me, Cyril. You have the charm, the wit, and the cheek. Use them equally, and remember, it's all about supply and demand. It comes down to one thing. You can sell anything, if the punter has a reason to buy and the means to pay. McKendrick has both. But, lad, remember this too: people buy people first. If he likes you, and please don't assume he does, but *if* he likes you, then he'll do business with you.'

Cyril paced the floor again. 'Really, I should just give Carlo Sandos his name and let the Colombians meet him and work out a deal.'

Mr Bates shook his head. 'That's not how the Colombians work, is it? They want you to do the first deal, until the client, in this case McKendrick, buys a few keys and safely pays up. Then you can hand over the details, and Sandos can do what the fuck he likes after that. You would have resolved your issue with him, and we won't have to look over our shoulders anymore.'

'So if it's that simple, why do I feel so bleedin' nervous? And you, Mr Bates, you look like you've shit yaself.'

'Cyril, shut up. Now then, that's the address. You've got a meeting in one hour. Don't fuck it up.'

Cyril snatched the piece of paper and hurried from the flat and down the stairs to Frank, Freddy, and Marcus, who were waiting by the car. He was surprised to see them all looking so smart and intimidating, and for a moment, he wondered if he ever came across them in a dark alley, he would run for his life. *Yeah*, he thought, *he would*. They didn't look like a bunch of teenagers; they looked like hard men. He just hoped he looked as tough as them.

Within half an hour, they arrived outside a dark dingy-looking pub just off Lewisham High Street.

'Cor, what a dump,' said Cyril, looking out of the car window.

Frank stared at the map. 'This is definitely it, Cyril.'

The four of them stepped out of the car and waited for Cyril to compose himself. Just as he was about to open the door into the pub, a man came flying out and landed on the pavement, right by Cyril's feet.

'Come back, and I'll fucking remove your liver with a rusty nail!'

Cyril glared at the giant of a man, dressed in a beige short-sleeved shirt, which showed all his muscles, and black slacks with braces. He had two gold teeth, and the rest were stained brown. And his face put Cyril in mind of a cauliflower with all its lumps and bumps.

The man turned his attention to Cyril and the men behind him. 'What the fuck are you all staring at?'

Cyril smiled genially. 'Nuffin, mate.' He stepped back and looked up at the sign. 'This *is* a pub, ain't it?'

'Are you being fucking funny, mate?' growled the man with the stained teeth.

'Nah, I just wanted to be sure I was at the right place.'

'Who are you after?'

'A bloke called Larry McKendrick.'

The man scoffed, looked Cyril up and down, and flicked his head for Cyril and the rest of them to go inside.

The pub was small and empty. A horseshoe bar, it had one barmaid behind it. The table and chairs were a mismatch, and the floor was covered in lino that had been worn bare in parts.

The ceiling and walls were brown from cigarette smoke, and the place stank of ash trays and stale beer. Cyril would have got a round in, but when he saw the colour of the barmaid's nails, he knew that if he and his firm were to have a drink, they'd be best having a shot of gin or vodka, to ensure they didn't catch anything.

As soon as they approached the bar, the man who had rudely met them outside the pub, appeared from an internal doorway and held a side door open. 'Well, come on, then. You said you wanted to meet me bruvver. I guess you've got a meeting, and he hates people being late.'

Cyril followed the man to the foot of a staircase. 'Go on up. He's in the room at the top of the stairs.'

This wasn't how Cyril had pictured a meeting with some hard gangster. Nevertheless, he climbed the smelly creaky staircase, trying not to grip the handrail, for fear of catching anything likely to kill him. This was nothing like going to Carlo Sandos' office.

Cyril was relieved to hear the others behind him, although they would probably look a bit silly with all of them squashed inside the room.

Once he reached the top, the room in front opened out. It seemed as large as the bar downstairs itself. The decor was a lot better too. The stale smell of fags and booze was replaced with a fruity aroma mixed with expensive aftershave. Cyril noticed the walls were cream and the floor was carpeted. Two large sash windows were open, and a gentle breeze of fresh air blew in. To the left of the long room, there was a sofa and a bookshelf, and to the right was a desk. Cyril tried to take everything in all at once. Beside the huge man seated behind the desk, who he assumed was McKendrick, there were two other men, who were not as smartly dressed as the man in the chair.

'I see you felt the need to bring the circus with you. Why, Mr Reardon, I do not know, since this isn't a business deal . . . yet.'

Cyril remained silent as he stared at McKendrick. He was probably in his late forties, a smoker, and a drinker. Cyril clocked the brown liquid in a brandy glass an inch away from McKendrick's hand and the ashtray with a few fag butts inside. But it was the gun, which was placed on the desk, that Cyril focused on. Just sitting there, it was as if it was a natural part of the furnishings, like a vase.

'Well, take a seat, Mr Reardon.'

Cyril sat down while Frank, Marcus, and Freddy stood behind him.

'I see you think you've got yourself a little firm, coming in here mob-handed. Is that what you think, little boy? So, which one of you clowns gets fired out of the cannon?'

Cyril felt the hairs on the back of his neck stand on end. He hated being patronised, but he had to hold his temper inside for now. 'So do you wanna talk business or did you just wanna take the piss out of me?'

'Hmm, cheeky bastard, aren't ya?'

Cyril held McKendrick's gaze for a few seconds until McKendrick leaned back on his chair and swigged the last of his drink. 'So Mr Bates said you want to talk about a supply of cocaine.'

Cyril nodded slowly, not taking his eyes off McKendrick's. 'I asked Mr Bates for the meeting. As I understand it, you already have a fair number of buyers yourself. Me, I have good connections and a regular supply of high-grade stuff that will make yours you're turning out look like talcum powder.'

McKendrick grinned. 'That's a fucking bold statement. I wanna sample this wonderful product, and if the rest of the gear isn't consistently the same as your sample, then you'd better surround yourself with a few more clowns and more clout than this lot.'

Cyril got up. 'I guarantee you, the supply will be as pure as the sample,' he said, as he pulled a packet from inside his top pocket and placed it on the table.

McKendrick snatched the packet and handed it to the lump of a man to his right, who used a tiny silver scoop and snorted the cocaine.

The man to his left then walked over to the door and stood in front of the doorway to block anyone's exit.

Everyone held their breath while the man sniffed and rubbed his nose. In no time, a huge grin spread across his face, and he nodded to McKendrick.

'Looks like we can do business, Mr Reardon.'

'I never doubted it. Now if James Cagney wants to get out of the way, we can all go down and celebrate with a drink on me.'

For the next half an hour, Cyril and McKendrick sat alone at a table discussing the deal, while Frank, Freddy, and Marcus stood at the bar with McKendrick's two heavies drinking whisky.

* * *

An hour later, Cyril's mob arrived back at the lock-up. They'd left the pub with a lot on their minds.

Cyril was a mix of emotions; he was angry that he couldn't slap the hell out of McKendrick for insulting his pals, but he was also relieved that he could now kiss his debt to the Colombian goodbye.

'Listen, I just wanna say this. I'm grateful to you all. And I will make it up to you, I promise.'

Frank knitted his brow. 'What are you on about, Cyril?'

'You know when that prick called you names? I wanted to flip the desk in his face, but I couldn't. I had to swallow his name-calling to get the deal done.'

'I for one am bloody glad you did. I didn't fancy a ruck with a gun. No doubt his two fire-breathing dragons had a weapon hidden in their jackets.'

Cyril sat down and looked at his friends. 'Even so, I just want you to know I appreciate your help and loyalty, and you'll all see soon enough when we'll have money, enough to buy our own pub.'

Freddy, who was quiet, sat next to Cyril. ‘Best you start making plans as you call ’em.’

CHAPTER SIXTEEN

By the end of the week, Cyril was summoned to meet Sandos. Once again, he was escorted by his men, but, this time, he felt less anxious because he had a buyer, and so, as far as he was concerned, the debt had been paid.

Sandos sat behind his desk. He looked just as smart as when Cyril had first met him; only, this time, he appeared concerned.

He waved Cyril in and nodded to his men to leave. Once they were alone, Sandos offered Cyril a bottle of Coke.

Cyril smiled. 'You remembered.'

'So, I am assuming that you have found a buyer?'

'I have, and he has sampled the goods and wants to have a deal.'

Sandos seemed preoccupied but nodded his head as if he was taking notice.

'Probably not my place to ask, but I will anyway. Are you okay, Mr Sandos?'

Sandos looked over Cyril's shoulder at the door and then directly into Cyril's eyes. 'About this deal. Are you sure the buyer will pay up? There won't be any funny business, will there?'

Cyril protruded his bottom lip. 'Carlo, I did say that this is all new to me, yeah? I've never sold a purple heart let alone kilos of cocaine, but the geezer does buy and sell drugs. He's a bit of a face, if you know what I mean.'

Sandos inclined his head in confusion.

'Oh, yeah, a "face" means a proper gangster. But don't worry. I don't think he'll do you over.'

Sandos put his hand to his chest. 'Me?'

Cyril was hoping that Sandos would take over the deal, but he guessed from that gesture that it wasn't going to happen. 'Okay, Carlo, I'll do the drop-off.' He sighed. 'Any chance I could take two of your big geezers with me?'

Sandos frowned. 'But I thought you said you had a deal? Why would you need two of my men? It should be straightforward unless you have any doubts about this buyer.'

Cyril grinned. 'Oh, come on, mate. Every deal will be a worry when that amount of money and drugs are involved, but then, I don't think I need to tell you, that, do I?'

From the angst on Sandos' face, Cyril realised that as much as the Colombian had plenty of bodyguards at his disposal, there was something on his mind, and he could only assume it was further up the food chain.

'Okay, then. Carlo, listen. Me and you, we are both young, and you can be honest with me. I bet you have the cartel breathing down your neck, and after the last bloke fucked up, you can't afford to mess up again, can ya?'

Sandos remained silent. He just stared at Cyril with eyes that saw nothing.

It was at that point Cyril knew that Sandos wanted to talk, but he had a reputation to uphold, and spilling his guts over his worries wouldn't sit right if he spoke about them with a young lad from Bermondsey.

'I get it, mate. I do, honestly, and I will do me best to help ya. I know London, I know people, and I know how it works. Lend me two of your men. I have me own as well, and I'll make the drop-off, and I will bring you back your money personally.'

'I like you, Cyril, and I do think you understand.' He poured himself a large brandy, swallowed it back, and then gritted his teeth. 'My father has high expectations. He put me in this position, and I was grateful. But you have, should I say, an uncanny knack, for hitting the nail on the head. Yes, with those drugs going missing, they have made the cartel question my position. This may make me sound weak, but, Cyril, I am not weak. It is not my safety or my life that concerns me. You see, if I mess up in this country, then it is my little brother who they will hurt.'

'Oh shit, mate. Now I get it, and I understand because I have a little brother as well, and he got hurt recently, and, well, I nearly killed the bloke who hurt him.'

'Really?'

Cyril nodded. 'Yeah, I fucking wished I had killed him as well. No one hurts my family and gets away with it.'

Sandos gave Cyril a smile that lifted his cheeks and showed his brilliant white teeth. 'You can take my men, then. I think we understand each other. But!' He held his hand up. 'Do *not* tell anyone of our conversation.' He lowered his voice. 'Those men – as much as they take orders from me – they will easily let their tongues wag, if they think I am weak. It's like the sick lion and the pride circling.'

'You have my word, Carlo. I won't let you down.'

'And, Cyril, I do believe that you won't.'

Getting up to shake Sandos' hand, Cyril was surprised when the young man rose and hugged him instead.

* * *

The arrangements were made for the drop-off twenty-four hours later on the Friday morning. There was no lock-up or secret place; Cyril agreed to do the deal in the upstairs office of Larry McKendrick's pub.

The two Colombians waited outside the pub. Frank, Blakey, and Marcus stood at the bar, and Cyril carried the suitcase with the drugs inside up the stairs and into McKendrick's office. As soon as he stepped inside, he was surprised to find McKendrick alone, and his gun wasn't on the table this time. Cyril smiled and nodded at the man.

'I love men that are on time and don't mess me about. I fucking hate messers. So you have the goods, I see.'

Cyril placed the suitcase on the desk. 'Everything's there.'

McKendrick opened it and gazed at the bags of white

powder. He then pulled a knife from his drawer, sliced open one of the bags, and used the same knife to scoop a small helping and snort it.

Cyril stared but didn't move.

'Good!'

McKendrick slammed the suitcase shut. Then, pushing his chair back, he got on the floor and grubbed about under his desk until he found what he was looking for. Dragging out a travel bag, he slid it towards Cyril. 'In there, they're all used notes. Check everything. You can count them all, if you like.'

Cyril unzipped the bag. He could see the bundles of used notes and quickly zipped the bag up.

'I'll take your word for it, as I am sure, mate, you'll be back for more.'

McKendrick clasped his hands together and grinned. He pointed over to the far right-hand corner of the room where there was a CCTV monitor showing Sandos' goons standing outside the pub. 'Those two men outside, they don't look Russian or Italian, so I can guess, Mr Reardon, that you are working for the Colombians.'

Cyril tapped the side of his nose. 'All you need to know is that you deal with me. The business is between us.'

McKendrick raised his brow and nodded very slowly. 'That's fine by me. You bring me top-grade powder, and I'll bring the readies.' He then stood up to shake the youngster's hand.

* * *

As soon as they were outside, one of the Colombians opened the Jag's door for Cyril to climb in.

But something made Cyril stop. 'No, I will go in that car.' He pointed to Frank's.

The bigger of the two Colombians grabbed Cyril by the collar, on the point of forcing him inside the car, but Frank and Marcus were onto him in a flash, pulling the Colombian away.

'You must come with us,' said the bigger Colombian, shaking Frank and Marcus off.

Cyril shook his head. 'You can follow me there, but your job is done, as far as I'm concerned. You big fucking oafs are here to protect me, not to protect our money. That was not the deal. Ask your boss!'

Giving Cyril an evil glare, the smaller Colombian flicked his head to the other one to get in the car.

As soon as Cyril's men were all back in Frank's car, Cyril wiped his brow. 'Fucking hell, I was shitting a brick just then.'

'I thought they were going to kidnap you. What was all that about, Cyril?' asked Frank.

'I don't know, but one thing I do know is I'm bloody glad you lot were there.' He shoved the bag of money in the footwell and leaned back in the seat. 'It was odd because it was as if the big geezer wanted to drag me inside the car, but the other fella looked nervous and uneasy about it all.'

'The only reason for that is the big prick was going to nick the money,' said Freddy.

Cyril shook his head. 'No. They know what happens if they fuck Carlo Sandos off. They end up taking a parachute jump without the parachute.'

'I'm coming with you when you face this Sandos fella again,' said Frank, concerned that the Colombian might end his mate's life, and he wasn't having any of it.

'He did say the business was just between me and him, though.'

'Yeah, but he didn't say his fucking lackeys could manhandle you, did he?'

Cyril nodded. 'True, true.'

* * *

As they pulled into the underground car park in the tall building, Frank parked next to the Colombians' flash Jag. 'Cor, one day, I'll be driving around in one of those.'

'Not long now, Frank. You'll see.'

Freddy and Marcus got out and waited by the car. Cyril and Frank both gave the Colombians a look that implied 'Don't mess with us.' The bigger Colombian huffed loudly and slapped his hand on the lift button.

Cyril gripped the heavy bag and waited. It was awkward. With all four men inside the lift, their arms touching, and with tensions still running high, the journey up seemed to take forever. Finally, the lift stopped, and the bigger of the two Colombians pulled open the inner cage door and then the outer door. Soon, they were inside Sandos' office.

Frank hadn't seen the place, so he stealthily gazed around, until his eyes clocked Sandos. He, like Cyril had been, was surprised that the man was so young and strikingly handsome, unlike his bodyguards, who were like monsters.

'So it all went well then, Cyril? No hiccups, and you checked the notes were used?'

Cyril placed the bag on the desk and shook Carlo's hand. 'All there, all good.' Slowly, he turned to face the two bodyguards and pointed a finger. 'Except for him. That great pillock wanted to drag me into his motor, and if it wasn't for me own mate' – he flicked his head to Frank – 'then I don't know what I would have done. It took Frank and me other pal, Marcus, to drag this prick off me. So what was that all about, Carlo? I mean, I did exactly as you asked. I set up the deal and executed it to perfection. Now you have a new buyer, *but*, I get treated like *that*?'

Sandos' eyes narrowed, and his face seemed to darken. Slowly, he turned towards the Colombian. 'Why, Johan?'

The Colombian appeared to shrivel up; his face lost its colour, and he looked terrified. 'Boss, I didn't trust him. I thought he may run off with the money. I wanted to make sure that he returned the money. He cannot be trusted.'

'You had no right to treat Mr Reardon in this way. I make the decisions, not you.' His voice and tone were heavy and deep, with an undercurrent of evil.

Cyril realised that Sandos may be a youngster, but he was like a general.

Johan held up his hand. 'I am sorry, Boss, very sorry. It won't happen again. I was just protecting you, as your uncle asked me to.'

The subtext of that remark was not lost on Sandos. Banging his fist on the desk, he shouted, 'And he also told you that you work for me now, not him.'

Unexpectedly, Johan looked at Cyril. 'I am very sorry if I have insulted you.'

Sandos glared. 'If Cyril accepts your apology then you live. If he doesn't, you die.'

'Whoa, whoa, whoa. No one needs to die. Shit! I accept his apology, but he owes me one.'

Sandos burst out laughing. He walked around the desk and hugged Cyril as he continued to laugh. 'Get my friend' – he turned to Johan – 'his Pepsi or Cola or whatever. And you' – he pointed to Frank – 'would you like a real man's drink with me?'

'Nah, mate, I'll have a Pepsi. We don't drink on any job do we, Mr Reardon?'

Cyril felt in charge and smiled. 'No, Frank, we don't drink on the job. None of my men drink on the job, do they, Frank?'

Frank knew what Cyril was up to and played along. 'No, Mr Reardon, none of us do.'

Fifteen minutes later, after some general chit-chat, which gave Sandos an opportunity to learn more about Cyril's business ideas, Sandos raised his brow and then smiled. 'Gentlemen, would you please leave us. Cyril and I have personal business to discuss.'

Frank glanced at Cyril, who nodded in response.

The minute Sandos' thugs and Frank left the room, Sandos laughed again, as he returned to his seat behind his desk. 'I don't know what it is about you, Cyril, but I think you have more than just charm.'

Cyril sipped the Pepsi-Cola that had been placed in front of him. 'I am only too pleased to have paid back in kind what I owed. I can now leave on good terms.'

Sandos' face dropped instantly. 'But I have an offer for you.'

Cyril got up and shook his head. 'Oh, no, no. I'm okay, thank you very much. We had a deal, and I kept up my end of the bargain, and I believe you are a man of your word, so you will keep yours.'

Sandos hurried around from his desk and gripped Cyril's arm. 'Wait, please, Cyril. Let's talk. You are right. I *am* a man of my word. But I have an offer, an excellent offer. Please, grace me with your presence to hear what I have to say.'

Sensing Sandos seemed genuine, Cyril sat down again. 'Fire away.'

Sandos turned to a landscape painting behind him on the wall. Pulling the right-hand side of the frame towards him, he entered the code to open a large safe, whose interior revealed bundles of notes. Sandos took three of these from the safe and slapped them on the desk. 'These, Cyril, are yours.'

Cyril's eyes widened, but he was conscious he shouldn't come across as too eager or excited.

'I need a business partner, and, to be honest, there are not many people I trust, but, for some reason, I do trust you. I have a product to sell, but I don't have many buyers.' He walked over to the window and stared across at the London landscape. 'There must be thousands of buyers out there, but, Cyril, I want the big dealers who, and I mean who, can be trusted. For every buyer you bring my way, there will be a package for you the size of this one.'

Cyril stared at all the money and felt his excitement climbing. 'Let me get this straight. I find you trustworthy buyers, I don't have to get my hands dirty, and you will give me a cut. Is that right?'

Sandos returned to his seat and nodded. 'Not just a cut. A big cut.'

'I don't want to work *for* you, Carlo, but I will work *with* you.'

Unexpectedly, Sandos leaped from his seat and hugged his new-found friend. 'Thank you, my friend, thank you.'

Cyril left the office with three giant bundles of money and a huge smile on his face. He was in business, and nothing was going to stand in his way now.

CHAPTER SEVENTEEN

Frank was waiting outside the room for Cyril, and as soon as he clocked the elation on Cyril's face, he knew that whatever had gone on in there was good news. They casually left the building and climbed into the car.

Cyril then pulled the bundles of money from inside his jacket. The second Frank was out of the car park and down the road, Cyril threw the money up in the air. It hit the headlining and scattered everywhere.

'What the hell is all this?' screeched Marcus.

Frank was trying to concentrate on his driving, but the notes had landed everywhere.

'We, gentlemen, are gonna be fucking raking it in. Go to the lock-up, Frank, so that we can share this up.'

'What? Is some of this coming our way, Cyril?' asked Freddy.

'This, my friend, is money that I owe you guys. You put your neck on the line, and so fair's fair. We split it four ways.'

Freddy and Marcus were grinning like Cheshire cats as they stared at the money. Neither of them had seen that much in all their lives.

'Now, lads, there's more where that came from. But, guys, it's a risky business. But, fuck me, we'll be loaded. Now, I've plans to make and scores to settle.'

'Scores to settle?' enquired Frank.

'Yep. That poxy Johnnie Carter ain't getting away with picking a fight with me in the street over his so-called bloody manor.'

* * *

The afternoon was spent counting the money and making plans. The excitement between the four of them had raised their confidence. The dynamics were established, and the set-up was perfect.

Frank had his stack tucked in his pocket and was off to take Trudy out for a meal. He dropped Cyril off at the foot of the tower block and then drove off.

Cyril was just glad to be back home so he could take his suit off. He was sure the sweat marks on his shirt would stand out. It had been a day of nerves, but the afternoon had finished with a smile.

As Cyril slid the key in the lock and turned the handle, he thought for a moment he heard a man's voice. But the walls were thin, and the old fella next door could be very loud, especially when he was hammered. Cyril didn't slam the door but quietly closed it and crept to his room. He didn't want to worry his mother by carrying bundles of cash or have her asking questions that, really, he couldn't answer without lying.

Then he heard the voice again, and it sounded as though it was actually coming from the kitchen. As he strained his ears, he thought he recognised who it was, yet it appeared as though the words were spat out through gritted teeth in a low mumble. Then he heard the anxious tone in his mother's voice.

'I swear to God, I don't have any more money. You took my last bloody shilling last week. I gave you everything you wanted. Now, leave me alone.'

'You, Peggy Reardon, tell lies, and we both know that, don't we? The dead landlord? That was you, and considering the past, I have no doubt about it. None at all.'

Cyril felt his throat tighten. He wanted to charge in and give whoever was talking to his mother a good bashing. However, something told him to stay put and just listen. If he heard his mother scream, he would run in. Then he had another thought; the gun was still behind the panel. Quickly, he grabbed the knife he kept under his pillow. Quietly, he prised the panel away from the bottom of the wardrobe, and then he retrieved the gun.

He could hear the man pacing the kitchen floor.

'I didn't kill the bloody landlord, and I had an alibi for that. Anyway, I had a good reason for what happened in the past, as well you know.'

'You were hauled in for the murdered landlord, though, weren't you? And it wouldn't have been the first time, would it? I bet the police don't know about your past back in Ireland, do they? Now, if you want it to stay that way, then you hand over the money. And don't you fucking lie to me again that you ain't got any. I know where you get yours. Your family are fucking loaded. Look at Cyril walking about in his flash suit. But I know he don't have a job, so where's he getting the money from, eh?'

'I had a few lucky games of poker, and I shared the money with him and Howie, so there ain't none. Now, leave me alone.'

'I'll leave you alone when I'm good and ready. You are me wife, after all, so who's gonna say anything to me? What goes on between man and wife stays between man and wife.'

'Get your fucking hands off me, you drunken bastard.'

That was all Cyril needed to hear to have him flying into the kitchen wielding a gun. 'Get away from my muvver!' he bellowed.

Cyril could see that Reginald Reardon was shocked to the core by his entrance. The man nearly jumped out of his skin. It was clear to Cyril that his father had aged more than his mother had. He was clean-shaven, but his hair needed a wash, and his teeth were rotten. He was a stranger and a memory that had faded so much over the years that he wondered if he'd only ever imagined having a father. He couldn't remember what exactly he looked like or even anything about his personality. But he still recalled his father shouting a lot and his mother crying when he had left them. He glared with spite.

'I said, get the fuck away from my muvver!'

Reginald let go of Peggy and stared his son up and down.

'I thought you'd be pleased to see me, Cyril. I'm your ol'

man, after all.'

'Well, you're mistaken,' spat Cyril, glaring at him, with a face like thunder.

Looking at the weapon in Cyril's hand, Reginald felt a little nervous. He really hadn't expected his eldest son to turn against him so much. He assumed that Cyril would be overjoyed to see him and welcome him with open arms.

He lashed back. 'A gun, is it, Cyril? You're holding a fucking shooter up at your farver's face? Is that right?'

Cyril was livid that his father was so cocky and yet nasty with it. He aimed the gun and tilted his head. '*Farver*? That's what you call yaself, is it? You ain't my farver. You mean fuck all to me.' He glanced at his mum to see if she was okay. 'And you mean fuck all to my mum. Now, unless you want a bullet put through that face of yours, you'd better get out. And don't you ever come back threatening and fucking blackmailing my mum, you low-life piece of dog shit!'

Reginald's arms were by his side, his shoulders stooped, but then he suddenly threw his head back and gave a fake laugh. 'Do you think you're some kinda gangster? Is that it, Cyril? The only thing different about you is that you ain't so scrawny now.'

Cyril didn't give him the courtesy of a response.

'Look at you, in your flash shoes and your gun. You'll be in prison soon enough.' He waved his hand at Peggy. 'Like she should have been. Well, I suppose you take after her side of the family, then.'

Cyril smirked. 'I guess I fucking do because I will never turn out like you. I will take care of my responsibilities, if I ever have any. I won't abandon my family like you abandoned your wife and two sons.'

'*Two*?'

Cyril frowned; he didn't quite follow what his father was implying. He glanced at his mother, who had her hands to her mouth.

'Well, if I ain't your boy, then that's one less thing to worry about, now, ain't it, *Reginald*? You thought you could hurt me that way. Wrong!'

The cocky grin and the mocking brow told Cyril there was more to this. 'Oh, Cyril, I ain't talking about *you*.'

'Shut up, Reginald, and leave! For Christ's sake, just leave it alone, will you!' screamed Peggy.

But Reginald was drunk, and he didn't care. 'They have a right to know.'

'No! Please, Reg, stop it!'

That was enough for Cyril. 'Get the fuck out of this flat, now. I don't care what you have to say. You ain't gonna upset my mum, you stinking rat. Now, fuck off.'

Reginald stared at Cyril as if he'd never seen him before, and at that moment, he knew that Cyril was going to be a handful. But the image of his son riled him up. In fact, he was jealous. Looking at this boy, with his boyish face and smart suit, but, most striking of all, the confidence in which he held himself, made Reginald feel depressed.

He should have worn that suit and that stance himself, not be standing here in a kitchen that wasn't even his, wearing a second-hand pair of trousers and shoes with holes in, while his son held a gun to his head. This wasn't how it was supposed to be.

He'd come back from Ireland when his fancy piece had thrown him out. He still thought he had the charm and the looks, but, clearly, he hadn't peered in the mirror lately because if he had, he would have seen that he was like a shadow of his former self.

'All right, I'll leave. But know this. That slut of a muvver of yours—'

He didn't get a chance to finish. Cyril swiped him hard across the mouth with his gun.

Reginald fell back but grabbed the work surface to stop himself from hitting the floor. Once he'd straightened up, he wiped his hand across his mouth, looked at the blood, and then at Cyril.

'You ever call my mum a slut again, and I'll throw you off this tower block, and they'll need a snow shovel to scrape you up.'

Reginald pushed himself away from the worktop and stormed towards the front door, but, just before he left, he shouted back like a child. 'Know this, Cyril. Howie ain't your bother.'

Peggy quickly grabbed Cyril's arm before he fired the gun.

The door slammed shut. Peggy let go of her son, lowered her head, and sobbed.

Cyril placed the gun on the table and an arm around her shoulders. 'He is my brother, Mum. I couldn't give a flying shit what that stinking, rotten bastard says. It's me, you, and Howie against the world, Mum.'

She sniffed and blew her nose on her apron. 'Oh my God, why would he do that to me? I never ever did him any wrong, never.'

'Well, let's hope he won't come back because I don't know if I can stop meself from shooting the bastard. Anyway, sit down, Mum. You've had a shock. I'll make us a cup of tea.'

Peggy sat and blew her nose once more. 'I . . . I.' She sighed.

'Mum, I don't care what me dad said. Howie's my brother. You don't have to say any more, not to me.'

'I think I owe it to you before that bastard comes back and tries to cause more problems.'

'You owe me nuffin, Mum. And as for him, if he comes back, I *will* kill him. Did he hurt you, Mum?'

'No, only with his spiteful tongue.'

Cyril got up to make the tea.

'It's true about Howie, bless his little heart. Well, he ain't your full brother.'

Cyril had his back to Peggy as he poured the hot water into the teapot. His heart ached not for the fact Howie was not his full blood brother but because his father had used this against her to blackmail her. It was true he didn't care that Howie was only his half-brother. As far as he was concerned, Howie was his only brother.

Cyril placed the teapot, the milk jug, and the cups on the table and then took his seat.

Peggy poured herself a cup, but her hands shook so much, she struggled to hold the cup high enough to take a sip.

'Why has he come back after all this time?' asked Cyril.

Stalling her answer, Peggy finally managed to sip her tea.

'Mum?'

'Okay, Cyril. Look, he needs money, and he has something over me that could have me locked up for a long time. He's threatened to share it with the police if I don't pay him off.'

'What does he have over you?'

She placed her cup on the saucer. 'I killed someone.'

Totally shocked by her response, Cyril could only stare at her in amazement. He just couldn't imagine his mother as a murderer. But then his mind went back to the fight with the Deacons, and the image of his mother hammering her stiletto heel into that bloke's head.

'But it was self-defence, surely?'

Slowly, she shook her head. 'No, well not directly. He was

your farver's friend, back in Ireland. I was alone at home. You were a baby, barely five months old. Your farver was out with . . .' She paused and stared into nothing. 'Well, I don't know who your farver was with. Anyway, your farver's friend was called Felix. He was really creepy, but a bold kind of lad. He was always ogling me, and I hated him. Your farver liked him, and when I told him that he was undressing me with his eyes, he said I imagined it, and I was not to encourage him. But I wasn't leading him on at all. I couldn't stand him.'

Cyril reached across and grabbed his mother's hand. 'I don't need to know any more, Mum. You don't have to say anything else.'

'Yeah, I think you should know what happened because I don't want you to think I'm a cold-blooded killer, and if your farver does shoot his mouth off to the police, then, at least, you would have heard the truth from me.'

Cyril nodded. 'Okay, Mum.'

'So your farver was out, and I was in my nightgown. You were in your cot that me dad had made for you.' She paused and swallowed hard to stop the tears. 'To cut a long story short, he overpowered me, and I couldn't stop him. All I kept thinking was that Reg would never believe me. He would think I led him on, because the fact was, your farver thought more of his mate than me. I was a fool to have fallen in love with such a deadbeat like Reginald.'

'So, it *was* self-defence, then?'

Peggy shook her head. 'No, wait. I didn't kill him then. It was three months later when I found I was expecting Howie and your farver was off up the pub to celebrate. That's when Felix came back to the house. He was drunk and laughing at me. He said the baby I was carrying was probably his, and he would tell Reg that I came on to him and that I was secretly in love with him, and if the baby had dark hair, then it would prove it was his.' She stopped to catch her breath.

'I had the iron in my hand. I remember I had just pulled it out of the fire, ready to iron your farver's shirt, when something inside me just exploded. One minute, I was feeling angry, and then the next, Felix was on the floor with his head caved in. I stood there frozen, thinking what the hell have I done. The blood was still dripping off the iron, and the smell of the burning blood was awful.'

'Oh, Mum, you must have been terrified. What a bastard.'

She sighed heavily. 'I was still staring at his face all smashed up and grotesque, when my dad came in through the back door with a sack of potatoes. I remember he dropped it, and the sack split, and one potato rolled across the floor and right through the pool of blood. It's funny what sticks in your mind.'

Cyril was on the edge of his seat listening to his mother. 'So how did you explain what had happened?'

'My dad didn't ask why or how or anything. He took the iron from me and sat me down. Then I remember him saying "I best get this mess cleaned up." And I thought, shit, yeah, it will ruin me best rug. I must've really hated that Felix, bloke, eh?'

Cyril was so shocked, all he could do was nod.

'Reginald walked in through the front door, just as my dad wrapped Felix up in a hessian sack. My farver went mad and said that Reginald had been warned about Felix and now he had to keep his mouth shut.'

'What happened then, Mum?'

Peggy took another sip of her tea. 'My dad took the body away and buried Felix somewhere. But I dunno where. Reginald was afraid of me dad. So all the time my dad was alive, I guess Reg went along with it. But it's different now. My dad, Gawd rest his soul, is no threat to Reginald, so now the bastard wants money to keep his mouth shut.'

Cyril gulped back his tea to loosen his tongue from the roof of his mouth. He was staggered beyond belief. But it certainly wasn't because this barrage of shocking information had dented his perfect picture of his mum. Far from it, in fact. It wasn't a case of seeing her as less than perfect. Rather, it had opened his eyes to the idea that his mother was a warrior – a woman who stood no nonsense and took no shit. Yet, what he couldn't come to terms with was why she was so afraid of his dad.

'Leave him to me, Mum. I'll deal with him. You don't still love him, though, do you?'

Staring at nothing, with her elbows on the table and holding the teacup to her chin, she said, 'No . . . I thought I did, though. I even waited and hoped every day for years, even beyond the time that I knew he wouldn't come back, that he would return. I fell in love with a young man who was, dare I say it, handsome. He was kind and sweet, so I thought. I guess the truth is, he was a user. He dated me because I was young, and I was my farver's daughter. He looked up to me dad, you see. Anyway, I loved him so much that I couldn't really see what was going on. I made excuses for his drinking and for his wandering eye. Not now, though. Now, it's different because now I realise that my boys grew up without a farver, without all the things they should have had. You and Howie went without far too much, and it was his fault. So to answer your question, Cyril, no, I don't still love him. Not a bit of it. I hate the man. He is a stranger to me. Do you hate him, Cyril?'

Cyril shrugged his shoulders. 'I never knew him, did I? All I knew was the aftermath. We couldn't go to the butcher's or the grocer's because that bastard owed money to everyone.'

Peggy felt tears well up in her eyes again as she glanced at the gun. 'It's all his fault, you know.'

Cyril followed her eyeline and frowned when he realised she was referring to the weapon on the table.

'If he hadn't buggered off and had found work here, then you would never have felt the need to do all the things you did and are still doing. You would probably be at university now, learning to be a solicitor, no doubt.'

A sudden chuckle left Cyril's mouth. 'Nah, Mum, that was never gonna 'appen. I told you I'm gonna be a lord in me own castle one day. You watch me.'

'Go and put that thing somewhere safe, in case your farver decides to call the Ol' Bill.'

Cyril nodded. Just as he got up to leave the kitchen, he spun around. 'Mum, how did he know where we live?'

She sighed again. 'You know when I went to the tea dance, in the lovely dress you got me? Well, he must have seen me there. I didn't see him, though, the sly bastard. I guess he saw the expensive dress and shoes and decided to follow me to see where we lived, and since then, he's spent time spying on me and you. I have already given him money to stay away, but he's come back for more. But I don't have any more to give him, and I don't want you to give him any because he'll always be coming back here for my money. It will be never-ending.'

'No, he flaming well won't. I'll make sure of it. Do you know where he's staying?'

Peggy moved the wisps of hair from her face and shook her head. 'No, I don't, but I do know he's following us. He knew when I last had a win on the poker.'

Cyril ground his back teeth in anger. 'I'll make sure he doesn't follow you again, Mum.'

'What are you gonna do, Cyril? I don't want you to get into any trouble.'

'Mum, leave it all to me, and don't worry.'

* * *

It was early evening when Cyril knocked at Mr Bates' door in the usual way with a bundle of notes tucked in his jacket.

Mr Bates answered the door and flicked his head as usual for Cyril to come in.

'So, what brings you here? I am guessing it all went well

with the Colombian?'

'Oh, that? Yeah, yeah, that went like a dream, but that's not why I'm here.'

Mr Bates frowned. 'Oh, really? What's the problem?'

Cyril pulled the money from his jacket and slapped it on the coffee table. 'I need someone taken care of.'

Mr Bates looked at the money and then at Cyril. 'Please don't tell me you want the Colombian . . .'

'No! Christ, no. It's me farver I want sorting out.'

Mr Bates stiffened. 'Reginald Reardon? Why?'

'Because he has come back to the area after all these bleedin' years, and he's now making me mum's life a nightmare.'

Mr Bates scrutinised Cyril's expression. 'Yeah, son, I can have him taken away, but only if you tell me the truth. I know your muvver well enough to know that someone like your farver wouldn't be a serious problem for a woman like her.'

'He's a pest, following her and me, and getting nosy . . .' He stopped when he saw Mr Bates shake his head. 'What?'

'He's blackmailing her, isn't he?'

Feeling in an uncomfortable predicament, Cyril realised he either came clean or pressed Mr Bates for what he knew.

'Why would you say that?'

Mr Bates went over to his favourite chair by the window and chuckled. 'I know more about your family's past than you do, son.'

'So, what would me farver blackmail her with?'

'Ah, I see your game, Cyril. Clever thinking, lad. Something happened when you were a baby. Let's just say it was a situation that should have been left dead and buried. But if it's what I think it is, then, yeah, I'll have a word with Reginald.'

'No!' blurted out Cyril. 'Sorry, I don't mean have a *word* with him. I want him got rid of. Permanently!'

Mr Bates looked at the money and shook his head.

Which riled up Cyril. He snatched up the notes. 'I'll find someone else, then.'

'Oi, stop having a strop like a child. I shook my head because I don't need the money.'

'Oh, er . . . sorry, Mr Bates. I'm just so fucking angry right now.'

'See, now that's another thing you need to work on, lad, your temper and impatience. Crikey, how the fuck you are gonna make any money, Gawd only knows. You'll make more enemies than mates.'

Cyril gave him a smug grin and sat down. 'My dad's a nasty piece of work. I've already smacked him one in the face. I really wanted to shoot him. Instead, I managed to catch him with the butt of me . . .'

He stopped when he realised what he'd said.

'A gun, eh?'

'Yeah. I found it when I found the drugs.'

'Don't ever keep that weapon in the house. If that gun is associated with previous murders, you'll get done for the lot.'

Cyril hadn't thought of that. He realised then he still had a lot to learn.

'Bring the gun to me, and I'll make sure he is seen to. But, Cyril, tell me, are you sure you want to do this? He *is* your farver.'

'Is he? The only thing that makes him my farver is the blood in my veins, but, other than that, he isn't a farver to me. And that's the only reason I didn't kill him, because, trust me, Mr Bates, if it had been any other man, then I wouldn't have hesitated. I would have knifed him right through the heart and laughed while I did it. But I'll tell ya this. If he comes back and upsets me mum, I won't give him another chance. I *will* kill him.'

CHAPTER EIGHTEEN

Every time Cyril met the lads at the lock-up, he would bring something to make the place more comfortable, and it became a regular occurrence. Frank even brought over an old but clean sofa. Cyril had a high-backed padded seat, which made him appear taller than the others, and Marcus brought a crate of Pepsi and a few beers.

They planned to sustain their money pot, and so the first thing was to make enquiries as to what the Carters were up to because word had it that Johnnie Carter was seen in the Cedar Arms with Red Deacon. And before Red's battering, Johnnie Carter and the Deacons were arch-enemies.

Frank chuckled. 'It seems to me, Cyril, that you pose a real threat to the likes of the Carters.'

Cyril put his feet up on the table and leaned back on the chair. 'Well, best I make sure Johnnie Carter knows I am. I mean, who the fuck do they think they are? Their turf! What a load of bollocks.'

'I heard that the landlord of the Red Lion pays Johnnie protection money,' said Frank.

Cyril grinned. 'Oh, really?'

‘So does the Queens Head and the Olive Tree,’ said Marcus, joining in.

Frank stared at Cyril. ‘Come on. What are you thinking?’

Cyril removed his feet from off the table and sat upright. ‘Freddy, do us a favour? Can you check that out? I wanna be a hundred per cent sure that’s the case before I go traipsing through there like a bull in a china shop.’

‘I get it. You wanna show that the Carters can’t protect the pubs, and so why are the landlords paying for protection?’ said Freddy, highly pleased with himself.

Cyril clapped. ‘Cor, Freddy, you ain’t slow, are ya?’

‘Fuck off,’ said Freddy, laughing.

‘Your brothers will know for sure, won’t they?’

Freddy nodded and jumped up from his chair. ‘Keith’s in, I think. I’ll have a word. Oh, yeah, by the way, me little sister has only got engaged to some toff. He’s a right knob he is, an’ all. He’s in the Army or the Navy. I dunno. Anyway, they’re having a big do up West London way. Me mum’s told me to invite you. It’s next month.’

‘Can I bring my Flossie and can Frank bring Trudy?’

Freddy suddenly blushed. ‘Yeah. I’m taking my girlfriend. And Marcus is with Tilly, so, yeah, I don’t see why not.’

Cyril smiled. ‘A girlfriend, eh, Freddy? You kept that quiet.’

It wasn’t surprising since Freddy was the best looking out

of the Blake family. He had a fashionable face much like Paul Newman, with his bright blue eyes and blond locks.

Freddy blushed again. 'We've only been courting for a month.'

Before the lads had a chance to tease him further, Freddy hurried out of the lock-up. There was a phone box a quarter of a mile away, so he made a call to his brother there.

They didn't have to wait long before he returned with the information confirming that the protection racket was true.

'Right, lads. First things first, I wanna stop that little con dead in its tracks.'

Frank chewed his lip and then sighed. 'Listen, Cyril. Are you sure about this, mate? I mean, the Carters are a big family of nutters.'

Cyril shrugged. 'I bet half of them are living off their uncle's name. And, let's be honest. You, Frank, on your own, could do that. Everyone knows your farver was a nutjob, and what about you, Freddy? You have a tribe at home all with criminal records. If your family clubbed together, they could take down half of London.'

'And what about you, Cyril?' asked Marcus.

'Me?' He laughed. 'Me, I have two fists, a hard head, and a fucking cocky attitude. And I ain't too bad looking either.'

The three lads laughed as they always did at Cyril's quips.

* * *

By 9.00 p.m., the Red Lion was packed to the rafters. Cyril walked through the crowd, with Marcus, Frank, and Freddy behind him.

As the landlord turned to face them, his expression changed. There among the youngsters having fun walked a young man with a confident swagger and a crafty expression on his face. Behind him were big, burly men ready for business, not there, obviously, to dance to 'Rock Around the Clock'.

'I take it you're the landlord?' enquired Cyril, as he stared unblinkingly at the man behind the bar.

The landlord noticed the man was putting on a pair of black leather gloves. 'Er, yeah. Why?'

'I wanna word with your security.'

Rufus Ruggle was a bony-framed man with deep-set eyes and a nervous twitch. He had taken over the pub from his father and hated every bit of it. His father, a domineering man, occupied the flat upstairs, and so Rufus couldn't just get out of the business; he had to bide his time. He didn't like the responsibility or the violence, which often occurred on a Saturday from a few of the local punters once they'd downed their six or seven pints.

Ruggle shot his eyes to the right to two men sitting at a table sipping beers.

Cyril wanted to laugh, but, instead, he nodded politely and made his way over to the two men.

The lads followed and surrounded the table. It took a few

seconds for the two seated men to work out that they were somewhat fenced in because the pub was so busy.

'Call yaself protection, yeah?' hissed Cyril, in the bald man's ear.

Suddenly the man jumped up and faced Cyril. He was bigger than Cyril had first anticipated, but not as big as Frank or Marcus. The other man who was seated also jumped up, but he was roughly the same size as Cyril.

'You'd best hop it,' said Cyril, flexing his fingers in the tight-fitting black leather gloves.

'What the fuck is this? You stupid kid. Leave, before I throw you out,' growled the bald man.

Cyril nodded. 'Is that right, *Mr Baldy*, 'cos I don't think you have the muscle behind your threat. Me, I have three men that will buckle you and your gormless pal there. So, like I said: hop it, and you can tell your boss that his silly protection racket is over. Me, I run this pub now. Got it?'

The bald man looked at the three men, and even though he and his mate were outnumbered, and they could easily receive a beating, he reckoned he had the experience, so he wasn't going to bow down to a bunch of kids. Silently, he narrowed his hooded eyes and squared up to Cyril. In a fast movement, he pulled his fist back and punched Cyril clean in the face.

Cyril didn't see the blow coming. The punch was hard and fast and knocked him over, and as he tried to get to his feet, he was booted in the ribs.

The other guy, who had been seated, now had the guts to

join in; he threw a punch that hit Marcus on the chin.

However, Marcus, unlike Cyril, didn't flinch. Instead, he returned a punch and sent the man somersaulting backwards over the chair and through the bay window.

The bald guy glanced to his side to see the devastation and held up his fists, ready to take them all on. But it was Frank who took on the challenge, and although he was clumped in the side of the face, he didn't go down and instantly landed a right hook that had the man wobbling. Two more quick jabs and his attacker was down.

Cyril was up and fingering his jaw when he noticed Frank pull out his knife. But Cyril was too late to intervene.

Frank ran the blade down the man's face. 'Now, you were told to hop it. So fucking hop it.'

When the punters saw blood, one woman screamed and a group of men slipped out. This fight wasn't a street brawl or a scuffle; this was business.

The bald guy got up, held his cheek, and glared at Frank. 'You fucking cockroach.'

Cyril was now steady on his feet, and so was the bald guy. They stared at each other until Cyril spoke. 'Go back and tell your boss that he has no protection racket anymore, and if he wants to argue the point, then he'll get the same treatment.'

The bald man narrowed his eyes. Still clutching his face, as the blood dripped between his fingers, he said, 'And who shall I say you are?'

'Cyril Reardon.'

The bald man had heard that name in connection with the battering that Johnnie Carter had received a while ago. He nodded and looked out of the broken window to see his pal limping away. He shook his head. 'I'll tell him.'

Cyril nodded. 'Good man. Oh, and I take it every other pub in this neck of the woods has two men like you sitting there in Johnnie Carter's name?'

'Not all of the pubs. Only the busy ones.' He pulled his hand away from his face and tried to wiggle his tight jaw. He guessed that not only had the big guy scarred his face, but he'd broken his jaw as well. 'It looks like I'll need a new boss, 'cos I can guess you and your men will be taking over.'

'Yep.'

He waited for an offer, but Cyril just stared him down and then nodded for him to leave.

Once everyone had left the pub, Cyril approached the bar, only to find the landlord as white as a ghost.

'So, Mr . . . ?'

'Ruggle. Rufus Ruggle.'

Frank sniggered, and Cyril elbowed him to stop laughing.

'Mr Ruggle, it appears that your protection need protection themselves, wouldn't you say?'

Ruggle, who was scared to death, nodded.

'Great, so I don't charge a lot. Tell me, how much did you pay the Carters?'

'Forty per cent of the night's takings.'

'What!' screeched Cyril.

'No, seriously, I swear, it is forty per cent. I really couldn't keep this pub open if I had to pay more than that. I am struggling as it is.'

Cyril wanted to laugh, but he held it in. He had no idea that protection rackets could rake in so much money. He wanted to test the water. 'So how much have you taken tonight?'

Ruggle nervously looked at the men. 'I haven't had a chance to count it out. Er, I can do it now, Mr . . . ?'

Cyril nodded. 'Mr Reardon. Yep, go on, then.'

Ruggle emptied the till and counted all the notes all the while glancing fearfully at the four men.

'Forty pounds.'

Cyril smiled. 'Okay, so you keep all the money tonight to pay for the window. I will have two of my men in here on a Friday and Saturday to make sure your pub stays aggro free.'

Ruggle was still in shock, but when he found his tongue, he asked, 'How much do you want?'

'If you get this pub done up a bit' – he looked down at the dirty lino and then at the tatty stools – 'I'll charge ya just twenty per cent.'

Suddenly, Ruggle's face lit up. 'Really?'

'Yep. Now, get that window boarded up, and if any of the Carters come knocking, you tell them to talk to me.'

Ruggle nodded and gazed in astonishment as the men left the pub.

* * *

Frank, as usual, drove back towards the lock-up. The firm were full of excitement with plans to take over the other pubs. Before Frank turned left just off the Old Kent Road, Cyril stopped him. 'Do us a favour. Can you drop me off at home first?'

'Are you sure, mate?'

'Yeah, you go back with Freddy and Marcus but drop us at the end of the road. I can walk. I need to do a bit of thinking.'

Frank chuckled. 'Thinking? You go and knock yourself out, mate.'

* * *

Walking casually to the tower block, Cyril clutched his jaw. That thump was hard, and it had knocked his confidence. It had him questioning if all this bravado was really him. Had he just got himself caught up in the moment every time and gained his thrills from the adrenaline rush, or was it the money he wanted? But more than any concerns for himself were those for his friends. He was leading them down the same pathway. They followed him, regardless of their own safety. He was now responsible for three lads, and he wondered if he was old enough, big enough, and had enough clout.

A commotion from the tower block stopped his musings. Glancing up, he suddenly turned stone cold. There on the balcony outside his front door were Frank's father and Shirley. His door was open, and they were shouting to someone inside. The circumstances looked odd to Cyril. Why would Henry be outside screaming down his hallway? A feeling of dread coiled around his stomach. In a blind panic, he tore up the stairs and along the outside walkway.

Shirley spotted him before he reached the door. She grabbed his arm and whispered, 'Don't go in there, Cyril.'

As Cyril looked past her, his breathing intensified. 'What the hell's happened? Where's me mum?' He tried to break free, but Shirley had a tight grip on his arm.

'Wait, Cyril. Don't go charging in. The geezer's got a fucking match.'

Cyril frowned. He had no idea what Shirley was talking about until the smell of petrol hit him. 'Fuck me, is me mum inside?'

Shirley's eyes were wide with terror. She nodded. 'There's a bloke in with her. He's in the living room, threatening to kill her, if we call the police. I think he's waiting for you, Cyril. But please don't run in, or he'll strike a fucking match. He's got a box of Swan Vestas, and you know how they spark.'

Cyril relaxed his arms and stared at Shirley as he quickly devised a plan. 'Shirley, go and fetch Mr Bates. Tell him to bring me tool. He'll know what I mean.'

Shirley let go of Cyril and ran like the clappers to the lift.

By now a few of the other neighbours had stepped onto the walkway in their dressing gowns, all wanting to know what the hell was going on.

Cyril tried to gesticulate they should go back inside. However, living next door was Mr Williams, who liked a few brandies in the evening and who then couldn't string two words together.

He swayed as he pointed a finger at Cyril. 'I know your shenaigananananags, up all hours parttyyying in, just you keep your doise nown.'

Cyril nodded, and, luckily, Mr Williams went back inside.

Taking a deep breath, Cyril was sweating buckets. He was terrified that whoever was inside would set his mother alight. He assumed it was one of the Carters or one of the Deacons, but as soon as he stepped inside the doorway, he knew it was none of them. It was his father who had returned, looking worse than ever.

His hair, thick with grease, was stuck to his face. His eyes were sunken and his cheeks sallow. His clothes were almost hanging off him.

Then Cyril's eyes diverted to his mother who was lying on the floor unconscious, but Cyril could see she was doused in petrol. Then he looked back at his father who held up a can of petrol and the box of matches. Cyril knew that he would never be able to run into the flat and grab the matches before his father could strike one. The hallway was too long.

He wanted to run, though. He wanted to kill his father. His evil sickly, smug grin was sending Cyril into a place where he was about to lose his mind and his senses, but he knew he must fight to keep his head clear. He had to think of his mother; he had to keep her alive, above all else.

'What do you want?'

Reginald smirked. 'You grovelling for a start! You fucking little shit. You should respect me. I'm your farver.'

Cyril felt Henry Marsden grab the back of his shirt. 'Easy, son,' he whispered.

'I've got money. Loads of it. You can have it. Please, Dad, let me help my mum. Is she hurt?'

Reginald looked down at Peggy. 'She's only knocked out. She's still alive. Now get down on your hands and knees and beg for forgiveness.'

'Do it, Cyril. This man means it,' whispered Henry.

Cyril dropped to his knees. 'I'm sorry, Dad. Please forgive me.' He would have said anything, if it meant his father wouldn't hurt his mother.

'Good. Now, you can stay on your hands and knees while we talk because I have things I want to say.'

'I know, Dad, and I know what happened, all right. Mum told me about Felix.'

Cyril noticed his father's face change. His bottom jaw protruded, his nostrils flared in anger, and the colour of his face turned a deep purple.

Cyril saw Reginald glance at Peggy, and Cyril could see his mouth was twitching. A frightening thought occurred to him. *Had his father just planned to murder his mother in front of him*?

'Why, Dad, why do you hate us so much?'

Reginald's eyes returned to Cyril. 'Hate you? I don't hate you. I don't even fucking know you. All I see is a wannabe gangster that your whore of a muvver raised. I guess she wanted you to be like her farver, eh? I bet she told you all about him. How he thought he ran fucking Bermondsey and then Kilkenny in Ireland. Well, he's dead now and no threat to anyone. He told me to keep my mouth shut or he would murder me. Ha! And this slut can't hide behind her farver now, can she? The bitch!'

Cyril remained focused on his father's hands, praying to God that all the while he was shouting his mouth off, he wouldn't strike that match, and the longer he kept talking, the more the petrol would evaporate. He could hear footsteps along the walkway, and he knew then Mr Bates was on his way. He didn't look away; he held his breath and waited. He was hoping to be able to get the gun from Mr Bates somehow and blow his father's head right off his shoulders. He knew how to hold the weapon – even how to fire it – but it would be pot luck as to whether he would be a good shot or not. Still, the only way to save his mum would be to blast Reginald away.

He heard a click of the gun and sensed the tension. All he could see as he remained on all fours was the tip of Mr Bates' shoes. He knew he needed to give Mr Bates a clue as to what he could see. 'Please, Dad. Keep those matches in the box. Don't do this. I know you hate Mum. I don't know why, but you will get hanged if you kill her.'

'Hanged? Me? Oh, no, no, Cyril, that was abolished years ago. But she, Cyril, she is the guilty one. She and her farver—'

Bang!

Cyril nearly jumped out of his skin from the sound of the gun; he couldn't believe the power of it. His father staggered back in total shock and then slumped to the floor. Cyril instantly jumped to his feet and ran along the hallway to his mother. He tapped her face. 'Mum! Mum, please wake up. Mum?'

She didn't move. Shirley pulled him away to help Peggy. She put her ear to Peggy's mouth. 'She's all right, Cyril, love.' As Shirley ran her hands around Peggy's head, she felt something wet and sticky, and so she tilted Peggy's head to one side to find the deep gash.

'We need an ambulance.'

'I'll go. You, Mr Bates, need to scarper a bit lively,' said Henry.

'No point!'

Cyril suddenly looked up to see Mr Bates standing with his legs apart, and the gun in his hand, but it was now lowered and hanging by his side. 'Go, Mr Bates. Go quick, before the police get here.'

Henry looked at Reginald, who was now dead. The bullet had passed straight through his neck and killed him almost instantaneously.

'Go, Mr Bates. Please, get out of here!' begged Cyril.

Peggy flicked her eyes open and tried to smile. 'Cyril,' she said, in a faint voice.

'Don't move, Peggy, love,' said Shirley. 'Cyril, fetch your mum some water.'

Cyril quickly ran into the kitchen and came back with a glass of water. He held it to his mum's lips as Shirley helped Peggy into a sitting position. He looked back at Mr Bates. 'Please, please, go.'

But Mr Bates still didn't move. Instead, he just stared at Peggy. 'I should have killed him before it got to this. It's my fault he hurt her.'

Cyril frowned, as he listened to Mr Bates, who appeared to be in a trance. It was eerie and strange.

Leaving Shirley to see to his mum, Cyril got up from the floor. He gripped Mr Bates' arm. 'Come on, get out of here. They'll fucking put you away for years.'

'Cyril, son, I'll be dead well before then. Go back and see to your lovely mum. You look after her.'

'What are you saying?' asked Cyril, as he ran his fingers through his hair and gulped back the lump in his throat.

'You know what I'm saying, lad. Now, go back, and see to

your mum. Leave everything else to me.'

Tears filled his eyes and then tumbled down his cheeks as Cyril tried to wipe them away. 'Please!'

Mr Bates shook his head. 'No, Cyril. Let the filth take me. It doesn't matter anymore.'

'Are you dying?'

Mr Bates nodded and placed a hand on Cyril's shoulder. 'Yeah, for real, this time, lad. You take care of her, like I know you will.'

Suddenly, Cyril flung his arms around Mr Bates' neck and hugged him while he sobbed. '*You* were me dad, Mr Bates. You were always a dad to me.'

Mr Bates hugged him back, and then, as they slowly drew apart, he smiled. 'You were the boy I never had. Now, then, don't you let me down. You go and make your mum proud.'

Cyril watched as Mr Bates walked towards the stairs. Cyril tried to stop the tears, but they just kept flowing. The sound of the sirens echoed somewhere in the back of his head. Everything seemed to be in slow motion. Then he saw Frank running along the walkway.

Before he could grasp what was happening, Frank grabbed Cyril and held him up. 'Cyril, Cyril, what the fuck's just happened?'

Cyril didn't have a chance to explain. Police and ambulancemen pushed both Frank and Cyril aside as they hurried inside the flat. As Cyril looked beyond Frank down the walkway, he saw two policemen handcuff Mr Bates and remove his gun. He stared as Mr Bates looked right into his eyes and nodded at him before the police escorted him away.

'Shit, who did Mr Bates shoot? Is your mum . . . ?' Frank stopped when he heard Shirley dishing out the orders.

'She needs a stretcher, the poor cow. She can't walk. She's been clumped around the head.'

'Who hurt your mum?'

Cyril took a few deep breaths to stop himself from fainting. 'Me dad. He did. He was going to set her alight, but Mr Bates shot him dead.'

Frank's eyes nearly popped out of his head. 'Jesus Christ, your *dad*?'

'Yes and no,' replied Cyril. 'The only man I ever saw as a farver figure was Mr Bates.'

CHAPTER NINETEEN

The talk of the year was the big flash engagement party between Freddy's sister, Gwynnie, and an Army lad called Campbell. Freddy's father, Vernon, wanted to put on a special do. The well-off folk would be coming, and he didn't want his little girl to be shown up.

When the protection racket business was all agreed, the pubs dropped the Carters like hot bricks, having taken on Cyril's firm. Marcus used some of the boxers from the clubs to watch the establishments for a little earner.

Paying for the party didn't prove to be quite so problematic as first thought. In lieu of payment for protecting their properties, the pub owners supplied almost all of the bottles of champagne and expensive wines. So the Blakes didn't have to dig deep to find the money for booze. The supply of the hall was a favour owing to Vernon, so that was already sorted. They just needed to find some cash for the food and the music. But Ronnie had just carried out a little job himself and was quids in, so he paid for most of the food and the DJ. All that was left to arrange was what everyone would be wearing.

* * *

Flossie was in her element, scouring the West End for a new

rig-out with the cash that Cyril had given her. She was easing into her new life with her fella and enjoying the presents and the respect. Even her mother had taken a shine to Cyril. Flossie knew it was because he bought her flowers when he came knocking. Her mother didn't care where the money came from, or how Cyril acquired it; money was money, and his was as good as anyone else's. As long as her Flossie wouldn't want for anything, then so be it. She had drummed that into her daughter's head for years, and now she could sit back and watch as her daughter flaunted her looks and her new knee-high patent boots, leather coat, and all the jewellery.

* * *

Cyril had been to Wormwood Scrubs at every opportunity he could because Mr Bates was on remand and was allowed frequent visits. Cyril was gutted every time he had to leave the old man behind because he could see he was deteriorating. It wouldn't be long before he would be visiting him for the last time.

It was precisely for this reason that Mr Bates wanted to give Cyril as much information on his contacts as the young man could store. He'd already given him plenty that had all been committed to memory on each visit: specifically, the names of drug dealers who Cyril could trust, and the names of the men involved in the protection rackets around South East London.

* * *

When the Saturday night of the engagement party arrived, Peggy was still very quiet. Seeing her husband dead in the flat and aware of the repercussions to her health following the blow to her head had left her withdrawn. Peggy knew she was a shell of a person she once was. She'd declined most social invitations, including the one to Gwynnie Blake and Heath Campbell's engagement party.

Instead, she had taken a warm bath, got into her nightwear, curled up on the sofa to watch the telly, and decided to finish the cardigan she'd been knitting forever. Cyril had bought her some fish and chips and a bottle of her favourite beer, Worthington 'E'. He'd also treated her to a bottle of perfume and a box of chocolates.

She smiled. 'Cyril, you've no need to spoil me. I quite like me own company, love. No doubt, I'll be asleep as soon as I've eaten these chips.'

'Well, you relax, Mum, and don't wait up.'

* * *

Cyril knocked at Flossie's door with a bunch of roses for her mum and a pretty gold necklace for her. Flossie appeared and twirled around in her new Mary Quant dress and light pink boots. Cyril smiled. 'Beautiful, my little princess.'

He handed her the necklace. It was a gold locket, and she quickly put it on. However, this time, she took it without a 'thank you', as if she'd expected a present.

Cyril felt a little hurt because he had spent more time than he should have searching for a unique gift, and if she had taken the time to look more closely, she would have seen it was engraved with her name on it. Yet Flossie was too excited and wanted to get going to show off her new clothes and her new hairstyle, cut and coloured by Vidal Sassoon, no less.

Frank had already picked up Trudy, and like Cyril, he'd handed his girlfriend a gold necklace, but he didn't want his engraved. He wasn't as sentimental as Cyril.

Trudy squealed with excitement and jumped two feet in the air to throw her arms around his neck. 'Oh, Frankie, I love it, babe. I really love it. I will wear it always.'

'All right, Trude, you don't have to burst me eardrums, girl.'

Trudy hadn't taken any money from Frank for this evening's new outfit. She was working hard and so could afford to buy what clothes she needed as well as save her pennies for the special day. However, when Frank told her that if she was out with him, she was never to put her hand in her pocket or else he would be offended, Trudy was grateful.

Frank was proud of the girl. He could see she didn't take everything for granted from him. He admired the fact that she was overjoyed with her job at the hairdresser's, despite it earning her very little income, and he couldn't be more pleased that she wanted to make her own way in life.

As the four of them made their way to the hall, the girls' chattering became more excitable. Guests were outside taking in the fresh night air; some were smoking, while others held a flute of champagne. It was evident that there were members of the upper class, just by the clothes and the way they held their drinks and cigarette holders. Cyril didn't care; he was there as a guest of the Blake family. As he worked his way through the crowd, gripping Flossie's hand, he was patted on the back and acknowledged by so many people. Flossie smiled too as if she was just as popular, but the fact was she was only greeted because she was Cyril's bird; otherwise, no one would have really known or even cared who she was.

Trudy couldn't care less who greeted Frank or her. She only wanted to have a good time with her fella, a few dances, a couple of glasses of Babycham, and a snog before she walked through her own front door.

Marcus appeared and waved at Cyril to join him at the bar. He ordered the drinks along with a glass of bubbly all round.

Vernon Blake, sporting a navy-blue suit and a white shirt, was the smartest Cyril had ever seen him.

'Cyril, me boy, have you got yaself and your lovely girl 'ere a drink?' His voice was deep and gruff.

Cyril nodded. 'Yes, Mr Blake.'

'Thanks, mate. Thank you so much for all the booze. It won't be forgotten.'

Cyril shook his head. 'You owe me nuffin, Mr Blake.'

Vernon patted Cyril's shoulder, smiled generously, and left.

Flossie had clocked the conversation. 'So did you pay for all this?'

Cyril wasn't sure of her tone. 'What, me? No, don't be daft. I just paid for a few bottles of champagne.'

'Why?'

'What d'ya mean?'

‘Well, why are you spending money on this? I mean, it’s not as if it’s *our* engagement, is it?’

Cyril was flummoxed. ‘Hold on a minute, Flossie. It was an engagement gift.’

Seeing the annoyed look on Cyril’s face, Flossie decided not to push the matter; instead, she sipped the champagne on offer and gazed around at the women. Pleased that she had the latest outfit, she knew she looked good.

Freddy was heading Cyril’s way with his hand firmly clutching a young, pretty, blonde girl. Cyril smiled to greet him. ‘And this is?’ asked Cyril, smiling.

‘This is Cindy. Cindy, this is Cyril.’

Cindy held out her hand as if she should shake Cyril’s, but Cyril just laughed and hugged her instead.

‘Nice to meet you, darling, and it looks like Freddy has bagged the top prize.’

As soon as Flossie heard that, she dug Cyril in the ribs.

‘Sorry, babe. You are an’ all, my princess.’

The girls got to know one another, while the men gathered around the bar.

Just as the men were about to talk shop, Cindy sidled up to Freddy. ‘Blakey, would you get me a drink, please?’

Cyril held his breath in to stop himself from laughing, but Frank couldn’t. He chuckled into his pint.

Freddy was embarrassed. 'Yes, yes, go over there with the girls, and I'll fetch one over.'

'All right, Blakey. I'll have a port and lemon,' she said, as she kissed Freddy on the cheek.

Cyril couldn't hold it in any longer, bursting out laughing. '*Blakey*?'

'Oh, fuck off,' said Freddy, now bright red.

But Frank and Cyril still found the term of endearment hilarious and wouldn't let it drop.

As the drinks flowed and the hall filled with more guests, it was apparent that there was a clear divide. Campbell's Army friends and his relations were so different from everyone else who had been invited. It wasn't so much because of their well-spoken accents but their demeanour.

Cyril noticed how Freddy's mum, Irene, tried hard to mingle with Campbell's family. Carefully, he watched how they were all polite to acknowledge her, but it was clear that they were not friendly enough to engage with her in their conversation.

Cyril kept his eye on the proceedings. Vernon was up on the stage, trying to get everyone's attention to make a toast. At the same time, Cyril watched as Irene hurried around the hall with a tray of champagne, ensuring everyone had their glasses topped up.

But Cyril felt a tinge of anger envelope him. A small group of men, dressed in classy dark suits, and their girlfriends, done up like Jackie Onassis, totally dismissed Irene as if she were a waitress. They waved her away, with not even a ‘please’ or a ‘thank you’. Cyril was about to go marching over and give them a piece of his mind when Vernon tapped his glass with a knife to make the all-important announcement.

Along with everyone else, Cyril held his glass up to congratulate the couple, but from behind came a mumble that he heard clearly.

‘I’ll give it a year,’ said a tall well-dressed man with close-cut fair hair.

‘Yes, Campbell will be onto the next bit of rough, in next to no time,’ said a shorter dark-haired man with protruding top teeth.

Cyril spun around to see who owned those sarcastic voices.

Both men were oblivious to the dirty look that Cyril was giving them because they were half-cut and too up themselves.

‘Oi, you need to watch what you say. Words like that can get a man hurt, you know,’ said Cyril, as he leaned into them.

The fair-haired man realised he was facing someone with clout.

Frank and Marcus leaned in over Cyril’s shoulder.

‘Oh, come on, lads. It was just said in jest. You know how it is.’

Cyril slammed his glass down on the bar. ‘No, mate, I don’t fucking know how it is, ’cos where we come from, we don’t insult our women. A “bit of rough”, you say, is she?’

growled Cyril, through gritted teeth.

The taller man shook his head. 'No, look, we're very sorry. We didn't mean to cause offence. Look, dear chaps, it's just the drink talking. We'll be off.' He tried to pull the shorter man away.

But Cyril grabbed the taller outspoken man's arm and pulled him closer. 'If I ever hear you two bad-mouth her again, I'll turn your guts inside out. Got it?'

Both men swallowed hard and shamefully nodded.

As the two tried to slip away from the bar, another one of their friends approached. He was a well-built gent, with dark hair parted on the side and held back with Brylcreem. Wearing a handmade suit, Italian leather shoes, and cufflinks that were studded with diamonds, with a Cartier watch to boot, he enquired, 'What's all the bother, chaps?'

Suddenly Frank nudged Cyril. 'Look who that is.'

Cyril stared but didn't recognise him.

'Look at the scar on his chin. D'you remember him now?'

Suddenly Cyril's eyes widened. 'Gawd, it's Lord Chambers' son.'

'Yep.'

'Frank, don't let on it was us that night, all right?'

'No way, Cyril. He got the biggest hiding, didn't he?'

Cyril laughed but stared at the three toffs, and then his

mother's words started to circle in his mind again. 'You have to be born a lord.' He looked down at his own Italian leather shoes and knew he had risked his liberty for these. However, Lord Chambers, with a display of high-hat cockiness had the best of everything because he was born with money. Intrigued, Cyril held his gaze at the scene in front of him. Two beautiful, highly fashionable women were now draped on Chambers' arm. It was as if they were there for show. Cyril then turned to look at Flossie. He concluded that although Lord Chambers had the money, he didn't have the girl. The prettiest one in the hall was his Flossie, and he knew it.

'Come on, lads, let's show 'em how it's done.'

Frank rolled his eyes. 'You can't dance, Cyril.'

'Shut up! Yes, I can. I can dance like the Isley Brothers.'

Frank laughed. 'More like the Beverley Sisters. But your Flossie can dance. Look at her move.'

'And your Trudy. Look at her an' all.'

Frank chuckled. 'What? Are you bleedin' blind, Cyril? My Trudy just wiggles her arse, and everyone has to get out of the way. Look at her.'

Cyril was laughing along now. 'You do like a big girl, though, Frank, eh?'

'You get more for ya money, mate,' he replied, as he clocked Trudy looking his way and smiling.

Before Frank and Cyril joined the girls, Cyril glanced once more at Lord Chambers, and, instantly, his shackles were up.

The bastard was eyeing up his Flossie.

Whether he could dance or not, Cyril was going to let everyone in the hall know that she was his girl.

At the end of the evening, slowly, but surely, everyone began to make their way home.

Irene had snapped a heel off one of her new shoes. She was limping around the hall with rubbish bags and collecting the bottles and paper plates of unfinished food.

'We did Gwynnie proud, though, didn't we, Cyril?' she said, as he walked past.

'You did her more than proud, Irene. Everyone had a good time, the food was great, and I ate ten vol-au-vents, I reckon.'

'Good. See, we can put on a do just as posh as that lot.'

'Better, Irene, better.'

Smiling to himself, he put his arm around Flossie's shoulder. 'It was a good night, eh?'

Flossie was quiet.

'Are you all right, princess?'

'Well, yeah, but we've been together a while now, Cyril, and, well, I just wonder sometimes if I am just, you know, just one of those things until someone better comes along.'

Cyril stopped and turned to face her. 'Listen, Flossie, I've had a couple of beers, and to be honest with ya, I have no idea what you're talking about. How about I take you out for a slap-up breakfast in the morning down at the Wimpy, and you can tell me what's on your mind?'

Flossie had had a few cherry brandies and was a little tipsy. Breakfast at the Wimpy seemed a good idea.

Frank waited on the other side of the road with the back door of his car open for Flossie and Cyril to climb in.

But as they walked across the road, no one could have predicted what would happen next.

Heading around the corner, with its tyres spinning and screeching, a car made straight for Cyril. Luckily for Flossie, Cyril had largely stuck to a few beers and not got himself drunk. Flinging Flossie to the kerb, he dived out of the way himself. The front wheel of the car missed his foot by an inch.

Flossie was livid. 'Now look at what's happened! Me fucking new boots are all scuffed to buggery. They cost me, well Cyril, a bleedin' arm and a leg!' she hollered, as Trudy helped her up off the pavement.

Cyril had bashed his hip when he fell, but he was more interested in who was driving that car. Frank was squinting, trying to see, but it was Freddy, who appeared from behind him, who clocked the driver's face.

'Red Deacon was driving that motor, but I know for a fact that's Johnnie Carter's car.'

'So that tells me that Red doesn't own a car, but he has guts, while Johnnie Carter owns a car, but he's too chicken to take me on himself,' said Cyril, as he stared up the road.

CHAPTER TWENTY

Flossie was cross with Cyril. It was the Sunday morning after the engagement party, and all she'd received was a quick 'goodbye', which wasn't acceptable. Having broken his promise to take her to the Wimpy, she now found herself at a loose end, just because, apparently, he had more pressing matters to deal with. She slammed the door shut and slumped onto her bed in a strop.

'What's the matter with you, my girl?' asked her mum, who came into the room and leaned against the doorway in her daughter's bedroom.

'Nuffin, Muvver. Just leave me alone.'

'Listen, Florence.'

'Mum, don't call me that. You know I hate it.'

'Flossie, Cyril is a good catch. You would be stupid to piss him off. Look at him. He's got money, and you'd do well to lower your stroppy tone. Because you watch, my girl. Soon enough, there will be hundreds of girls after him and some prettier than you.'

Flossie sat up straight and sighed. 'I am fed up with always coming second to his mates or his "bit of business", as he calls it.'

'You need to grow up, Flossie. The boy's making a name

and money for himself. Leave him to do what he has to do. Money don't grow on trees. He's out earning, and you, Flossie, need to be the dutiful girlfriend, if you want him to put a ring on that finger of yours. Trust me, when he's swimming in it, you'll have a nice home, nice clobber, and want for nuffin. Take a look around you, Flossie. This isn't the life you want, stuck in a poxy high-rise council flat, with not a blade of grass for a dog to wipe its arse.'

'Yeah, but I'm too young to be waiting in for when he feels like calling. And, Muvver, I ain't gonna be at his beck and call for ever.'

With a loud huff and a puff, Sonia left the doorway and clip-clopped up the hallway to the kitchen.

As she looked around her bedroom, Flossie spied her new coat with the fur trim hanging from the wardrobe door that Cyril had given her the money for. Then she looked across at her new boots and her kid gloves that he'd bought because the weather was a little chilly. She stood up and walked over to her teak dressing table that was covered in lace doilies and stared at the neatly arranged collection of small square boxes. Each one contained a piece of jewellery, and each one was a gift from Cyril. Even the reflection in the mirror had Cyril's stamp on it. The new haircut by Vidal Sassoon himself and the gold hairclip were all courtesy of Cyril. *Perhaps her mother was right*, she thought. She glared for a second in response to one remark her mother had made, though – that there were prettier girls out there. A cold feeling crept through her. But she shrugged it off. Cyril wasn't that kind of guy. He didn't have a wandering eye, unless it was for a new business venture. Picking up the new bottle of Oh! de London perfume – another treat from Cyril – she sprayed a touch just behind her ears. Her mind went back to the engagement party and how Gwynnie Blake had paraded around like a doll, with everyone praising her and making a big fuss. There he was, her fiancé, an Army sergeant in his uniform, looking smart, and his friends with him, all dripping in money. That's what *she* wanted. However, there was already a ring on Gwynnie's finger. But she knew that if Cyril didn't pop the question soon, she would find herself another suitor – a rich one.

* * *

Cyril was gutted that he couldn't take Flossie to the Wimpy. But Mr Bates' solicitor had knocked earlier with a message that his client was at the Royal London Hospital and he didn't have long to live. The prison authorities had moved him from Wormwood Scrubs; there was no point in keeping him on remand when he was dying.

Frank offered to drive Cyril to the hospital. He knew how close Cyril was to Mr Bates. Although there wasn't much that bothered Cyril, Frank knew that once Mr Bates had popped his clogs, it would cut Cyril deeply.

Frank had barely parked the car when Cyril got out.

Cyril ran up the steps, through the main entrance, and then stared gormlessly at the list of wards. He found Turner Ward and ran along the corridor only to find the ward entrance door shut.

He banged hard until a ward sister opened the door with a face like thunder and glared at Cyril. 'What on earth are you doing? Visiting is not until after three this afternoon.'

Cyril was anxious, and no vinegar-faced sister was going

to stop him. 'Mr Bates, I've come to see him.'

The sister raised her brow defiantly. 'Are you a relative?'

Cyril nodded but didn't answer.

'We have placed Mr Bates in a room at the end. He shouldn't be disturbed.'

Cyril didn't like her tone or her smug face. 'What? You mean he should be left to die on his own, then?'

With her hands on her hips, she replied, 'The patients prefer to be left in peace.'

'Nah, love, not Mr Bates, because he has asked for me, so if he's changed his mind, then I want to hear it from his own lips.'

'I don't have to let you in. It's up to my discretion, and you appear to be rather excitable to me.'

'Listen, love, that man in there is on his last legs. We both know that, and all he wanted was to talk to me. Are you gonna refuse his dying wish?'

'Er, what is all this about?' came another stern female voice, from behind Cyril. He watched as the sister stiffened in surprise.

Cyril turned to face the woman and was taken aback himself. She was a large woman, taller than himself, in a uniform that if it was starched any more, it would grow legs and walk away on its own.

'Look, all I'm trying to do is to give a dying man his last

wish. His solicitor told me this morning that he needs to see me before he . . . well, you know.' He swallowed hard, stopping himself from choking on his words.

The matron stared at the sister. 'And what is the problem?'

The sister shuffled nervously and looked down. 'I . . . er, well, I assumed Mr Bates would want to be left alone. He is in the final stages.' She had no sooner got the words out of her mouth than the matron almost pushed her aside.

'Come with me, sir, please, and let's see if we can find you a chair so that you can speak to Mr Bates. A police officer is outside the room, but don't be put off.'

Cyril sensed her tone had softened. 'Thank you. This means such a lot to me. He's been like a farver to me, you see.'

The matron gripped his shoulder. 'You go along inside, and I'll fetch a chair and make you a nice cuppa tea. How about that?'

A sudden feeling of relief hit him. He had no idea what to expect. He'd never seen anyone actually dying like this. The policeman outside was reading a newspaper. He didn't even look up at Cyril as he walked into the dimly lit room. The curtains were drawn, and a small lamp glowed a soft orange colour. Mr Bates was in his striped pyjamas, sitting up, but his head was back on the pillows all propped up.

'Mr Bates, it's me. It's Cyril,' he whispered.

Mr Bates opened his eyes and smiled. 'Hello, son. Did you get here all right? Wasn't a bother, was it?'

Cyril smiled back, but he was fighting to keep the tears at bay.

Just at that moment, the matron brought in a chair and a cup of tea. 'There you are, love.'

'Thank you,' replied Cyril.

'I haven't got long, so you need to listen.' He gasped and winced.

'Are you in pain? I'll get a nurse.'

Mr Bates waved his hand. 'Nah, the nurses get on my wick, and the painkillers knock me out.'

Cyril knew that Mr Bates was struggling to talk; he looked exhausted, and now seeing him so painfully thin, Cyril only just managed to control the tears that were welling up.

''Ere, take these,' Mr Bates said, pointing to a ring of keys on the bedside cabinet. 'They're the keys to me flat. It's all yours in there. Take the lot. Don't leave anything of value to the council.'

Cyril looked at Mr Bates' thin and veiny hand. He remembered when they were both huge and powerful.

'Your grandfarver, Dillon, he died before I had the chance to say I was sorry. I never made it up to him, so listen to me. The cottage, I have left it to you. Your muvver doesn't want to move there. She likes the flat, for some reason. And the shop, lad. Half of that business is yours now. Those McNalleys, the bastards, they were supposed to pay me for the loan on the shop, but they just hoped I would die. I went to see them a few weeks ago, but they fucked me off, and I didn't have the strength to fight. In fact, I used me last bit of strength to shoot your ol' man. You do forgive me, don't ya?'

'Of course, I do. I would have shot him meself, but, look, Mr Bates, I don't need . . .'

'Stop, Cyril. Please, just listen. The cottage is yours. Half of it belonged to your grandfarver, anyway. I loved him like a brother. We shared everything. Whatever we stole, conned, or blagged, we shared fifty-fifty.'

'Like Frank and me, then.'

Mr Bates nodded. 'If you say so. But I got caught robbing the building society. Dillon managed to scarper. I never grassed even though they beat me black and fucking blue. 'Cos, well, you just didn't squeal on your mates. So I got a long sentence. All I asked was he took care of me fiancée, my . . .' He paused and wiped a tear away.

Cyril was gobsmacked; he'd never seen Mr Bates so emotional.

'He did take care of her, so much so, that he got her pregnant. He didn't hang about, mind you. My Annie was a beautiful woman, sweeter than the first honeysuckle blooms. I loved her with all my being. I guess he did as well. Anyway, they got wed. And me? Well, I spent a few years stewing inside. I wanted to hurt your grandfarver badly. I did something terrible, and I can't forgive meself for it.'

'It don't matter now, Mr Bates. It's all in the past. Me grandfarver's dead.'

Mr Bates coughed, and choked, and gasped until he caught his breath. 'No, I have to tell you something else. I can't go to my grave without telling you.'

Cyril nodded.

'I came out of prison a few years later. Your grandmuvver couldn't look me in the eye, but, no matter, I still loved her. And your muvver was a little girl running around with her pigtails. I loved her too, you know, but it made me sick to think that Annie and your muvver should have been mine.' Another tear fell, and he wiped it away with his bony hand.

'I pretended we were fine and there were no hard feelings. So, we arranged another job. This one was the post office. Your grandfarver was a gambling man in more than the obvious sense of the word. He was reckless and sometimes went in without thinking. I think his stint in the Army had made him an angry man, so he would fight anyone who stood in his way.' He stopped and coughed again.

Cyril pulled a tissue out of the box on top of the cabinet and handed it to Mr Bates, but the coughing wouldn't stop. His whole body shot forward as he almost coughed the remains of his lungs up. Cyril jumped up from his seat and screamed from the doorway for a nurse to help.

As soon as one came into the room, she tried to place a mask over Mr Bates' face so that he could breathe.

But he couldn't stop coughing and gasping. He thrashed around, making it impossible for her to help him. She pressed a bell, and, right away, a doctor rushed into the room.

He also tried to get the mask over Mr Batcs' face, but,

suddenly, everything went quiet.

Mr Bates lay at an odd angle with his mouth wide open.

Cyril couldn't believe he was dead. *No way*, he thought. *Mr Bates has stuff to tell me. He couldn't just die, not now. And he himself hadn't even had the chance to say his goodbyes. This wasn't happening, surely*?

The police officer was up on his feet peering inside the room, which pissed Cyril right off.

''Ere, get your fucking nose out,' he snapped.

The officer soon stepped back when the doctor came out of the room. The medic looked at Cyril and shook his head.

'What? Is that *it*? Is he *dead*?'

'I'm so very sorry. Yes, he has passed away.'

'But?'

'I know it seemed very sudden to you, I am sure, but he was a very sick man and in a lot of pain.'

Cyril lowered his head, consumed with grief. He hadn't realised just how fond he was of Mr Bates until that very moment. He didn't care what Mr Bates had done to his grandfather. As far as he was concerned, Mr Bates was kind to him and his mother, and if it hadn't been for Mr Bates, then they may well have all starved to death.

As he marched through the hospital corridors, he felt every fibre of his being alight with anger. Mr Bates should never have spent his last few weeks in a stinking prison cell, and he shouldn't have died in pain like that.

Frank was waiting by the car smoking a cigarette when he saw Cyril storm out of the hospital. He guessed the news wasn't good, and so he decided to keep quiet and wait for Cyril to talk. They drove home in silence.

As Cyril got out of the car, he turned to Frank. 'Would you ask Freddy and his brothers if they have that Red Deacon's address? I'm gonna pay the bastard a visit.'

Frank watched Cyril walk over towards the flat, with his head down. Quickly, he stepped out of his car, slammed the door shut, and hurried after him. 'Listen, mate, I know you're upset, but venting your anger on the likes of Red Deacon will have you locked up in seconds.'

Cyril stopped in his tracks and took a few deep breaths. 'I was angry last night, and now Mr Bates is dead, I am even more angry. The fight was done and dusted a long time ago, right? Red Deacon tried it on and got fucked up. Me little bruvver has never been the same since, and now Deacon seems to be pushing his fucking luck. As I see it, what happened after the engagement party was cowardly, and me bird could've been killed.'

'Okay, okay, listen. You're upset, mate. You need to calm down. We'll set up a meeting with the Deacons and find out what the hell they're playing at because, like you, Cyril, I agree. If they want a fucking war, then a war they shall have. And, see, me, I won't be just cutting off ears. I'll take a few limbs off, this time.'

'Good, right, but not yet, because, Frank, we have another

meeting, this time with a bloke called Christian Cooper. He appears a decent geezer, a buyer, for Sandos.'

Frank smiled. 'Another big earner, Cyril?'

Cyril nodded, but he wasn't thinking about the money. He was now thinking about making a firm statement and ensuring that the Carters and the Deacons backed right off.

'And another thing, my friend. We'll be paying the cheeky no-good cocky pricks the McNalleys a visit.'

'Who? The butchers?'

'Yes, Frank, the butchers. And I will teach those bastards how to use a fucking butcher's knife.'

'Jesus, Cyril, what the hell happened back there in the hospital?'

'McNalley owed Mr Bates a lot of money, and he and his sons told him to fuck off. Well, Frank, I own half that business now, and I will show them what it means to fuck me about.'

Frank had never seen Cyril look so dark and angry. He realised the new expression was one of bitterness.

* * *

By the time Cyril had climbed the staircase, he had calmed down and was in a better place to break the sad news to his mother. She was sitting in front of the telly in her Brentford nylon dressing gown. The bright yellow suited her dark hair.

'Oh, 'ello, love. How'd it go? I was gonna pop up there tomorrow and take him some lovely grapes from the market.'

Cyril sat heavily in the chair. 'Mum, there's no point now. He's gone.'

Peggy sat bolt upright spilling her tea into the saucer. 'You *what*?'

'He died while I was there, poor ol' fella.'

'Oh, no! I didn't get to say goodbye. I . . .'

'He said to say goodbye and that it was lovely knowing you.'

'Did he, Cyril? Did he really?'

'Yeah, Mum. He said you were the daughter he never had, and you made his last few years really nice for him.'

'Oh, love him. Well, the truth is, Cyril, it was the other way around. I really loved the old sod. He was so good to me, you know. He would have given me the world. But you know me, Son. I wouldn't take it. He even offered me his cottage in the country. But the thing is, I do like me flat. I couldn't be stuck out in the sticks, with just sheep and rabbits.'

Cyril smiled. 'He did see us all right, even to the end, didn't he, Mum?'

Peggy was staring out of the window. 'Yeah, Son, he did.'

They sat there together, each drinking a glass of brandy and reminiscing over the past and talking about Mr Bates until the skies darkened and the day came to an end. Cyril didn't mention the conversation about his grandfather; he didn't want to press his mother. However, it did play on his mind. Mr

Bates was dead, and now he would never know why the man had felt so guilty.

CHAPTER TWENTY-ONE

It was two weeks later, on a Monday, bang on 9.00 a.m., when Frank knocked at the door. He hoped to see a smile on Cyril's face, but that bitterness was still there.

'Are the lads coming?' Cyril asked, as he marched along the walkway.

Frank nodded. 'I don't mean to be nosy, but do you really need the money from McNalley?'

Cyril stopped dead. 'Frank, it ain't all about the money, mate. There's a fucking principle involved 'ere. That McNalley family were eager to take the loan to keep their butcher business going. But they never paid Mr Bates back, and when the ol' boy turned up to collect what was owing, they fucked him off. Well, the debt didn't die when Mr Bates did. 'Cos I've just found out that Mr Bates left the premises to me, as well as half of the business, so I'm gonna collect what's owing . . . every fucking last penny.'

Frank knew then that he either shut his mouth and went along or backed out completely.

'Right, Cyril, the boys will follow us in Marcus' car. Cyril, the McNalleys will have an advantage over us, you know.'

Cyril was still marching along, his head bobbing from side to side. 'Oh, yeah, and what's that, then?'

'A fucking shop full of meat cleavers and axes, and shit like that, if ya get my drift.'

Suddenly Cyril stopped dead and slid his hand inside his jacket. That old familiar grin appeared across his face as he pulled out a gun.

Frank's eyes nearly popped out of his head. 'Where the fuck did you get *that*?'

'Mr Bates' garage. He said the contents were mine, so now this little weapon has my name on it, and the fucking bullet inside has McNalley's himself, if he starts to kick off.'

* * *

Once Frank's car drew up outside the butcher's in Bermondsey, Cyril's anger increased at the sight of the shop having been completely overhauled with shiny new signage and a recently tiled floor. Not waiting for Marcus or Blakey, as Freddy was commonly called, he stormed in, ready to pull out his gun, when he saw two old ladies, almost identical in appearance, in their green overcoats and with blue scarves around their heads, eyeing up the contents of the chilled cabinets.

'Mildred, look, love, they've got ham on the bone. Now what about that for a nice change when your Violet comes over on Sunday?'

'Hmm, I dunno, Maud. Not sure she likes ham on the bone.'

'She likes ham, though, doesn't she?'

'Yeah, but I'm not sure if she likes it on the bone.'

Cyril glared at Frank, who had a grin on his face. He knew the two old ladies could be fussing for ages, and Cyril's idea of charging in with all guns blazing had suddenly gone to pot.

Cyril's impatience was being tested to the limit; he wanted to go to town on the place. He knew Malcolm McNalley, otherwise known as Mac, who was bigger than ever, and who was now even more of an arrogant bastard. He had his back to the shop while he chopped away at a slab of meat. His son Ernest was filling sausages and totally ignoring the two old ladies. The youngest son, Gerald, Cyril assumed was out in the back room somewhere, but it was McNalley and Ernest who Cyril intended to wage war on first.

Uptight but yet pragmatic, Cyril placed his arm around Mildred's shoulder and said, 'How about I treat you to the whole joint on me, darling, 'cos I'm in a very generous mood today.'

Mildred looked up and smiled. 'Well, I never. Did you hear that, Maud? This handsome young man is going to treat us.'

Maud frowned, but when her eyes met Cyril's, she too smiled. 'Well, I won't look a gift horse in the mouth, now, will I?'

McNalley stopped chopping and turned around. He hadn't realised that anyone else was inside the shop. He wiped his eyes because he thought he was seeing things. *It couldn't be Cyril Reardon and Frank Marsden, could it? Surely not*, he thought.

'These two lovely ladies would like that ham on the bone.'

Mac didn't quite know what to make of Cyril or Frank standing there. He'd heard the rumours that Cyril and Henry Marsden's lad were a force to be reckoned with, but he'd never really taken much notice. He didn't like to listen to hearsay, but he had a cold feeling inside. It wasn't the size of Frank Marsden; it was more the look in Cyril Reardon's eyes. Without saying a word, he wrapped the meat in the paper and handed it to Maud.

'Good man,' grinned Cyril. He turned to face the old ladies, who were as pleased as punch with their free parcel of ham. 'Let's hope your Violet likes it, eh?'

The women chuckled and left the shop, leaving Cyril with a smirk and an air of mischief about him. Frank sized up Ernest and clocked the knives and meathooks dangling above Ernest's head.

'That'll be three shillings,' said Mac, in his deep croaky voice.

Cyril looked at McNalley's open hand and mockingly shook his head.

'Ah, dear, dear me, you're a proper joker, ain't ya.'

Holding a meat cleaver, Ernest had the mad assumption that he had the upper hand. Reputation or not, Marsden and Reardon couldn't fight against a sharp weapon that would literally cut through bone with ease.

‘What do you want?’ growled Ernest.

‘It ain’t about what I want, mate! It’s about what’s mine.’

Mac’s eyes began to twitch, but he said nothing and just gaped.

‘You three fucking bastards told the one man who helped you build your sausage empire to fuck off. And, see, me. Well’ – he poked himself in the chest while his temper began to rise – ‘I fucking know that man wanted only what was owing. But, no, you three greedy fuckers told him to fuck off. You thought he was too old and sick to take back what was rightfully his. Ha! And you thought that when he died his debt died too.’

‘That’s right, Reardon, the debt died too, so you can fuck off, an’ all.’

Frank weighed up his options because he assumed that any second now Cyril was going to lose the plot and bash seven colours of shit out of McNalley.

‘Fuck off, can I? Yeah, well let me tell you, ya fucking greasy, ugly fat pig. The debt *would* have died with him, if he’d had no one to leave the business to. But guess what, you wanker? He left it to me. So, seeing that you ain’t paid up, and yet you’ve managed to open up yet *another* shop and have this one all refurbed, you, Mr fucking McNalley, can fuck right off yourself. And see the sign above this shop? It’s gonna say “Reardon” on it. Oh, and by the way, you’re *still* in debt. I’ll have me accountant draw up the figures, and you can use your fat trotter fingers to count out me money.’

McNalley listened, but he wasn’t going to take that lying down. ‘You don’t know what you’re talking about. There was no such contract.' He nervously looked at Ernest, who was now growing red in the face with anger.

'Oh, there was, but you took the piss. And me, I ain't having any of it. Mr Bates came to you when he was dying, and you fucked him off. I've taken a real offence to that and—'

Before Cyril could finish, Ernest pulled his father back and leaned across the counter. Holding the meat cleaver up to Cyril's face, he growled, 'Fuck off, Reardon, and take your gorilla with you.'

Frank was still eyeing up the tools above Ernest. As soon as Ernest made that move, albeit from behind the counter, Frank snatched the meathook from the steel rack above, and, in the blink of an eye, he thrust the hook straight into Ernest's arm, pinning it to the wooden block.

The shock made Ernest drop the meat cleaver, and as soon as his eyes rested on his arm nailed to the butcher's block, he let out a howl like an injured wolf.

McNalley jumped back in horror. 'What the fucking hell!'

Gerald heard the noise from the back room and hurried through to see what all the fuss was about. But he stopped dead when he saw Cyril Reardon and Frank Marsden venting their anger on his dad, and his brother pinned to the block, with blood pooling around his arm.

'Jesus, what's going on?'

'Gerald, you, your farver, and your brother will be vacating this shop. You don't own it anymore, and I would have been a bit patient and fair with ya, but seeing that you took the liberty to tell Mr Bates to fuck off, I've changed me mind. So help your brother to detach himself from the block, get your stuff, and go.'

McNalley was using an old towel to stop the bleeding while desperately trying to pull the hook from the wooden block. 'Help me, Gerald!' he hollered, in a panic.

Looking at Ernest, Gerald could see that he had turned from white to grey. He was such a lump that if Ernest fainted, his own weight would rip his arm from the block.

Gerald gently pushed his father aside and slid his hand under his brother's arm. With the other hand, he held the hook and yanked it free. He then wrapped his brother's wound in the towel.

'You fucking animal, Marsden!' bellowed Gerald.

Frank nodded calmly. In a flash, he leaned over the counter and snatched the meat cleaver. 'Wanna lose a hand, you cheeky fucker?'

Gerald stepped away from Frank, who was now swinging the tool menacingly.

But from nowhere, McNalley had suddenly found some courage. He spun around, grabbed the bacon slicer, held it above his head, and then launched it. 'You want a fight, Reardon? Well, a fight you shall have.'

Cyril managed to dodge the bacon slicer, and, to add insult to injury, he laughed. 'Is that the best you can do?'

McNalley then grabbed a knife that was hidden under the counter and moved fast for a fat man. He shuffled quickly through the bar flap and launched himself at Cyril.

Cyril, though, was laughing by now and taunting him. ‘Come on, then, old man. Let’s see what you’re made of before I run you through that mincing machine.’

McNalley waved the knife like a Kung Fu fighter, but all he managed to do was to wear himself out.

Cyril was nimble and laughed when he managed to sidestep McNalley like a matador in a bullring. Then Cyril heard more laughter. As he looked towards Frank, he saw Marcus and Blakey standing there watching, as if this was a theatrical performance put on for their benefit.

Frank remained glaring at Ernest and Gerald, daring them to move.

Hanging up in the window behind Cyril were three large geese. Dodging yet another attempt to decapitate him, Cyril managed to swing up and grab one of the geese and swipe it at McNalley. It was a joke, until McNalley, in one spin, completely cut the goose in half. Cyril instantly realised this was no laughing matter anymore.

McNalley may have been out of breath and shattered, but he was still swinging the lethal weapon as well as any stuntman.

One false move, Cyril reckoned, and it could be curtains for him.

Cyril decided enough was enough. Reaching inside his

pocket, he pulled out his own weapon – his new tool left to him by Mr Bates. 'Now, fuck right off, all of you, or I'll put a fucking hole in your heads.'

Everyone froze to the spot. Not even Marcus or Blakey expected Cyril to be so brazen and in broad daylight too.

'I said, fuck right off. Go on, get out, and don't come back, 'cos, see this gun? It ain't a toy.'

McNalley was still out of breath when he dropped the knife.

'You will get locked up for this.'

Blakey wasted no time in dropping the shutters, closing the door, and putting up the 'We Are Closed' sign in the window.

'Good man, Blakey. Now, then, McNalley, this is what's gonna happen. I am gonna let you keep your new shop that's yours, but, see, these premises, well, they're now mine. Mr Bates lent you a lot of money to help you get started, with the promise that you'd pay back what you owe in the form of a percentage, but you hoped he'd die and you'd not have to pay a penny. Well, it's all in black and white in the contract you signed. He may not have had an heir then, but he has one now, and that's me.'

McNalley glared at the gun. 'And you're hoping that I won't argue with a gun pointing at my face?'

Cyril shrugged his shoulders. 'You can argue with what the fuck you like, but the solicitor and Mr Bates had all the papers drawn up with my name on it, so, gun or no gun, this butcher's new proprietor is me. Now, I can be fair and let you leave with your bollocks still attached to you, or you can all be squeezed through a mincer and shoved into sausages. It's your choice. But don't make me wanna have to start putting bullets all in me new shop.'

Fuming, McNalley glanced down at the gun, but Frank was fast.

He bolted over to Cyril, slid on the tiles, and managed to ram McNalley into the tiled wall. Holding the meat cleaver close to McNalley's neck, Frank said, 'Now you know how a turkey feels before you cut its throat.'

McNalley didn't move. All he could feel was his pulse in the side of his head and the cold blade pressed hard against his throat.

'All right,' he croaked.

Frank looked at Cyril, who nodded to him to let McNalley go.

'How are you so sure I ain't gonna call the police and have you lot nicked?'

Cyril laughed and cocked the gun. 'Because if you do, ya fat prick, I'll have someone pay you' – he rudely pointed to McNalley's chest – 'a visit, and it won't be with a shooter, next time. It will be with a rope and a noose wide enough to fit all of your fucking fat heads through.'

Not another word was said. McNalley removed his apron and handed it to Cyril. 'I knew you'd turn out to be trouble, the day you asked for a job.'

Cyril grinned. 'And I knew one day I'd bring you, you bastard, and Tweedledum and Tweedledee, 'ere, down. And, oh boy, does it feel fucking good.'

'You are just like your farver.'

Cyril grinned once more. 'No, I ain't, 'cos he's dead. But I'm very much alive and kicking.'

As soon as the three McNalleys left the shop, Cyril placed his gun back inside his jacket. 'So, lads, now I have me a butcher's shop.' He watched Frank eyeing up all the meat-cutting tools.

'Cor, Frank, you're like a kid in a sweet shop.'

'Me dad was a butcher,' said Frank, turning a skewer over in his hand.

Blakey laughed. 'Frank, your dad, was a butcher, but he didn't cut up sausages or pork chops, did he?'

'Nah, seriously, years ago, he was a butcher.'

Cyril looked around the shop. 'Does he wanna job? 'Cos what the hell do I know about a lamb chop except I like it with mint sauce?'

Blakey wandered into the back of the shop to find two cows hanging from the meathooks and larger lumps of meat stacked on shelves. 'You've got a lot of stock an' all, Cyril. Fuck me, I could hide meself inside this fucking cow.'

The rest of the lads joined Blakey.

'What are ya staring at, Cyril?'

‘Hmm, nuffin much. It’s just good to know what’s back here. You never know if we might need this room.’

CHAPTER TWENTY-TWO

Christian Cooper was in his early forties. He'd gained his reputation by using his brains rather than his brawn. The Russians had been his leading supplier, but they were getting greedy, and he'd heard that, in any case, the Colombian cocaine was of a far better quality.

Mr Bates had put Cyril Reardon's name forward as a person who would act as a middleman for the Colombian cocaine, and after a brief meeting with Cyril on the phone, they'd all agreed a price and when the meeting was to take place.

The only issue Cooper had was he didn't know much about Cyril or his firm. There was a debt to be paid to Mr Bates, but he felt confident that now the old man was dead, it wouldn't matter if it was left unpaid.

The meeting was to take place in a barn in Kent. Cyril arrived promptly at around 2.00 p.m. He was still in a foul mood, and his sombre expression showed. However, Cooper knew no different. Cyril clocked the one car and felt his gun inside his jacket pocket. Frank had his knife and his new meat cleaver, Blakey had his cosh, and Marcus had his fists.

What Cyril or Frank hadn't spotted was the black car

following them.

As soon as they parked next to a Rover, a side door to the barn opened. There, waving them in, was a slim man in a cream suit. Cyril squinted in the poor light to see more clearly, but he didn't recognise him.

'Is that Christian Cooper?' asked Frank.

'I dunno who he is, but he looks harmless enough.'

Blakey laughed. 'And so do you, Cyril, but you ain't.'

'Yeah, but going by the state of him, a stick insect has more meat on its bones. Jesus.' His tone turned serious. 'Frank, leave the case in the boot for a minute, and lock the car, will ya?'

Without questioning Cyril, Frank did as he was asked.

Cyril and his firm all walked together into the barn through the side door. Inside were haystacks and nothing else. Then another man appeared. He was grey-haired, of medium build, wearing a black polo neck, white jacket, and black slacks. He reminded Cyril of the toffs at Gwynnie's engagement party. Yet he wasn't a toff. There was something very effeminate about him.

'I'm Christian Cooper. Glad you could make it.' He looked at Cyril. 'I assume you are Cyril Reardon, right?'

Cyril nodded. 'So, do you have the cash?'

Cooper nodded. 'Yeah, but it looks as though your hands are empty.'

‘No, the gear’s in the car. And the money?’

Cooper snapped his fingers, and a meathead of a man miraculously appeared from behind a haystack holding a canvas sack. Cyril felt uneasy. His eyes skimmed the tall straw structures, and then it dawned on him: the haystacks were a partition. Slowly, he reached inside his pocket and held his hand there.

‘So what’s going on, Mr Cooper?’ Cyril asked, as he flicked his eyes from the skinny young man in the cream suit, who looked petrified, to the bigger meathead holding the canvas sack.

With an irritating chuckle, Cooper flicked his long fringe out of his eyes. ‘That Mr Bates . . . Now, there’s an interesting fellow.’

Cyril didn’t like the way Cooper was talking. ‘What are ya saying, mate?’

Cooper flicked his hair again and smoothed down his lapels. ‘I owed him a debt. He helped me out once upon a time. He said as part of the repayment I should do business with you, and the debt would then be cleared completely. But I have since been informed that he’s dead, so now I have decided I am not obliged to do business with you.’

Cyril felt his neck getting hot. He was taking a severe dislike to this Christian Cooper and wanted nothing more than to butcher the bastard, but he kept his nerve and glared back. ‘Fine, no skin off my nose. In fact, Mr Cooper, you have it all wrong. He was doing you a favour, not the other way around, had you done your homework on me. I have enough buyers out there, and the powder is top quality, as well you know, if, as I assume, you've tried it yourself. So, if you're not interested, then, why bring the money?' He nodded in the direction of the canvas sack.

'Oh that? That was left over from the last supplier.'

Cyril inclined his head, confused, until the penny dropped. Cooper had done over the last dealer. Cyril wondered how the hell he'd got away with it. Then his thoughts turned to making a plan . . . and a bit lively too.

Frank was to his right, as always, while Marcus and Blakey stood to his left.

Cyril assumed that behind those haystacks were more of Cooper's men. The slim one in the cream suit was nothing to worry about. Cyril could see he was still visibly shaking. But the meathead, he suspected, could be a handful. Even more worrying was the idea that he himself was surrounded, and he had no clue as to how many men or what tools they had.

'Well, Cooper, tell your men to show themselves, before they start neighing like donkeys.'

'You were stupid, Reardon. I was told you're a youngster, and I was also told that you had a lot of bottle, but what you don't have is a decent firm.' He laughed. 'You have taken on more than you can chew, Reardon. Just because you knocked seven bells out of Johnnie Carter and Red Deacon doesn't mean you can now take over the manor.' He shook his head and tutted. '*I* run the fucking manor, *I* say who buys and who sells, and you, Reardon, have taken the piss. Putting boxers in the pubs for protection, taking the business from the Russians, you really think you're a big man, don't you?'

'Listen, city boy, stop with the fucking lectures. You ain't me teacher or me farver. You either wanna do business with me or you don't. But I ain't got the time or the patience to fuck about. I have missed me breakfast, I've missed me haircut, and I ain't gonna miss me evening pint. So, what's it to be? A fair deal or a fucking fight? And tell your men to show themselves, the weasels. Because the one thing I ain't is stupid.'

Cooper laughed again. 'You know nothing about me, Reardon. I am rich because I am smart. And, to be honest, I couldn't give a fuck about people like you or anyone else, for that matter. I have no feelings. I take the best offer, and, right now, that ain't from you.'

Cyril was angry; he didn't even bother to answer Cooper. He spun around. 'Come on, lads. I've had enough. I ain't dealing with guinea pigs. I have other shit to take care of.'

Frank followed him, but Marcus glared at Cooper, for a few seconds longer. 'Wanker,' he mumbled, under his breath, as he turned to leave.

'Stop right there, Reardon!' came a voice they all recognised as Johnnie Carter's.

Cyril instantly halted and then he heard the sound of a gun being cocked. He just hoped that his mates had heard it too and could second-guess what he was about to do.

Sliding his hand back inside his pocket, he gripped his gun, and in an instant, he spun round and fired shots while ducking and running towards cover.

Luckily, Frank, Blakey, and Marcus instantly ran for the man with the gun, while he was trying to shoot Cyril. Frank was the first to reach Cooper, and with a fierce plunge of his meat cleaver into the man's head, Cooper went down like a sack of shit.

Then, Red Deacon appeared from behind the haystack partition. He lunged forward swinging a scythe, but as soon as he realised their man with the shooter had gone down, he stopped and stared at Cyril, who was pointing his gun at him.

'You weren't the only ones who brought a gun to the barn dance.' Cyril glared at Deacon and then at Carter. 'You fucked up, didn't ya?'

Blakey reached down and picked up Cooper's gun. He used it to smash Johnnie Carter in the face.

Marcus clumped Deacon so hard in the side of the head that he was knocked out cold. He then went for the meathead, whose right hook was so well telegraphed in advance that Marcus easily dodged its intended path. That gave Marcus his opportunity. With the meathead's stance wide open, it only took a short jab into the gut to have the man on his knees gasping for breath.

Cyril was still pointing his gun at Deacon. 'Frank, give that wanker a permanent reminder of what it's like to cross us.'

Frank pulled out his fisherman's knife from his inside pocket and grinned malevolently. Deacon started to run, but Marcus put his foot out and tripped him over. Deacon, for all his previous bravado, screamed like a baby. But Frank didn't care; he turned him over and ran the knife down his face.

'Now then, every time you have a shave in the morning, you'll be reminded that you don't fuck with me or mine ever again. Got it?'

Unexpectedly, the side door flew open and there like a grizzly bear stood the big ugly Colombian, Johan, brandishing a sawn-off shotgun.

Cyril stared in horror. He knew that one blast from that gun, and he would be embedded in the haystack, but Johan turned the weapon on Johnnie Carter. 'Sorry, Mr Reardon. I heard shots and . . .'

Cyril was gobsmacked. He hadn't expected this at all, but like Maud had said, he wasn't about to look a gift horse in the mouth.

'All under control, mate.'

The slender man in the cheap cream suit looked like a limp fish. He stood shivering, but Cyril knew he was harmless enough. 'You, fetch me the sack with the money in it.'

The man's eyes widened. 'I am sorry, Mr Reardon, but there is no money. This was all a set-up.'

'And you are?'

'Er, me? No one, really. Can I ask that you shoot me in the head? Don't torture me, please,' he cried.

'I asked who you are, not how you wanna die.'

'Oh, er, I'm Augustin, Christian's, er . . .'

'What? He's gay, is he?'

‘I dunno. He paid me on a weekly basis.’ His face dropped as his eyes glazed over.

‘Come here,’ demanded Cyril.

Augustin slowly walked towards Cyril, believing that he too would get a beating.

Cyril leaned into his ear. ‘Was he a cunt?’

Augustin nodded. ‘I can show you the scars if you’d like, Mr Reardon.’

‘Do you know who his buyers are?’

‘Yes, he made me go everywhere with him.’

‘Right, me and you will have words later. I need to clean this mess up first. You keep your mouth shut and do as you’re told. Then you, Augustin, will come out of this intact and with a few quid in your back pocket.’

‘Yes, of course, Mr Reardon.’

Deacon was still clutching his face and moaning like a child, but Johnnie Carter stood firm, although his head now had a lump the size of a golf ball.

‘You came here wearing your big girl knickers to have me set up. Cooper was gonna shoot me in the back. You brought your little army, but you fucked up, and now everyone on the manor is gonna know what’s happened. And you, Johnnie Carter, and your family had best up sticks and move out of South East London, or, I swear to God, I will make it known to every villain this side of the water that you and your lot are wrong 'uns. Oh, and no one will question it because, as you can see, Deacon, the prick, there, will be wearing a nice strip as a permanent reminder. I tell you this now, Johnnie Carter, if you ever try to cross me again, I'll make sure that you'll end up like Cooper.'

Carter stared down at the meat cleaver stuck in Cooper's head. The blood still oozed, but it was the grotesque, hideous expression on Cooper's face that affected Johnnie the most. No mortician would be able to make that face look presentable.

'You!' Cyril pointed to Carter. 'And you.' He looked across to the meathead. 'You both are gonna bury Cooper. If the police ever come knocking at my door, then I'll have you and your family buried as well. Got me?'

Carter and the meathead both nodded. They knew that Cyril Reardon was not messing around.

* * *

Augustin was still quaking in his boots when Cyril pulled him outside. 'Right, mate, me and you are gonna go for a drive, and you are going to tell me who Cooper was selling the gear to.'

Augustin nodded so fast that Cyril suddenly laughed. 'Calm down, will ya, for fuck's sake. I ain't gonna blast you away.'

'Sorry, it's just all been rather scary. He was an evil man.'

'Was he, mate?'

'Yes, I mean, well, actually, I'm at a loss for words, but thank you, Mr Reardon. Thank you.'

'So where did he live and where did he keep his money? 'Cos the drugs still have to be paid for.'

Augustin was silent for a minute. Cyril guessed the lad was contemplating keeping that bit of information to himself.

'Where, Augustin?' he bellowed in his ear. Augustin's eyes flicked to the Rover. 'In the boot.'

'Good lad. Now I need that list of names because the punters will want their gear, and since Cooper has more pressing things to deal with, like making a deal with Him upstairs, he's not in a position to do so, is he?'

'Of course, Mr Reardon. You are quite right.'

Cyril noticed that Augustin was very white, and his lips were turning a shade bluer than he assumed they should. Then, like a sack of potatoes, he hit the ground.

It took a little time before he regained consciousness.

'Blimey, was it all a bit of a shock for ya?' asked Cyril, helping the lad to his feet.

Augustin shook his head. 'No, I haven't eaten for a few days. I just feel . . .' He fainted again.

Johan, who was standing by his car, came over. 'Everything okay?'

Cyril wondered why he was there. After the last fiasco, when the Colombian had tried to drag him into the car, he was intrigued. 'So why did you follow me?'

'Extra security. Mr Sandos told me to keep my distance but to look out for you. I heard the gunshot, and I was protecting the drugs.'

Cyril grinned. 'Well, cheers, mate, anyway.'

'No, thank *you*, Mr Reardon. You could have sent me off the building, but you didn't.'

'Have you got any nosh? This little runt, 'ere, looks as if he's starving.'

Johan helped Augustin to the car, where he gave him a bottle of water and a sandwich.

Augustin was feeling very sheepish; this wasn't how he imagined his life would end up. However, he realised Cyril Reardon and his mob were seriously dangerous men. So he would say and do whatever it took so that he wouldn't end up with a meat cleaver in his head like his boyfriend had. He felt sick; all he could visualise was Christian's head literally split in half. It was so gross that he knew he would never have a good night's sleep again.

* * *

It took nearly two hours for Carter, the meathead, and Deacon to dig a grave and bury Cooper while Cyril took down a list of Cooper's dealers' names from Augustin. Once dusk had fully set in, it was time to call it a day.

Johan stayed to ensure Carter and his men were kept at the barn so that Cyril and his firm had sufficient time to get away and hide the drugs, the money, and the gun.

They didn't have to drive too far away at all because Mr Bates' cottage was conveniently close by. It had been a long time since Cyril had been inside, but nothing had changed at all. He knew that Mr Bates had often driven down to the house to make sure it wasn't going to rack and ruin.

It was Marcus who was blown away with it. 'Cor, why didn't he live here? I mean, it's beautiful, so cosy.'

Frank laughed. 'Listen to you, Marcus. You sound like an old man. All you need is your pipe and slippers.'

Marcus ignored the sarcasm. 'All I need is my Tilly living with me 'ere, and I'll be as snug as a bug in a rug.'

'Fucking 'ell.' Frank laughed.

'Shut up, Frank. I'd live here with my Cindy an' all. It beats fucking Camberwell.'

'Ooooh, *Blakey*.'

Blakey rolled his eyes, and the others grinned, until, that was, they spotted Cyril, who wasn't joining in with the banter.

'Come on, mate. Let's get this gear pugged away and head back to London,' said Frank, nudging Cyril.

Cyril pulled the sofa away from the wall and then lifted the loose floorboards. 'It'll be safe down there, lads, until we find another buyer.'

The room fell silent for a moment as everyone noticed Cyril's dismal tone.

'Are you all right, mate?' asked Frank.

Cyril nodded. 'Still gutted about Mr Bates.'

''Ere, don't your Howie live near here?'

'Yeah, on that pig farm near to where we went hopping. Let's pay him a visit on the way back.'

* * *

As they drove into the farm, Cyril's former mood instantly transformed into his usual laid-back self. He could just see Howie, under the outside lights, with that ruddy complexion, happily walking across the pigpen with two piglets under his arm.

'Howie!' waved Cyril, as the others joined him.

Howie placed the piglets on the ground and hurried over. He climbed over the pigpen and flung his arms around Cyril.

Frank could smell him before he'd even arrived and didn't envy Cyril being hugged by his brother, who was covered in pig shit. But as soon as he'd let go of Cyril and turned to hug Frank, Frank felt he could hardly object, really. Making sure he didn't breathe in, Frank returned the hug.

'Cor, look at you, Howie. You've grown some more.'

Howie smiled. 'Yep, another two inches.'

'How are ya doing?' asked Cyril.

Howie looked behind him towards the farmhouse. 'I'm a bit worried about Mrs Muggeridge. She's not well. She won't get out of her bed.'

Cyril sighed. He knew if she died then Howie would lose his job and his home that he loved so much. 'Does Mrs Muggeridge wanna sell the farm? Because if she does, we could buy it, Howie.'

Slowly, Howie turned his head and frowned. 'Buy it?'

Cyril nodded. 'I'll have enough saved in a few weeks.'

Howie shook his head. 'No need to buy it, Cyril. Mrs Muggeridge says the farm is mine. She had a lawyer make me sign some papers.'

Cyril tutted and sighed. 'Aw, for fuck's sake, Howie. What are you doing signing papers?'

'It's all right. She says the farm is mine as long as I don't sell ol' Rose and Daisy, or eat 'em.'

Cyril was still anxious about his brother signing documents, and so he made him fetch a copy of the agreement for them both to pore over.

While Cyril and Howie went over the details, Frank, Blakey, and Marcus looked at the pigs in the pen. They stank to high heaven, but the surroundings – those that they could see under the outside lights – were beautiful. And although the farmhouse wasn't huge, it was full of character with a thatched roof and small Georgian windows.

'Ah, Howie, yeah, you're right. You do own this lot, as long as Mrs Muggeridge can live out her life here, and you don't sell or kill the two ol' sows.'

'See, Cyril, I told ya. Mrs Muggeridge has been good to me, and, of course, I won't eat Rose or Daisy. They are sweet ol' girls. They can't 'alf eat, though, bones an' all.'

Cyril glanced at Frank, who didn't twig what he was thinking.

'So, Howie, they eat anything, then?'

Howie laughed. 'Yep, they even ate me old wellies. Lucky me feet weren't in them at the time.'

'I might have some meat for them.'

Howie grinned and his eyes twinkled as they used to do all those years ago.

* * *

Frank drove the firm back to the barn, only to find Johnnie Carter, Red Deacon, and the meathead had all vanished. Johan was asleep in the front of the car and Augustin was out for the count on the back seat.

Working by torchlight, the firm spotted some shovels leaning against the barn door, and the grave now easily detectable by the fresh earth on the top of the mound.

Cyril turned to his mates. 'Sorry, lads, but we'd best dig up the body. I don't trust Johnnie Carter. He may just lie low for a bit and later grass us up. If there's no body, then there's no evidence, right?'

Frank shook his head. 'Jesus, I already smell like pig shit, and now I'm gonna smell of sweat.' He sighed heavily and grasped a shovel.

Since the grave was filled with loose earth, it didn't take too long to exhume Cooper's body and have him in the boot of the car before the Colombian and Augustin woke up. The grave was restored to its former state, so it looked authentic, and then the firm drove away again. Blakey looked through the back window, but all he saw was Johan with his mouth open catching flies.

* * *

As soon as they returned to the farm, Howie took Cyril to another pen. It was enclosed, but he climbed up on the metal fence. 'These pigs, they're hungry, Cyril. They'll eat whatever you have for them.'

Cyril didn't want to tell his brother a dead body was going to be fed to the pigs, but Howie seemed to get the gist of it, all the same. Howie winked and headed for the house. 'I'll make us all a drink.'

Marcus shook his head. 'Are you sure about this, Cyril?'

'Well, listen. We killed this bastard, right? And murder carries a hefty sentence. Me, I don't want to be inside for the best years of me life, so the sensible thing we can do is to get rid of the evidence.'

Blakey suddenly felt queasy. 'D'ya mind, lads, if you kinda do this bit alone?'

Marcus pushed Blakey aside. 'Aw, for fuck's sake, you bloody big girl's blouse.' He popped the boot open, grabbed the body, threw it over his shoulder, and marched towards the pen.

Frank and Cyril were wide-eyed. 'Ok, er . . . just throw him in then, I guess,' said Cyril.

Marcus literally hurled Cooper into the pen and instantly some pigs appeared. They were not sweet, pretty piglets but huge pigs, with their long ugly snouts and teeth like bricks. The sounds were horrific.

Cyril guessed where the saying 'Stop eating like a pig' came from.

By the time Howie returned with a tray full of mugs of tea and a huge smile on his face, Cooper's body was completely devoured.

Blakey was holding the contents of his stomach down and Frank was trying to brush off some of the muck on his jacket.

Cyril searched every inch of the pigpen using his torch, but he couldn't find a shred of Cooper's remains. He smiled to himself. He hated bullies and he hated double-crossing men. Cooper was both, but now he was dead.

CHAPTER TWENTY-THREE

Cyril didn't want a party for his twenty-second birthday. He just wanted the keys to his new pad.

But the solicitors were making a big fuss over the equity Cyril was putting into the purchase of the new property. Cyril wasn't stupid; he used the butcher business to launder money and a top-drawer accountant to cook the books.

However, the accountant was taking his time, by ensuring that he couldn't end up in the shit himself, and so the completion date was delayed.

Cyril sighed heavily and kicked the wall outside the solicitor's office.

He'd arranged to pick Flossie up from the hairdresser's, and, as a massive surprise, to take her to their new home, but without the completion in place, he couldn't, and he was feeling more than a little disappointed. She had no idea that he'd been viewing houses in Chislehurst, and that he had his heart set on a smart-looking property. It wasn't huge, but it had its own drive, three bedrooms, and a conservatory to the rear. He'd even bartered with the owners over the furniture, because if he was being honest with himself, he didn't really have a good eye for design. So, having all the furnishings that matched the decor still in place meant this was one less hurdle to overcome. The master bedroom had obviously been designed by the lady of the house because it was pink. It wasn't to Cyril's taste, but he knew Flossie would be in her element. The bed was high and draped in a pink nylon ruffled bedspread. The wall-to-wall carpet was pink, and the wardrobe that stretched across one wall was in cream and edged in ornate gold trim.

He knew Flossie would be thrilled, although she didn't have a ring on her finger yet. He had saved all his money from the drugs and the protection rackets to afford a beautiful palace fit for his princess. She would be so excited, and he assumed that living in Chislehurst would beat having any ring on her finger. He was saving for that and only wanted the best for her. She'd hinted for years about getting married or at least engaged. Cyril, though, wanted to make sure she had a lovely home and a decent car first, and so when he did pop the question, they could get married within a year and live in a charming house. He never wanted to scrimp and scrape like his mother had done for all those years. He wanted to be a lord in his own pad and have his lady by his side.

He had learned to drive, and he'd bought a new Ford Cortina, but the driving test was a real stumbling block: he'd failed it three times. He'd decided it wasn't worth taking a fourth one, after he almost shot the instructor through the window when doing an emergency stop.

Now, pulling up outside the hairdresser's, he noticed that the lights were off. He checked his watch; he was only ten minutes late. Surely Flossie would have waited for him? He'd told her that he would pick her up. He tutted and drove to the tower block. She'd been getting stroppy lately, and as much as he'd tried to pacify her moods, she was still giving him a hard time. He had business to attend to and couldn't always be at her beck and call. There were times when he was late, but he couldn't help that. He made up for it, though, with a gift or a lovely evening out. Sitting in his car, he stared up at the tower block.

His mother still lived in the flat, even though he'd offered to buy her a house. She loved the flat: it was like a sanctuary to her. Henry and Shirley lived a few doors along from him, and they were happy enough. Henry loved working in the butcher's and living a quiet life. Frank had moved into a flat in Lewisham above a hairdresser's that his Trudy was running. Marcus had married his Tilly and was saving up to buy the cottage in Otford that had once belonged to Mr Bates. Blakey, now known as Blakey, although he hated the name, was living in a flat in Bromley with Cindy, and yet the firm all managed to meet up and get down to business at least five days a week.

It had taken Cyril several months to cope with Mr Bates' death, and even when he could smile again, he wondered if he would ever surmount that feeling of being so angry. He thought perhaps he had made a wrong decision when he'd taken a few shots at Cooper. The whole thing had been a mess, and if he hadn't been in mourning, maybe he would have done things differently. However, the one thing that did come out of it was the realisation that the four of them – his firm – were so close and trusted each other implicitly.

As he opened his car door, the cold air bit his face. Winter was around the corner, and so the sooner he was in his new home, the better. He hated the sound of the wind swirling around the bins, along with the loose rubbish left outside by the recent tenants. To him, the flats weren't the same. The new residents were louder, and, in some ways, disrespectful, but not to him, though. He had to laugh when they gave him a wide berth or almost bowed when they addressed him. But he knew the tenants weren't doing it out of respect: they were convinced that his notoriety – he was described as the right-hand man to a Mafia don – was in fact true.

As he was about to slam his car door shut, he saw his Flossie hurrying along the walkway. She had her new coat on, and her hair was piled high in a fashionable beehive. He smiled as he watched her clip-clopping along. Then she stopped at the lifts. He waited by the entrance, ready to greet her with a big hug when the lift door opened.

However, once the door finally slid aside, Flossie looked shocked to see him there. 'Oh, hello, Cyril.'

'I went to the hairdresser's, babe, but you'd already left. Did they wanna shut up shop early?'

'Er, yeah, that's right. I got away before five.'

He stood and stared, feeling uneasy. 'So, what are you up to, all dolled up, babe? I thought we were off out tonight in the local?'

'Oh, well, the girls are off up the Pagoda for a few. I said I'd join them. You don't mind, do ya? Only, we didn't have firm plans, did we?'

Cyril gave her a broad smile. 'Nah. You have a good time. I'll see you later, babe.'

She gave him a quick kiss on the cheek and hurried off towards the bus stop.

Cyril looked over his shoulder and watched her skip away. He loved everything about her – her red hair, her almond eyes, and how she could chuck anything on and still look a million dollars. He knew she was a good-looking woman because every time they were out, other men always eyed her up. No one in his company or where they drank would dare try to chat her up, though. She was his bird, and that was a known fact.

* * *

Feeling slightly disappointed, he casually strolled to his flat, put the key in the door, and wandered inside.

'Cyril, babe, is that you?'

Cyril smiled to himself. 'Who else has a key?'

'Me!' came a deep voice.

Cyril hurried along the hallway and straight into the kitchen to find Howie at the table and a gift-wrapped present in front of him.

Peggy was in her pale blue floral dress that sat just above the knee. She wasn't a teenager anymore, but she still had long slender legs and could get away with wearing a shorter dress. She felt far more at ease at last, and even more so, now that she'd been promoted to shop steward. She turned around and smiled. 'Happy Birthday, Son.'

'Thanks, Mum. Well, this is a surprise. What are you doing here, Howie?'

Howie blushed. 'I've got me a car. The farm has been officially signed over to me, and I wanted to see me brother on his birthday.'

Cyril hugged him and looked at the present on the table. 'For me?'

'Yeah. Go on, open it.'

Cyril peeled off the blue paper and then removed the lid from the box. He clocked the stamp first, though. It was Royal Doulton.

As he scanned what was inside, his eyes lit up. 'Blimey, ah, Howie, thank you so much. It must have cost a fortune.' He stared at the beautiful mug with the horses and hounds and the script – 'The Lord's Mug'.

'Oh, Howie, it's bloody perfect, mate.'

'Yep. Well, you always wanted to be a lord, didn't ya?'

Cyril winked. 'And, little bruvver, one day I will be.'

Peggy removed her pinny and opened the fridge door.

Cyril noticed Howie's eyes widen. As Cyril looked over his shoulder, his did too. His mother was balancing a large cake.

'Blimey, Mum, the size of that! It's like a wedding cake.'

'Yeah, well, it's your birthday, babe, and even though you're a grown man, you're still my little boy, and it makes up for all the years I couldn't make you a big cake.'

She placed the cake on the table and looked at her sons in turn. Howie's face was still the same. His huge beaming innocent smile and ruddy cheeks still shone like a baby's. Cyril had changed a lot. His former slight frame and huge silver eyes had transformed him. He was a big, solid lad now. His face was fuller, and his eyes could change in a second to become dark and threatening. Yet Cyril as a man was still a comical charmer and could even get away with murder.

As much as he was smiling and laughing, she could tell he was hurting inside. She knew about facial expressions: her father had taught her so well. It was a part of being a top poker player. The poker face was one thing, but any facial movements could give the game away, and she had studied them for years. Ninety per cent of her wins were the result of reading other people's expressions.

When Howie got up to use the toilet, Peggy nudged her son. 'What's up, Cyril?'

He knew he couldn't fob his mother off; she knew him too well. 'I dunno, Mum. I thought Flossie would have remembered me birthday. Not that I wanted anything,' he quickly added. 'It's just the way she said . . . Oh, it don't matter now what she said. Anyway, Mum, seeing Howie was my birthday treat. He looks well, Mum, eh?'

'Yeah, he does, like a pig in shit. I wish I could say the same about you, babe.'

'I'm fine, Mum. Next week, I should have completed on the house. The current owners have agreed to leave everything. So, I don't have to go shopping for all that stuff, and I nearly have enough money put by for that ring I told you about.'

Peggy's face dropped. 'Are you sure about all of this, Cyril?'

'Yeah, of course I am. Me and Flossie have been together for ages, and all me mates are married or getting married. Marcus' Tilly is pregnant already. They'll be moving into Mr Bates' cottage soon enough. I think they'll stay with her mum for a few weeks first, though.'

Peggy laughed. 'As if Irene hasn't had enough practice with her brood. But just 'cos they're all getting hitched, it don't mean you have to do the same.'

'I know, Mum, but I do love my Flossie. She's the only girl for me.'

Peggy bit her bottom lip and felt a wave of sadness come over her. She looked at her son's handsome face, and she knew in her heart that Flossie wasn't the one for him. But he didn't know any different; she was his first girlfriend. 'Son, you haven't exactly courted any other girls to compare, have you?'

Cyril's brows snapped together. 'I don't need to when she's perfect.'

Peggy knew then to shut up. He loved Flossie and would never have a bad word said about her.

'Ah, well, what do I bleedin' know, eh? I've been on me own for years now. Mind you, I have the only two men in my life that I need. That's you and Howie.'

Cyril felt he might have been a bit sharp and sighed. 'Sorry, Mum. I didn't mean to get shirty. I thought she would have wished me a happy birthday, though, that's all.'

Peggy wanted to say '*She should do a lot of things, but she only thinks of herself.*' But she kept quiet and cut him another slice of cake.

Howie returned from the bathroom just as there was a knock at the door.

Cyril hoped that Flossie had had a change of heart and remembered his birthday, but when Howie opened the door, Cyril could hear his mates, Frank and Blakey, call out, 'Oi, oi, birthday boy.'

Cyril got up from his chair to greet them.

'Cyril, get ya best suit on, mate. We're off up West. It's ya birthday.'

'How did you know I was home? We didn't plan anything, did we?'

Frank looked at Blakey. 'Nah, but my Trudy said all the girls are going up the Pagoda tonight, so I thought, great, we can have a few sherbets up town and have a real lads' night out.' He saw the flat expression on Cyril's face. 'What's up with you, mate? I thought you'd prefer a night up the Dilly than sitting in a restaurant with Flossie getting all sentimental over a candle and a prawn cocktail.'

Cyril laughed. 'I don't know about sentimental, but, yeah, let's go up West and get mental.'

Frank glanced at Howie. 'You're coming, mate, ain't ya?'

Howie blushed. 'Oh me, nah. I've gotta get back and see to the pigs. I don't like to leave them for too long.'

'Oh, shut up, Howie. They're hardly likely to be having a party while you're away,' said Frank, almost convulsing with laughter.

'It's not my thing really, Frank. I like me farm and me bird.'

Suddenly everyone gasped. 'A bird, Howie? You've got yaself a bird?' choked Cyril.

'Oh, my word, why didn't you say? You could have brought her for tea,' said Peggy.

'What's she like, blonde, brunette, big ti? . . . Oops, sorry,' said Blakey, as he looked at Howie's mum.

Howie was frowning as he noticed all the eager eyes on him. 'She's a parrot.'

Suddenly they all roared with laughter, and, fortunately, even Howie saw the joke and joined in.

* * *

The Playground nightclub inside Hatchetts in Piccadilly was heaving. A queue had formed, and it was raining heavily by the time Cyril, Frank, and Blakey had arrived.

'Aw, you're kidding me,' said Frank, as he looked at the long line of umbrellas.

'Hang on, it's Bernie on the door,' said Blakey, when he noticed his Ronnie's friend.

'Have a word. See if we can jump that queue.'

Blakey pulled his jacket over his head and ran over to the doorman. 'All right, Bernie, it's Cyril's birthday, and you know what he's like when he's got his new ones and twos on.'

Bernie laughed and nodded Cyril's way as the lads appeared. 'Get in, lads. You've no need to queue.' He looked down at Cyril's shoes. 'We can't have you getting them wet, can we?'

Cyril gently slapped Bernie's cheek. 'Nice one, Bernie.'

A few men recognised Cyril and called out in respect, secretly hoping he would get them in before they got drenched. However, Cyril wasn't one for taking out-and-out liberties, so he hurried inside, shook off the excess rain, and headed for the bar. 'On me, lads. It's me birthday after all.'

Frank put his wallet away. 'If you insist, mate, I won't argue. I'll have a vodka and lemon. In fact, make it a double.'

A new group were up on stage blasting out an old Searchers tune, and the glass dance floor that was shaped like a honeycomb was buzzing with young women in crepe dresses swinging their hips.

Cyril sipped his champagne and laughed at a couple of men trying their best to get the attention of two very attractive young ladies. ''Ere, clock that geezer there. That twat, he can't dance to save his life. I mean, I thought I had two left feet, but, fuck me, he looks like he's being electrocuted.'

Frank peered over Cyril's shoulder. ''Ere, ain't that Lord Chambers?'

Blakey peered closer. 'He's one of Campbell's mates. All the toffs are hanging about up here, ya know. Fucking Lord this and Viscount that and Lady Penelope Creighton-Ward.'

Cyril laughed. 'Thunderbirds?'

'Well, fuck me, it's all Tarquin-Radcliffe or some posh double-barrelled name.'

Cyril screwed his nose up. 'Double-barrelled?'

'Yeah, like two names, like Cartwright-Myers, or something like that.'

'I have something double-barrelled, but I keep it locked up in me bruvver's barn. It fires two rounds. Fucking double-barrelled names. Those greedy bastards have to have two surnames, not just the one.'

As they were laughing, and generally taking the mickey out of Lord Chambers, he stopped dancing and walked across to the bar.

Chambers had spotted Blakey, who he recalled had been at the engagement party. 'Hello, there. It's Gwynnie's brother, isn't it?'

Blakey was leaning with one arm on the bar and holding his drink with the other. He nodded. 'Yeah, that's right, and you are Lord . . . ?'

The man stepped forward, extending his hand. 'Call me Byron. I tend to drop the "Lord" bit when I'm among friends.' He glanced at Blakey's friends and smiled.

Blakey placed his drink on the counter and shook Chambers' hand. 'Nice to see ya. So, do you and your lot drink here, then?'

Chambers nodded. 'Yes, often. It's a lively scene, and we meet up most weekends. The Salvador is a little quieter, and I do like to play a few games of roulette. Do you go yourself?'

Cyril turned to face Chambers. 'I go sometimes. They have a poker school downstairs, don't they?'

Chambers inclined his head. 'Yes, indeed they do. Do you play, then, er . . . ?'

'It's Cyril, Cyril Reardon, and, no, I don't play. I can just about get me head around Fish.'

Chambers threw his head back and laughed, but it was all a bit over the top. 'Oh, I say. That's so funny.'

Cyril stared intensely at him with one eyebrow raised. 'Nah, mate, it's true. I don't play poker.'

'Oh, my good chap, you should come along. I often play.'

Cyril nodded. 'Yeah, one day, maybe.'

Frank was knocking back the vodkas and smiling to himself at the scar on Chambers' chin, all the while thinking what a flash, pompous prick he was.

'So are those friends of yours?' asked Cyril, as he pointed to the two pretty women on the dance floor.

'Oh, gosh no. They're just a couple of tarts. I'll probably meet up with them later for a good rogering.'

Cyril felt his throat tighten at this outrageous show of disrespect by Chambers to two young ladies he obviously didn't know.

The club was now filling up, and more people were strutting their stuff on the dance floor. A few men either patted Cyril on the shoulder, offered to buy him a drink, or just nodded out of respect.

Chambers was surprised that such a young man with no sense of real style and who spoke with a rough London accent could know so many people. Intrigued, he decided to stay in the man's company.

'Let me get the next round in, lads.'

Cyril held up his champagne flute. 'I should warn you that mine's the best in the house.'

Chambers scoffed. 'Yes, I will join you. Shall we say champagne all round?'

Frank was still smirking. 'Nah, not for me. But a double vodka and lemon would go down a treat, though.'

Chambers nodded, and then, as he stared for a second at Frank, he did a double take.

'You were at the engagement party too, weren't you?'

With a deadpan face now, Frank slowly nodded, while glaring at the man he loathed.

'Have I ever seen you before that? It's just that I feel our paths may have crossed.'

Frank watched Chambers run his forefinger along the scar on his chin.

'Have you ever been to Otford?' asked Chambers.

Frank shook his head. 'I've not been outside of London, mate. Why?'

Chambers' long forehead crinkled up. 'Oh, no reason. I just thought perhaps we had met a long time ago.'

Cyril was laughing inside at Chambers' obvious failure to get Frank to talk and at Frank's considerable talent for displaying such a good statuelike face.

The moment was interrupted by the two girls who had been dancing. They were now making their way towards the bar.

Chambers had spotted them, and he was eagerly grinning, assuming they were heading his way, but when they stopped by Cyril, he was taken aback.

'Well, if it ain't Cyril Reardon,' said the girl with short blonde hair and wearing a bright red dress. 'I'm Liberty. I lived just along from yours, in Bermondsey. I heard you've done well for yaself.' She sidled up to him. 'This is me mate, Wendy. She's out of Poplar, ain't ya, Wend?'

Wendy, a tiny slip of a girl, with red hair that was stiff from so much hair lacquer, smiled coyly. 'Hiya, Cyril. And you must be Frank Marsden,' she said, as she smiled at Frank.

'Yeah, love. Do I know you?' he asked politely.

'No, but I wouldn't mind getting to know you.'

At that, Frank chuckled and blushed. It wasn't in his nature to flirt. 'Go on, girls, run along. I'll send over some Babycham. How about that?'

Liberty broke into a laugh. 'Spoilsport.'

'Let *me* get you that drink, ladies. My name is Lord Byron Chambers. Pleased to meet you.'

The girls looked him up and down. 'A lord, yeah? Blimey, I've never met a real lord before,' said Wendy.

'Really? Well, I *am* the real thing. I have my Bentley outside, and I could show you around my stately home if you'd like.'

Cyril nudged Frank and moved him away from Chambers. 'Get a load of him, will ya. *My name is Lord Byron Chambers*,' mimicked Cyril, in a posh voice.

Frank spat out his drink and roared with laughter.

As Blakey also moved a few feet away out of earshot from the girls and Chambers, he said quietly, 'Fucking twat.'

While Chambers' attention was focused on Wendy, Liberty was still eyeing up Cyril. She knew who he was and how much clout he had, and she wanted to be the girl on his arm. Leaving Chambers to chat up Wendy, she came up to Cyril. 'I have no interest in lords meself.'

Cyril raised his chin. 'Well, he obviously likes you. Now, sorry to sound rude, darling, but I'm having a private conversation with me mates.'

'Cor blimey, she must be worth it, is all I can say.'

Cyril beamed. 'Oh, yeah, she is.'

Frank was still staring daggers at Chambers when Cyril nudged him again. 'You hate that geezer, don't ya?'

Frank gulped back his vodka. 'I do, mate, I fucking do. He's such a prick, and he really wanted his ol' man to shoot us that day, all over a few fucking fish.'

'It's more than that though, Frank, ain't it, mate?'

Frank took a deep breath. 'It's the way he fucking looks at us, like we're nuffin. He did it at Gwynnie's engagement, and he's doing it here. He only wants to join our company because we probably know more people in here than he does. 'Cos, Cyril, I didn't see anyone fucking shaking his hand or patting his back.'

'Frank, he's a knobhead and nuffin to us, so I wouldn't worry about him and his lot. They ain't our cup o' tea, so let's get another round in and have a wiggle on the dance floor.'

Frank rolled his eyes. 'That's it, mate, you'll go and throw all your kudos right out the window when you start flicking your hooves and showing us all up. Blimey, the last time you did that I had to tell everyone you were paralytic.'

Cyril waved his hand, demonstrating that he didn't care what people thought. There weren't many men who would dare to say too much. Especially not after the rumours going around that he had pretty much sown up every racket in South

East London and had the Colombian's backing.

CHAPTER TWENTY-FOUR

Cyril awoke the next morning with a stinking hangover. His tongue was glued to the roof of his mouth, and his head felt as though it was in a vice. He wondered where the hell the grumbling noise was coming from inside his bedroom. Turning over, he realised that Frank was crashed out on Howie's bed, still fully clothed. Then Cyril noticed he himself was as well.

Snippets from last night popped into his head, and he cringed. He'd drunk way too much, danced way too much, and probably pissed off a few people in the process.

Slowly, he sat upright and felt a wave of sickness envelope him. Then he had to run to the bathroom. Whatever he'd drunk that evening was now down the toilet. He gasped for breath and then felt his pockets. They were empty. 'Bloody hell's bells,' he said to himself. All the money he had taken out last night, he'd obviously spent, and the worst of it was, he couldn't remember much about it.

As soon as he got up and wiped his face, Frank appeared in the doorway.

'Shit me, you look rough, mate.'

Frank sighed. 'I don't feel the best. Me mouth's like the bottom of a parrot's cage.'

'What the fuck did we get up to last night, Frank?'

Frank laughed. 'Well, you downed a bottle of champagne and got on the table to show the girls how to dance. You fell off and landed arse over tit, knocking a group of lads over. They took umbrage and one of 'em tried to land you a right hook. Blakey ended up smashing the life out of the geezer. I larruped two of 'em, and then the bouncers threw the lads out. At least, I think that's what happened. Hang on, Cyril, did I drive us back here?'

Cyril shrugged his shoulders. 'Beats me, mate, but you don't live here anymore. Remember, you moved above the hairdresser's with Trudy.'

'Oh, shit! I bet I don't anymore. She'll be bleedin' fuming.'

Cyril shook his head. 'Go and buy her a bunch of flowers. She'll be all right about it.'

Just as Cyril stepped aside for Frank to use the bathroom, a very loud bang made them both freeze.

'Open the door and come out with your hands above your heads!'

Frank glared at Cyril. 'Oh fuck!'

'Shit! Did anyone end up brown bread last night?' asked Cyril, as he looked at his knuckles.

Frank shrugged. 'Fucked if I know, Cyril. I don't even remember getting home.'

Peggy appeared from her bedroom and glanced at the two young men. 'Listen, whatever you've done, you were at home playing cards. You know the sequence.' She nodded firmly.

Frank had to go over it in his head. It was an alibi they had joked about with Peggy, if ever they'd find themselves in bother, but now, it seemed suddenly to have become a real possibility.

Peggy pulled the front door open to find the walkway swarming with police. And there, looking her up and down, was Chief Inspector Cummins.

'Well, hello, Peggy.'

'How dare you call me, Peggy. If you, mate, want to address me, then it's Mrs Reardon to you.'

'And it's Chief Inspector to you, Peggy Reardon.'

'I don't do polite when it comes to the likes of you, Cummins.'

Leon Cummins was in his late fifties. He'd been in the force since he'd left school and had worked the area for years. Everyone on the estate and from around the area knew him. He was a nasty piece of work. Once he got a suspect inside the station, he would have his 'alone time', as he called it, and use a snooker ball in his fist to punch the hell out of them, but only along their midriff. He left no facial bruising.

His green eyes stared intensely, daring Peggy. He wasn't

particularly tall, but he was heavily built and had thick wiry grey hair and profuse bushy eyebrows. He moved quite fast for an overweight man of his age. 'Now, Peggy, no obstructing the justice system. We are here to arrest your son.' He grinned.

'Oh, yeah? What for, Cuntins?'

Cummins growled. 'It's Cummins. And I thought you were more of a woman than that, using foul language that doesn't suit you.'

'Nah, and being a chief inspector don't suit you either. You ain't got the smile for it.'

'Move aside, Peggy,' he bellowed, as his eyes focused on her son and Frank Marsden in the hallway. He then whispered in her ear, 'Shame you haven't got ol' Mr Bates to cover your arse now.'

Peggy looked at him expressionless. Just one eyebrow rose by a mere half an inch, but, otherwise, there was not even a muscle twitch on her face.

'You may have got away with the landlord's murder, all those years ago, Peggy Reardon, but you watch me, I'll have your son for murder, and fucking banged to rights.'

She continued to stare at him. 'And what a prize prick you will look when you have the wrong man.'

'Oh, I have the right man all right, Peggy. In fact' – he pointed his finger at her – 'I have *both* of the men.'

'Well, Cuntins, good luck with that.' She stepped aside, allowing Cummins to enter.

Two police officers pushed past and handcuffed both Frank and Cyril. The officers tried to drag Cyril and Frank away, but it was Cyril who bellowed.

'Oi, you div, you've no need to pull me arms out of me sockets. I'll happily help you with any inquiries.' He stopped and looked at Cummins. 'I don't believe that you have read me my rights.'

Cummins rolled his eyes. 'I see we've got a right cocky one 'ere. Mr Cyril Reardon, I am arresting you for the murder of Christian Cooper. Anything you do say can and will . . .'

'That's better. Now I know why I am being shackled and dragged outta me house. Sorry, Mum, I'll be home by teatime. Call my solicitor for me, will you, please?'

Cummins took an instant dislike to Cyril Reardon; he was cocky and charmingly confident. Cummins thought Frank Marsden, however, looked nervous, but then he wasn't sure if Marsden was always so quiet and dark-eyed.

He tauntingly grinned. 'Right, lads, turn this place upside down. We're looking for a shooter,' he said, as he presented Peggy with a search warrant.

She sighed heavily. 'You make sure none of your fucking drips break anything. That's my bedroom, and so that's out of bounds, unless I'm a suspect.'

A young officer was just about to go inside.

'Oi, drippy bollocks, that room is out of bounds. I know my rights.'

The young officer looked at Cummins, who nodded.

'You, Peggy Reardon, used to be quite sweet. I see you have changed.'

'And you, Cummins, have always been a monster, so I speak a language that you understand.'

As Cummins turned to walk away, he whispered in her ear, 'I know you killed the landlord, and I know Mr Bates went back to clean up your mess. You would never have had the strength to throw him down the cellar. And, one day, I'll prove it.'

Peggy had her arms crossed as she leaned against the hallway wall. 'Mr Bates is dead, the landlord is dead, and like I said, I never killed him, so you'll be scratching your bonce for a very long time.'

'And that boy of yours, I bet you're proud of him, aren't you?'

Peggy allowed a full smile to crawl its way across her face. 'Very proud.'

'Peggy, your son may have gotten away with a lot over the years, but, trust me, that smile on your face will soon disappear when he's locked up on a murder charge.'

'My son hasn't murdered anyone.' She glanced around at the police as they completed the search of the rooms – all except hers. 'They don't seem to have found this "shooter", as you put it. My boy is no gangster. He's a kid.'

'A kid? Seriously, Peggy, a kid, yeah? Frank Marsden and

your son robbed the factory wages runners. We know that. And the protection racket has your boy's name all over it. *And*, Peggy, you are walking around with your head up your arse, if you think that your son is as innocent as they come.'

Peggy shrugged. 'You call it a protection racket. He calls it a security company.'

Cummins' eyes twitched in anger. 'I don't care. I will have that boy locked up. You just watch me.'

* * *

Frank looked over at Cyril, who was being pushed inside the police car. He felt more confident when he saw Cyril wink, and then he smiled.

As the police car drove around the tower block to join the main road, Cyril spotted Johnnie Carter. He was alone and marching towards the estate. Carter looked nervous. He had his hands in his pockets and his head down.

As Carter glanced up, he could see Cyril in a police car. His eyes widened when he saw Cyril wave at him.

What was Carter doing alone and walking onto his estate? Cyril wondered. Cyril was on the point of turning his head to have a proper look back until an officer told him to keep his eyes forward. Something in his gut told Cyril that it wasn't Johnnie Carter who'd grassed. He guessed it was more likely to be Red Deacon or the only other person would be Augustin.

It wouldn't be long before he would get to know exactly what the filth had on him because he knew the one thing they didn't have was a dead body. If there was no body, how could a murder have taken place?

The cold and rather drab interview room contained a table and four chairs. Cyril was pushed inside and told to sit down. He did as he was told; he wasn't in the mood for mental gymnastics because he was still nursing a hangover. As he composed himself, he heard Frank's deep voice bellow, 'All right, you don't have to fucking push me.'

It wasn't too long before Cummins and another detective entered the room Cyril was in.

'Right, Mr Cyril Reardon, I am Chief Inspector Cummins, and this is Detective Inspector Bracken.'

Cyril smiled but noticed that Bracken had a habit of rubbing his nose and then flicking his hair back.

Cummins sat with his hands on the desk, twirling his wedding ring. 'So, you know why you're here, I'm sure.'

Cyril didn't answer; he simply glared.

'You're not going to answer me then, Cyril?'

'I didn't hear you ask a question. All you've told me is that I know why I am here.'

'Oh, I see. So we've got a right fucking clever clogs here, have we? Where were you around 2.00 p.m. on Friday the fourth of November?'

Cyril looked at the empty seat beside him. 'I'll wait until my brief arrives, if you don't mind, Mr Cummins.'

'So, Cyril. So you're frightened you might say the wrong

thing, is that it? Not man enough to answer on your own, are you? Well, my son, if you think that a brief will get you out of this, mate, then you are wrong. We have so much on you that you are going down for a very long time.'

Cyril raised his eyebrow. 'Son, eh? Let's get something straight, right. You may be the head poncho in here, but I ain't your son *or* your fucking mate.'

Bracken piped up before Cummins had a chance to speak. 'Honcho. You mean *honcho*.'

Cyril grinned malevolently. 'Nope, poncho. I meant *poncho*.'

Cummins flared his nostrils and gritted his teeth. Placing his hands palm down on the desk, he pushed himself up. 'Well, Cyril, you can wait for your brief, and while you do, you can mentally prepare your statement. And, as you're doing that, I'll be taking a statement from the key witness. Oh, I bet you didn't imagine that the man who saw everything would grass on the likes of Cyril Reardon, did you? Wrong!'

Cyril guessed then that it wasn't Johnnie Carter because he saw him in the street. He naturally assumed it was Red Deacon. Especially after they had left the man in such a mess.

* * *

Peggy paced the floor, her nerves in tatters. She hoped and prayed that they genuinely had nothing on her son. She had a good idea what Cyril had been up to, but she'd tried not to ask questions, as it wasn't her place to do so.

Just as she stubbed out her second cigarette, there was a

knock at the door. She assumed it was Henry or Shirley, but as she pulled the door open it was a young man she'd never seen before. Probably a little older than her son, he was well dressed in black slacks and a black blazer and his hair was neatly cut around his ears.

Nervously, he looked along the walkway before asking if he could come in.

Peggy sensed the urgency in the young man and allowed him in without much thought. Her main worry was her son.

'Sorry to bother you, Mrs Reardon, but I saw Cyril and Frank being carted away in the police cars. I was on me way over to warn Cyril that someone had grassed on him. Is there any way you can get a message to him, to let him know that it wasn't me or Red Deacon?'

'And you are?'

'Johnnie Carter. Mrs Reardon, me and Cyril are enemies, yeah. He took my protection racket and we've had a couple of barneys, but I ain't a grass. Red Deacon may be bad news and a right twat, but he never grassed neither, 'cos he has a family now and a new baby, and no one in their right mind would mess with Cyril, not in that way.'

Peggy snatched her packet of cigarettes from her apron pocket. She was down to her last one, but she decided to light it up all the same. 'And how can I believe you?'

'I dunno, Mrs Reardon, but all I can say is I was in the pub with Deacon when the fuzz came in and dragged us out. They said they had reason to believe that Cyril Reardon and Frank Marsden killed a bloke and made us bury him.'

Peggy took a deep drag on her third cigarette in the space of ten minutes. Really, she didn't want to know if what Johnnie Carter had just said was true or not.

'We both said to the filth we had no idea what they were on about. But they said they would be back, after they'd had a word with Cyril.'

Peggy nodded. 'All right, Johnnie, I will be sure to pass on the message.'

'It's urgent, Mrs Reardon, because if Cyril knows it ain't us that's grassed, then he'll know what to do, and he won't confess.'

Peggy nodded. 'Okay, I'll let him know what you've told me.'

Carter nodded politely and left with his hands still in his pockets.

As soon as Peggy closed the door, she hurried to the new phone that Cyril had had installed for her. She dialled the solicitor's number, and, luckily, he answered right away.

'Percy, it's Peggy Reardon again. I am so glad you haven't left yet. I have just had a visit from a chap called Johnnie Carter. Apparently, the police pulled him and Red Deacon out of a pub and questioned them about a murder they were implicated in. He says that neither he nor Deacon grassed up Cyril. He said to be sure Cyril gets the message because then he would know what to do next.'

'Okay, Peggy. I was just gathering my things. I'm on my way now. What did this Johnnie Carter look like?'

Light brown hair, slim build, black blazer and black slacks, around twenty-five years old, and he has a front tooth missing and an old bruise around his temple.'

'I will call you as soon as I can, hopefully with good news.'

'Thank you so much, Percy.'

* * *

Cyril's mouth was bone dry, his head was still thumping, and his anger was rising until it was nearly off the charts. Percy Milton was taking his time, and now the reality was kicking in. If they had Deacon in the next room, then they would at least have the full account of what had happened. He took a deep breath and put his hands under the table. He didn't want to appear nervous at all.

The door opened and there in a smart suit with a gold chain dangling from his watch pocket stood Milton. His attire was immaculate. The pinstriped suit was tailor-made to fit his slim but tall frame. With his black hair parted in the middle and cut above his ears, his face was framed. His distinguished moustache didn't have a hair out of place and even his thick dark eyebrows were neatly trimmed.

He settled his briefcase on the table, sat down, and shuffled his chair to face Cyril, but any useful moment between the two was short-lived when the door was thrown open and Cummins stormed in and sat down opposite Cyril and Milton.

'So we are all ready to go, then, are we?'

Milton threw a death glare at Cummins. 'No, we are not. I

have a few papers for Mr Reardon to sign before we begin.'

Cummins rolled his eyes, shot up from his chair, which was sent sprawling across the room, and slammed the door shut behind him.

'Your mother called, Cyril. Apparently, Johnnie Carter gave her a message for her to pass on to you via me. The gist of it was that Carter said he didn't grass, and neither did Red Deacon. It seems that the police had pulled them out of the pub and questioned them.'

Cyril nodded and frowned. 'So, what happens now?'

'What happens now is that you say nothing. Nothing at all. Not unless I tell you to. Say "no comment". I will do most of the talking because I want to ascertain what evidence they have on you.'

'What about Frank?'

Milton waved his hand. 'I am looking after him as well, so don't you worry about Frank. Let's get you sorted out first.'

Cyril nodded. Not for the first time, Percy Milton was proving to be top class.

'Is there any chance I could get a drink? I am hung-over. My head is pounding.'

Milton dived into his briefcase and pulled out two tablets. 'Here you go. I'll organise a drink.'

Cyril tried hard to swallow the tablets but almost threw up when they wouldn't go down because his mouth was so dry, and the taste was vile.

Milton got up and left the room, leaving Cyril battling with the tablets.

He had only gone a few minutes when he returned with three plastic cups, one with water and the other two containing tea. 'Bloody-minded ignoramuses. Quick, take these, before I bloody scold myself.'

Cyril quickly retrieved the teas and took a mouthful to get rid of the lingering taste.

'Ah, thank you, Mr Milton.'

'Please call me Percy. Now then, the lawyer-client privilege states that whatever you say to me stays between us. That said, though, I don't want to know if you have killed this chap or not. I will take it that you didn't, unless you want to confess, which I strongly recommend at this stage you don't.'

Cyril cupped the tea with both hands and sipped as much as he could without burning his mouth. 'I don't intend to confess to—'

'To something I didn't do,' said Milton, finishing off Cyril's sentence for him.

* * *

'Ready now, are we?' asked Cummins, as he barged into the room once more.

Milton nodded and indicated for Cummins to take a seat. Cummins huffed at the insult. This was his station after all.

‘Hmm, I thought you would’ve retired by now, Mr Milton.’

‘Likewise, Mr Cummins.’

Cyril could sense the long-term dislike between the two men.

Cummins sat down opposite Cyril while Bracken sat opposite Milton.

The tape was inserted in the tape recorder and Cummins began with a broad smile. ‘For the tape, what is your full name?’

‘Cyril Reardon.’

‘Where were you around 2.00 p.m. on Friday the fourth of November?’

Cyril put his finger to his lips and stared up at the ceiling. ‘Let me see . . . Oh, yeah, I was at home with my mum and Frank Marsden.’

‘And she will corroborate that, will she?’

Cyril chuckled. ‘She will unless she’s developed amnesia or dementia or whatever.’

‘Just answer the question.’

‘Yeah, of course she will. She don’t tell lies.’

Cummins huffed sarcastically, which got Cyril’s back up. However, he knew he must never lose his temper while being questioned. It showed a violent tendency. Mr Bates had taught him about that, among a hundred other things.

'So what were you doing?'

'Playing cards,' said Cyril.

'Poker, I'm guessing. Right?'

Cyril didn't answer.

'Well?'

'Sorry, I didn't hear a question.'

Cummins loosened his collar. 'Still showing your cocky side, eh? What game were you playing? In fact, Cyril, take me through the afternoon and evening, minute by minute.'

'I was tired, so I didn't get up until late afternoon. Me mum made a round of sandwiches and then Frank knocked at the door. It's uncanny, Mr Cummins. Do you know that whenever there's food about to be brought to the table, Frank appears like magic.'

'Cyril, I'm not especially interested in the habits of any of your friends. Let me repeat what I said for the record. What game were you playing? And I want you to take me through that afternoon, early evening, minute by minute, with no bullshit this time.'

'We sat down in the kitchen, ate the sandwiches, drank some tea, and then played poker. I won two games, Mum won three, and Frank lost every game.'

'You've a good memory, Cyril. It's so good it sounded as if you've practiced it. Have you?'

Cyril stared into Cummins' eyes, not saying a word.

'So what hand did your mother win with? Can you remember that?'

Cyril looked nervously at Milton who said, 'You don't have to answer that, Cyril. Not everyone has a perfect memory, not from a few weeks ago.'

'Uh, I am trying to remember.'

'Well, you remember eating sandwiches. Do you remember what was in them?' asked Cummins, looking pleased with himself.

'Oh, that was it. Yeah, me mum won her first game with four kings, her second game with a royal flush, and her final game with three queens and a pair of aces . . . Oh yes, and we had cheese and pickle sandwiches. Is that good enough for ya?'

'And Frank will say the same, will he?'

Cyril laughed. 'How do I know?'

'What is your association with Christian Cooper?'

'*Who*?'

'Oh, come on, Cyril. Christian Cooper was a well-known drug dealer. You had a meeting with him on that Friday afternoon. We've got a witness who put you there.'

Cyril shrugged his shoulders. 'Like I said, I've never heard of him.'

'What is your relationship with Johnnie Carter?'

Cyril shrugged his shoulders again. 'I don't have one.'

'And Red Deacon?'

Once more, Cyril shrugged his shoulders. 'I don't really know him.'

'Well, Johnnie Carter seems to know you. We questioned him, you see.'

Cyril stayed silent.

'Chief Inspector, we don't seem to be getting anywhere, and the clock is ticking. What exactly do you have in the way of evidence that my client has murdered this chap Christian Cooper?'

'We have a witness that says so.'

'Hmm, a reliable witness, is he or she? And where did this murder take place and at what time? Because my client seems to have a firm alibi for the afternoon and early evening of the fourth of November.'

Cummins ground his teeth and leaned back on his chair. 'The murder took place in a barn on the outskirts of Eynsford. Oh, and trust me, I have a very reliable witness.'

'And would your witness have any grudge against my client?'

'What? No, of course not. He doesn't have a grudge with Mr Reardon or Mr Marsden.'

'Who is this so-called witness? Tell us that, and then maybe my client can confirm whether or not he had a grudge with them.'

'You know I can't tell you that.'

'My client has rights. So, tell me, how was the victim murdered?'

'He was either shot or he died from a meat cleaver to the head.'

Milton grinned and leaned forward. Deliberately, he whispered, 'You don't have a body, do you? All you have is someone out to cause trouble. That's right, isn't it, Chief Inspector?'

'We have a witness, a grave, and several shell cases, but we have a man who saw it all happen, and who has described the incident in graphic detail.'

Milton stood up. 'Hmm, well, you have nothing to charge my client with at the present time. Confirm his alibi, with his mother, and/or Mr Marsden, and then you must either charge Mr Reardon or let him go. I would personally have my money on you letting him go.' He laughed and patted Cummins' shoulder. 'Nice try, Leon, nice try. Now show me to my next client, Frank Marsden. Oh, and I want time alone to fill out the necessary paperwork. You know how it all works.'

CHAPTER TWENTY-FIVE

Leon Cummins was livid because he knew that Cyril and Frank had been involved in Cooper's disappearance and the details given by Augustin were too clear and descriptive for him to be making it all up. The only thing they had was his statement of accounts and the shell casings, but, again, it was a barn, and the gun could have belonged to the local farmer. The barn itself was as clean as a whistle, although the site of what looked like a grave that had been filled in was a strange thing.

If only Augustin had contacted them earlier, they may have been able to lift prints at least to prove that Reardon and Marsden were there. He shuddered when he thought of Augustin. The skinny man was a creep. His suit was way too large for him, and the floral shirt was over the top for a man who acted so shyly and submissively. He wondered if it was an act, and a thought crossed his mind that Augustin was wearing a dead man's clothes. Either that or he had killed Cooper himself.

* * *

Cyril stayed low for a while. The lads were counting themselves lucky that they hadn't been charged with murder or aiding and abetting. It was a sharp reminder that they were not infallible. Cyril was grateful to Johnnie Carter, although somewhat begrudgingly. But Cyril's view was simple: if you do good by me, I will see you all right.

They had held a meeting in the Mitcham Mint. Red Deacon had promised to stay well away and get on with his life as a family man, and Johnnie Carter was given free rein to run his business in North London. He wanted to jump on the bandwagon of this new cocaine craze, and so he agreed to buy the drugs from Cyril.

When Carter had cheekily offered a partnership, Cyril had laughed in his face. He'd told him firmly that the only relationship he would entertain with Carter would be if the man bought the drugs from him and no one else. The Carters and the Deacons knew only too well not to push their luck, after rumours went around that a skinny man dressed in an oversized cream suit was left hanging by his feet from the new Breydon Bridge the day before it opened, and he was screaming for hours, until someone cut his throat with a fisherman's knife.

Although Cyril was called in for questioning over Augustin's death, he'd had the perfect alibi and so had Frank. They had been playing cards at Peggy's flat. And why would they want to murder a complete stranger? They were never told that Augustin had been the police informant.

* * *

It was time for Marcus and Tilly to move into the cottage, but before Cyril handed over the keys, he went to the house and removed the most personal belongings.

There was something about the cottage that made Cyril feel warm inside. He wasn't sure if it was the feeling of safety when Mr Bates had taken him and Howie from the farm and kept them there until the police had released his mother from the station. Whatever it was, he knew that the cottage was going to the perfect couple. The garden was long and well established, with plants and bushes. Their child would have such a wonderful time. It would be a huge difference from how he grew up with all the dark and damp and sooty walls inside his house in Bermondsey.

Inside the cottage, it was cold. But it always was until the open fire took a hold. The walls were stone, and if the property was left empty for long periods of time, it could get pretty chilly inside.

He climbed the stairs and turned left into the bedroom at the front of the house. This was the largest one. There against the wall on the right was a double bed covered with a thick eiderdown. The mahogany wardrobes didn't have a scratch on them. At the foot of the bed was a trunk, and underneath the bed was a suitcase; it was an old Army suitcase. First, he lifted the lid of the trunk, which contained only blankets. Then he pulled out the suitcase from under the bed. He assumed it would just contain a few old papers and memorabilia from the war. But it was much heavier than he'd expected, and as he lifted it and placed it on the bed, he felt a chill creep up his spine. It was as if he was uncovering Mr Bates' grave. He flipped the lid open and stared at the neatly placed boxes that were all filled with letters. Many of them had been unopened. Closing the lid, he carried the suitcase down to the living room. He lit the fire and waited for the flames to dance up the chimney. The house needed to be warmed up before Tilly could comfortably move in with her new baby. He added another log and could feel the room warming up. The feeling of comfort enveloped him, and he went on to light the log burner in the kitchen. Before long, the house was so inviting that Cyril didn't want to go outside and face the bitter wind. He sat on the floor with the suitcase open, pondering over the letters; after five minutes, he was still unsure if he should burn them or keep them. They were Mr Bates' most private belongings; he got that. But his inner voice was telling him to read them. His gut instinct won the day.

When he removed the first letter and saw that it was addressed to Arthur Bates, his curiosity was piqued by the handwriting on the envelope. It was ornate, written in a cursive style, and Cyril guessed the letter was written by a woman. The address was 'Wormwood Scrubs'. This was confirmed by the prison approval stamp when he looked on the back of the envelope. For some strange reason, he held the letter to his nose and smelled the faint perfume. He sighed. This was Mr Bates' very personal relationship. He hesitated before he removed the letter from the envelope. But, suddenly, as if a woman's voice had just jumped off the page, he read and almost heard the words.

Dear Arthur,

It's so very hard for me because mother isn't at all well. I would love to come more often, my darling, but she needs my constant attention. And God forbid she ever found out that you, my beloved, were in prison. Dillon has been by and dropped in a basket of food. He really has been a blessing and a godsend for me and Mother.

I do hope you are coping in there and it is not as terrible as I imagine it to be.

Please write soon as I do look forward to your letters.

All my love

Annie

Cyril stared at the delicate handwriting and could hear her saying those words. It was so bizarre to read a love letter to Mr Bates, knowing that it was from his grandmother, before she married his grandfather Dillon. He paused, in thought, before he moved on to the next letter.

Dear Arthur,

I received your letter; you do sound ever so upbeat. I wish I could respond in such a jolly manner, but Mother is quite difficult these days. I am sure she is up and about when I am out of the house. However, she is demanding so much of my attention that I find it impossible to leave her alone. The last time I did, she knocked the vase over and soaked her slippers.

Dillon has been over. He stayed with Mother while I went shopping; he has been ever so wonderful. He told me he has sent you some money. I wish I could help in some way, my darling, but I am simply broke. Mother refuses to open her purse, and since I will not marry Lord Carroway, she is cutting me out of her will. Oh, it's all rather a mess, but I will try to visit you next week. I am missing you awfully.

All my love

Annie

Cyril felt strange: he was reading history – his family history. Annie was his grandmother, and by the way she wrote, she was fairly well educated. He thought back to when he was very young, to when his mother took a china cup and saucer to the market.

It had belonged to her mother, and he remembered she had carefully wrapped it in newspaper, and when she presented it to the china man, he had marvelled at its quality. 'It's worth a lot,' she had told him. 'It was me muvver's.'

He'd never pressed his mum for information about their family history, but, now, after reading the two letters, he wanted to know more. Surely, Annie could only have married a lord if she herself had been some type of aristocrat? His mother had never mentioned any of that to him.

He opened the next letter but realised someone had ripped it to pieces and then stuck it back together again.

Dear Arthur,

Things have become very difficult here. My brother has now moved into the house and my mother has ordered me out. The Claremonts have put me up for a week, but then I shall have to find my own lodgings. Dillon has offered me rooms at his house. He has been so generous and kind. Would you mind awfully if I took up his offer of the tenancy? It's not ideal but beggars simply can't be choosers.

I don't know when I will see you or be able to write. I am so terribly sorry. I miss you, my darling Arthur.

All my love

Annie

Cyril could see where this was leading, and he really felt for Mr Bates. He had to read on. However, the next letter in the series was written in different handwriting, with a firm style.

Hello Arthur,

Sorry to write this. I hope you can understand. Annie and me have gone and gotten wed. Man to man, I had to write and tell you myself. I couldn't help falling in love with her, Arthur. You weren't around, her mother's been a right bitch, and I was all she had. She did say that you hadn't asked for her hand in marriage. That's not an excuse, I know, but I just hope you understand.

Yours

Dillon

That was harsh, thought Cyril. Even though the words were from his grandfather, he still felt sorry for Mr Bates. After all, he'd never known his grandfather, but Mr Bates had been there teaching him everything he knew. Getting up from the floor, Cyril walked about in deep thought. He'd never felt like this before. It was as if he was going back in time and seeing a story unfold. Then he recalled Mr Bates wanting to tell him about what he'd done to his grandfather, but then he had died. He stared down at the suitcase. *Were the answers contained in those letters*? he wondered.

He noticed a bundle of letters tied up with string all unopened. As he held the letters in his hands, he knew that whatever they conveyed inside would mean he would be the first to read them. A flood of anticipation and excitement ripped through him. His mouth turned dry. *Did he have the right to read them*? he questioned. Glancing around the room, he felt the stillness and the peace. Slowly, he eased himself onto the sofa and carefully untied the string. The first letter was from Annie; he could tell by the handwriting. Taking a deep breath, he cautiously opened it, taking care not to rip it.

Unfolding it, he held his breath as if he knew the words would have an effect on him. Slowly, he read them, and he could almost imagine hearing her voice again, but what he read made his heart skip a beat. In fact, he had to blink twice before he reread the letter.

Dear Arthur,

I am writing this letter with a very heavy heart. The time is coming close that I should leave this world. I know how much I have hurt you. It showed in your eyes when we last met at the time of Dillon's arrest.

I know you thought me cold and heartless, when I decided to abandon you and agreed to marry Dillon, but I want you to know that I always loved you. I had no choice but to marry Dillon. I was a single woman with a child on the way. At that time, you had only just received your eight-year sentence, and my mother agreed to welcome me and the child back into her life if I was married. She couldn't bear the shame of having an unmarried mother as a daughter. It would have resulted in the ultimate humiliation for the family.

I have lived with the guilt and the embarrassment all my life. I will die having lived a lie. For the hurt this will cause you, I am sorry. No doubt, God will see fit to punish me when I finally meet Him.

My little Peggy brought joy for Dillon and myself, but she should have brought you joy. After all, she was your child. I should have told you the truth when Dillon was in prison and you were still looking out for us. I know you will never forgive me, but please don't take it out on her. She is returning to Bermondsey with her husband and her sons. Life has become very hard for us in Ireland.

I know I cannot ask anything of you, but please find it in your heart to look out for her, your own daughter, and her two sons. I fear that her husband will let her down.

I still love you and I always will.

God bless

Annie

Cyril sat back and stared into space. Huge tears filled his eyes, and he allowed them to tumble down his cheeks. 'Jesus, Mr Bates, you never knew. How sad, so sad.'

After wiping his tears away, he thumbed through the letters until he found just one more written by Dillon. It had been opened and folded back down. He quickly unfolded the letter and read the words.

To my dearest friend,

It is with much sadness that I tell you that Annie passed away this morning.

Time is a healer, as they say. I know you set me up for that job, Arthur, and, yes, at first, I was angry. I served time away from my Annie and Peggy, but I realised why you did it, and the truth is, Arthur, I would have done the same. But I forgive you for it all, and I am sorry for the pain I caused you.

I need a favour, my friend. My Peggy is returning to Bermondsey. Please would you look out for her? That husband of hers is no good. As you would call him, Arthur, a right shitbag.

One day we'll meet again and perhaps laugh over the old days – the good, the bad, and the ugly.

Take care of yourself, Arthur.

Yours faithfully

Dillon

Another tear rolled down Cyril's cheek. 'You never knew, Dillon, that Peggy was Mr Bates' child, and you, Mr Bates, never knew either.'

The grandfather clock in the hallway chimed four times. *Where had the time gone*? thought Cyril, as he stared at the letters. He knew he should throw them in the fire and leave all the secrets to go to ashes as Mr Bates and Annie had done. Yet they were a part of him. Mr Bates was his flesh and blood. He had taught him he all he knew, and it was true what he had said to the man in the hospital – that he was like a father to him. He suddenly laughed. 'Grandad, eh!'

Just as he placed the letters back inside the suitcase, he noticed a photograph of a man in baggy trousers and a loose cream shirt. He was leaning against a wall and smoking a cigarette. Cyril stared in shock; it was like looking at himself. It couldn't be Mr Bates, surely? But as he read what was written on the back, it was there in black and white. He turned the photo back over and stared, unable to take it in. Mr Bates was a big man; his hair was fair, his face was fuller, and his eyes were lighter. Perhaps sadness had made him lose weight and left him so sallow and gaunt looking in his later years. Yet in that photo, he really smiled, almost beaming, as if his face was alive with pleasure. He put the photo back in the suitcase.

Cyril decided there and then that there was no way he was going to burn any of the letters. He just couldn't throw the past away. And the one lesson he'd learned was that he wouldn't waste away his days and end up like his real grandfather; he would fill his life with happiness, as much as he could.

He thought about his mother, and it made sense how Mr Bates had helped her. Of course it was him who had thrown the landlord's body down the cellar. He would have done it to protect her because he loved her. Maybe he knew all along that she was his daughter. However, Cyril knew that his mother loved Dillon as her father, and so he surmised that if Mr Bates knew this as well, he had decided never to tell her the truth. It wouldn't be fair to shatter her illusions of the man who had raised her.

Before he left to return home, he took one last look around to make sure he had cleared all of Mr Bates' personal effects away. He'd already donated the clothes to the poor. The trunk in the spare bedroom was empty, but as Cyril turned to leave, he noticed a loose floorboard like the one downstairs. At first, he assumed it was only loose, but as he looked more closely, he noticed that a nail was newer than the others. He pulled a penknife from his jeans and prised the board free. Putting his hand inside the cavity, he felt some papers. It was a surprise because he thought he might find a gun. As soon as he dragged the papers out, he realised that they were drawings made by a professional, probably an architect. At first, he couldn't make head nor tail of them. But then, when he studied the details, he could see they were technical drawings of two different buildings from different positions. He unrolled the first sheet of paper and studied it carefully, and then he looked in the margins where there were a series of annotated notes connected by hand-drawn arrows to key points on the drawing. Sitting on his haunches, he laughed out loud. 'Well, bugger me, Mr Bates. You were a brilliant man.'

The drawings were plans to break into two different depositories, one done by entering through the shop next door. He shook his head when he remembered on one of the last prison visits Mr Bates telling him to look under the floorboards in his cottage, but he'd only found the one in the living room where there were guns, money, and all sorts. He'd never in his wildest dreams expected Mr Bates to mean this one as well. Excitement built up like a tsunami as he realised he could execute this undertaking with careful planning. Blakey was shit-hot at blowing things up. Frank could stop anyone in their tracks who got in the way. And he could organise the whole set-up. They were a good team.

Perhaps he was like his real grandfather after all.

CHAPTER TWENTY-SIX

Marcus and Tilly were over the moon to be moving from their grotty flat so soon with their new baby daughter. Cyril had left all the furnishings so they could replace them if and when they chose to. Marcus was even more thrilled that he was now the proud owner of Mr Bates' former cottage, which he had bought for a fraction of the price.

With the exchange and completion on his own property having reached a successful conclusion, Cyril received the all-important call.

Cyril and the estate agent had agreed that they would meet at Cyril's new property, where the latter would hand over the keys. He thanked the estate agent as soon as the keys were in his hand.

But the minute the estate agent left, Cyril sighed. All his plans had been building up to this point. He should be standing in the front garden of his very own palace with a brandy in his hand and his arm around his Flossie's waist. He should be ecstatic. But he wasn't.

He still hadn't broken the news to Flossie about the purchase of the house in Chislehurst. Things seemed different between them, but he couldn't put his finger on why. Flossie seemed to be miles away most of the time. He'd taken her to all the top restaurants, all the ones she loved. He'd spoiled her rotten and still she was so distant. He wondered if she was pregnant and didn't know how to tell him. Not that he was ready for kids just yet, but it wouldn't have changed anything. He loved her with all his heart. He thought that perhaps taking her out and buying her things wasn't enough, and maybe she wanted to know where their relationship was going.

Looking up at the big house, he smiled. She would be as proud as punch to be living at this highly sought-after address. What woman in their right mind wouldn't? He went inside just to check that the previous owners had left all the furnishings, especially the bedding with all its frills. True to their word, they had left the contents in situ. He wandered from room to room and admired all the finishes. It was perfect. Now all he needed was to collect the ring.

Locking the door behind him, he raced across the drive to his car and had a burst of excitable energy. He tore away and drove to Mr Ezra's shop to make the final payment for the engagement ring. He imagined Flossie's face when he handed it to her. His thoughts turned to how he would propose. Should it be in their new home on bended knee? Or should he organise a huge party in a hall, like Gwynnie had?

Ezra was behind the counter, which was unusual; normally, it was his pretty wife.

'I was hoping to see you myself, Mr Reardon. I suppose you're here to make the last payment on the diamond. A very, very lucky girl.'

'How are you, Mr Ezra?'

'Good, very good. Now, Mr Reardon, as you may already

know.' He looked over Cyril's shoulder and narrowed his dark beady eyes. 'I am a man who has, shall we say, my fingers in many pies. And it has come to my attention that you have a product of top quality.'

Cyril looked the man over. 'Don't know what you're talking about, Mr Ezra.'

'I believe it comes from Colombia.'

'Still don't know what you're on about.'

Ezra nodded and smiled. 'Good, I like to deal with people who know when to keep schtum. Mr Bates, God rest his soul, he told me I could trust you.'

Cyril inclined his head and raised his chin. 'Oh, yeah? So what else did Mr Bates say about me?'

Ezra looked over Cyril's shoulder again. 'He said that I was to look out for you. Let's just say that Arthur, Dillon, and myself knew each other a long time ago. There are very few people who I trust. However, I am told that I can trust you.'

Cyril smirked. 'Well, that is true, but how can I say the same about you?'

'Because I will tell you something that only Arthur and I know, and it's probably a question that has circled your mind more than once. This will prove to you I can be trusted, and, by the way, I will offer no other proof.'

Cyril leaned closer. 'Go on, then. Try me.'

Ezra smiled, before he looked deadly serious. 'It was Mr

Bates who threw the landlord's body down the cellar.'

Cyril felt his body prickle with goosebumps. It was the eerie way in which the jeweller had said those words. But he knew then that Ezra could be trusted. He was right: Mr Bates would have told no one.

'So, Mr Ezra, it looks like we may be in business. I can send a sample to you tonight. If you like it, then we can come to some arrangement.'

Ezra was nodding. 'Good, I won't tread on your toes, and, please, don't tread on mine.'

Cyril nodded politely back. 'Perfect. Now, then, the ring.'

Ezra retrieved a small box from inside his jacket pocket. He placed it on the counter and popped open the lid. 'There you are.'

Cyril held the diamond ring up to the light and admired its sparkle. 'She's gonna love it.'

Ezra laughed. 'Never underestimate a woman, Mr Reardon. Never believe you know what goes on inside their mind. But she has to be insane if she doesn't fall in love with that piece. It once belonged to an Arabian princess all the way—'

'Cut the crap, Mr Ezra. I don't give a flying fig. It's a big diamond that shines. That's all I want. Leave all the ol' flannel to me. I am sure I can concoct a better story than an Arabian princess.'

Ezra's face was a picture as he laughed along and patted

Cyril's arm. 'Me and you will do well in business.'

Just as Cyril was about to close the door behind him, Ezra called him back. 'Mr Reardon, if you ever decide to pay the depository a visit, please give me prior warning. There are a few things I would like to remove from there first.'

Cyril's eyes widened. It was true then: Mr Ezra really did know Mr Bates very well.

Cyril left the shop with so much on his mind: the landlord, the safe deposit building's footprint, and the story he should make up about the ring, so that his Flossie would feel a million dollars.

* * *

Once he was back in the flat, he had a quick bath, put on his best aftershave and suit, and headed up the concrete steps to meet Flossie. He would have to find out what type of engagement do she would like without giving away the fact that he intended to propose to her. He would have asked Trudy, but he was worried that she would spill the beans and ruin the surprise. He banged on the door and waited.

He could hear the familiar clip-clop of heels before the door opened, and there in her fluffy high-heeled slippers and wearing an almost see-through negligee stood not Flossy but Sonia. Cyril felt embarrassed and wanted to look away, but there was nowhere to look. 'Er, is Flossie in?' he asked, staring at the floor.

'No, Cyril, she's, er . . .'

He looked up, sensing she was faltering.

‘Where is she?’

‘Oh, I dunno. The hairdresser’s, maybe, or . . .’ She paused. ‘I dunno, love. I’m sorry.’

Cyril smiled and walked away. It was odd, since Sonia was always so loud and brash, but today, for some reason, she was quiet and almost withdrawn.

* * *

Two days passed, and Cyril tried again, but, once more, Flossie was out. Deciding to get down to business, he left a message with her mother for Flossie to meet him at The Talk of the Town on Saturday. He told Sonia to inform her daughter that she was to put on her best dress as she would be met by a chauffeur who would be taking her for a celebratory night out. He didn’t let on, though, that the chauffeur would be driving a Rolls Royce.

Strangely, the planning details were not Cyril’s at all: they were Frank’s. It was his idea that his best friend should book a table for all of them, the lads and their other halves. And when the black forest gateau was served, he would get down on one knee and propose to Flossie. Once the formalities were over with, the two of them would be whisked away by their chauffeur to their new house. There, Cyril would have a beautiful bunch of red roses in the bedroom, and then, if his intended wanted to have a huge do for all their friends and families later on, he would book a decent hall and invite everyone. He would have caterers and a constant flow of champagne. Frank had surprised Cyril with his very romantic ideas.

Saturday evening came but Cyril still hadn't heard from Flossie. He assumed that she would catch up with him at the restaurant. The Talk of the Town was one of their regular haunts, and as far as he was aware, she loved the place.

Cyril arrived with Frank and Trudy and was shortly joined by Marcus and Tilly. Blakey hurried in with Cindy on his arm.

But in contrast to the others, Cyril wasn't in a relaxed state at all. He was so anxious about the proposal that he'd downed two shots of vodka before he'd even got a round in for everyone else.

Eventually, he took his seat, and Tramon, the waiter, who made it his job to serve Cyril because he always gave the best tips, was seen hovering. 'Mr Reardon, shall I pop some champagne for you?'

Cyril looked up. 'Oh . . . Er, well, no, not just yet. I am waiting for Flossie.'

Everyone chit-chatted over their plans while Cyril made a series of nervous glances towards the door. He looked at his watch; it was 7.30 p.m. She was half an hour late.

Tramon hovered again. 'Can I bring over some hors d'oeuvres, Mr Reardon?'

Cyril nodded.

'Blimey, I'm starving. Can you get some bread on the table, sweetheart?' asked Trudy.

'Trude,' tutted Frank.

'What did I do? I can't help it if I'm hungry. All I had were two sandwiches and an angel cake at lunchtime.'

'You could wait for Flossie, for starters, Trude.'

Trudy looked around the table. 'Bleedin' Nora, she's late.' She glanced at her watch and then frowned at Frank.

Another half an hour passed, and Cyril was now feeling sick. 'I hope nuffin's happened. I sent a car for her an' all.'

'She's probably still getting ready, mate. You know what girls are like,' said Blakey.

'Not my Flossie. She's never late,' replied Cyril, as he rose from the table. 'Look, all of you stay here. I'll square up the bill. I'm off to see if I can find her.'

'Marcus, love, you go with him. I'll be all right here,' said Tilly. 'In fact, why don't you boys all go and us girls will stay, in case she arrives 'ere.'

Frank stood up and kissed Trudy on the forehead. ''Ere, girl, use that to help pay the bill. Just in case we're not back in time,' he said, as he placed a five-pound note on the table. It was obvious that Cyril was getting worried. Marcus and Blakey also slapped a few pounds on the table and followed Cyril to the door.

Frank held the door open for Cyril to climb into his car. 'She's probably on her way, mate. Don't worry too much.'

'I've got a bad feeling about all this, Frank.'

Marcus and Blakey climbed into the back seats and

remained quiet. They were concerned more about Cyril. His positive, almost carefree state of mind was not present now. In fact, neither of them could recall ever seeing him look so worried. Normally, nothing ever seemed to bother the man.

Frank drove to the estate and stopped in a space below the tower block. 'Are you gonna go up and see if she's in? She might be unwell.'

Cyril nodded but didn't reply. He hurried up the steps and banged on the door. Giving no thought to who was in there, his impatience had him banging hard again before he heard a voice. 'All right all right, keep your hair on.'

Flossie's mother opened the door, dressed this time in a puffy nylon dressing gown.

Cyril leaned against the wall, out of breath. 'Where is she? You gave her the message, didn't you?' he asked accusingly. But it was the sympathetic expression on her face that told Cyril that Sonia knew more than she had been letting on earlier.

'Yes, love, I did.'

'Well?' snapped Cyril.

'All I know is that she said she was off out, and she would be back later.'

'So was she meeting me at the restaurant then or what?'

She shrugged her shoulders. 'I dunno what she's flaming well playing at, love. A driver came knocking, and I had to send him away, 'cos she'd already gone. But I got him to fetch me some fish and chips first, though. I hope you don't mind.'

'Where did she go and who the fuck with? 'Cos all her friends are at the restaurant waiting for her.'

'Cyril, I have no idea. She ain't been the same lately. The stuck-up cow.'

With a heavy sigh, Cyril was about to walk away when he noticed a small case to the left of her feet.

'Going away, is she?'

Sonia looked just as surprised as Cyril when she saw the case. 'Well, I'll be fucking buggered. What the hell is that girl of mine up to? Oh, Cyril, love. I am so sorry.'

'Don't worry. Just tell her I called.'

* * *

By 9.30 p.m., they were heading back to the restaurant to meet the girls. Cyril had hoped that Flossie would have had a change of heart and would be there to greet him with some satisfactory explanation.

Unexpectedly, Frank slammed on the brakes and pulled over. 'Is that *her*?'

Cyril glanced in the direction of Frank's eyeline. He couldn't believe it. Almost directly across from their car was a posh restaurant with floor-to-ceiling windows. Cyril stared, squinting his eyes. He felt his heart pounding, and a wave of sickness rushed over him. He jumped out of the car, to be followed by Marcus, Blakey, and Frank. They all stared as

Flossie rose from her seat and allowed a man to wrap a mink fur coat around her shoulders.

Flossie hadn't seen them. She was obviously far too busy to notice anyone other than the man she was with. She tilted her head, blushing, but held his hands to her neck longer than a friend would.

Then Cyril felt a lump in his throat when he saw the man kiss her neck. It was exactly what he used to do when he would fasten on a new necklace.

Rooted to the spot, he just gazed at his girl. The woman who he treasured, the woman who he loved so much was being touched and caressed by another man. With his hand in his pocket, he turned the small engagement box over and over. He had seen enough and needed to look away before he did something stupid.

'Fuck me, Cyril, let's give that cunt a good larruping. I've wanted to do that for years to the flash bastard.'

Cyril then twigged that Frank knew who the guy was. Cyril straightened up, and as soon as he realised who was fussing over his bird, every muscle in his body went rigid. The anger raged inside him, and if he could have breathed fire, he would. But, instead, he took a few rapid breaths to calm his heartbeat before he had a coronary. 'Let's go, lads.'

Frank spun around. 'What? You mean you're gonna let that pompous, flash prick get away with taking your bird? Oh, come on, Cyril. Everyone knows she's your bird, including that cunt.'

'I won't fight over a woman. I don't care who he is. Leave

it, Frank.'

'I thought more of you, Cyril. You're not gonna let him get away with that, are ya?'

Cyril flared his nostrils. 'You what, Frank? You thought *more* of me, did ya?'

Frank lowered his shoulders and ran his hands through his hair. 'Look, mate, I'm sorry. Really sorry. It's just that I am so fucking mad.'

'Frank, leave it to me, eh?' said Cyril, as he lowered his voice.

Frank nodded and pulled Cyril close, placing an arm around his shoulders. 'Her loss, mate, her fucking loss.'

They all climbed back into Frank's car, and as they drove away, Cyril saw his Flossie with the one man he secretly hated – Lord Chambers. It seemed as though he had it all: the mansion, the Bentley, the clothes, the money, and now he had his girl. He may have been born rich, but he wasn't born with the right to take any girl he liked. He sighed out loud as they drove away, feeling sick with heartache.

* * *

Frank knew his best buddy would want to go home. He could sense the sadness and could feel his anguish. He would feel the same if it was Lord Chambers slobbering over his Trudy. He wanted to go and hunt the man down, but it seemed as though Cyril had something up his sleeve. He knew Cyril only too well. He had seen the lengths Cyril would go to, to have a principle established and honoured.

God help Lord Chambers, thought Frank.

* * *

Cyril thanked the lads and walked slowly back up the steps to the flat. Every step was heavy as if his shoulders were weighed down with a ton of bricks. It wasn't until he reached the door that he realised his cheeks were sodden.

Peggy was shocked to hear him come in. She assumed he would go straight to his new place since that had been the plan. 'How did it go, love?' she asked tentatively.

Cyril wandered into the kitchen where his mother was sitting at the table, adding up her Green Shield stamps. 'It didn't, Mum.'

She looked up and saw the devastating expression on her son's face. It was a look she'd never seen before.

'Oh, Cyril, what's happened, love?' she asked, assuming that Flossie had turned his proposal down.

He pulled a chair out and sat down. 'She didn't turn up for the meal, so we came back. Her mother told me she'd gone out. I hoped she was just late, so we drove back to the restaurant. But, on the way, we saw her . . . in another restaurant.'

Peggy stubbed her cigarette out. 'And what did she have to say for herself?'

Cyril took a deep breath. 'She didn't have to say anything because I didn't go into the restaurant to ask her. But it was obvious what was going on. She was with another man. It was

Lord fucking Chambers.'

Peggy threw her hands to her mouth in utter shock. 'Oh, my God, you are kidding me?'

Cyril shook his head and pulled out the box from his pocket. 'I saved up for months for this, and she didn't even get to see it or the house that's all pink and frilly, just the way she would've liked it.'

Peggy's blood was boiling, her heart rampaging. 'Are you sure, darling, that it wasn't just a friendship with this Lord whatshisface?'

'No, he was draping her in some flash fur coat and snogging her neck in the fucking process.' He jumped up. 'Sorry. Mum, I just wanna be alone.'

'I know, Son, I'm so sorry, babe . . .' She didn't know what else to say as she watched him slope off to his room. She picked up the box and opened the lid. The ring was stunning, the diamond was huge, and the ring mount itself was shaped in an amazing intricate pattern.

Biting her lip, Peggy tried to stop the sob that had stuck in her throat. It would hurt her poor lad for some time. She knew exactly how much he loved Flossie. When her son was in pain, then so was she. Young woman or not, Peggy would give the girl a piece of her mind. She'd always tried herself to act the lady, but she was too incensed to worry about lowering herself right now. Snatching her cigarettes, she went outside. She stood on the walkway and peered over, watching for the tart. If it meant she would stand there all night, then so be it. Flossie would get both barrels.

Now feeling cold, Peggy slipped back inside, grabbed her coat and a scarf, and returned to the walkway. It was late and quiet, which was unusual for the estate. Rarely had she been outside at this hour in the morning; she was always tucked up in bed. Her hands shook with the chill that had reached her bones, but she lit another cigarette and watched the smoke and her warm breath produce large white clouds. She stared along the walkway at the empty milk bottles put out for the milkman, at the makeshift washing lines hanging from the rafters above, and at the pristine doorsteps. It amazed Peggy how the two older ladies who lived here always polished their doorsteps every week. She wondered if it was a competition, or whether they just couldn't get out of the old ways when they'd all lived in Bermondsey and Poplar, in houses with their pristine doorsteps brought to a shine with red boot polish.

Peggy didn't miss the old ways at all. She'd never found scraping for pennies for coal and milk much fun. She could never sit back and laugh at how it was back in the good old days. It wasn't good at all: it was cold, harsh, and cruel. She had done things that she should never have had to do. And if it hadn't been for the need to feed her two little boys, then she would have died before earning money that way. The thought of that man's dirty hands made her shudder, and she pulled a deep drag on her cigarette. It had only been the once, and she had been paid a few shillings for what she'd had to perform on the man. The money had, however, bought food and filled her sons' tummies, but the memory would never leave her and the disgust for herself would always soil her dreams. She'd smiled at Cyril when he said she would one day be the duchess of his castle, but the truth was, she never could be, and he could never know the truth behind her past. She would die having her sons believe she was a good person.

A rush of anger filled her veins when she thought of how Flossie had treated her son. There were so many young women out there who would have given their right arm to be spoiled and loved by a man like her Cyril. She wasn't blinded by motherly love either. She had watched him wrap presents and get excited when he bought the latest fashionable dress in the shop. He would spread it out on his bed and ask for her opinion. Peggy would admire the material and the stitching, and, every time, she would think how lucky Flossie was. Now she was livid. Everything her Cyril had done for the girl, and she'd had the brass neck to treat him like a throwaway toy. And to make matters worse, she'd publicly humiliated him in the process.

A gentle rumbling made Peggy stare up the road. There in the distance, she could see powerful headlights from a car heading towards the tower block. She watched the big car pull up and a tall man in a suit get out. He walked around to the passenger side and opened the door. And there wearing a fur coat and with her signature hairstyle was Flossie.

Peggy was now raging. She ran along the walkway and down the stairwell. The sound of her slippers slapping the cold concrete would have woken some of the tenants, but she didn't care. She wanted to rip Flossie's hair off her head.

By the time she reached the bottom, the flash Bentley had driven away, leaving Flossie waving as if she were a queen.

'Why, you fucking no-good tart. How could you do that to Cyril!' screamed Peggy.

Flossie spun around in horror to find Peggy with an expression like that of a monster's. Even in the poor light,

Peggy's face was dark red and her jaw was tightly clenched. But it was those eyes of hers that made Flossie tremble. They were flashing in the moonlight, so piercing and narrow.

'Peggy, look, it . . . er.'

'Oh, shut up. Don't you dare try to make an excuse for what you've done. That lad saved for months for a fucking ring for you, and he was going to propose and then take you to the house he'd bought for you and him.'

Flossie didn't know where to look or where to go because Peggy was blocking her way to the safety of her mum's flat.

'I didn't know,' said Flossie, in a tone of voice that was both flat and uncaring.

'You fucking liar. Why else would my boy send a car to take you to the restaurant and tell you to wear something nice? You fucking knew, all right, but no, you didn't care, did ya, eh?'

'It's not like that, Peggy. We were just growing apart. I didn't know he was buying a ring or a bleedin' house. He should have said.'

'You should have told my boy it was over, before throwing your legs in the air for another man.'

Flossie gasped. 'I haven't slept with . . .'

'What? You mean you think the posh meal and the mink coat are free? Are you that fucking stupid?'

Peggy marched forward until she was a few inches from

Flossie's nose. She snatched at the necklace that hung around Flossie's neck, and, in one quick movement, ripped if off. 'But you fucking took this from Cyril, and you had the gall to wear it when you went out with another man, didn't ya? Well, didn't ya?'

Peggy looked down at Flossie's boots. 'Even those boots were bought for you by my Cyril. You're one fucking 'orrible cow.'

Flossie tried to push past Peggy, but it got her nowhere. Peggy was still on a mission. Grabbing Flossie's hand, she said, 'And look at those. Those two rings – *gold* fucking rings at that.' Then Peggy's eyes were drawn to what else Flossie was wearing. Peggy was now incandescent with rage. 'And you, you uncaring bitch – those *gold* earrings were bought by my lad because he loved you, and he thought you loved him an' all.'

As Peggy continued to tear into the young woman, her voice steadily became louder and louder until the more angry she got, the more neighbours appeared to see what the ruckus was all about.

* * *

Flossie's mother had heard enough. In her negligee and fluffy slippers, Sonia tore along the walkway and hurtled down the steps to get to her daughter before Peggy bashed the hell out of her. She knew Peggy had a fierce temper, and if Flossie wasn't careful, she suspected her daughter may just lose her looks.

'All right, Peggy, that's enough. You've made your point, and I 'ave to say, I don't disagree with a word you've said. My

Flossie was wrong, but she's only a kid. Come on, love.' She tried to soften her tone before Peggy smacked her one in the face.

Peggy turned to face Sonia. 'She's only a kid, is she? Is she? No! She ain't! She's a conniving whore, a backstabbing, low-life excuse for a woman. And she must have fucking learned that from *you*. 'Cos let's not be shy about it. You've been around the fucking block yaself, and the apple obviously ain't fallen far from the tree, has it?'

Peggy looked back at Flossie, who was now crying. The mascara ran down her cheeks, and she looked a mess. 'You're fucking pathetic, girl.'

She spun back to Sonia. 'She could have been living in a beautiful house in Chislehurst with a fucking great rock on her finger, but, oh, no! She buggered off with a pompous prick and kissed goodbye to everything my Cyril had built for her.'

Sonia stood open-mouthed and speechless until a voice behind made them all look.

'Mum, come on back to the flat. You've no need to get upset on my account. There is nothing more to say,' said Cyril, as he put his meaty arm around her shoulders and pulled her away.

Sonia grabbed her daughter's arm and hissed in her ear. 'You have well and truly pissed on your chips now. This lord won't buy you a bloody house in Chislehurst. You just remember this, Florence. A lord will see you as his bit on the bloody side, and if that life suits you, then so be it. But you understand this, my girl. Never try to be his wife, 'cos they only marry their own kind. They never marry beneath them, so get any idea of being a real lady out of your head.'

'No, Mum, he loves me. He said he would buy me the world. He lives in a mansion, and one day, I will live in it. He has a flat in Chelsea. He said we can live there until we get married. I've packed me case and everything.'

'So why didn't he take you to this flat in Chelsea?'

'Oh, well, it's being decorated at the moment, but, in a few weeks, we will move in, and then, we'll be arranging the wedding.'

Sonia looked at her daughter and wondered how the hell she'd brought up someone as thick as shit. She shook her head. 'You silly, silly girl. If the flat isn't ready, then why doesn't he move you into his mansion? In fact, it would have been ideal wouldn't it, Flossie? With so many bedrooms, you could have slept in separate beds until the wedding day.'

Her mother's sarcastic tone began to resonate with her daughter. At last, the penny had dropped. She looked up and saw Cyril with his arm around his mother. He didn't look back, and that was the moment she knew he never would. The one thing she'd learned about Cyril was that he would never be mugged off. Well, she had royally mugged him off – and in the worst way possible.

* * *

Frank didn't mention anything to Trudy until they were inside their flat.

'Trudy, babe, put the kettle on, love, will ya,' said Frank, as he sat down in the living room on their new velvet sofa.

Trudy looked down at his shoes. 'Aw, Frank, you know I like you to take ya shoes off at the door. Bloody hell, I wanna keep this little place of ours clean and tidy.'

Frank looked around the room. It wasn't huge, but it was spotlessly clean and contained all modern furnishings, just how Trudy liked it. He thought about Cyril and felt sick for him. If only he had a bird like Trudy. She was a good girl, keeping a good home, working hard, cooking him dinners, and ironing his shirts. He smiled as he watched her busy in the kitchen not only making a cup of tea but frying up some bacon and buttering some bread.

'Blimey, Trude, it's two in the morning. Why are you cooking?'

''Cos, I'm starving. The portions in that restaurant are all right for the skinny Mary Quants of this world, but I am a larger woman. I need more to fill me up, and also, Frank, you have something to say, and I want to have a proper sit down for a tell-all.'

Frank stood back up and took his shoes off, walking across the room, and leaving them at the door. He loosened his belt and sat back down; he didn't start talking until Trudy was settled with a cup of tea in one hand and a bacon sandwich in the other.

'So, Trude, I ain't having you on when I say I was gonna propose to you next week after Cyril had proposed to Flossie first.' He stopped and studied the look on Trudy's face. The bacon suddenly slid out of the sandwich and dropped on the plate.

'Propose? What!' she squealed.

Frank smiled. 'Well, yes, I wanted it to be a surprise, but maybe we should wait a couple of months, under the circumstances.'

Trudy quickly plonked the cup and plate on the pouffe and launched herself at Frank, flinging her arms around him. 'Marriage? What, me?'

'Yeah, of course, you, ya silly mare. But wait, babe. I wanna propose, and I want it to be a surprise. So I thought I'd tell you now, in case you had ideas of buggering off with some fucking poncy lord.'

Trudy peeled herself away and sat back down, looking thoroughly confused. 'What are you on about? What's actually happened? None of you lads will say. I rarely ask you about ya business, Frank, but Flossie is me mate.'

Frank nodded. 'Yeah, well, she was seeing Lord Chambers behind Cyril's back. He was gonna propose tonight and take her back to his big house he's just bought for her in Chislehurst.'

'Chislehurst?'

Frank nodded. 'Yes and the ring, babe, cost as much as the house. Anyway, we saw her in a restaurant up the road with the lord. He was kissing her in full fucking view. I swear to God, I would have put him straight through that window and scarred his face so it looked like the London Underground map, if he'd done that to me.'

It shocked Trudy to the core. All this was new to her. 'I'd never favour a lord over you, Frank. You're all the man I want, and a wedding, eh? Me and you getting married. Oh, Frank, I can't wait. Listen, don't go spending a lot on a ring. I don't need an engagement ring. Just a wedding ring will do me fine, and then, if you want, we can start a family, and . . .'

'Hang on, Trude. We ain't even walked down the bleedin' aisle yet. The reason I am saying all this is that I feel Cyril dragged his heels for far too long. If only he'd proposed sooner, then maybe she wouldn't have gone off with this lord.'

'Yeah, I don't know what she sees in him. I told him to get lost, the last time we saw him.'

Frank was confused. 'Er, what do you mean by "the last time we saw him"? I thought the only time you saw him was at Gwynnie's engagement party.'

Trudy took a sip of her tea. 'Oh no, that posh lot are always hanging around the clubs that us girls go to on a Friday night.'

'You never said, Trude.'

'Why would I, Frank? You have your boys' nights out and us girls do the same. I don't ask you who you speak to. I trust you, Frank.'

Frank nodded, looking at his girl in a fresh light. *She was a good 'un and no mistake*, he thought. 'I trust you, girl, but what's that lord hanging around you lot for?'

'Oh, he's a chancer. He tried it on with me a few times. I told him I had a fella. He said he knew you and Cyril. He said you go way back. Something about a fish farm. But he was too pissed at the time, though, to tell me any more about it.'

Frank felt the heat rising on the back of his neck. 'Why, that fucking wanker!'

'Frank, whatever is the matter, darling?'

'Lord Chambers. Did he really try it on with you?'

'Yeah, but I didn't do anything, I swear. He was just a bit drunk, I guess. And he offered to take me out. I promise you, though, love, I said *no* to him, and that I loved you.'

Frank detected the panic in her voice. 'Listen, Trude, I believe you. Please, just tell me everything. I swear to you, I won't get cross with you.'

'Well, he offered to buy me a drink, and I refused. I don't like to be owing. You know me. Anyway, he kept joining me on the dance floor, and it got on me nerves a bit. The next time we were at the club, he was going on about how you knew each other from Kent and something about a lake. I dunno. Like I said, I think he was pissed. Then, a few weeks later, he was telling me how he could take me away from London, and I could live in a beautiful mansion in the countryside with its own woods and a lake, and I would live like a princess. I said to him "If you're friends with my Frank, then why would you dare chat me up?" He sniggered and wiped his moustache and said, "Because, sweet Trudy, I like you more." I thought then what a dickhead, and that was that, really. I never said anything to the girls because, well, let's be honest, look at me. I assumed he was just having a bet with his pals. I did hear one of them mention a game called Pull a Pig Night.'

Frank got up from his seat and snatched Trudy's hands, pulling her to her feet. 'You, my special girl, are the most beautiful woman this side of the water, and don't you forget it. I'll have that ring on your finger so no other fella can take you off me.'

'Make sure you get a large one, Frank. And only this side of the water?' She chuckled.

'Well, I ain't never been north of Watford, so I don't know, but south of the river is good enough for me.'

She hugged him tight before they made their way to the bedroom. 'I feel so sorry for Cyril. He really was besotted with Flossie. D'ya reckon he will have Lord Chambers secretly buried someplace?'

Frank pulled her onto the bed. 'If he doesn't, I fucking will, chatting up my missus.'

'What about Flossie, though? 'Cos I tell ya right now, Frank, I won't be having anything to do with her, and once the other girls know what she's done, I don't expect they will either. Cindy ain't keen on her. She never has been.'

'Well, let's try to make Cyril feel better. I don't know how, but I hate seeing him so hurt.'

Trudy agreed. 'God help anyone who upsets him now, with all that fire in his belly.'

PART THREE

CHAPTER TWENTY-SEVEN

Most of the South London club scene had security on the doors, and most of it was undertaken by Cyril's men. If they weren't Cyril's, they were those employed by him. The rave scene had proved to be very lucrative as well as a testing time with rival businessmen trying to get in on the game.

The Cedar Arms was now his pub, and any drugs, whether it be ecstasy or cocaine, were run through Cyril's firm, unless, of course, someone was stupid enough to get on the wrong side of him.

The days of the post office jobs and bank jobs and even the pavement work were ending with the installation of cameras and this new DNA testing.

So with all these scientific developments giving the police

force more options in fighting crime, Cyril had to devise more detailed and cunning plans. He had also taken on additional men, and one, in particular, was beginning to make a name for himself. Eddie Raven.

Cyril caught him breaking into his car, but when he held the youngster at gunpoint, the lad just laughed in his face and said, 'So it worked, Mr Reardon. I have finally caught your attention.'

Seeing a bit of himself in the young lad, Cyril took him into his fold and slowly taught him everything he knew. And it wasn't long before Eddie had gained respect beyond South East London.

Cyril thought that one day he could hand over all the business to Eddie. He would then sit back and put his feet up with a regular poke coming his way to keep him in summer holidays and flash cars for the rest of his days. Eddie had already asked to buy the Cedar Arms and for a good price, and Cyril was giving it serious consideration.

Now in his forties, Cyril didn't have children of his own; in fact, he hadn't settled down with any one woman. The truth was, he had never really gotten over Flossie. Marcus had a daughter, and so did Frank. Even reckless Eddie had a daughter. Blakey didn't have children and neither did he want any. But Cyril felt lucky to call all these children his nieces. And, as far as he was concerned, they were all his family, along with his own mother and brother.

* * *

It was late July when Cyril turned up at his mother's with a huge bouquet of flowers. He was in his new Jaguar XJ40 series, although the side panel did have a nasty dent in it. Once again, Cyril had misjudged the turning and taken it a bit too late. On his way along the walkway, he passed Sonia, who was now bent over with arthritis.

'Hello, Sonia, how are ya, love?'

She tried to straighten up as much as she could and lift her cheeks to give him a smile, but it was hard, and she was in pain. 'Okay, Cyril, I guess. As good as can be expected.'

He looked down and saw she had a rubbish bag in her hand. ''Ere, give us that, love, and I'll take it down for you.'

Sonia handed Cyril the bag and sighed. 'You're a good lad, Cyril. My Florence was a fool, a bloody fool.'

Cyril gave her a sympathetic smile. 'I am sure your Flossie is doing all right for herself. It was a long time ago, Sonia, and people move on.'

'Some of us don't, Cyril,' she replied, before cautiously walking away.

Cyril knew exactly what she meant. Taking a moment's silent reflection, he glanced at the grey concrete step that he and Flossie had sat on in all weathers talking, kissing, and planning for their future together. He sighed and hurried to dispose of Sonia's rubbish before he ran along the walkway to his mother's flat. She had refused to move into his house with him; she enjoyed the community of the tower block. He didn't, though; he much preferred his landscaped garden and the bar inside his house. On his to-do list was to install a pool, but he couldn't swim, and he knew he'd probably drown. But that wasn't the point. Cyril had reached a stage in his life when a man in his position opted for status.

'Happy Birthday, Mum!' he called out, as he opened the front door.

Peggy was sitting by the window with a pink cardigan around her shoulders.

'Cor, Mum. It's baking in here. Open a bloody window, will ya?' He put the flowers on the table and rushed over to open the window.

'No, Cyril, love, leave it. I've got a chill.'

Cyril turned to see his mother's pale face. 'Blimey, you look rough, Mum. Are you all right?'

Peggy shivered. 'I've got this bloody flu and a chest with it. Do us a favour, babe. Steam up some Vick, will you, in a bowl and fetch us a towel.'

Cyril knew the routine. It had been the same whenever Howie got a chesty cough. She would fill the bowl with hot water and drop in some balsam. He himself could never explain how it worked. But it did: it worked a treat.

'Shit way to spend your birthday, Mum.'

'Never mind, lad. I will have plenty more to celebrate. I was out last night playing cards. I only lost 'cos I couldn't concentrate. And all to that bloody lord an' all.'

Cyril's blood ran cold and a chill shot down his back. As he took a deep breath, he loosened the tightness in his neck.

All the aristocrats who had once frequented the same places as he had had moved away from the London scene. The action was now taking place in Brighton. But, nevertheless, he had heard that there were a few who had returned to their former London haunts and who liked to snort cocaine.

'Where did you play, Mum?'

'The Salvador, but they're playing downstairs for big money, and I *mean* big money. It's all chips and shit now. Me, I like a good old-fashioned game. Still, I didn't lose too much. I know when to stop.'

'You should be a millionaire by now, Mum, what with all the games you've played and won.'

Peggy laughed, but then she coughed violently, much to her son's concern.

He hurried over with the bowl, removed the flowers, and put the bowl on the table. 'There you go, Mum. Just take a few deep breaths. Do you want me to get you anything else?'

Peggy had the towel over her head but waved her hand, saying 'no'.

Cyril put the flowers into water and put the kettle on again to make them both a cup of tea.

Peggy stopped coughing and removed the towel.

Cyril noticed how red and shiny her face was from the steam. 'Are you sure you won't move into my house? I could do with a cleaner. I mean Val's all right, but she's refused point-blank to do any washing, and she hates ironing.'

Peggy shook her head. 'No, Son. It's a waste of breath asking me to leave this flat. I like it here, and if Val's not pulling her weight, then get another cleaner.'

As she looked her son up and down, she noticed how his hair had changed colour over the years from blond to fair to dark, and now, a few strands of grey were appearing at the sides. But as he'd aged, he hadn't gained a beer belly, like some men. In fact, he still looked distinguished in his navy suit and white shirt. He'd even got his cheeky grin back. But there was one feature missing: he'd lost that particular charm he'd been renowned for, for many years now. Flossie had knocked it out of him. Peggy wondered if time really was a healer, or whether that saying was a load of claptrap.

'So what about you, Cyril? Will you follow in my footsteps?'

He smiled and winked. 'I might do. I've had enough practice over the years with the best teacher.'

Peggy nodded, understandingly. 'You need a hobby, love. All work and no play makes Jack a dull boy.'

He chuckled. 'I'd hardly call my work dull. I don't think I've ever had two days the same.'

'No, I guess you're right there, babe. Life's never dull when you're around.'

'So the toffs are playing cards at the Salvador, then, are they?'

Peggy pulled a handkerchief from her apron pocket and coughed into it. 'I wish this cough would bloody go soon. I need to get back on me feet. Oh, sorry, Son. Yeah, the posh lot are back in the club.'

'Mum, would you know if a Lord Chambers plays cards there?'

Peggy inclined her head and frowned. 'Yes, he was the man I lost the game to. That's what I was about to tell you.'

'Bloody hell, so he's back then. I knew he couldn't have disappeared off the face of the earth. I'm gonna go and play that bastard and win all your money back.'

'What? All twenty-five quid?'

Cyril laughed. 'Oh, blimey, Mum. Is that all you lost?'

Peggy coughed again. 'It's all about the principle, not how much you lose by.'

The hairs on the back of Cyril's neck stood on end. His mother was right: it was all about the principle.

'He was the bloke that dated Flossie,' she said, as she stopped coughing.

'Yep, that's him. And he did it deliberately to get back at me. It doesn't matter now. It was too long ago.'

'If it hadn't been him, it would have been someone else, love.'

Cyril agreed, but, deep down, he knew the truth. Flossie went with him because of the money, and if he'd had more money than Lord Chambers, then he knew, in his heart, she wouldn't have buggered off so easily.

* * *

Cyril drove his car to the lock-up. He smiled to himself every time he reached the garage door. The firm could meet anywhere, but, for some reason, they still loved to meet there as if they were kids again.

'Frank, me ol' friend, we're gonna have a real good earner. And you, Blakey, are gonna get your ballistic skills in tune.'

Frank rolled his eyes. 'Cyril, we have plenty of money. Marcus is sunning it in Spain with his family. I've got me villa almost built, although,' he said, laughingly, 'the bank manager keeps asking me how the hell I earn the money for it.'

'You wanna tell him to mind his own fucking business. I tell you what, Frank. If he gets too nosy, we'll rob his bank, and then, when he asks again, you can just smile at him.'

'So what did you have in mind?' asked Frank.

Cyril pulled out what looked to Frank like a scroll from a cardboard tube.

'What's that?' asked Frank, as he stood up from his chair.

Cyril placed the rolled-up sheet of paper on the table and put a few tools on the corners to keep it flat. 'That there, my son, is probably five million quids' worth of goodies.'

Frank and Blakey stared at the drawings, trying to make them out. They'd never seen an architect's set of drawings before.

'It's the safe deposit building in New Street,' said Cyril,

pleased with himself. 'Mr Bates left these to me years ago and I've sat on them.'

'Them?' queried Frank.

'Yeah, this is just one. I have another one, the main safe deposit box building up the West End, but I was thinking, let's do this one first and leave it a couple of years before going for the biggy.'

Blakey turned the sheet around until he could visualise the building. 'That's the fruit and veg shop next door.'

'Yes, Blakey, although it's not attached. Shame, 'cos that would be too easy. But look at the drawing. The cellars are attached.'

Frank shook his head. 'I don't have a clue what you're on about.'

Ignoring Frank, Blakey was studying the drawing carefully. 'Cyril, look here. See, that wall is what they call a single brick facade. The wall will have two skins separated by a cavity for ventilation. Look there.' Blakey pointed at a particular spot on the plan. 'There are no metal structures in the footings. None that I can see, anyway. All we wanna hope is that they haven't made any major changes since the building was built.'

'Well, I've already paid the place a visit and opened an account, so I've been inside. And judging by the building, none of it looks new. It's all old solid wood, no metal, no new tiled floor. The skirting looks original as well, so I reckon the footprint ain't been changed one bit.'

'I can blow through two walls – that's piss-easy – although I'll need a couple of heavy-duty jacks or the whole lot will fall in. That's a tall and heavy building. I wanna look at the cellar. It looks to me like it follows the structures of the main walls, which means I can blow through underground.'

'What else do you need?'

Blakey was still studying the drawing. 'I dunno yet, Cyril, but we need more than us three.'

'I can bring Tommy on board.'

'No way. I believe he stitched up Eddie Raven when he did the last heist for Mickey and Jack. Eddie may be in the slammer, but God help Tommy when he gets out, if Eddie ever finds him. He fucked up Jack and Mickey big time, the reckless bastard. No more talk about Eddie. We need to think of someone else we can trust.'

'What about Ronnie?' suggested Blakey.

'Yep, and Keith,' replied Frank.

'Right, then, let's get to work, lads. I'll sort out a plan and organise a van.'

Blakey and Frank each shot Cyril a questioning look. 'You ain't driving it, though, Cyril, are ya?' asked Frank.

Looking somewhat shocked, Cyril said, 'I'll have you know my driving has mightily improved.'

'Mate, the last job we did, you fucking did more damage to the motors in the street than Blakey could have done with his single stick of gelignite.'

'It was the gloves. They made the steering wheel slippery. Jesus, we got away, didn't we?'

Frank shook his head. 'I'm driving this time.'

'Whatever.'

* * *

Cyril's plan fell into place, as always. The fruit and veg shop, run by Mr Lamp, needed revamping, but Ronnie owned a building company. He had gone in with a quote to turn the greengrocer's place into a modern, inviting shop, with a fashionable open-plan effect. He intended to take down the partition wall, put a lintel in, and have it all plastered smooth. He'd build a waist-high small wall and worktop for the till and for Mr Lamp to wrap the fruit and veg. He would also build new racks for shelving so Mr Lamp could offer more variety of produce.

Ronnie and Keith had each grown a moustache, coloured their hair, and worn fake glasses every day Mr Lamp was there. Mr Lamp and his wife were an elderly couple anyway and wouldn't have noticed much about the men's appearance – certainly not enough to pick them out in an ID parade.

When she saw the quote, Mrs Lamp was chomping at the bit, and so the work began.

The back of the shop was opened up and a steel lintel put in. To be on the safe side, they kept the machinery and the building materials down in the cellar during the time that the work wasn't supposedly being carried out. However, it was being done through the cellar. They had parked a white builder's van at the back for two weeks, and so it became part of the furniture, with nothing looking odd or out of place. Meanwhile, Ronnie and Keith had taken it in turns to tunnel through the single brick facade between the two buildings. The tunnel with its makeshift supports was crude, but the lads thought they would hold up long enough to do the job. Mr Lamp rarely ventured into the cellar because he was too frail and also because he had no need to. He just assumed the builders knew exactly what they were doing. That being the case, Mr and Mrs Lamp went down to their daughter's place in Devon, since the plaster dust was affecting Mr Lamp's emphysema.

When the time came to blast through the final concrete and steel wall, Blakey was ready.

Ronnie and Keith made sure the walls were safely held up since even a blast would make the supports wobble. They wouldn't risk Blakey, their youngest brother, suffering a cave-in.

Frank was ready to drive the van. He'd already set out his route and done a dummy run in his car.

Cyril had bought the van. It was an old Ford Transit, but he'd made sure that the engine was brand new, along with new tyres, and he'd filled the van up with fuel.

Their only concern was that the night guard would hear the bang and go to investigate, or, worse, set the alarm off. It was connected directly to the nearest police station. Blakey only had one chance to blow a hole big enough for Cyril and his shotgun to get through.

Bang on midnight, the work began. Frank had the van pulled up to the back of the shop with the rear doors open. Blakey had the gelignite poked into the cracks that his brothers had made, and then they all stepped back and waited for the bang. Once they could see beyond the dust, Cyril tried to climb through the gap, but he struggled. 'Well, fucking help, will ya?'

Blakey, Ronnie, and Keith used all their efforts to push him through.

'Get in there, you fat bastard!' said Blakey, jokingly, as he pushed and pushed. Then, like popping a spot, Cyril was in. With his balaclava pulled down, he ran up the stairwell and into the room where he knew the security guard would be. Ready to hold a gun to his head, Cyril was fired up, only to find the guard was asleep with his feet up on the desk, a half-eaten sandwich left on the side, and his mouth open.

Cyril crept back to the hole to find Blakey inserting more gelignite to make the hole bigger.

'The guard's soundo. So let's be quick, lads. I'll watch the guard while you fill the potato sacks.'

He then hurried back upstairs.

Cyril heard another bang, but moments later, Blakey came into the guard's room. 'The fucking door has a code on it.'

Cyril couldn't remember the door having a code. Then he realised that when he had deposited his goods, the door was open. 'Oh, shit. Right, have you got your shooter?'

'Yeah.'

'ell, Blakey, just fucking blast it off. If fat boy, 'ere, wakes up, then I'll have a word in his shell-like.'

Blakey looked at the guard. ''Ere, are you sure he's not dead? He doesn't look right to me.'

Cyril leaned closer to the guard and smelled his breath. 'He's fucking drunk, that's why. Get a move on, mate, before he wakes up.'

The bang from the gun didn't stir the guard at all, so Cyril gave the lads a hand in emptying the boxes. After fifteen minutes, they had cleared the contents of every box and made their way back through the hole in the wall.

Frank helped them load the van.

Before Ronnie left the shop, he grabbed a handful of notes from his coat pocket and popped them into Mr Lamp's till. They locked the shop up and drove away.

They didn't go to the lock-up; instead, they went to the butcher's shop, where they used the back room to unload their potato sacks. Then it was a waiting game until Frank had driven the van to the arches, changed the number plates, collected his own car, and returned to the butcher's shop.

'Well, lads, let's divide this lot up,' said Cyril, rubbing his hands together.

'How do we divvy up this jewellery?' asked Ronnie, staring at the gems.

'Right, me, I don't know much about gems. I think the fairest way is to roll the dice. Let's say I get a six. That means

I get first dibs. If Frank gets a four, and let's say Keith gets a three, then Frank gets second dibs, and so on. So we'll put all the tom in the middle and go around, each taking a piece we fancy.'

Everyone agreed, and for an hour they went around the table as if they were playing a board game. After all the jewellery was divided up, they then got to work counting the money.

Once they were all done, they sat back and smiled, but Cyril nudged Blakey. ''Ere, and I just wanna clear something up. I ain't fucking fat,' he said, as he looked down at his flat toned stomach.

Frank roared, 'Jesus, Cyril, you are easy to wind up.'

By the next morning, they had all gone their separate ways. They decided to keep it that way for a few weeks and agreed not to flog any of the jewellery for a while.

CHAPTER TWENTY-EIGHT

Three months later

Cyril stashed his money away in a briefcase. He had plans for that.

Mr Ezra had valued his pieces of jewellery and Cyril was chuffed that he'd chosen the right ones. Not that the others had lost out – far from it – as they were all in for at least a million. Mr Ezra was grateful to Cyril that he was able to get his jewellery out of the place before it was robbed. He shook Cyril's hand. 'Business is good, Cyril. You must be a very happy man.'

Cyril smiled. 'Soon, Izzy. Very soon, I will be.'

Mr Ezra frowned. 'A man with money has no problems and must be happy. No?'

'Izzy, it's all about status.'

Izzy laughed. 'Yes, my son, you are right. This jewellery, I have paid you half now, and so I will pay you the other half next week.'

'I need the rest next week. You won't let me down, Izzy, will you, now?'

'Have I ever?'

'No, but that don't mean you won't in the future.'

'Good lad. I see you haven't changed. You trust no one.'

Cyril winked, smiled, and left.

* * *

By 8.00 p.m., Cyril was ready.

Frank sensed that Cyril was nervous because he was quiet and kept sighing. 'Look, are you sure about this, mate?'

'Frank, I am going to play poker and win back me mum's twenty-five quid from Lord Chambers.'

Frank took a deep breath. 'I know you never got over what he did, but, really, mate, winning twenty-five quid means fuck all, and if he wins, you may lose your rag and wallop him one.'

'Frank, it's all about the principle. You know that. And you know me from a little lad at primary school that that's how I've lived my life. Take this Lord fucking Chambers guy, for example. He knew she was my mother, and what is it with him, hey? Taking me bird wasn't enough, now, was it? He wanted to win a game of poker against my mum. That's true. But I would bet my last quid, he did it because he got a hard-on knowing that he was also sticking two fucking fingers up at me.'

'Cyril, he may not have known it was your mum. I've heard that he gambles a lot these days. His farver pegged it and left him a fortune. And now he's back in London and acting like a right flash prick.'

'Well, I wanna see what Lord Chambers looks like now, and I wanna win back that twenty-five quid. Come on, Frank, he has an issue with us. You know he does. He went after your Trudy and ended up with Flossie. When word went around that I was after his blood, although I never started that rumour, he fucked off. And now the prick's back and making a point by playing fucking poker with me ol' lady.'

'All right, all right, we'll go to the Salvador, but, please, Cyril, leave the shooter behind. I don't want you going all silly and taking chances, all because you're holding a grudge.'

'I ain't that reckless, Frank.'

Frank sensed Cyril's tone had changed and decided not to push the matter.

* * *

Luca Phylen, the owner of the Salvador, was a man in his late fifties. His mother was Italian and his father was Irish, so he was an odd-looking chap with white skin but jet-black hair. He was short in stature, with bright-green eyes and a prominent long nose. He always stood like a waiter with his hands behind his back. 'Good evening, Mr Reardon. It's been a long time, my friend.'

Cyril nodded. 'How's it going, Luca?'

'As you can see, Mr Reardon, the place has changed. The real poker games,' he confided with a wink, 'are held in my private quarters. Will your mother be joining you this evening?'

'No, she's at home watching some programme about cooking.'

'And will you be playing poker yourself, Mr Reardon?'

Cyril looked around the room. It was a sight, that was for sure, what with the expensive newly laid red and gold carpet, the endless rows of fruit machines, and the roulette tables. 'I'll play roulette for a while, and then, if there are any serious players around, I'll join the poker in your quarters.'

'Very well, Mr Reardon. There are a few serious players downstairs already.'

Cyril inclined his head. 'A bit early for that, wouldn't you say?'

Phylen smiled. 'Some have more money than sense.'

'I'll have a drink and a few chips on the wheel.'

'Very well, Mr Reardon. And you, Mr Marsden. Will you be paying poker?'

Frank smiled. 'Luca, my Trudy would box my ears if I got into gambling. But she don't know about the money tucked inside me boot, so I might just have a little flutter.'

'Good, good, please, gentlemen, go through, and Lucy, here, will take care of you.' He snapped his fingers at the blonde girl in the low-cut dress, with the long diamond earrings and hair that was pulled tightly away from her catlike face.

‘How many chips would you like, sir?’ she asked Cyril.

He handed her his jacket. ‘Fetch us a thousand and two brandies, would you, darlin’?’

It wasn’t her job to carry jackets and fetch drinks. Still, with one glance from her boss, she knew she had to keep these two men catered for. ‘Certainly, sir,’ she replied, with a smile, displaying small, even teeth, before hurrying away.

It was to be Cyril’s lucky night, but not so much for Frank. After four brandies, Cyril was up five thousand pounds and decided to head down to the poker room to the rear of the building. Phylen was only too pleased to escort the men. The doors were unlocked and inside stood two bouncers. Four large poker tables covered in green baize and surrounded by padded chairs dominated the room. A bar in the corner, manned by two very beautiful women, was a little hazy from where Cyril stood, due to the cigar smoke, which lingered several feet above the tables.

As soon as Cyril clapped eyes on the man at the second table, his breathing increased.

Lord Byron Chambers hadn’t aged too well. He looked a little haggard from all the smoking and drinking. His hair was thin and grey and his skin was wrinkled from the sun. As soon as he clocked Cyril, he leaned back on his chair, took a long drag on his cigar, and chuckled. ‘Well, well, if it isn’t Cyril Reardon. Long time no see. And your sidekick Frank Marsden is here, I see.’

Frank flared his nostrils; he hated everything about Chambers. His cocky attitude, with his over-the-top, plum-in-his-mouth accent, made Frank grit his teeth in rage.

'All right, Byron? I didn't know you were back in London.'

Chambers scoffed. 'I thought your mother would have told you. I do believe I won her last few pennies. But I have to say, gentlemen, she plays very well for a woman, and an old dear at that. A sweet thing, isn't she? I bet she was a very good-looking woman in her day.'

Cyril took Chambers' comments on the chin. He knew he was deliberately trying to wind him up, and if he hadn't had a plan in place, he was adamant he would have smashed the living shit out of the man. So, instead, he mumbled under his breath to Frank, 'Leave it, Frank, please.'

Frank knew then that the minute Cyril had said 'please', it was a signal to keep his neck well and truly reeled in.

'So, fancy a game do you? The thing is, Cyril, I am playing for high stakes, but, then, it's entirely up to you.'

Cyril removed his gloves and loosened his tie before he sat down at the table. The two other men who sat on either side of Chambers looked upper class. Cyril could tell right away, just from the way they held themselves, with their snotty expressions.

'This is Tristan Simons and this dear old fellow is Lord Parker-Green.'

Cyril was silent but nodded to the dealer. 'Deal me in, mate. And the stakes are?'

Lord Parker-Green got up. 'I'm done for, this evening. See you later, Byron.'

'See you, old chap, but next week, don't bring pennies. There's no fun in that.'

Cyril didn't even look Parker-Green's way or say goodbye.

Chambers smirked. 'Let's start with a thousand pounds.'

The dealer coughed in surprise. No one started with a bet of a thousand pounds.

Cyril sniffed up through his nose and nodded. 'Sure.' He looked at Frank, who reached inside his jacket pocket; he pulled out the chips and slapped them in front of Cyril.

'Oooh, so you have come prepared, I see, Cyril.'

Cyril just smiled. He really didn't want to get into a conversation with the lord. He knew if he did, he would end up punching the bastard.

As the dealer dealt the cards, Cyril studied every inch of Chambers' face. As if the world was rolling in slow motion, he focused on the man's cheek bones and particularly the muscles that reveal the true feelings of a man. The muscle that cannot fake a smile and the muscle just below that can. He stared at the man's eyelids, scrutinising how creased and crinkled they'd become, and then he looked at the pulse in his opponent's temple. It was steady, a regular beat. There were no beads of sweat, no surges of pressure even. The man appeared quite relaxed.

The dealer dealt the cards to the three men, and then Cyril

watched as Chambers studied his. His true facial muscle lifted into a genuine smile. The pulse quickened but returned to normal. Cyril knew then that Chambers had a good hand so far. He looked at his own two cards; there was nothing of any value to get excited about. He could lose the grand by folding, which meant throwing his cards in and exiting the game. But he decided not to do this. He wanted to see Chambers' cards, to ensure he had the measure of the man.

Cyril waited and called the next round by matching the stakes. The dealer then dealt the flop, where three cards are placed face up on the table. The two cards in Cyril's hands, along with the three cards on the table, still did not make up a good hand, but he could see that Chambers' excitement had just upped a level. Cyril decided to fold. He wanted to make sure he was right about him.

Simons also folded.

Bingo! Chambers won. He held two kings in his hand, so, with the third king on the table, he had three of a kind.

'It seems that Lady Luck is not on your side tonight, Cyril. Are you sure you want to play with the big boys for even bigger money?'

Cyril gave his opponent an inscrutable stare and remained silent except for a firm nod in acknowledgement.

Chambers nodded. 'Okay, dealer.'

Cyril threw his chips on the pile, and, again, he watched the look on Chambers' face.

The pulse quickened in Chambers' temple and remained

fast. Then, a tiny twitch appeared in the crease of his eye. He smiled at Cyril, but it was the under muscle, the one that lied. The fake smile.

Cyril knew then that the start of his opponent's hand was rubbish. But he had to see this for himself. Once again, he folded his cards to end the game. He was spot on: Chambers did have a shit hand.

Feeling the butterflies in his stomach, Cyril was ready to start the next game, and although he had kept Frank in the dark, he knew that it had to be that way for now.

Simons was nervous and kept glancing at Reardon. He lit up a cigar and was mindful not to blow the smoke in Reardon's direction. It was the intense level of dark concentration on the younger man's face that bothered him the most.

The game started with Chambers' sarcastic comment, 'I don't want to win your shoes off your feet. Are you sure about this, ol' fellow?'

'Just play!' growled Cyril.

The cards were dealt, and Cyril glanced at the two in his hand, a seven of spades and an eight of spades. He rolled his eyes and then caught Chambers staring at him.

But he had already summed up his opponents. Chambers most likely held two good cards, but he couldn't suss out Simons' hand.

The dealer then placed the flop in the middle.

Right away, Cyril knew that he couldn't win with what was on the table. Even if the fourth card or the fifth, called the river, was a good one, his own were far worse. It was Chambers' turn, and he raised the bet.

Simons matched and then Cyril did likewise.

It was frustrating because Simons was such a cautious player.

Chambers raised again, and this time, Simons raised, so Cyril knew he had to raise as well. After a good hour of staring, smoking, and drinking, the size of the pot became a significant amount of money.

Luca Phylen was now in the room, anxious about the outcome of the game between three very different individuals. He knew of Lord Chambers very well. Tristan Simons, a minor royal, came in, once in a while, and he could usually be relied on to play a good hand. Cyril Reardon was less well known to him, but he had no doubts in betting that the man was a gangster.

Frank was hot under the collar because it was as if Cyril was playing just to prove a point, but if that was the case, then the stakes were getting silly. Cyril was running out of chips. Frank had even cashed in all of his own money and handed it to Cyril, and now there were no more chips left.

Chambers sighed. 'Oh dear, what do we do now, Cyril? Shall we just call "all in" and see the cards? Only it appears you have no chips left to play.'

His voice was so defined, and each word was so crisp and deliberate that Cyril wanted to throw up, but, instead, he pulled a set of keys from his pocket. 'We'll use my car, my brand-new Jaguar, as collateral.'

Simons threw his cards in. 'I fold.' He really couldn't afford to lose any more money.

Chambers beamed. 'A new Jaguar it is, then. I'll see you and raise you one hundred thousand pounds.'

Cyril stared at his cards and then glanced up at Frank. Frank shook his head, letting Cyril know he wasn't happy. But Cyril just gave him his trademark smirk and retrieved another set of keys. 'My home in Chislehurst – it's worth over a hundred thousand pounds – and I will see you.'

'Your house! Yes, I know it, and your car, eh, Cyril. Well, I'll accept.' When a huge smile lifted Chambers' cheeks, his mouth showed a gold back tooth. 'Dear me, ol' fellow, I hate to say it, but I am sure you cannot beat my hand.' He slapped the cards face up. He had a queen and a jack of hearts.

Cyril stared at the five cards on the table – the ten, nine, and eight of hearts, as well as the five and six of spades. So regardless of Cyril's seven and eight of spades, which could have made a good hand with the five and six of spades, Chambers beat him with a higher straight flush.

Cyril threw his cards on the table. There was nothing in his hand that he could have won with.

He snatched his brandy, downed it in one, and rose to leave.

'Thank you, Cyril. I'll have the deeds transferred. Oh, you'll see to that, won't you, Luca? There's a good man.'

Cyril glanced back at Lord Chambers, who was laughing his head off, watching him slip away.

'Why the fuck did you do that?' hissed Frank in Cyril's ear, once they were out of earshot of Chambers. 'You've lost everything. I can't believe you ever thought you could stand a chance with such a shit hand. What the hell has got into you? Fuck me. Your lovely house.' He slapped his hands down to his sides and marched on ahead, out of the club.

Once he reached his car, he stopped, pulled out a cigarette, and began smoking furiously. He waited for Cyril, who had been delayed while he collected his jacket. As soon as Cyril was in sight, he saw the beaming smile on his face. Frank sighed; he might have known – Cyril had something up his sleeve.

'Get in the car, Frank, and drive.'

Once they were along the road, Cyril laughed. 'That went like a fucking dream.'

Frank craned his neck across at his friend. 'A dream? What are you on about? He'll be living the *dream* in your posh pad in Chislehurst, as well as driving your new Jag.'

'Good, he can have it all.'

'*What*?'

'He can have it all. Let the twat get used to the idea that he is invincible, that he's ruined me.'

Frank shook his head. 'You are unbelievable, and, dare I say it, Cyril, fucking reckless, mate.'

‘Don’t get so upset, Frank. You’ll be laughing this time next week. In fact, Frank, you will be hysterical.’

Frank couldn’t be bothered to ask any more questions. He was going home a few quid light, but his best mate was a house and a car down.

CHAPTER TWENTY-NINE

With Cyril's house now the property of Lord Chambers, Cyril spent the next week at his mother's flat. It was during that time he realised she wasn't well at all. He had lain in bed on the Friday morning listening to her coughing her lungs up. She was always up by 6.00 a.m., but it was gone 7.00 a.m., and she was still in bed.

He got up, slid his feet into his old slippers, which his mother had kept at the end of his bed, and ambled into the kitchen. He then noticed that the worktop and the table, which normally were always immaculately clean, were now a little grubby. And looking more closely around the kitchen, he noticed a few burned water stains on the cooker. *This wasn't like his mother*, he thought.

He boiled the kettle, popped some bread in the toaster, and sat down on a kitchen chair. He wondered if maybe Howie and himself leaving home had had a knock-on effect. Perhaps his mother had kept a spotless house for her sons, and now she lived here alone, she didn't feel she needed to worry so much.

After making a pot of tea and buttering the toast, he placed everything on a tray and took it through to his mother.

''Ere you go, Mum. Sit yourself up.'

Peggy's eyes looked half-closed, and her hair was a mess.

'Mum, are you sure you've just got the flu? You don't look well at all.'

She waved her hand. 'I'm fine. It's just the flu. It's taken a while to shift. Now then, you put that tray on me bedside table and go and have yourself some breakfast. Don't be catching my lurgy.'

Cyril was about to do as she asked, but before he left the room, he opened the curtains and the small window to let in the light and a bit of fresh air.

As he turned around, he found his mum squinting and raising her arm to shield her eyes. 'Bloody hell, Cyril. I've not even woken up properly yet.'

At that moment, Cyril realised that his mother was getting old. With no make-up and the light shining on her skin, he could see she was ageing. He just hadn't noticed it before.

'Do you want anything else, Mum?'

Peggy was now sitting upright and had pulled a cardigan around her shoulders. 'No, love, this is fine.' She sighed, her voice sounding breathless.

'I have to go out tonight, Mum, and when I come home, I will be a different person.'

'Oh, yeah? Good. Would you fetch me some paracetamol and a bit of cough mixture, or Vicks VapoRub?'

'Mum, you need the doctor, not a couple of tablets. I'll

take you there meself.'

'No, you won't. I'll call him out. I don't wanna spread all these germs over the weak and sick.'

Cyril left his mum to herself and went back into the kitchen where he made a coffee, quickly downed it, and jumped into the bath. He wanted a very clear head, and a carefully thought-out plan.

Following a relaxing soak and with just a towel around his waist, he headed back to his bedroom. He smiled to himself. The two beds were still the same, and even Howie's slippers remained at the foot of his bed, like his. *Howie would never fit into those now, though*, he thought.

By 10.00 a.m., Cyril was ready, and Frank was on time. They drove first to Izzy Ezra's place to collect the briefcase of money that Izzy had promised him. The shop was closed, so Cyril went to the office at the back.

He was confronted with Izzy in a long coat with his hand held up to stop Cyril walking too close to him. 'Do not stand on the rug. Please walk around it.'

Cyril rolled his eyes. 'I ain't got time to fuck about, Izzy. Have you got me money?'

Izzy pulled a briefcase from behind the desk at the back of the room.

'All in used notes.'

Cyril smiled. 'Thank you, Izzy, mate.'

'Aren't you going to count it all?'

Cyril looked back over his shoulder and winked. 'I know where you live.'

'Good luck, Cyril, and I mean it. I wish you well.'

Cyril gripped the case and hurried to Frank's car. 'Right, tonight, remember I will go in with one briefcase, and you, Frank, will handle the other one. Act like it's yours.'

Frank sighed heavily. 'And if it all goes wrong, mate, then what?'

Cyril grinned like a kid. 'Then I will have to shoot the bastard.'

* * *

It was 8.30 p.m. by the time they reached the Salvador. Frank held the door open for Cyril to breeze through.

Luca Phylen spotted the men each holding a black briefcase and hurried over. 'Back again so soon, Cyril? I hope everything's okay?'

Cyril sensed that Phylen was worried that he had returned to cause trouble. He tried to give him a reassuring nod. 'Let's hope you have enough chips, Luca, me ol' mucker.'

Phylen smiled but almost lost his balance when Cyril tapped his shoulder.

'Er, Mr Reardon. Will you be using the high roller table?'

Cyril nudged Frank and laughed. 'Yep, I think I just might

be. So, who's down there? Anyone we know?'

Phylen swallowed hard. 'Well, Lord Chambers, Lord Parker-Green, and another chap called Brighton-Shaw.'

'Good,' said Cyril, as he rubbed his hands together; he'd known full well his nemesis was there.

'Will anyone be joining you?'

Cyril shrugged his shoulders. 'Freddy Blake might join us if the game goes on until late.'

Once Phylen had taken Cyril Reardon's coat, he walked him and Frank Marsden down to his private quarters and to the large green baize table up on the stand, with the overhead lights. It was known as the high roller table.

Chambers didn't spot Reardon and Marsden right away. He was busy playing a game with Parker-Green and another friend of his father's, Oliver Brighton-Shaw, a wealthy aristocrat from Surrey.

Just as Cyril was approaching the table, he spotted Parker-Green, and for a moment he stopped in his tracks. On his previous visit to the club, his inner voice told him that he should know the man. Now he was almost certain he did. There was something very familiar about him, and it made his stomach turn over. *But how could he know him*? he wondered. He stepped closer, all the while staring at the man and feeling disconcerted.

'Well, if it isn't Mr Cyril Reardon. Please don't tell me you have returned hoping to win your home back?' said Chambers, mockingly.

Cyril smiled. 'Not necessarily. I just thought you might like to play cards, and if it gets as far as winning back my house, then I would have had a good night, eh?'

Chambers laughed. 'Oh, chaps, this is the man I was telling you about. I won his brand-new Jag, his home, and now, I guess, I will win the shoes off his feet.' He glanced at Reardon's watch. 'And the Cartier.' He peered closer. 'An ancient but valuable Cartier, I see.'

Cyril clenched his fist as he brought the watch closer to Chambers' face. 'Yeah, this is a valuable piece, but I won't offer this up. This is a personal gift from an old friend of mine.' And he meant it: Carlo had given it to him as a trust reward.

Chambers raised his brow. 'Really, I am, as you can see' – he pointed to his pile of chips – 'a gambling man, and I bet it won't be long before you will offer up your watch.' His smile fell to a look of annoyance. 'In fact, I will have everything you own by the end of the evening.'

It surprised Cyril that Lord Chambers would say such a daring thing, to him or to anyone, for that matter. Still, he didn't care; he was here to win a game, and with his head clear and his mind sober, he would swallow every snide comment. But as he sat down, his eyes flicked to Parker-Green again.

Now an older man, probably in his seventies, his eyes were round and darted around suspiciously. As he leaned forward to shake Cyril's hand, he smiled in a way that made Cyril go rigid.

Cyril knew that smile, but he still couldn't recall from

where. That was until the man spoke.

'Excuse me, gentlemen, I wish to use the bathroom.'

Cyril watched Parker-Green get up from his seat and walk towards the men's toilets, his gait slow and stiff and his frame slightly bent to the side.

'Why does that bloke walk like that?'

Chambers was busily putting his chips into piles when he looked up. 'Oh, Parker-Green? He was stabbed many years ago, and an infection got the better of him. The poor old fellow, he had to have most of his innards removed. Apparently, he's lucky to be alive.'

Cyril felt sick. Everything was falling into place about the bastard: the smile, the voice, and the man's injuries. He had called himself Dulcie at the time, but Cyril knew it was definitely him. He would never forget the man, or the fear, or the impression he had left on him when he was only a young lad who wanted to use his fishing rod. Now, as a grown man, Cyril realised what Lord Parker-Green was all about, and he would make sure that once this game of poker was over, this shithead would never hurt another child.

After taking a few deep but inconspicuous breaths, Cyril awaited his pile of chips.

Phylen had them brought to the table, and with his white gloves on, he carefully placed them in front of Cyril.

'I see,' said Chambers, 'you are very serious about winning back the house. Well, it looks like it will be a long night. Care for a brandy?'

Cyril shook his head. ‘No, but I’ll have a Pepsi.’

‘It might sharpen your mind.’

‘No, Byron, I don’t fancy a brandy just yet. Now, how about we play?’

‘Slow down, old chap. Let’s act like gentlemen and wait for Parker-Green.’

Cyril needed to take another deep breath. Two of his enemies – two complete wasters – would be in his company tonight. He would need a calm and cool head.

As soon as Parker-Green returned to his seat, the game began. The dealer, a rotund man with rosy cheeks and a shock of red curly hair, shuffled the pack with his long gloved fingers, ensuring each player received two cards. He paused and waited for the betting to begin. However, the first game was over in a few minutes. The three card flop was useless and no one had a decent hand.

The dealer decided to give the pack of cards an extra shuffle before he dealt two cards to each player. With one thousand pounds each in the pot, the men were poised again.

As soon as Cyril saw Chambers look at his two cards, he watched the man’s facial muscles and saw his temple pulse. The hand wasn’t brilliant; he knew that, from the pulse not calming down so rapidly. Then he saw the crease in the man’s eye slightly twitch. Cyril knew then that the two cards in front of Chambers were definitely not good. He looked at his own cards and saw the nine and jack of hearts. He wondered if Lady Luck was now on his side. ‘I’ll see you and raise you two thousand.’

Chambers laughed. 'I thought you were a serious player, Cyril. A couple of thousand chips will not win your house back. Come on, man.'

Cyril shook his head. 'Mind your own business, Chambers, and just play.'

Parker-Green stared at his two cards for ages before he then placed them face down and lit up a cigar.

'Don't blow that shit in my face,' demanded Cyril.

Parker-Green stopped sucking on the cigar and glared for a moment before he realised that Reardon was no gentleman from his stable. He looked a rough kind of man who fancied his chances at poker. The look he'd given him was one that made Parker-Green shudder. It was as if he had seen that dark expression before. Stubbing out the cigar, he raised the bet by three thousand.

Cyril matched Parker-Green and Chambers followed suit. Then the dealer placed the three card flop on the table. Cyril stared at Chambers and noticed that his eyes were alive. He then glanced at the cards: an eight of hearts, an ace of diamonds, and the queen of hearts.

From his position, Frank could see the men looking at their own two cards again to see how well they would fit with the three cards on the table to make a good five-card hand, and his heart rose a beat. The game was at last coming alive.

The surge of excitement on Chambers' face had Cyril wondering if he held a pair of aces, which would give him three, including the one on the table. Yet, even so, he knew that if that was the case, three aces would not beat a straight flush. Cyril then glanced at Parker-Green, who appeared to be very nervous. His eyes and his lips seemed to twitch.

The betting stakes were raised, and the dealer laid the fourth card face up on the table – the ten of hearts.

Cyril felt absolute elation. No matter what Chambers had in his hand, he couldn't beat his – not now.

Chambers' top cheek muscles twitched, and Cyril knew then that Chambers had a good hand. But it was never going to be good enough. That was the moment when Cyril nearly gave the game away, but he remained still with no expression.

He waited, but it was Parker-Green who folded. 'Good lunch earlier today, Byron. It's all yours now,' he said, as he rose from the table and tottered off towards the bar.

A waitress approached and offered both Cyril and Chambers a drink. Cyril shook his head, but Chambers opted for a large brandy.

Suddenly, Chambers pushed five chips forward. 'I'll raise you by fifty thousand pounds.'

Cyril looked at his cards once more and then at the ones on the table. He stared in deep thought. He had to act as if he was troubled. Then he watched Chambers doing the same thing. Cyril clocked the pulse in the man's temple quicken and it wasn't letting up.

'I'll see you—'

'See me?' interrupted Chambers.

'No, I'll see you and *raise* you a hundred thousand pounds.'

A tiny bead of sweat appeared on Chambers' hairline. Cyril watched it trickle down to his sideburn.

'Well?' said Cyril.

Chambers smiled with his lower cheek muscle; it was a fake and nervous smile. 'I'll see you and raise you *two* hundred thousand pounds.'

Cyril stared at the man. 'Two hundred grand?'

Chambers nodded slowly – almost seductively.

The waitress appeared again with Chambers' brandy. She offered both men a cigar, which Chambers took from her without even moving his eyes away from Reardon's. She lit the end and stepped back.

'Do you want to fold, old chap?'

'Shut up and wait. If I want to fold, you will be the first to know. Now you' – he pointed to the waitress – 'can I have a cold orange and bitter lemon and a packet of plain crisps?' The waitress hurried away to fetch the refreshments.

Meanwhile, Frank, who was still standing away from the table, just watching, stepped forward and whispered in Cyril's ear, 'Are you fucking sure, mate?'

Cyril turned to the side and whispered back in Frank's ear, 'Oh, yeah, and if I run out of money, go and get me some more.'

Chambers didn't like Reardon's smirk, and he hated even more the fact that he was so well respected for being a villain. And he knew he was a gangster; he had monitored him and Frank Marsden. He detested them. As far as he was concerned, the two lads who had scarred his chin, resulting in him having to flee through the barbed wire fence, leaving him ripped to shreds and even losing a testicle in the process, should not be swanning around in flash cars, wearing expensive watches, and having the respect they so didn't deserve – in his eyes anyway. He assumed that once Reardon had lost his house and car, he would be gutted and withdraw with his tail between his legs – not come back for more. So Chambers was not having it; he would make sure both men would crawl back under the rocks they came from.

He nodded to one of his old drinking partners, an Etonian buddy called Ivan Fairbanks.

Fairbanks scooted over, only too eager to hear what his friend had to say and also to be nosy. He could see the pile of chips accumulating on the table.

'Ivan, call Flossie and tell her to join me, there's a good chap,' Chambers instructed, hoping that the sight of Flossie would have Reardon less cocksure, and when he won the pot, he would also be able to rub Reardon's nose well and truly in it.

Fairbanks nodded and left the room. Checking his mobile phone, he found the number to his friend Byron's London pad, where Flossie was kept as Byron's bit on the side. He called her and also called a taxi firm to pick her up.

Chambers then smiled sarcastically at Reardon. 'I thought

you were a daring man, Cyril Reardon.'

'I'll see your two hundred grand and I'll raise you four hundred grand,' said Cyril, coldly.

Chambers worked his cigar and waited until a strong plume of smoke spiralled high above the table. He then gulped back his brandy. But seeing his opponent grin at him, he said, 'I'll raise you seven hundred grand and offer up the house in Chislehurst.'

Cyril picked up the house keys that Chambers had slung into the pot, and he turned them over in his hands. He huffed and threw them back onto the pile of chips, 'Sure,' he said, amiably.

Half an hour passed. It was an anxious time for Frank and everyone else, since it appeared that Cyril was in a quandary and couldn't decide whether to call the bet or raise it.

But unknown to the players and a few onlookers, who had suddenly appeared, almost by magic, Cyril was in the zone. He leaned back on his chair and continued to stare, noting every involuntary muscle movement on Chambers' face. He knew his opponent was tense and not as confident as the last time they had played against each other a week earlier. But instructing his friend to bring Flossie onto the scene was something he had not banked on. Chambers had obviously decided to up the stakes by such an audacious act.

Twenty minutes later, the sound of the door opening and closing briefly caused Chambers to look up and smile.

Cyril, though, had his back to the door, and so he didn't see who had just walked in.

But Frank had, and it took only a second before he realised it was Flossie. She had aged so much, but, then, it was over twenty years ago when they were all living in the same tower block.

Flossie, in a black tight-fitting dress and long black boots, walked over to Chambers. She had no idea that opposite him was Cyril Reardon. That was until she leaned down to kiss Byron's cheek, and then she saw Cyril. Slowly, she stood up straight and blinked. It really was Cyril. He was bigger and fuller in the face, but there was not an inch of fat on his ripped body. His hair was darker but his eyes still sparkled. Compared to Byron, Cyril was like a handsome movie star. He had certainly aged well. She thought in fact he had got better looking with age. His navy-blue suit was worn loose and his crisp white shirt fitted him like a glove. She could smell his aftershave and noticed how smooth his freshly shaven face was.

She tried to look coy, like when they'd first met, because she remembered how he was so willing to please her. For a moment, she longed to swap places – to be with Cyril and to feel his big strong arms around her waist. However, she noticed that when Cyril recognised her, he simply gave her a cold nod in acknowledgement. She had always thought if one day they ever met up again he would beg and plead to get back with her. So his complete lack of interest in her now was mind-blowing. Never in her wildest dreams had she imagined he would look at her as if she was a nobody.

Chambers wrapped his arm around her waist and then slapped her bum, like she was a piece of meat to him.

She tutted and pulled away. Keen to try to make another

impression on Cyril, Flossie caught his eye and smiled, but she had a rude awakening when he waved a waitress over to fill up his orange and bitter lemon, acting as if she really wasn't even in the room.

Meanwhile, Chambers was staring at the pot again. He then flipped the corners of his own two cards, and with a smile he nodded. 'I'll see you and I'll raise you.'

A few gasps from even more people who had gathered to watch made Cyril chuckle. 'Let me see, Byron. I can raise you, but I am looking at your chips, and they are a bit on the low side, wouldn't you say?'

Chambers looked at the space in front of Cyril. 'And what will you raise, Cyril? Because, dear chap, it appears that you have run out of your hard-earned savings.'

Cyril turned sideways to see Blakey arrive and make his way over to where Frank was standing. Cyril winked at Blakey, who appeared excited since he had no idea about poker. Cyril then gave Frank the nod; it was as if they could communicate without words.

Frank left the room with the briefcase, and Phylen returned with the chips on a tray and piled them in front of Cyril.

Flossie watched the enormous amount of money on the table; she then glanced across to Cyril, who seemed as cool as a cucumber. She was now on Cyril's side. If she hadn't been, she would have told Byron that he was playing against a professional. She'd spent many an evening with Peggy and Cyril playing cards, and she knew how good he was because he had been taught by the best. She had also learned to detest

Byron over the years and had only put up with his carryings-on because she had nowhere else to go; she couldn't face going back to her mother's. She had no job, and, in reality, she was a prostitute, selling her arse to one man who was vile in the bedroom. All the gifts he had thrown at her for a quick, rough shag were nothing compared to the pretty pendants with the engraved words that Cyril had bought her. She had been a fool and knew she would never get over it unless Cyril could forgive her. She desperately hoped he would, and then, perhaps, they could make another go of it.

'I tell you what, Byron,' said Cyril. 'Like you said in that last game we played, let's play like daring men, eh. You're not a chicken, are you?'

Chambers gulped back another brandy and glared at the man and then at one of Reardon's friends, but as soon as his eyes met Marsden's, he felt that familiar surge of anger he'd experienced earlier this evening. He would not let Reardon win; he would strip him of everything.

Shooting a look back at Reardon, he felt his head was going to explode. With wet palms, a dry throat – despite consuming the most expensive brandy – and now feeling an anxious rush to go to the lavatory, he was struggling to maintain his composure. Looking at his cards, he knew he had a chance, and so he had to call. There was no way he was going to fold – not now – not with all the money on the table. 'Go on, then, I am going to call.'

And when the dealer turned over the river card, there, staring Chambers in the face, was his fourth ace. He knew it would take one hell of a hand to beat that. All of a sudden, his whole aura changed. He felt alive. He had Reardon's former girlfriend here just for this moment. He was going to win and win big. He couldn't wait to see Reardon's final cards because he believed he had won the game.

The room was still. Onlookers were staring at the players in disbelief, mesmerised by the kind of game that they would probably never ever have the privilege to witness again in their lifetime. This was a game for huge winners and no one could call it.

Suddenly, Cyril pushed all his chips into the middle. 'I'll bet you, Lord fucking Chambers, one million pounds.'

Chambers laughed nervously. 'A million? Er, are you sure?'

Cyril leaned forward. 'I thought you were a real man. A man of your word. Really, you are just Mickey fucking Mouse. I wanted a real game, but I guess a lord like you is all mouth and trousers.'

Byron grinned at Flossie. 'I can match you, Cyril Reardon. I have far more money than you.'

Looking relaxed, Cyril smiled and eased himself back on his chair. 'Prove it.'

Everyone waited, wondering if Lord Chambers would make a few calls to raise the money, but, suddenly, he pulled two sets of keys from his suit pocket. 'My house is worth almost a million, and these are the keys to my Bentley.'

Cyril looked around the room at all the open mouths and then he stared at the pot. 'I'd rather you write me out a chitty and pay me the million tomorrow.'

'I . . . er, I don't have a million pounds. All I have is my mansion and my car.'

Cyril gave an exaggerated gasp. 'And there I was thinking you were a rich geezer. Ah, well, ya can't have it all, eh, Chambers. Your poncy title, it seems to me, ain't worth jack shit, really, is it, mate? So, down to business. To match my million, I want the keys to my Jag in that pile, as well as everything inside that mansion, including the garages and the land, and then we can call "all in", unless you want to see me and raise the bet again. But, oh dear, you can't, can you?'

'Yes, okay, the mansion, the land, and all the contents.'

'And your garages, and, don't forget, I want my car in the pot as well.'

Cockily, Chambers pulled out another set of keys from his suit pocket and threw them on the table.

'Yes, yes, and the garages and your former car. There,' he said, impatiently, 'are the keys. Now, come on, man, let's just do this. If we are both all in, then let's show our cards.'

Cyril smiled and faced Phylen. 'You are the witness to this gentlemen's agreement.'

Phylen nodded, and, in turn, he was acknowledged by Lord Chambers.

Both players nodded to each other, but Chambers, with a wide cheesy smile, slapped his two aces on the table, and then he rudely pointed to the other two aces on the table before leaning forward to scoop up the chips.

‘Oi, hold up!’ demanded Cyril, as he slowly turned over his two cards. The nine and jack of hearts went perfectly with the cards on the table to make a straight flush.

Gasps from the room were met with shock from Chambers as Reardon’s cards turned him a deathly pale. It couldn’t be. He was sure, with four aces, that he would beat Reardon’s hand. Swallowing hard, he suddenly had to turn to the side to throw up.

Both Frank and Blakey cheered, and Cyril spun round to look at them, his face creased in that familiar massive grin of his. Then, all three men were jumping up and down like kids and high-fiving each other.

Chambers had disgusted Flossie by throwing up, and so she moved away and gently navigated herself towards Cyril, who was still laughing as Phylen instructed two men with trays to take the chips away to be counted.

‘Hello, Cyril,’ said Flossie, in her most provocative voice.

Instantly, Frank and Blakey stopped laughing and the room became quiet once more. Both men stared coldly at her, but this was Cyril’s call; they would stay out of it.

‘Hello, Flossie.’

‘It’s been a long time, Cyril.’

Cyril nodded, equably. ‘Yeah, I guess it has.’

‘I didn’t want it to end the way it did, you know,’ she whispered, as she watched Byron from the corner of her eye stagger to his feet and flee towards the men’s toilets.

‘Ah, well, shit happens, but I don’t hold a grudge, Flossie. You, of all people, would know that.’

‘Oh, that’s good because I thought perhaps we could go for a drink sometime. You know, to catch up and talk about the old times.’

Cyril stepped back and looked Flossie up and down. He sighed. ‘I would do, doll, but I am a very busy man, you see, and I wouldn’t see the point. I mean, I don’t need to go over the old times. I remember them very well.’

Flossie wasn’t sure what he meant, or if he was being sarcastic because he was never sarcastic with her. ‘Cyril, I always loved you, ya know. I never loved Byron.’

Cyril put his arms out and pulled her close. Flossie didn’t struggle. She embraced Cyril and was about to whisper in his ear again when he said to her. ‘You could never love anyone, Flossie. Ya see, your only love is money.’

He let her go then, like a hot brick, and smiled sweetly at her, before joining Frank and Blakey.

It was the smug look on Frank’s face that really told her she was hated.

CHAPTER THIRTY

It was 2.00 a.m., by the time the money had been counted and bagged up.

Chambers was now knocking back the Scotch and growling under his breath as he watched Cyril laughing and jumping about with his mates, who were joining in with the excitement.

'It may be best for you to leave now, Mr Chambers, er, sorry, I mean Lord Chambers,' said Phylen.

'I will go when I am fucking good and ready.'

Cyril looked back at Chambers. 'I would never have played you for your home. But you know what? You are one nasty piece of shit. You wanted me and me pal Frank shot. Oh, I remember it well, Byron, and so do you. We were kids, but you, ya sick bastard, wanted your farver to shoot us, all 'cos we chored a few fish to eat. And you knew it was us at Gwynnie's engagement party. Then you tried to meddle with Frank's Trudy, but she would have none of it.' He stopped when he saw Flossie appear, with her head down. 'And then you managed to take Flossie from me.'

Flossie looked up in hope, but Cyril wasn't looking at her. He was glaring at Chambers, who could just about stand up.

'You probably did me a favour on that score. But you then played me mum for twenty-five quid, and, to top it all, you wanted to take my house. I would never have taken a man's home, you know, never! But, see, you, in my eyes, Byron, you may be a so-called gentleman, all 'cos you were born the son of a lord, but you are no real gentleman. You have the title, but, see, me, I have the mansion, the Bentley, and the land, and if ever a young man fished in the lake or took from the land, I'd let them. I'd even carry it to their home.'

As soon as he stopped with the speech, Frank and Blakey clapped.

'I'll have the papers drawn up tomorrow and the deeds signed over. Luca is the legal witness and you have until tonight to collect your smalls, and nothing else. Got me?'

Chambers nodded in defeat.

On a high, Cyril left the Salvador and drove back to the flat, to be followed by Frank and Blakey.

But as soon as they all arrived, Shirley came hurtling along the walkway to meet them. 'It's Peggy. She's been rushed into the Royal London Hospital. I went to see if she was all right, but she was so poorly. I didn't know where you were, Cyril. I've called Howie. He's at the hospital now.'

The excitement of the evening plummeted in a single heartbeat. Now, for the first time in his life, Cyril felt an overwhelming feeling of fear. 'Frank, please get me there as quick as you can.'

The drive to the hospital was quicker than when they carried out any robberies. Frank finally skidded to a halt outside the entrance. The door was already open before he'd stopped, and Cyril was running towards reception. 'Please, my mum, Peggy Reardon, where is she?'

The receptionist scrolled down the lists and shook her head. 'There's no *Peggy* here.'

Cyril gasped. '*What*? But she was brought in here. Hold on. Can you check for *Margaret* Reardon?'

Cyril drummed the receptionist's desk with his fingers as he watched anxiously for her to check the admissions on the screen in front of her.

'Oh, yes, sir, we have a *Margaret* Reardon. Go up to the second floor, turn left, and she is on that ward.'

Cyril flew up the stairs, followed by Frank and Blakey, hot on his heels. All three men tore along the corridor and onto the ward, only to be stopped by a nurse. 'Slow down, gentlemen. It's three in the morning. Who are you here to see?'

'Peggy, er, Margaret Reardon, my mum. She was rushed in.'

The young nurse suddenly bit her lip. 'Oh, sir, er.'

'Cyril,' came a voice from a room on the left.

'Howie, where's Mum?'

But Howie didn't answer. Rushing out of the room, he grabbed Cyril's arms. 'She's gone.'

Cyril stood in disbelief at his brother, not taking in the words because his brain wouldn't process them. And for good reason. It was only yesterday morning he was making her a cup of tea. She was sitting up in bed.

'No, no' – he looked past Howie – 'no, she can't be. She doesn't know that I won the bet. I won the mansion. She can live like a queen. No, Howie, please.'

Howie gripped Cyril tighter until he felt Cyril's body go limp, and then he felt every deep sob escape as Cyril fell to his knees and cried like a baby.

Frank and Blakey tried to help their best friend to his feet as the nurse guided them into the family room. Once the door was closed behind them, Cyril let out a wailing sound that none of the men had ever heard before. Frank wrapped his arms around Cyril and rocked him while he broke his heart crying into Frank's shoulder.

It was a while before the room was quiet and Cyril could take anything in. After sitting down, he looked up at the nurse, who was hovering by the door, almost in tears herself, so overcome by the emotion in the room. 'Please, tell me why she died?'

'Let me fetch the doctor. He can explain everything to you,' she said, as she left the room.

Howie crouched down by his brother. 'She went peacefully, Cyril. She just went to sleep. She said to tell you she loved you very much, and that I was to look after you.'

Cyril suddenly sat up straight and grinned. 'Did she?' He knew Howie was telling the truth because it was the sort of thing she would say.

'She never got to know that I won the mansion.'

Howie chuckled. 'Mum always knew you would be a king of your castle one day. She always said it to me, anyway, and she would always say I would live like a pig in shit.'

The door to the family room opened and a doctor appeared; he was a young man with a stern expression. Politely acknowledging everyone, his eyes fell to Cyril. 'Mr Reardon?'

Cyril stood up, but he was still unsteady from the shock.

'I am Dr Grant. I am very sorry. We couldn't save her. Even if we had started the chemotherapy, the pneumonia would have devastated her lungs.'

Cyril twisted his head to the side and his brow puckered in shock. '*Chemotherapy*?'

Grant assumed that Peggy's son would have known. 'Oh, you didn't know? I am so very sorry. Your mother had cancer, and we were looking at the option of chemotherapy, although her prognosis was terminal, and, well, she died of pneumonia.'

Cyril ran his hands through his hair. He found it hard to take all this in. 'If I'd brought her in yesterday morning, would she still be alive?'

Grant gave Mr Reardon a sympathetic smile but shook his head. 'No, no, the pneumonia was too far advanced.'

'I wanna see her.'

The doctor nodded. 'Of course. Nurse, please take Mr

Reardon to say goodbye to his mother.'

Those words hit Cyril hard; he couldn't imagine saying 'goodbye' for good.

Cyril straightened his jacket and tightened his tie before he walked in. He could feel Howie's breath on the back of his neck and then hear him whisper, 'I'm right with you, Cyril.'

Slowly, Cyril stepped forward, afraid to see his mother lifeless, but, as he stepped closer, he could somehow sense she was at peace. She looked asleep. Her soft features were relaxed, her eyes were closed, and her hands were by her side.

He sat next to her on the bed and allowed the tears to run down his cheeks and drip onto her pink nightdress.

'Oh, Mum, you weren't supposed to leave us yet. I wanted to show you that I am finally a king of my castle. I am a lord, Mum, and you should have been there as the duchess.'

He stopped when he heard Howie snivelling and turned to grab his brother's hand. 'We will make you proud, Mum. We will look after each other. I promise.'

Howie leaned forward. 'Yeah, we promise, Mum.'

'You were the best mum ever.'

'Yeah, you were, Mum,' said Howie.

Cyril stared at his mother for a while. He never wanted to forget his mother's sweet face; he never wanted the memory of her to fade. As he got up, he leaned down and kissed her forehead.

Howie did the same, and the Reardon brothers left the room with their arms around each other.

Frank, who loved Peggy, was being comforted by Blakey, but as soon as Cyril and Howie were back in the room, Frank straightened up. 'Can I go and say goodbye?'

Cyril nodded. ''Course, mate. You were like her own son.'

Frank sniffed back the tears and trudged out of the room to see Peggy.

Cyril sat down and Howie sat next to him while Blakey offered to get them all a coffee.

'I'm glad you were with her, Howie.'

'Yeah, me too, Cyril. So you won the mansion from Lord Chambers, then?'

Cyril nodded. 'How do you know about him?'

''Cos Mum said she'd heard that a Lord Chambers was in a London poker club, and she wanted to win big and clean him out after what he'd done to you with Flossie.'

Cyril let out a big sigh. 'So that's why she let him win twenty-five quid. I wondered how she had lost to a prick like that. I bet she was going back to take him to the cleaners.'

'Yeah, she said something about that last week, but I didn't really understand what she was on about. But she did say something about money she had saved to play on the high rolls table. I don't know what that means, but I guess you do.'

'High roller table, you mean.'

‘Yeah, that’s it,’ said Howie.

‘Well, Howie, I have just finished what she tried to start. I just wish our lovely mum had lived to see it.’

* * *

The day arrived when the deeds were signed over to Cyril. He’d already made sure that when the lord left the mansion by the deadline after the poker game, he left with only his clothes. Blakey and Ronnie had made sure of that.

Cyril decided to go to the mansion alone. He drove up the long drive that seemed to go on forever, and there, in all its glory, was the very imposing building. He stopped and stared. It was so different in the daylight from that night he and Frank ran for their lives. He looked up at the windows on the second floor and smiled; there had to be at least thirteen bedrooms. The massive pillars that stood either side of the door reminded him of a Roman feature. He continued on and parked directly outside the main huge oak door. For a moment, he had a feeling of trespassing, but then he smiled. He wasn’t trespassing; no one was suddenly going to appear with a gun and blow his brains out. Not this time.

Stepping out of his car, with the keys to his new home in his hand, he thought he would rattle around in it because of the sheer size of the place.

As he walked up three grand limestone steps, he felt the weight of the large brass knocker, but he didn’t have to knock – he had the key. And soon, as the key went into the lock and he felt the click, he pushed the two oak doors wide open and stared incredulously at the grand entrance hall, which he could easily have fitted his mother's entire flat into.

Frozen to the spot, he absorbed every inch before deciding to enter the drawing room. It was every bit as plush as he had imagined it would be. The vast Chinese rugs, the velvet chairs and sofas, the large mahogany coffee tables, and the enormous open fireplace were a sight to behold. His eyes were then drawn to the oil painting above the fireplace. The man on the horse was Lord Chambers senior; Cyril felt his blood run cold, and, in an instant, he wanted to rip the painting down.

As he was taking in all the finery, he heard the sound of footsteps clip-clopping through the house and getting closer. He spun around, and there in the doorway stood a woman with a furious expression on her otherwise pretty face.

'And what are you doing here?'

'I am the lord of this mansion.' He smiled because he had always wanted to say that and because this dainty woman looked like she was ready for battle.

She looked Cyril up and down. 'You a lord? Well, I am the bloody Queen of Sheba. Lord Chambers, bless his heart, told me I would have a new boss.'

Cyril put his hands on his hips and laughed. 'Oh, did he? Well, I never said anything about employing you.'

'He said you won a bet, this mansion and everything in it. I am the housekeeper. I have worked for years looking after this place, and now, I suppose, I am out of work.'

Cyril sensed something rather warm about the woman and was surprised she was so young.

‘Can you cook a roast dinner?’

‘What, right now?’

Cyril laughed again. ‘No, you daft bat. Anyway’ – he stepped forward with his hand out – ‘I’m Cyril Reardon, and you are?’

She dismissed his hand. ‘I’m Mary, and, yes, of course I can cook a roast dinner.’

‘Right, Maggie, you can stay on. I am not always here, so you can swan around like the lady of the manor if you like, but when I am here, I do like a nice dinner. And can you iron a shirt or two?’

‘It’s Mary, and the answer to the second question is yes. Now, about me wages. Lord Chambers paid me fifty, er, I mean a hundred pounds a week.’

That blush and attempt to conceal an obvious lie stood her in good stead, had she but known it. Of course Cyril had sussed it right away. *You can’t kid a kidder*, he thought. ‘Maggie, if me and you are gonna get along, you must always tell me the truth. So the lord paid you fifty quid a week, but, see, me, I am a generous man. I’ll up that to a hundred pounds a week.’

Mary smiled. ‘Okay, and I have Saturdays off.’

Cyril nodded. ‘Yeah, no worries. One rule, though, girl. What goes on in this house stays in this house.’

Mary backed away. ‘Oh, Jesus. You ain’t into any funny business like those swingers parties, are you?’

For the first time in ages, Cyril threw his head back and roared. 'Oh my Gawd, Maggie, no, no, nuffin like that.'

'I have a room, upstairs. The post is a live-in one, although I do spend time with me sister, you understand.'

Cyril was warming to the woman even more. He liked the way when she blushed, her pretty blue eyes sparkled. She was plainly dressed, but he could see she had a good figure. He wanted to pull the pin from her bun and watch her hair tumble down, but he didn't. He just smiled and nodded. 'I think, Maggie, me and you will get along just fine.'

Mary huffed as she walked away mumbling under her breath, 'Lord, my arse. Lord Fuckwit, maybe.'

'I heard that!' shouted Cyril, as he chuckled to himself. 'I'll have a cup of tea. Er . . . please.'

By the time Mary had returned with a tray of tea and biscuits, Cyril had ripped the oil painting down from the mantelpiece and had flung it out of the front door.

'What on earth have you done, Mr Reardon?' said Mary, as she quickly placed the tray on the table, on the point of turning on her heel to rescue the oil painting.

'Hold up, Maggie. Leave that pile of shit out there. It will never come into this mansion again.'

Mary frowned but was intrigued. 'Why do you hate that painting so much?'

Cyril gestured to her to take a seat. 'You worked for this family, but I bet you don't know what they represented, do ya?

Did you ever know a man called Lord Parker-Green?'

Mary nodded. 'Of course, I did. He was a very close friend of Lord Harold Chambers. They often went hunting and fishing together. But he's dead now. It was in our local newspaper, this morning. He was found hanging from a rafter in his barn. He killed himself.' She paused and put her hand to her face, giving Cyril a questioning look. Although, in truth, she couldn't stand Parker-Green and had always had her suspicions about the man.

'Maggie, they were not nice men, trust me. I personally know how bad they were.'

Mary saw the sincerity in Cyril's eyes, and she guessed whatever it was they had got up to, Cyril had learned about it first-hand. She sighed. 'It's a big house for just me and you to be rattling around in.'

'You never know, Maggie. One day, this mansion will be filled with love and laughter.'

'I do hope so. This house was always pretty dark and lifeless, and there were always formalities and etiquette, but I guess you have to be born with that,' she said, as she looked at Cyril dunking a ginger nut biscuit.

'I may not have been raised a lord but I am a gentleman.'

Mary looked at Cyril from the corner of her eye. Although she would never admit it, she did find him attractive. Aware that he hadn't been raised a lord, she suspected he probably was raised a gangster, but, nevertheless, he was indeed a gentleman.

Printed in Great Britain
by Amazon

45967216R00303